NEVERMIND

Nevermind

The Last Temptation of Frank

by JOHN CLIMENHAGA

Writers Club Press

New York Lincoln Shanghai

Nevermind

The Last Temptation of Frank

Writers Club Press
an imprint of iUniverse, Inc.

For information address:
iUniverse, Inc.
2021 Pine Lake Road, Suite 100
Lincoln, NE 68512
www.iuniverse.com

ISBN: 0-595-26522-7

Printed in the United States of America

To Camille: For being frank when I needed her to be.

BOOK 1

STRANGE LACK OF INTEREST IN SEX THROUGH THE
EXISTENCE OF A SPIRITUAL PROGENY

Art is born of coitus between the male and female elements of which we are all composed, and they are more balanced in the case of artists than of other men. It results from a kind of incest, of love of self for self, of parthenogenesis. It is this that makes marriage so dangerous among artists, for whom it represents a pleonasm, a monstrous effort towards the norm. The 'poor specimen' look which is the mark of so many men of genius arises from the fact that the creative instinct is satisfied elsewhere and leaves sexual pleasure free to exert itself in the pure domain of aesthetics, inclining it also towards unfruitful forms of expression.

Jean Cocteau–Opium

PART I

▼

5/11/86

I made a deal with the devil.

I hate to say it, because it sounds so ridiculous, but that's the only conclusion I can come to. It wasn't your normal deal by any means. There wasn't any talk of souls or anything. I didn't even know he was the devil at the time. I was walking through Central Park trying to recapture the energy it once had for me. I hadn't slept for a couple of days, that was due to anxiety mostly, but I'm sure the cocaine had something to do with it, too. I had recently sold a painting for an ungodly sum and I was extremely anxious. Yeah, anxious. So, I was walking through the park at sunrise trying to feel good about something. I was failing miserably. You see I had been the proverbial starving artist. My stuff was being showed, but I still had to work at McGarrety's Market to afford my small Eastside studio. When I sold that first painting for a hundred dollars I spent it all (and then some) on liquor for some friends and me. I was twenty-five at the time, I guess it took a couple years for the theoretical constipation of school to clear up. I liked what I was doing, but still saw some room for improvement. One day, I was stocking canned goods in aisle three when an elderly woman came into the store. She turned out to be a long, lost, friend of the McGarrety's. I remember her as just aglow with warmth and happiness. It's hard to believe that she single-handedly destroyed my life.

What a sweet woman, too.

Mrs. Solomon was a neighbor of the McGarrety's from way back. She had led a modest life up until 1965 when she happened to meet Jacob Solomon, a wealthy investment counselor. When she eventually married ole Jake, she moved out of her lower Eastside digs of thirty years and headed for the Hamptons and the high life. That day when she walked into the McGarrety's shop was the first they had seen of her in over twenty years. Now, it seems, Mr. Solomon had died and left everything to Irene. This was difficult for her because, even though she had been living in the lap of luxury, she had managed to keep her modest lifestyle in tact. It was one of the things Jacob liked about her most. He was particularly frugal also. Now that she had this enormous cash surplus to deal with, she was at a loss. Particularly when her advisors told her that she needed to spend to keep her taxes down. Irene Solomon, nee Marsh, had come back to her old neighborhood to find a way to spend that money. She didn't just want to spend it though; she wanted to feel good about spending it. She had never felt good about spending money and she was hoping that the folks in the neighborhood that was so dear to her would help.

"Excuse me," I popped up, "Where are those green beans?"

"Frank" Maureen McGarrety motioned for me, "this is Irene Solomon. Irene, this is Frank Teeman." We shook hands. "Frank is an artist!" Maureen pointed to my small acrylic piece that was hanging behind the register.

"It's nice to meet you Mr. Teeman," Irene said as she stared at the painting. It was an earth tone thing with an abstract human figure kind of floating in a vague background. I called it "Ahhh…" It was one of the first pieces I had done after being hired and it came from a sense of relief. I finally had an income. So, I gave it to the McGarretys and whenever I met one of their friends "Ahhh…" was peremptorily displayed. I didn't really like it that much. It was more of a doodle than anything, but I didn't want to spoil their enthusiasm. It did make me feel good.

"I like that very much," Irene said emphatically, *"Do you have any more?"*

"Well, none like that, really…"

"Frank's got lots of them. He's very prolific," Maureen piped in like a proud mother.

"Really? Are any being shown?"

"Well, I'm kind of between shows right now, but there are a few up at the Purple Dragon."

"That's where Franklin's used to be," Maureen was nostalgic, *"Remember when we used to meet there after school?"*

"That's where I met Jacob," Irene was distant.

"Yes, I remember," there was a pause as both women left for a moment.

"It was nice to meet you," I broke, *"I'll be getting back to work, now. Where are those beans?"*

"Look by the back door or maybe under the paper towels."

"All right. So, long," I waived.

"Nice to meet you, Mr. Teeman," Irene called after me. *"What a nice young man,"* I heard her say to Maureen before I entered the storeroom.

I have to admit that after overhearing the conversation between those two old friends, I made an appearance intentionally. It was kind of a habit I was in. When you live in New York and you don't have a lot of money, you're constantly reminded of the difference between you and those who do. When you're paying your bills and filling your stomach and entertaining yourself that's not so bad.

You're happy…satisfied.

Well, it's not bad anyway.

But when you see those folks who are paying their bills and filling their stomachs and entertaining themselves and furnishing their houses and have romance and…It's like an annoying itch. At least for me it is. And I scratch that itch by meeting as many people of the other kind as possible. Some people play the lottery. I play the pool. The pool of liquid assets. That ocean of surplus cash that happens to be pretty deep in this area. So, I do a little swimming. That's it. It's not like I'm fishing. I'm just swimming. Nothing ever had really come of it, before.

Ed Tiegle called me two days later. I was in my loft and I remember it vividly. I had just finished a couple of hits of some dirt weed after my usual boring dinner. I had easeled a canvas months ago, but I couldn't get started on it. I had budgeted the time for that express purpose. Still, I was diddling around washing dishes when my cassette deck took a dump. It was one of those awful moments that culminate a lousy day. I had bought the stereo while in college and had grown very attached to it. The turntable was a piece of shit and I'm not sure if it even worked. I loved my tape deck. It was one of those reversible direction things so I could put in something like Carmina Burana and paint for hours. Suddenly, there was this high screech and then a pop and when I turned I saw a small plume of white smoke come out the back. I knew it was gone and I was sitting there mourning the loss of a good friend. I knew I wasn't going to be able to replace it for a long while. Not unless something miraculous happened.

"Man, this is it," Ed Tiegle said when I answered the phone. Ed had been running the Purple Dragon forever and was very supportive of the arts. Paintings hung there always and music and poetry and theater…it was a cool place. Ed was a little spun, but harmless just the same.

"What's up, Ed?" I was dejected because of the tape deck.

"Man, Cheer up. You're on top."

"What?"

"I just got in and Kara, you know her, right, well she takes me back to the office and shows me this wad of cash," Ed fades and I hear him tell somebody something about grinding coffee.

"And?" I'm trying to restrain my enthusiasm because I want that wad of cash to be related to me, some how, but I know that if I assume that it is, it won't be.

"Well, we sold all your stuff!" Ed laughs. I can't tell if he's joking or not.

"What?"

"That's Right. Full price, too. I've never seen anything like it." There's an excitement in his voice that infects me.

"You've got the cash?" I practically screamed into the phone.

"Twenty eight hundred samoleans, right here." We both chuckled.

"I'll be right down," I slam the phone down and leave with a skip.

By the time I hit the street I'm really high. I'm kind of inside myself. Really inside myself. Like my eyes are focusing on the bridge of my nose and my ears are listening to my brain work overtime. When you're at the bottom and looking up the top is always visible, but usually distant. Then something like this happens to bring it into close proximity and it's frightening. So, I'm thinking about this sale and what it could mean and it dawns on me that it could mean nothing. That maybe Ed sold everything in the cafe or the whole cafe. It had been rumored. The next thing I know I'm at the Purple Dragon and I'm practically stiff from nervousness. When I step through the doors everything goes into slow motion, but as soon as Ed says, "Frankie, Frank, Frank!" and slaps me on the back, I snap out of it. Ed gestures towards the walls and I can see the six blank spots where my pieces used to be.

"This is great," Ed is exuberant and he looks towards me for agreement.

"Yeah," I kind of chuckle.

"C'mon back to the office and take a look at that dough!" Ed laughs heartily.

You'd think I'd be ecstatic at this time. Instead, I'm just kind of blah. Maybe it was that cheap weed. I don't know. I just felt like a pile of Jell-O. Ed had to take me by the arm to get me back to the office. When I got there I started to laugh.

"Just my stuff?" I asked with some uncertainty.

"Only your stuff," Ed held out a stack of one hundred dollar bills. Time stood still for me then. I got a lump in my throat and tears welled in my eyes. I counted through the bills, but kept losing track. It was nice to just leaf through them. I started to think about the last time I had that kind of money. God, I remember it so well.

I was standing at Phillip's Grill waiting for the bus.
The sky was so blue I couldn't take my eyes off of it.
Just deep blue, no clouds.
And with my head leaning back a small sense of comfort.
I was leaving my hometown of Dilon, Kansas for good. I knew it then. Both my parents had died. They were hit head on by a drunken truck driver. I had been going through the motions of settling the estate. I was a robot. In the middle of it all I found my adoption papers. I had been adopted as an infant in nearby Kansas City. The papers said, "Mother: unknown. Father: unknown." I was pretty numb at the time. This information just seemed like another minor detail in the surrealistic bent that my life had taken. When all the business had been completed I was left with $5,000.00 in traveler's checks and a one-way bus ticket to New York and I was standing there waiting for that bus to come and take me away. And then all the pain would be gone.
Or so I thought.

Now, standing in Ed Tiegle's office, I have just realized that I've been in pain ever since. I never dealt with it and being in New York was not helping. My parents would've never approved. I graduated from Kansas State with a degree in communications. I always loved painting. I minored in art. My folks weren't going to pay for my education if I was going to major in art. So, I got my degree in communications and had started work at Dad's grocery store. He had put me in charge of advertisement. I was going to rescue him. When he died a chain snatched the store up. Something he should have done years before. Kroger's were pretty generous, I guess. There was a pile of bills and a couple of mortgages. I did leave town with 5 G's. I knew that Mom and Dad wouldn't have understood me going to New York to be an artist, so, I kept telling myself that if I made it I would be vindicated in their eyes. And if they were looking down on me, here I was with $2,800 cash. From my art!

"I guess the art frenzy has spread from Christy's to the Purple Dragon," Ed laughed. He was referring to the ridiculous prices art was getting at the auction houses. Everyone was wondering when that same price hike would happen in the galleries. It snapped me out of my daydream.

"Yeah, I guess so," I was still dazed. Normally I'd have a lot to say on the topic. I counted out three hundred dollars and plunked it on Ed's desk. "There's your commission, Ed. Thanks."

"Hey man, you know we don't charge commission," Ed held his hands up as if the money were suddenly radioactive.

"Consider it a donation, then."

"All right," Ed was humbled, "Thanks, that's really cool." Ed was touched, "Hey, I need you to sign a receipt."

He got out his receipt book and while he was filling it out he was saying how great this was and although he didn't know who the buyer was it meant something. I just agreed at the appropriate moments and tried to be happy. Part of me was and I tried to focus on that. It was a chore. Still, I managed to smile when Ed turned the receipt book towards me and handed me the pen. My smile quickly faded as I looked down at that receipt book. It was one of those books with several receipts per page and I saw that the receipt directly above the one I was to sign had Irene Solomon's name on it.

"Irene Solomon?" I looked at Ed for confirmation, but I knew what it meant. It meant that instead of being discovered by a buyer for a gallery or auction house, I had been the recipient of a tax write off.

Or worse yet—a favor.

"You know her?" Ed was intrigued.

"Yeah, I met her once," the sinking feeling was about to consume me and I felt a pressing need to leave. Fresh air was all I could think about. I scribbled my signature in Ed's book and exited hastily.

"Hey! Who is she?" he called after me. I did not respond. "Frank your receipt," I heard him calling.

I just wanted to breathe.

3/11/79

Manhattan is alive. I stand on the street outside my studio soaking up the energy. It keeps me alive. Whenever I feel weak I must get outside. I'm not sure what it is. I know that if I just look out the window that doesn't do it for me. I mean, I thought that my perception of what New York was, was the source of that well spring so that if I just thought about it, New York, I would be rejuvenated, but no. That doesn't work. It's something in the air. I have to stand on the street, even the most desolate street, I have to stand there and let it come to me. When I'm walking I can tell it's there and that's a comfort, but, unless I stand there and soak it in, only then, am I young again.

When I'm standing there, I become aware of humanity. I don't hear voices, per se; my ears are still hearing the din of four million people busy at life. I still smell the normal Manhattan air, I don't even see anything, but I become aware and it's humanity I'm aware of. I know that because my mind wanders and I think about people and I know that I'm not alone. Sometimes, I think that I am alone, but these encounter sessions with humanity convince me that I'm not. Sometimes, I'm convinced that I'm alone and like a junkie runs for the needle I run for the outdoors. Does this sound crazy? It is. At the same time it keeps me from going crazy.

I had this feeling first when I was very young. I didn't really note it until much later. The first time I was aware of it was when I stepped off the bus as a recent addition to the New York artists' pool. At the time I was feeling pretty lonely, what with the death of my folks. And then finding out they weren't my parents. And then riding on a bus for a couple of days. And then arriving at the New York Port Authority! I was pretty lonely. But when I stepped on to the pavement from the last step of the bus, I was seized by a fervor. I just assumed that it had something to do with the newness of the situation but have since found that there is more to it than that.

I was drunk the first time that I realized that this fervor was not simply excitement with the newness of everything. I had been involved with the drudgery of life. You know, finding a place to live, getting utilities, getting some furniture, finding your way around. Once I got set up I was doing a lot of painting. My money had run a little faster than I had originally hoped, so I started looking into selling some of my stuff. I started to find out just how many people have artistic aspirations in the New York metropolitan area and I was beginning to wonder if maybe I hadn't bitten off more than I could chew. The more I doubted myself the more I drank and it was easy to find "friends" in that state of mind. Through all the doubt I managed to persevere. I started on a large canvas and it seemed like each stroke was painful. Sometimes I would stare at it for hours just adding a touch here and there. Other times, I would paint furiously for a half hour and then go drink. I always drank a lot after those bursts. Inevitably I would be called home to take a look at what I'd done. I would be sitting in a bar and it would call me. "What have you done?" it would cry and I would be compelled to leave whatever I was doing and return to the scene to witness the mess. Eventually it was done. Then it sat there for a week until I showed it to Brian Mosten, one of my drinking buddies/artist friends. We left McSorley's arm in arm and ended up at my place to smoke a joint. It wasn't until we opened the door and that huge canvas greeted us that I realized that Brian would be its first visitor and mine, too!

"*Wow,*" *Brian was gawking. I was embarrassed so I didn't say anything, "Kind of a deMoline/Wyeth thing, huh?"*

"*Not really,*" *I didn't know deMoline and I couldn't figure the Wyeth angle at all.*

"*I like it, though. Particularly the way the person is obscured. The whole insignificance of life thing...*"

"*Actually, you know, the human is the largest part even though it is minimally detailed.*"

"*Yeah, I suppose. It's just obscured. For me, anyways. Maybe if you put a little more red behind it...*"

"*It's done.*" *I barked. I think Brian could sense my aggravation because he moved on to idle chat. I lit the joint and we smoked. I was distant. I kept thinking about adding red to it. It seemed like a good idea, but something, someone, was barking at me, "It's done".*

Brian left eventually and I sat there and stared and wondered and wished that I had someone I could talk to about it or about anything and a chill went up my back. It wasn't from being cold. The thermometer read 72. It was loneliness. And I couldn't shake that feeling of desperation. And I started pacing around the studio, but everywhere I went its eyes were on me. So, I left. And as soon as I hit the street I stopped and was relaxed. I closed my eyes and my head was spinning so, I laid down but the sidewalk was cold so, I sat up. A nausea came over me then and the desperation returned with a vengeance and I felt as if I were going to die. I gritted my teeth and started to fight. I growled and gritted and I felt like I was losing. But, right before I passed, it became easy. The awareness had come. I sat there soaking it up.

Oh, what peace.

I woke up the next morning in a blanket of whiskey sweat. My head felt like it had been hatcheted. I felt great, though. My first thoughts were about my last thoughts. That peace was still with me and I knew that I had experienced something special. I wasn't sure if that specialness was the result of some intoxicated hallucination or whether my body had overcome the pollutants in some miraculous serge of well-being. I crawled out of my bed, which took me by surprise since I last remembered the sidewalk as a blanket. As I made my way to the drain hole that huge canvas leaped on me.

I couldn't believe it!

There was a red line!

"That fucking Brian Mosten came in here and put a fucking red line on my painting!"

He had outlined, ever so lightly, the human form in that painting, I thought. And then I saw the broken brush on the floor. I always broke my brush when I was done and I realized that I had done it. I wanted to be depressed, but couldn't. All I knew was that I felt whole in the morning when I usually felt empty. So I walked the sunlit streets of New York that day. I loved it. Just walking. I was reminded of my first stroll through the concrete jungle. After I stepped off that Greyhound I just walked and walked. Now that I was gobbling up sidewalk again I had to wonder, "What provided that energy?"

5/13/86

When I left the Purple Dragon that night after receiving Irene Solomon's beneficence, I had a tremendous sense of horror. By the time I got back to my place I had calmed down. "Maybe she did like my stuff," I was thinking. It mattered to me, but I couldn't find out for sure so, I sat there, in my studio, looking at that cash and trying to decide how to feel about it. Part of me wanted to jump for joy. Twenty five hundred bucks is twenty five hundred bucks! Another part of me felt like it had just sold its children for peanuts. Finally, I decided to feel drunk about it. It's the easiest. So, I took a couple hundred bucks and hit the streets.

First it was a couple seven and sevens at McSorley's. I didn't know anybody there, except Jim, the bartender. I left him a nice tip and headed for the Blarney Stone. Harry, the bartender there, was always jovial; he'd cheer me up. After a couple of glasses of twelve year old scotch I was feeling a little looser, but not much more enthusiastic. None of my regular pals were at the Blarney Stone either. I never did mention my windfall to Harry so everything had a very normal feel to it. I was supposed to be celebrating, though, so that mundane quality became boredom. I tried to think of some one I could call. I had never been celebrating in New York. I didn't have anyone. I looked around the bar. I wanted to tell someone that I had just come into a pile of money, but you have to be careful about spreading that kind of news. It's a good way to get stabbed. Besides, I wasn't sure if I was proud of it or not so, it wasn't exactly bursting from within. "What to do?" I had to do something. *That much was clear. I left the Blarney Stone and decided to look for Brian at some of our regular spots. The Blue Room was empty and Lillie's was hosting a bachelor party. Much too festive for me. Brian wasn't there anyway. I remembered Brian talking about a strip joint on 42nd that he liked—Tommy's Topless or something like that. I had never been there even though Brian had encouraged me to go. It's not like I have anything against strippers it's just that they're so damn expensive. I had money to burn so off I went. Finally the night was getting a little exciting. I flagged a cab and as it stopped I realized that this would be my first cab ride since I became a resident.*

This was exciting!

"Good evening," the cabby said in a very subdued tone as I crawled into the back seat. I was reveling in the experience. The feel of the seat, the divider. Finally the cabby turned around and said, "Where to?" What a pleasant face and demeanor this guy had.

"Oh, I don't know! Forty second street somewhere," I was giddy.

"I need a destination," he was firm yet polite. I was intrigued. I thought cabbies were rude.

"Say, do you know a place called Tommy's Topless or something like that," I had a lilt in my voice that made me sound like a teenager, "It's on forty second," I was oblivious.

"Get out! Your drunk!" I wasn't that drunk. Not on alcohol anyways. It took me a while to hear what he was saying, still. I thought about getting out but I couldn't believe that I was getting kicked out of my first cab ride. Before it even started! I liked this cab and I wanted to go to Forty-second Street in it. I tossed a twenty into the front seat, "Drive straight. I'll tell you when to turn. Let me know if that runs out."

He looked at me real hard and I waved my little wad of cash and he turned around with a sigh and drove on.

"Hey Ernie, this is Jack," he said over his mic, "I've got a goose here."

"10-4" squawked the dashboard back.

I watched my money slowly tick away on the meter. Every time it jumped I'd get this tremendous urge to savor the moment. I mean, this ride was costing so I'd better get my money's worth. The more it ticked, though, the less fulfilled I felt. Eventually I had resigned myself to flushing that twenty away. With that realization I was able to take my eyes off that meter although I never missed a tick. I saw the cabby's ID on the dash next to the meter. That photo looked like a mug shot of a mass murderer. Was that the same guy driving? He seemed so nice. The ID said his name was Jacsun Pranesh. Was this guy a foreigner? He seemed so American. I couldn't get a look at him now. He was facing forward and there was no light, so I leaned forward to see if I could get a view. He turned and caught me staring.

"You wanna take seventh? It'll probably be faster," he was very polite. I was embarrassed.

"Yeah. That's fine," the alcohol was wearing off and that combined with my faux pas made my stomach a little queasy. I slumped in the back, cracked the window, and started sniffing the cool air. My head was still a little light, but my stomach had stopped kicking anyways.

"You OK?" Jacsun asked through the rear view mirror. He had such a concerned tone that I was touched.

"No. Not really," I moaned. I felt like telling this guy my life story, or at least the last day's worth.

"You're not gonna puke back there?" He was straining to see me.

"No. I'm fine," I sat up so that he could see. And when he did see, I saw how relieved he was and I felt ashamed. I was being an annoyance and that's the one thing I never wanted to be.

"Here's forty second. Which way?"

"I don't fucking know," I groaned, "Go down to Times Square." There was a certain amount of tension in my voice. The light turned green and we didn't move. Horns started blasting immediately. "What's the matter?" I shrieked as I jutted into the front seat. Jacsun calmly turned and looked at me with wide eyes.

"Ask nicely," he said in a dark whisper. I was reminded of that maniacal picture on his ID. I saw that he was indeed that criminal foreigner portrayed on the dash. All those horns blaring combined with my newfound

fear made me panic. I couldn't remember what I was supposed to ask nicely for. Finally I said, "Times Square, please," in my most plaintiff voice and the cab turned left on Forty-second Street. "Listen, I'm sorry about that. I'm just a little frustrated," that came out unwittingly. I was scared.

"Yeah. It must be tough to have money," Jacsun was sarcastic.

I opened my mouth to correct him. He thought I was rich. I wanted to tell him that I was poor like him, but couldn't. I thought about launching into a full explanation. The words didn't come.

I just sighed.

"Well? Is it tough?" Jacsun was insistent. Why? I couldn't figure.

"Yeah. It's tough," I finally blurted.

He just laughed, "Here's Tommy's." He pulled up in front of a small storefront with an old lighted sign that said "Tommy's". I looked out the window and was hesitant. Tommy's looked all right. I just felt like we had more to say to each other.

"What's the total?" I was procrastinating. I knew the total.

"Twelve ninety," Jacsun shoved some money through the divider, "here's your change."

"No. That's OK," I waved my hand and got out of the cab. I stuck my head in the door before closing it. "Thanks," I was trying to be as genuine as possible.

"Thank you," he said genuinely with a smile, "any time you need a cab just call. Here's my card." He handed me a Checker Cab business card. On the back, in a loose hand writing it said, "Ask for Jack P."

"All right," I said with a smile and he drove off. I stuck the card in my breast pocket and headed for Tommy's with a new lease on the night. I was determined to celebrate.

When I opened the door to Tommy's I was slapped with the din of clinking glasses, loud music, and drunken whoops. This looked like fun! I was going to have a good time! I saw the naked back of one of the women dancers and was intrigued. She looked beautiful. From the back anyways. Before I could get a closer look a big, round, man with a shaved head and black goatee grabbed my shoulder. I turned with a start.

"Five dollar cover, two drink minimum," he said with out moving at all. I reached for my cash and so did he, "It's ten dollars total. You want some ones?" He lightened up considerably. I was glad about that. I handed him a twenty and said, "Sure." I didn't really want those ones. I didn't want to piss him off. I took my ones and drink tickets and made my way towards the bar. There was a woman dancing on each end of the bar as well as two others on platforms in the room. They were all bouncing their tits variously wearing only G-strings and pumps. The bar was filled with drunken men. A few were shouting obscenities at the dancers, but everybody was having fun. I was kind of oblivious to everything. The red head at the far end of the bar transfixed me. It was her back that I saw in a mirror at the front door. Once I saw her face...I couldn't take my eyes off of her. She was exquisitely beautiful. I mean, she looked great, but she was enveloped in an aura of joy that seemed to light her up. I found a seat at the bar near her and the bartender was there.

"What's it gonna be?" she said in a gravely voice.

"Scotch rocks," I said without missing a step by my red head.

"Those tickets are for draft beer only. Scotch is another two bucks each."

I thought for a second. This was precisely why I hate these joints, but I was out celebrating so, I laid my ones down and two scotch rocks appeared.

Ahhh, scotch...

Naked women...

Loud music.

This was fun.

I was celebrating.

The song ended and "The Stripper" came up and everybody started cheering madly. This was great. The girls on the platform began walking down the steps and into the audience and the girls on the bar started making their way across. Guys were flashing money madly and there was such excitement. I downed my scotch and started in on number two. I could see guys shoving ones in the G-strings of the girls on the floor and the guy next to me had caught my red head's attention with a five-dollar bill. She made her way over and danced right in front of him. He put the bill between his lips and a small crowd gathered around and started whooping. I was enthralled. She was right in front of me! She started to crouch down in front of my neighbor and as her face got closer my heart beat raced. She was crouched so low she was almost face to face with that five. Her knee was in my face. I could smell it. It smelled like sweat. She shoved her tits in that guy's face and gave them a shake and then pressed them together and took that five spot. It kind of took me by surprise. I had heard tale of strip joints and this was, by no means, as wild as some of the stories I had heard. Still, I was surprised. I was watching her face through all this. She laughed, but there was this look in her eyes. It was like hatred or disgust. Something unpleasant. It made me tense. She stood up and everybody cheered, but I was gawking. Open mouth gawking! And she turned and saw me! She looked straight through me. I saw that anger inside of her vividly. I was embarrassed. I took my ones and held them out and she snatched them from my hand and made her way down the bar.

I heard some one behind me say, "What an idiot."

Well, now I was cold. I felt a shiver in my back and I couldn't look up even though I heard someone yelling, "Take it off." People started pounding on the bar and it seemed like everyone was watching my red head. I had to see so I took a big gulp of liquor and I forced my neck to move. It felt like rigor mortis had almost set in, but I got my head to look up and over just in time to see her totally naked now. She was going into her crouch again. She was holding her hair up over her head. As she made her way lower and lower I finally saw the Budweiser long neck on the bar underneath her. I knew what was coming. I braced myself, but when that bottle entered her pussy and the crowd erupted I had to close my eyes. I sat there drinking with my eyes shut until that song ended and then I polished the rest of that scotch and split.

I started walking down 42nd. I had lost my desire to party. Still, I felt like there was something that needed to be done. Before I could move on I had to figure out what had just happened. I mean, why did that stripper freak me out? So, I was walking along thinking about what had just happened. The prostitution of her body. And I thought I was prostituting myself! I have no problem with selling my art. I always thought that the only people who would buy it would really like it, though. Why did Irene Solomon buy those paintings? Was she hanging them in her house right now? Doubtful. Well, at least I was a high-class whore. That red head did that bottle for a twenty. I kicked a can on the street. It felt good. When I caught up with it I kicked it again, only harder. I watched it bounce a long the sidewalk and roll into a pool of light that was an open storefront. As I was getting ready to kick it again, I noticed all the electronic equipment in the store's window. Right up front was a dual well, dual direction, cassette deck. I walked into the store, laid down all the cash I had and it was mine. God that felt great. That was the kind of celebrating I needed. I don't know what made me think it was drinking and debauchery. Yes, now I could go home. Whoring is profitable. I called Checker and had them send Jack over. He arrived promptly. I was happy to see him.

"Long time no see," I said with a giggle as I hopped into the back seat. I was still a little drunk.

"Djou win the door prize?"

"Nah. Tommy's was a drag."

"I never heard that about a strip joint before," we laughed.

"I guess I wasn't in the right frame of mind."

"You seem to be now."

"Yeah. I just got a new tape deck." I held it up. Jack was not jiving with me on that one. "Mine broke today," I offered as an explanation.

"Oh," Jack thought I was some rich guy frivolously spending, "Where to now?" I could tell he was still a little put off. I gave him directions to my place and settled back. I felt relaxed but something was still missing. I was still a little disappointed that Jack and I weren't meshing that well, but that was no big deal. I guess I was just out of practice at feeling happy. We rode in silence until we stopped in front of my studio.

"OK, that's fifteen forty," Jack turned around with a smile.

"I don't have any cash on me. You want to wait here or would you like to come up with me? I have a little weed," I whispered that last bit. Jack was hesitant and I could see that. I didn't blame him. "I'll leave the tape deck here. I'll be right back." I didn't want to be any more of an annoyance than I already had been. Jack shifted into park and killed the engine. I headed up the stairs.

"Wait up," I heard Jack say and I turned to see him following me with the tape deck under his arm.

That made me feel good. Genuinely good.

Jack left after a joint. He is a nice guy and I think he liked me. We had a couple of laughs. He admitted that he thought I was some wealthy wacko, so I was glad to let him know the reality of the situation. When he left I felt complete. I still had that new canvas that I was supposed to have started earlier so, I started in on it.

Sometimes painting is just the most joyful thing you can do.

3/11/80

I paint people. Not portraiture. People.

I had to do still life and landscape and other stuff in school. Now that I'm on my own, I paint people. Sometimes I think I'm limiting myself so I'll try something with out a human figure in it. I always find a place for a person, though. Is that so bad? I like people and there's so much you can do with the human form. It's amazing how a strong hand changes a bowl of fruit or a minute decaying corpse interrupts a pastoral landscape. And as far as abstract things go—Nothing is more abstract and yet concrete.

When I first got to New York I went through this elderly person thing. Obsession I guess you'd call it. I suppose it had something to do with the death of my parents. I would go down to Penn Station, or somewhere, and find an elderly person and offer them money to sit for me. Most of the men were open to it. Elderly women were harder to find. I found Gladys Rowe outside of Waldbaum's. She was pan handling. I told her that I was an artist and that I was looking for a subject. Once the price was agreed upon we were off. Gladys was a delight to work with. That first time, she stripped naked the moment we got in the door.

"This is what you want, right?" She was coy. I laughed to myself. That little girl's voice coming from that decrepit old body was funny.

"No, that's not necessary. Why don't you take a shower now that you're nude," Gladys really smelled bad. She covered her sagging breasts with her arms and she actually looked hurt.

"I'm on the clock," she said with a pout. We had agreed to ten dollars an hour.

"OK, OK," I just wanted her to shower. When she left the room I put her smelly clothes out on the window ledge. I ran down to the Salvation Army thrift store and bought her a maroon velour bathrobe and ran back. Gladys was just getting out of the shower then and I handed her the robe through the door. She was all smiles when she came out; still she was a little embarrassed. She wouldn't look at me.

"Are you gonna fuck me?" She whispered.

"No, Gladys," I choked out. I had the feeling she had been raped. "No, I just want to paint you. Would you sit in that arm chair please," I tried to say in my softest voice. She did and I started painting. She had the saddest eyes I had ever seen so I started with her face. After a couple hours I was exhausted, but I thought I had captured that melancholy well.

Irene Solomon now owns "Glad" (that's what I titled that painting of Gladys Rowe). I was always particularly proud of it and even though it was old and simple I would include it in some of my shows. So, I put it at the Purple Dragon. It was mostly maroon and I thought that was appropriate for the Purple Dragon. I put a seven hundred dollar price tag on it figuring nobody would pay that much for it.

Unless they really liked it.

I painted Gladys a few times after that. I did do a nude of her. It was interesting, I guess, but not as much as that first one. The last time I did Gladys I just used her feet and lower legs. It was a thing that had a bunch of feet and legs in it. So many, it became difficult to tell what any of them were. Two days after that session, Mary Everett knocked on my door. She was a social worker and introduced herself as such.

"I'm a social worker," she said with outstretched hand and a grim smile. She was a good-looking woman. Nothing outstanding. Just wholesome goodness and the fire of determination in her eye. For a Kansas boy like me she was gorgeous.

"I'm not in trouble I hope," I said coyly back to her as I shook her hand warmly and gestured her in.

"Are you Frank?" she said without even the hint of a response to my comment.

"Yes. Frank Teeman," I was actually a little concerned and had slipped into that business tone.

"When was the last time you saw Gladys Rowe?" She sounded like a policewoman.

"I painted her two days ago," I pointed to the leg piece as evidence, "Is she missing?"

"No, Mr. Teeman, she's dead. She was stabbed down near Waldbaum's." Mary was choked up. That got to me. I wasn't that shocked when I heard, but to hear Mary choke on Waldbaum's really got to me. Suddenly, I felt the weight of that moment intensely and just sat where I was standing, bewildered.

"Damn," I kind of whispered. It was all I could think of. My head started to move slowly from side to side. "Damn," I said again.

"I found your name and address with her personal affects," Mary said soothingly.

"Yeah, I painted her," I pointed to the leg thing again. I was just kind of blank. I mean, I wasn't screaming with anguish or grief. Just kind of blank. I had a tear in my eye!

Huh?

"That's Gladys?" Mary was confused. I laughed and so did she. That was good because the air cleared instantly.

"No. Her legs are in there, though."

"Oh, legs. I see," Mary was intrigued. She moved closer. I got up and pointed to Gladys' toe.

"See?" Gladys had this gnarled toenail. Mary was not making the connection. Oh well. "Look at this," I hopped over to my storage rack and pulled out "Glad". Mary looked at it for a long second and then burst into tears. I ran to comfort her.

"There, there," as I patted her back. The whole bit.

"That's Gladys," she said with a nod as she got herself together and turned her back to me. "Would you please call me if you remember anything or find out anything that might help the police," she turned and handed me her card with a straight face. Her eyes were still red.

"Certainly," I didn't want her to leave, but she was walking towards the door still.

"Thank you," she said honestly and she was gone.

I couldn't stop thinking about Mary after that. I pinned her card up by the phone and thought about calling her every time I saw it. She wasn't very friendly to me. There was something that was memorable. Maybe it was the circumstances around our meeting. I didn't meet many women that intrigued me like Mary had. So, I called. I was a little nervous, actually, but, when I said, "Could we get together for lunch sometime?" and she said, "How 'bout tomorrow," I was more relieved than I had been in days. Months.

I found some "good" clothes still in a suitcase and headed to lunch with hope and butterflies. I made it to Arnie's deli by 11:55 and Mary showed promptly at noon. She looked happy to see me and that made me feel good. She was also as captivatingly beautiful as I remembered her and that made me feel good, too.

This was the right thing to do!

"So, did you find out something about Gladys?" she jumped right in after the initial pleasantries. It hadn't occurred to me that she would think that I had information on Gladys.

"No," I blurted, and then I thought about lying.

"No?" Mary was confused and disappointed.

"No, I just wanted to see you again," I said to the floor. Mary was embarrassed. I saw her face go red. "I'm sorry if I misled you. It wasn't intentional."

"Let's order," she said with a bright smile and so, we did, and we talked over lunch and I got her home phone number and we parted with a hug. What a wonderful day that was. I still remember it as one of the happiest feelings I've ever had.

Unfortunately, things never worked out between us. We got together frequently over the next six months and we had lots of fun. I was falling in love with Mary. It was obvious that she was not reciprocating. Finally, after a fun day at Coney Island, I tried to kiss her good night. It was one of the most awkward good night kisses the world has ever seen, I'm sure of it. I got this painful cramp in my throat and a chill went up my spine. It was plain—she was not romantically inclined towards me.

"Frank, I'm sorry," she could tell that I was getting the message, "I like you very much, and I enjoy being with you, but…"

"I know, 'Just friends,'" I said with a "cut and dry" motion of the hands. I just had to leave at that point. What else can be said?

"Frank, I don't want to lose our friendship," I heard her call after me, earnestly. I turned and saw a distressed look on her face. I just waved and kept walking.

5/14/86

I dreamt about Irene Solomon that night. I woke up thinking about her money. I woke up thinking that I liked having her money and the two G's that I had left would not last long. I got up thinking that that transient nature is the thing that I liked about money. One minute a hundred-dollar bill, the next ... nothing ... a full toilet and the spins. Or maybe a new dual well, dual direction tape deck! And then more money and more toilet fodder. Yes, spending is what makes money great. Having it is only nice because you can spend it. Some people spend it without having it. That must be like having sex with half a hard-on. Some people have it and never spend it. That must be like having sex without orgasm. Well, I had been abstinent for so long, I was ready for more. I didn't have to work until late. Ralph, the janitor at McGarrety's, was on vacation and I was filling in, sweeping and mopping after hours. Yes, a whole day of spending was in order. I phoned Mary for a lunch date. I usually called a couple days in advance to invite her to lunch. I told her that this was special. She had to appear in court in the afternoon, so we agreed to meet at Arnie's. God, it had been a long time. I phoned Checker on the off chance that Jack could take me there. My lucky day! Jack was on his way. I put on my "good" clothes. I had that festive mood and dressing up always went with that. Those damn dress shoes were always too tight. So, I wore my boots. Paint and all! I knew it looked weird, but I was comfortable. Yes, I was very comfortable and ready to go. Then the phone rang. My heart sank. I thought for sure it was Mary canceling. Who else could it be?

"Hello?" I was almost afraid to answer.

"Hello, Mr. Teeman?" a thin voice came over the line.

"Yes," at least it wasn't Mary canceling so I spoke a bit more freely.

"This is Irene Solomon. We met at McGarrety's…"

"Yes, I remember," I was half angry, half embarrassed. "What can I do for you?" Thoughts of her asking for her money back flashed through my head and scared me.

"I'm opening my own gallery here in East Hampton and I want you to be our first featured artist," she said so sweetly.

"What?" Now I was confused.

"I want to feature your work at my gallery." She was very businesslike now.

"Really?" I was timid.

"Yes, really. We hope to have our kickoff in a month, or so, and we want you to be the feature artist. We have a budget of one hundred thousand dollars and we expect to use half of that on advertisement. It would be good exposure for you."

"Why me?" I knew saying that was a mistake. It was out before I knew it.

"Does it matter? Will you do it?" A horn honked outside and I realized it was Jack. I hesitated. "I'm sure you need to speak with your agent, or manager so please have them call me at 516-485-1999," I scrambled to write the number down. Jack honked again. "Have you got that?" Irene sounded worried

"Yeah. 485-1999," I was distracted trying to signal Jack that I would be right there.

"I hope we can work this out," Irene returned to her old woman voice.

"I'm sure we can," I said as confidently as my nervous excitement would let me.

"Goood. Nice to speak with you Mr. Teeman."

"Likewise, Mrs. Solomon, good-by."

I hung up and the horn honked again. I ran out the door in a cloud.

"Sorry about that," I said between gasps as I climbed into the back of Jack's cab. I hadn't run that far, still I was mysteriously out of breath.

"No prob. Where to?" Jack smiled. I gave him cross streets for Arnie's and we were off.

"Hey Jack, did you ever have something so great happen to you that it scared you?" I finally said after collecting my breath and thoughts.

"Well, I never had a twenty eight hundred dollar fare, if that's what you mean," Jack laughed. I didn't laugh along with him. I was ill. I was sitting in the back with a cramp in my stomach.

"No, that's not what I meant," I had actually forgotten about that little windfall.

"What then?" Jack sounded genuinely interested.

"That woman who bought my paintings, now wants to take me on at her new gallery," I said with horror.

"And?" Jack couldn't relate.

"She's going to spend fifty G's on advertisement," I said in exaggerated disbelief.

"Whooo boy, that does sound rough. Fame, fortune…the torture," he was teasing. I could see why, too. I was still uncomfortable and Jack could see that in his rear view mirror, "Jeez, lighten up. Sounds like the opportunity of a lifetime."

"Yeah, I suppose." I tried to relax. "It's just that it's a new gallery and she's never been in the business before and I guess, I'm worried that she'll muck it all up."

"Well, you have to be careful, but you could benefit even if she does go under," Jack had such a reassuring tone. He had a lot of practice counseling in the cab.

"Yeah, that's true," I was relaxing! The buildings passing by had a fresh appearance suddenly. They had seemed so big before. Now, they were enormous. I sat there watching them, awe-struck. I smiled.

"God! Fifty G's on advertisement," I actually laughed. Jack laughed, too.

"You're not a native are you?"

"What?"

"The way you said 'Gawd'. You're not a New Yorker, are you?"

"Nope. Kansas," it's difficult to admit you're not a native. Probably because natives hate transplants so much.

"So you came here to be an artist," here it came, the patronizing rhetoric, the "How nice" smile, "and now you've made it and you're not even happy? Do you realize how many people would kill to be in your shoes?" I was speechless. I was dumfounded. Jack had such anger in his voice, like I was taking something from him. "Here you are your majesty. Thirteen dollars even," his anger had disappeared, but I was still numb. I handed him some money.

"Could you pick me up in an hour?" I thought, for sure, that he would say no.

"No prob," he smiled, waved and left me standing on the curb scratching my head. I always thought of myself as different from all those glory hounds that had made their obligatory pilgrimage to New York to be discovered. I didn't really have any expectations. I just wanted to do it. Why New York?

I had a friend when I was young, John Rogers. He was several years older than me, but out in the country a friend is a friend. John was a bundle of energy who was frequently out of control. He was always getting me into sticky situations and then getting me out. Sometimes I think that he used to try things, like climbing the silo, just to get me to follow him. He used to laugh hard when I got scared.

When John was twelve he fell in love with New York. Something he heard on the radio had really pushed his buttons. I never really figured out what it was, but he was infected. After that, he was always wondering about "the city". His parents finally took him to Kansas City so that he could see. When he came back he told me this story about waking up in the family station wagon while it was parked out front of the hotel. He had slept through most of the trip there and was catching his first eye full when he saw "the most incredible set of gozangas, ever". They were walking down the street toward him, thinly veiled behind a red T-shirt. Evidently, their owner caught him gawking because she pulled up her T-shirt and showed him those "mammoth globes" for a second. John hid his eyes, but he could hear that woman laughing and laughing.

"That kind of shit doesn't happen in Dildo, Kansas!"

I lost touch with him shortly after that trip. He befriended some kids his own age that lived in town. In the morning they smoked cigarettes together right outside of school grounds. That was the most decadent thing in Dilon, Kansas at the time. I would bump into John occasionally and he would still rave about New York. "Man, you just can't believe it 'til you see it," he used to say.

After he graduated High School he split. I knew that he went to New York although he didn't tell me he was going. My folks wouldn't listen to me during the investigation of his disappearance. Mr. and Mrs. Rogers were convinced that John had been kidnapped. They just couldn't believe he would leave without a word. I left for New York ten years later. It was the place where Dilonites went when they didn't fit in.

"Hey, stranger," Mary's voice brought me back to Arnie's. She gave me a big hug, but I was still thinking about John Rogers. "Are you all right?"

"Huh?"

"What's up? You seem so distant." I finally focused on Mary. She always asked about me. I liked that so much.

"Good news," I said with a smile. I was just bursting with happiness now, and it was because of Mary. I was glad to be able to share this with her.

"Whaat?" She was impatient.

"Let's get a table."

"Oh Frank, don't tease me," I just grabbed her hand and walked towards the patio. God that felt good. Her hand. Her hand in mine. And I was about to share my good fortune with her. I knew she'd be glad for me.

The best thing about good fortune is being able to share it.

Share it with someone who cares.

"I've been discovered," I said triumphantly before we even sat down. I couldn't contain it.

"What?" Mary has the brightest blue eyes. She opened them wide.

"A new gallery bought several of my things and now they want to feature me," I was practically shouting with joy.

"Frank, you're kidding," she actually thought I was kidding. I just smiled and shook my head. "Frank, congratulations," we hugged again, "you must be so happy."

"Yeah. A little scared, too."

"What's the gallery?"

"I don't know," I laughed.

"How did this come about?"

"I don't know," I laughed some more.

"C'mon Frank, you're teasing me."

"Well, actually when I called you it was because I had some money. She bought six paintings yesterday at the Purple Dragon."

"Who?"

"Irene Solomon. She's the woman behind all this. Anyways, she bought all my stuff at the Purple Dragon, you remember that place?"

"Sure."

"Then, this morning, right before I left to come here, she calls and says she's opening a new gallery and wants me to be the opener."

"Wow! That's great," she was vibrant.

"And get this—she's got a budget of one hundred thousand dollars!"

"Oh Frank, I'm so happy for you!" We were holding hands across the table and beaming at each other. My head was spinning at this point. It was the first time I really believed any of that. And here I was being happy with the woman of my dreams. Dreams!?! Maybe this wasn't real.

"Will you marry me?" God, I was dreaming. I would never say that in real life. But there I was holding her hand and staring into her eyes and saying, "Will you marry me?" Her eyes looked away and she withdrew her hand.

"Frank," she said in a hushed tone. I waited for something to follow. There was nothing. This definitely wasn't a dream. The waiter saved the awkward moment with a friendly, "What can I get you?" That gave Mary some one to look at. I couldn't take my eyes off of her. After the waiter left with our order, Mary was stranded with me again.

"God damn it," I finally gave in, "I'm such an idiot, sometimes."

"Frank, I'm sorry," she said with this begging quality.

It made me angry. Sick? Revolted.

"I always thought it was my poverty that you didn't like," I looked for some recognition. She barely looked at me. "Something else, huh?"

"Frank, we should be celebrating. You just had the most wonderful news."

"Yeah, it was great news. It was only good news until I told you, then it was great news. You made it great," now I had that begging tone. I was even more revolted.

"Sharing is always nice. Surely you have some one else you can share this with."

"Yeah, sure," I swallowed my nausea and put on a smile. We ate and chatted. I don't even remember what.

Just when you think things are good something pops up to remind you otherwise.

That's what I said to Jack when he picked me up. Mary left early to get to court and I had a good long time to brood. I was really dark by the time I got into that cab.

"Not a good time, eh?" Jack was sympathetic.

"I don't even know why I said it," I saw that Jack was confused by that non-sequitor, "I asked her to marry me," I admitted in shame.

"At lunch?"

"I know, I know. I can screw things up, if I don't try," now I was babbling. "Home please."

We jumped into traffic and I started thinking about what I was going to do. I still had that anxious desire to be productive. Or at least spend some money. I couldn't think of anything to do or to buy.

"Hey, Jack? Where can I spend some money?" I asked with determination. He looked at me like I was crazy.

"This is Manhattan. Where can't you spend money? You're spending money right now," he hit the meter. He was pissed again.

"I'm sorry. I guess I'm just not very good at this. Help me do this, Jack. If you had a thousand bucks what would you do with it?"

"Man, don't you need anything?" I tried to think. Nothing. "What about a new pair of shoes or something?"

Shoes? I looked down and saw the paint splattered shells of boots that covered my feet and had been doing so for the last eight years. Yeah, some new shoes.

"OK. New shoes. These boots do look pretty silly with this suit. Stop at the first shoe store." I declared with regal authority.

"Yes your majesty," Jack growled under his breath and lo and behold— Thom McAnn. "Would you like me to wait, your highness?"

"OK, OK, lighten up a little. I'll be right back."

I remembered shoe shopping as really fun. I hadn't done it in a while, though. What to get? I started looking around trying to decide what might feel comfortable and I started thinking that my feet were very comfortable now. Maybe I should get another pair of boots. Well, there's cowboy boots and there's boots with lots of buckles. Where are the Redwings? No Redwings? "No" the salesman confirmed. Oh, well. No new shoes today. Jack saw that I was empty handed when I got back in the cab.

"What's the matter?"

"No Redwings. Just take me home."

"You sure you don't want to try another store?" Jack said in disbelief.

"Nah. These boots are fine," I said in frustration.

"Man. I ain't never seen nothin' like this before. You don't know how to spend money!"

"Huh?"

"You got cash. Just buy a pair of shoes and if you don't like 'em, toss 'em. Or give 'em to the Salvation Army or something."

"Nah. That wouldn't be any fun."

"Fun? You want fun?"

"Yeah, that's what I want!"

"Then I'll take you down to forty second again. That's fun."

"Nah. That strip joint thing doesn't do it for me."

"C'mon Frank. You don't have to be a spectator. You can get a private show for just two hundred."

"I know. I coulda done that last night, if I wanted."

"Oh, I forgot. Kansas boy. You need to do it right."

"What?"

"Just go to a bar, find a pretty lady and buy her a drink. Wave some cash around, buy her dinner and you're in there."

"Hmmmm."

"Frank, if doin' the boingo ain't fun, I don't know what is."

"I suppose."

"You suppose!?!"

"You're right." What the hell was I thinking? Doing "The boingo" was fun. *"You are right."*

"It's Friday Frank. Hit some yuppie joint at happy hour."

"You know a good one?" I felt like a tourist.

"What do I look like? Just go down to that new market on the lower eastside. I hear all those Wall Street types hang out there."

"Can you pick me up?"

"Nah. I gotta boingo, too." We laughed, but I was growing more frustrated by the moment. For all these years I had been saying, *"If only I had the money."* What was I talking about? I needed sedation. Just get me home so I could relax. Yes, a couple bong hits and I'd figure this all out.

3/11/81

I did a self-portrait, once. I was never very keen on the idea and I'm still not. For one thing, I always try to get some expression of the person's character that I'm painting. When I look in a mirror I don't see any character. I'm too obsessed with the physical form of the object I'm seeing. It's always been that way, though. Ever since I can remember I've loved staring into the mirror particularly looking at my face. There are so many parts of your body that you know the look of intimately, but your face is not one of them. It's always on a two-dimensional plane of a mirror or a photograph. I look at my face and I can't help staring at it like a long lost brother. So, painting it is difficult and, I think, unproductive.

It was spring and I was coming out of a particularly cloistered winter. Things hadn't worked out between Mary and me and I was depressed about it. Not in any extreme fashion. I kept myself pretty pickled, though, so it's hard to say what my honest reaction was. When the holidays hit, I went for the full lonely-hearts club routine. I convinced myself that I was helping the people at those bars by providing companionship when they really needed it. I suppose there's some truth to that. While we were drinking we were happy. At least we pretended to be. I had just started working at McGarrety's so, I would work during the day and drink at night. My painting took a back seat for a while and I started fancying myself a real working class Joe. That was all part of my reaction to my failure with Mary. I was trying to build myself into the kind of person that I thought she wanted me to be. I had some spending money and a regular schedule and a carefree attitude, and lo and behold I started scoring! Yup, I would take a women home from those bars as often as I cared to and that was pretty often. I even spent a couple days with a few, but those were the longest. Most would show up at one of the local saloons a day or two later and I would greet her with a hug and then go back to conversation as if nothing had happened. Most of those were drunken slobber sessions anyways so nothing had happened. Once I had done my bit I wasn't interested anymore. I guess it was part of the "charity" I was doing and I wanted to spread it around. Anyhow, I had several women hounding me New Year's Eve. All those "charity cases" had come back and they were all at McSorley's looking for a hand out. I ended up watching the ball drop at Times Square by myself. It was nice to stand in that throng and feel that kind of energy—drunken people kissing everywhere.

I just watched.

It was over. I would go to work, still. But the rest of the time I was either painting or eating or sleeping. I did go to Central Park a few times. Once Spring sprang, I developed a bit of youthful exuberance and I wasn't able to vent that newfound energy. I started out trying to figure out what I could do for recreation and ended up on this intense self-introspection trip. That's when I decided to do the self-portrait. Once I had made the decision to do it, it consumed me and I would find myself relishing the slightest reflection. I did a bunch of sketches and I even bought a couple extra mirrors so that I could see myself from all angles. I was obsessing with the form again, you see. Consequently, I never felt ready to go to paint. I never force myself to paint. I wait for the paint to force me. And even though I had decided to do a self-portrait a month ago I was not yet possessed with the passion to do it. I did buy a canvas and I found myself looking at that blank canvas, somehow, expecting to see myself in it and then I would just have to paint between the lines. I never saw anything. I started to really question who I was. I had avoided having to answer any serious questions on the last trip. I figured the self-portrait would answer them for me. Now it was clear that I needed to answer those questions before I could do that painting. Top of the list was the whole relationship thing. I knew that when I had met Mary it had renewed something in me that I hadn't felt since college. Would I ever feel that again? If so, would I botch it again? I decided to call Mary and talk to her. It had been a year since we had first met.

"Mary?" I still had her work number, "it's Frank Teeman," I was short of breath with excitement.

"Frank! What a surprise," she sounded happy.

"How've you been?" I hate idle chat, but felt obliged.

"Not bad. Yourself?" She was tentative.

"Not bad," then the silence, "listen, I was wondering if we could get together for a cup of coffee or something."

"Well, I have an opening tomorrow at two o'clock." I could hear her looking through her calendar.

"No, this isn't a…listen, I was thinking about you and I wanted to see you."

"Frank that's sweet." There was a small amount of relief in her tone and consequently in my shoulders. "What about Saturday afternoon?"

"That sounds great. How about one?"

"Pick me up at my place?"

"See you then."

As I hung up the phone I caught a glimpse of myself in one of the mirrors that were lying around. It was the first time I had noticed that particular image. It was a kind of happiness. More like relief, but certainly, there was a happiness element there. I stepped closer to the mirror, but it was gone. I tried to recreate it. It didn't work. Still, I felt like I was already on my way towards completing that self-portrait.

My date with Mary started out with a hard-on. It popped up right there at the front door. I was really self-conscious about it. I didn't want Mary to think I was out for a quick roll in the hay. So, I gave her a top only hug and kept my hands in my pockets while we strolled and chatted. Eventually it went away, but sure enough it would pop up again. We ended up at an outdoor cafe and I was able to hide my protruding crotch under the table. There was a growing sense of intensity, I remember. I had a specific purpose for seeing Mary and I wanted to get to it.

"Mary, what's the matter with me?" I just blurted after some comment she had made about the cappuccino. I had taken her by surprise and it had made her feel uncomfortable, I could tell.

"Frank," she looked away, "I don't know what to tell you about that."

"Are you attracted to me at all?"

"I like you, Frank."

"I know," I collected myself.

"And I am attracted to you…"

"Have you ever thought about sex with me?" I was growing insistent.

"Not really."

"Either you have or you haven't."

"Well, I've thought that you probably wanted to," I nodded, "and there was a time when I might have…" I felt my ears start to glow, "but now, I'd rather not. I like you."

That made no sense to me.

"So,…what? It's just a chemistry thing? It's just not there for you?"

"Yeah. I guess you could say that."

"Well has it happened with anyone else?" She nodded. "Oh," was all I could say. "So, it wasn't that she's frigid. She's just not attracted to me. Why?" was all I could think.

By this time my previously protruding penis had lost its zeal and, if anything, it was more like an anti-hard-on. I felt cold for a second, but took a deep breath and was all right. I guess it was a harder realization than I had expected, but I was over it. I needed to do that self-portrait.

"Mary, I can deal with that. Can we talk about why? Be honest with me."

"Frank I've already said that I didn't know. I like you. You're a nice person. I'm sorry that the romance didn't happen," she looked at me with

plaintiff eyes. I didn't want to torture her, but I needed to know. "You'll meet someone. I'm sure of it," she tried to be reassuring. It didn't help.

"What about you?...Have you met someone?" I tried to sound like I was moving on.

"Well, yes. I have," she was embarrassed to admit it.

"Good for you," I tried to be happy, "tell me about him."

"Well, he was the PD for one of my people."

"A lawyer?"

"He's really dedicated to his work."

"So, are you two living together?"

"Noooo," she looked down, "As a matter of fact, I hardly ever see him."

"What?" I was outraged.

"Well he's so busy and tired at the end of the day."

"Oh, I see," I didn't see, but what else could I say. "When did you meet him?"

"Oh, about four months ago."

"And you love him?"

"Well our relationship is still growing. I think I love him."

"Have you slept together?" She just nodded.

I could tell that she was embarrassed and that made me melt. I really liked that about Mary. "Hey have you seen the new Woody Allen film?" I had put her through enough. She was distant, but returned soon enough. We talked about movies and then went our way. I didn't even escort her home.

So, there I was, alone again, sitting in front of that blank canvas, staring. I hadn't learned enough and now all I could think about was Mary. I have to admit that part of me hoped that Mary would profess her love for me. And then to hear about some other guy who doesn't even seem to care! That was brutal. I ended up at McSorley's that night. Whiskey is the best salve for a broken heart. After seven, seven and sevens I heard that blank canvas calling. I was surprised that it was still blank. When I got home I still expected to see those lines for me to paint between. I painted the whole thing black and then proceeded to the toilet for a prayer session to the porcelain god, after which I curled up on my bed and held on.

I woke up hurt. I could barely move, but I had a real desire to paint. That black canvas possessed a new dimension for me. Even though I couldn't see those proverbial lines, I picked up my brush and started. I called in sick to work and spent the whole day painstakingly painting. The pain was from my hangover. I really had to concentrate, but the motivation was there, so I persevered. Once the images started forming I was swept with an excitement that bordered on fear. It took me a good three weeks to finish. I went to work and everything. My thoughts were always on that picture. I would look at it from different angles and in mirrors and in my dreams. When it was done I slept a lot. I left it on the easel for a while. Then I developed a growing dislike for it so, I stowed it behind some other stuff. Occasionally I would be tempted to take it out and look at it. Those times I would go out drinking.

5/14/86

I showed up at McGarrety's, that night, at 10:15. I was late. I didn't even go gallivanting like I wanted to. I just sat home and painted. Fed the munchies and painted. It was one of those sessions where I would think eternally between strokes. I thought a lot about the people I knew in Kansas. I tried to imagine what they were doing at that precise moment. I even thought about calling a couple to find out.

I thought about it.

I thought about Irene Solomon's offer. There wasn't much to think about. It was too absurd. It would fall through, anyways. I didn't even know what she was talking about. Spending that kind of money on an unknown like me. It was a tax write off. That bothered me. I couldn't do that. No, she could find some one else. Yup, just forget about it—not the right thing.

"Frank!" Bill McGarrety bellowed when I walked into the store.
"Oh boy, he's pissed," I thought as I hid by the time clock. Bill's a real bear when he's pissed. And he gets pissed easily late at night. I heard him approaching and figured I'd cut him off. "Sorry Bill, I…" I saw his smiling face and it shocked me.
"You were out celebrating. I heard the good news. You lucky dog, you."
He wrapped his arm around me and squeezed. I was a little confused. I

was repressing the Irene Solomon thing so, it made it difficult to relate to his jubilance. "C'mon, don't be shy. Irene called us before she called you."

"Oh, that," I hung my head, "I'm not going to do that."

"What? Did I hear right?" Bill was shocked. I knew he would be. I couldn't look at him. I just nodded my head. "What are you, crazy? What's the matter?"

"It just doesn't feel right."

"Why the hell not?"

"It's a tax write off, Bill, I can't do that."

"What are you talking about?"

"Irene is lovely…" I tried to clock in.

"Frank, Frank, Frank," Bill was aghast, "C'mon back to the office we need to have a talk."

This was not a request. He had a firm hold on my arm and practically dragged me back there. I knew what was coming. The whiskey, the stories about the depression. It wasn't going to change my mind. Bill poured two glasses of whiskey and handed me one.

"You know Frank, that Mo and me think of you as a son," I looked up for the first time and saw Bill in all his sincerity. He had never said that before. "And we want you to be happy, and we won't be runnin' this store forever, and this is an opportunity." He stressed opportunity.

"I know," opportunity was always the key word in Bill's depression era parables.

"Now, it may not be ideal, but I know Irene and she's a good person…"

"Irene is a good person?"

"A real good person! She would never use you just to get a tax break."

"I heard her telling Maureen about her tax problems. Money changes people, Bill."

"Not Irene." He was incensed, "Besides, what have you got to lose?"

"My good name," I stung him with one of his own lines.

"Well, I suppose that's true," I set him back for just a second, "but, how do you know? Have you seen her plan?"

"No."

"Well there you go. Me and Mo are goin' out to visit Irene on Sunday. Why don't you come along?"

"I don't know," I had a hard time resisting his enthusiasm.

"Just think about it. We'll be leavin' at two in the afternoon."

"OK. I'll think about it"

"That's a boy," Bill laughed. That made me feel good. "Here's to it," Bill held up his glass.

I did likewise.

Then we drank.

Bill wrapped his arm around me as he did his post-shot laugh/growl.

"One more for good luck!" and we went through the routine again complete with laugh/growl at the end of which came "All right get to work. You're fifteen minutes late," he was back to his bearish self.

I was so humbled I was on the brink of tears.

"Thanks Bill," I said from the doorway of the office.

"For what?"

"For caring," I choked.

Bill gave me a big hug then.

The verve I had in the morning returned.

Change the mops. Change the dust mop. Get out the mop bucket. Put in some soap. Find some gloves and some rags, too. Plug in the radio. Clear a path to the dumpster. Throw out all those boxes. Move the aisle display racks. Start dust mopping. Back and forth. Twist of the wrist. End of the aisle and shake it clean. Next aisle, ditto. Op, a piece of gum. Where the hell is that scraper? Storage closet? No. Toolbox? No. It's in the bathroom! Of course! More mopping. Back and forth. End of the aisle shake. Yeah, I remember how to do this. It has been a long time. Get under the bread rack. Shake. It's amazing how much piles up. Once all eight aisles are done, mop up the eight piles at the end of the aisle and dispose.

"All right, Bill. Good night. Yeah, I'll think about it. G'night."

Doors locked. Crank that radio. "Talkin 'bout my generation!" Time for a coke and some chips. Bill is such a nice boss. He really was happy for me. I suppose I owe it to him to check it out. Maybe I'll ask him to be my agent. He runs a business. Maybe I will. OK, get out the scrubber. Park it at the end of aisle one. Hot water in the mop bucket. Wet aisle one. Back and forth. "Swab the deck matie!" I can't believe I asked Mary to marry me. Why am I so attached to her? Could it be that she's perfect for me? I don't know. Maybe I'm wrong about that. She certainly thinks I am. Maybe she's a lesbian. God, I never thought about that. Nah, she just doesn't like me. Why can't I accept that? Hmmmm. OK, time to scrub. How does this thing work? It says "on". It's plugged in. On, off, on, off, on—Damn! This thing's broken. Damn it! I have to finish by three for the Remzi delivery. I guess I'll have to take this piece of shit apart. Damn! I don't know anything about this. Off, on, off, on—nothing. Damn. The plug's in. Maybe there's another switch. On the cord? No. On the machine? No. Aaarrrgh. Guess I'd better get the toolbox. DAMN! Maybe the circuit breaker is off. God, I hope this doesn't turn out to be one of those days. What am I talking about? It's already been one of those days. I just need to get through this night with as little aggravation as possible. I can already feel the tension welling inside. Yeah, I'm pretty sick of this place. Bill's right. Opportunity knocks. Let's see, circuit panel, circuit panel? Ah yes, here we are right under the picture of Bill and Maureen. Well I'll be! One of them is off all right. Yes! It's working. I can hear it. Oh shit! What the hell was that? Aarrrgh. The pickles! Smashed by the scrubber. Shit! Turn it off. At least I didn't have to take it apart. This sucks. Glass everywhere. Pickle juice everywhere. Awww. Pickles ground up in the brushes. This sucks. I better clean it up. I got that damn Remzi at three. Let's see, it's already midnight. There goes my break. Damn! This sucks. I guess it's better than doin' beer bottles, though. Or is it? There's got to be days when you just don't feel like doin' that bottle. Although twenty bucks a pop ain't bad. I have to work three hours to get twenty bucks. I was at Tommy's for half an hour and "Red" made at least fifty bucks in that time. That's a hundred bucks an hour! Holy shit! I don't know what I'm surprised for. Whoring is profitable. I guess I just never thought of it in terms of numbers—cash per hour. I wonder what my cash per hour quotient is for my latest slutfest. Let's see, six paintings at twenty eight hundred bucks that's four fifty a painting and with an average of...how many hours? "Glad" I did in a couple or four hours, and "Shine on" was a major endeavor, maybe a hundred hours long. So, around fifty hours average per and that's not counting framing or transportation or all the hours I spent thinking about it. Thinking doesn't count. Everyone thinks about their job during off hours, right? So, I guess it works out to nine dollars an hour. Not bad. That's only for six, though. I wonder if "Red" ever does any bottles and doesn't get paid for it. God! I've done a hundred paintings that haven't sold. So, let's see, a hundred and ten paintings with a total income of thirty five hundred or so, that's about thirty bucks each, with an average time spent of oh, let's say for ease, thirty hours each, that's a big fat dollar an hour. Yeah, well, I better get this scrubber going. I certainly can't afford to lose this job. Jeez, it looks like the pickle juice bleached out part of the floor. Great. How the hell am I going to fix that? Aaarrrgh. Oh well. What's a light spot on the floor? No big deal. Back to the scrubber. Damn! The water's dried up. OK, back to the mop. Boy this thing is heavy. I'm tired. Can't be tired now, still plenty of work to do. Work, work, work, work. Work, work, work, work. Work is great. I love it. I live for it. If I keep telling myself that, maybe I'll believe it some day. Aaarrrgh. OK, Mister Scrubber time to go to work. What the fuck!?! Threw the breaker again. God damn it! Make sure it's off this time. Let's go check that breaker. What a pain in the ass. Well sure enough that fucker's off. OK, Mister Scrubber, please, please work for me. On. Nothing. Fuck! Off, on, off, on. Fuck! Did that breaker go again? Aaarrrgh. I don't need this. "I...do...not...neeeed...this!" Sure enough that damn circuit breaker. It's got to be the switch. It's got to be. The damn thing worked long enough to plow the pickles. So, if I leave it on…and…plug it in. Yes! OK, OK. Jeez I do not believe this shit. OK, unplug it, turn the circuit breaker on, leave the machine on and plug it in. Yesss. Here we go. Finally. That pickle juice is scrubbing out. Cool! Whew. What a hassle. OK, if I hustle I can finish this by three.

Will this ever end? Bill McGarrety has been running this market for thirty years. Before that, he worked here. I've been working here for six years now, and in a couple more I suppose Bill and Maureen will retire and I'll be next in line. Wow! I had been working at my folks market for six years when they died. I was next in line there, too. Is this a second chance? I can't imagine doing it. How do they pull it off? They have each other. That must help a lot. Yeah, it must be nice to have someone to be with. Maybe I should have taken Ellen Tamoritz up on her offer. It seemed so completely absurd at the time.

Ellen was the same age as me. We met in kindergarten and spent our entire schooling together. This was nothing extraordinary. Dilon is a small town of about four thousand and there were only a hundred, or so, kids in my grade. The thing that was special about Ellen was that she always sat in front of me. Alphabetizing the pupils was big then. Ellen and I never really interacted on any kind of social level except for idle chat before class. For thirteen years I chatted with Ellen Tamoritz. I never considered her my friend, though. I guess I knew her pretty well after all those snippets of conversation. She felt like she knew me, anyways. After I received my diploma from Roosevelt High, Ellen gave me a big hug and we laughed and cheered and that was the last I saw of her. And the last I thought of her. I hate to say it, but I was never much taken with her. So, Ellen spent thirteen years right next to me and I didn't even notice her absence. Then she popped up at my folks' funeral and I didn't even recognize her. She was pregnant at the time. Still, when she was giving her condolences I was thinking, "Who the hell is this?"

"Frank, if you need anything call me," she said and handed me a slip of paper with her name and phone number on it. When I read "Ellen Tamoritz" I got this picture of a little girl in pigtails. That's why I couldn't recognize her. I remembered her as a five-year-old, but not as a fifteen-year-old. Hmmmm?

Ellen showed up at the house a couple days after the services. I hadn't called.

"I was just concerned," she said when I greeted her with a question mark. I invited her in and we started our idle chat like usual. I was glad she was there. I had just found the papers about my adoption and it gave me a chance to forget about it for a while. Ellen talked and talked, mostly about town gossip. Never about my folks. I appreciated that. She asked me about college and then I talked while she listened. It was very therapeutic for both of us. I thought about asking her about her pregnancy, but couldn't quite put the words together. She finally said, "Don't you want to know about my baby?" with a pat on her protruding belly.

"When are you due?" I tried to sound enthusiastic.

"Eight more weeks," she tried to sound enthusiastic.

"You must be excited."

"I'm not sure excited is the right word." Then it dawned on me.

She had no rings on. She was at the funeral alone. There was a silence then. I didn't know what else to say.

"I've decided to give him up for adoption," Ellen was somber.

"I was adopted," flew out of my mouth for the first time. It sounded weird particularly since there was an element of pride in there. I did mean it to be consoling.

"Really?" Ellen looked up with astonishment. I just nodded because I knew that if I tried to speak I would cry. It didn't matter. I started to cry anyways. Then Ellen started crying. I gave her a hug and we both started wailing. We eventually fell asleep in our tears, holding each other tightly.

In the morning we woke with the sun. We didn't have much to say to each other. I offered her coffee and she accepted. We sat at the kitchen table sipping. I asked her about Bob Benjamin and we started reminiscing about old times. Even managed a couple of laughs.

"Well, I've got to go," she finally said. I was relieved. As she got to the front door she turned, took a deep breath and hit me with it.

"Frank, I would make you a...you'll need help at the store. We know each other so well. Please say you'll think about it." She looked at me with the sorriest eyes I'd ever seen. I was in shock. I wasn't even sure what she was talking about. I heard her words, but I couldn't make sense out of them.

"Thanks for listening. You're sweet," she gave me a kiss on the cheek and left.

I just stood there scratching my head. It took a little while, but I finally figured it out. Ellen wanted to marry me and we would live happily ever after, raising her illegitimate child, living in my folks' house, running my folks' store. I tried to picture it. I couldn't. I could see Ellen with the baby in her arms standing on the porch waiting the return of her husband from a hard days work. And I would try to insert myself in that scenario, pulling up in the family wagon...That's as far as I got. I didn't even have a driver's license. Never wanted one, either. Nope, just not do-able. I called Ellen directly. No answer. I tried to imagine my life in Dilon, Kansas if it wasn't going to be with Ellen. I could run the store. At least I knew how. Bob Benjamin was running his dad's hardware store, practically. He had a wife and a newborn. I could get a job at the munitions plant like so many of my classmates. Or maybe the brewery. I like beer. Wait! "I have a degree in communications."

The radio station?

The newspaper?

Boring.

Whew! Finally done. And just in time for that Remzi. Maybe I'll have a chance to relax a little bit. Only if he's running late. Well, get this infernal machine away as fast as possible anyways. God, I hope there's not much on the truck. I'm whipped already. If I were running my own grocery store I wouldn't be doing this, that's for sure. I'd be home in bed, with my wife. God, that sounds so appealing. It's amazing how a few years can change your perspective. Op, there's that truck. Damn. Why does he have to be on time today? Better get out there and help him. I know it's a tight squeeze. What the hell? He's already in place.

"Hey, kid," Ralph, *the janitor, was behind me.*

"Ralph? What are you doing here?" He was supposed to be on vacation.

"I'm your Remzi," he pointed to the emblem on his shirt. I was confused. "I usually deliver during the day and I'm here at night." He took a swig of beer, "Let's do it."

"You work two jobs?" I couldn't believe it.

"Yup. Got bills to pay," he was so casual, "C'mon let's go," he headed for the truck.

"I thought you were on vacation," I was still shocked.

"I am," he threw open the truck door, "After two jobs, working only one is a vacation," he laughed and handed me the invoice. It was thick. I was sick. By the time I looked up boxes were rolling towards me. Boxes rolled steadily out of that truck for two hours. There were times when I was shuffling boxes that I thought I was going to drop. I would start cursing under my breath, but another wind would come and I'd pop back into gear. Finally everything was in and Ralph was closing up the truck.

"God damn, Ralph. How the hell do you do it?"

"What's that?" Ralph was a big guy and had been laboring for years. He didn't know what I was talking about.

"Let me buy you a drink," I gestured towards the store. Ralph looked at his watch.

"Does the old man have any whiskey in the desk?"

"I had some when I came in," I said in confirmation. Ralph headed towards the office and I followed.

"Ralph! How long have you been doing this?"

"Only about eight years," he was so casual. My knees went weak then.

We picked up a couple of beers on the way while cursing the size of the load. By the time we got the whiskey out I was back to Ralph's double life. He told me how he and his wife decided to move out of their fastly decaying neighborhood so, he took the night job at McGarrety's in order to afford their new place.

"How do you do it?" I said with an aching.

"I don't mind it," he was still so casual, "I'm never bored."

We laughed.

"Neither am I," I thought.

3/11/66

We were doing finger painting one day when I was in kindergarten. Our teacher encouraged us to do a picture of our parents. So, I did. I actually did a family portrait with me in the middle. I brought it home and I remember how pleased my folks were. I also remember how orange it was. It went right up on the fridge. And it stayed there. That finger painting was still hanging there when I graduated grammar school. I don't remember the circumstances around its removal, but once it was gone I felt a real need to replace it. I guess that was the start of my "career" as an artist. I got a hold of some watercolors, somehow, and started dabbling, but became frustrated quickly. I wanted to do extremely realistic portrayals of my family and surroundings and the watercolors weren't doing it. I didn't know about oils or acrylics, I guess I was ten or eleven.

"Why don't you try drawing, dear," Mom said, once, to try and quiet me when I got frustrated. I couldn't draw, though. I couldn't even write legibly so, I knew I wouldn't be able to draw. I gave it a shot, though, and I was surprised how well I did. I was still not satisfied. I liked colors! That's when Mom got me a set of Crayolas. That kept me quiet for a while. I still wasn't able to capture the realism that I was looking for. I was convinced that paint was the answer. It was actually John Rogers who told me about oil and canvas.

"Painting is cool, man," John said with a reverent awe. I could talk to John about things and when I ran into him I told him I was painting. "I saw this wild piece when I was in KC. It was oil on wood. Completely different from canvas. And it had a bunch of toothpicks glued in there, too. W-i-i-ld." That had become his favorite word. "What are you working in?" I wasn't sure what he was talking about so, I spewed something that included the words "oil" and "canvas". As soon as I got home I told my mom that I wanted "oil and canvas" hoping she would know what that meant.

"Honey, let's talk about this when your father gets home," was all I got. Maybe she didn't know, either. Dad's response was a little frightening.

"Sounds like you need a job so you can buy yourself some supplies." Not exactly what I was looking for. I wasn't following him, though. "I know a grocery store that could use some help." I still wasn't following. I thought we had left the original topic completely.

"What about paint, dad?"

"Well, when you get your own money you can do with it what you like," he said with a smile.

Finally, I understood.

I went to dad's store after school the next day and he immediately took me to the storeroom. I was surprised to find a little corner cleared out with a homemade easel standing in the middle of it.

"Wow, dad, thanks," I rushed over to it.

"Don't thank me until you hear it all. Look! Here's paint and some brushes," he showed me several silver quart cans and several varied brushes and a feeling of excitement filled me until I laughed out loud. "Now hold on," he kept me from opening one of the paint cans, "here's some stencils and here's a list," my enthusiasm plummeted, "this list is all the signs that I need made," he handed it to me and I read all those items that were on sale, "now, you can do these signs however you want, but they're going up in the store so, I won't put 'em up unless they're readable," I looked at him, confused. I hadn't expected this at all. "Can you do it?"

"Yes sir," I never turned down a challenge.

"All right," dad chuckled as he gave me a hug, "go at it. Oh, and I'll give you fifty cents for every one that goes up. Here's a big roll of paper so, if you make a mistake just start over. Neatness counts so, take your time. OK?"

"OK," I wasn't too confident. I didn't know where to start.

"I've got to go up front. I'll check to see how you're doing in a little bit," and he was gone. I sat there looking at that list and that excitement returned. Not only did I have a neat set up, I was getting paid to paint and it was all because of my dad. I could hardly believe it. I spent the longest time just looking at everything. I still wasn't sure where, or how, to start. Eventually, I opened that first can of red paint. I remember the tingle that went up my spine as I dipped the brush for the first time. The glistening paint. I remember the sheen. It seemed so shiny. I was grinning with delight, but as soon as I applied the brush to the paper a big drip ran down it. Hmmmm? Not so easy. So, I crumpled up that paper and started again. I managed to get the brush sufficiently dry so as to be able to paint without dripping. I painted an Ess. Scott paper towels were on sale. The Ess was crooked and the paint thinned out halfway through. I crumpled up that sheet, too. I tried holding the stencil with one hand and painting with the other. That worked for the Ess and the Cee, but I slipped on the Oh. Another crumpled wad and the disappearance of my grin. I was deter-mined, though, so, I tore off another piece and tried it again, but my arms were getting tired and I slipped on the Ess. Dad showed up then and saw the pile of failed attempts. There was paint on the floor and on me, too. I hadn't even noticed that. He got me an old apron and tied it up to fit. He laid a bunch of cardboard on the floor and that's when we decided to do away with the easel. I was afraid that he would be angry with my slow progress and I could see that he was aggravated over the spilt paint, still he had a patient and encouraging tone so, I continued with resolve, if not enthusiasm. Dad had gotten me some masking tape so that I could hold everything in place. That worked nicely. I painted as slowly as I could, but when I removed the stencil I found that the paint had bled underneath it and instead of the neat Ess I thought I had accomplished, a red blotch *appeared. I screamed and tore up that paper. Fran, a cashier, came running back. She thought I was hurt. She found me just pouting. She laid out a new piece of paper, laid down a stencil and traced its shape with a pencil. When she lifted the stencil, I realized where I had gone wrong and grabbed the brush.*

"Do the whole sign first. Paint last. OK?"

"OK," I was embarrassed at my ignorance. She handed me the pencil and tousled my hair. We both laughed. I started tracing immediately and soon I was filling those lines with glistening red paint. I finished that sign and got paid fifty cents.

When I showed up the next day "Scott Paper Towels 39c" read brightly in the front window. I stood in the parking lot admiring. It was a beautiful sign, I thought. I went back in and started on the applesauce sign. I decided I would put an apple on this one. Dad liked it so well he gave me seventy-five cents. I had benefited tremendously from a suggestion of Fran's. She came back right when I was starting, complimented me on the Scott sign, and then mentioned outlining the letters with a thin brush, "to smooth out the edges." I was ecstatic. The next day I took Emily Parker to the soda shop for a malt after school. When I got home I was in trouble. Dad expected me to show up for "work." Then when he found out I had blown the whole dollar twenty-five on confections…

"I thought you wanted oil and canvas," dad wasn't shouting, but it was clear that he was angry. Mom was grinning from ear to ear. She eventually convinced him that it was all right for me to have celebrated a little, but also emphasized that I had "a job" now. Every day after school I went to the store to paint. So, painting had now become a chore.

I started getting restless pretty quickly and started getting creative. One sign had all the words reading from top to bottom. Dad accepted that one, begrudgingly. The next one had all the letters crooked. That one didn't go up. Then I found a piece of plywood behind the paint cans and decided that I was going to work on a family portrait. No words, no sale price, just a picture. When dad found me kneeling in front of that board he freaked. We got in a big argument and I stomped out of the store. We rode home together in silence.

Over dinner dad gave me my "pink slip". He said that I wasn't ready for the responsibility of a job and I agreed. That was the end of my interest in painting. I thought about that family portrait I had started, but only occasionally. I hadn't gotten much done on it so, it was more of a recollection of the vision I had for that painting. It was a clear vision. That's why I had started it. It presented itself to me. When I pulled out that wood I was compelled to do it. Dad didn't understand that. Neither did I. It kind of frightened me. I had never been intentionally disobedient before. That's why I steered clear of painting for almost five years.

A force guiding you into previously unventured territory?

A force from within?!? No one else to blame?

Just a crazy feeling that it has to be done?!

That's frightening.

5/15/86

Another Saturday night and I ain't got nobody. But, I still got that damn cash. I thought about giving some of it to Ralph, actually. When I woke up that afternoon, cursing the C shift, I thought about Ralph. "I don't mind it," I could hear him saying so casually. Well I do mind it. And I realized it that morning. I went right to the phone, called Bill, and told him that I would join them on their visit to Irene. He suggested I call Irene and tell her that. I didn't want to. My revulsion with work gave me the strength. Fortunately, there was an answering machine. I was relieved. I didn't want to talk with Irene just then. I was still uncomfortable with the idea even though I had resigned myself to it. That resignation was very obvious, once I had left that message.

"It has begun," I said aloud as I hung up the phone. I turned around and saw my humble abode in an entirely new light. It seemed so small and mundane. The hole in the wall where I had fallen in a drunken stupor two years ago seemed like a gross wound. The harshness of the lighting fixture was unbearable. That blank canvas beckoned me from the easel, but I turned my back on it. I dialed Checker to find Jack off duty. I felt that wad of cash filling my front pocket and my desire to have some fun with it returned vigorously. I just started walking. It was a nice day and that was a good thing because I left without a jacket. As a matter of fact, I had left without my keys or sunglasses. The place was open. The radio was on. The light was on. Who knows what else was left on? I didn't. I didn't care. I was glad to be walking. And seeing people. It was time for another dose of energy. So, I stopped on Seventh Avenue to soak. I could hear, "Jesus is the

savior!" It was bellowing from a well-dressed old man. There was a sense of desperation in his voice as he sang the Christian rhetoric. I watched him intently. Hundreds of people streamed by him. Not one of them even looked at him. He was invisible. Only I could see him. And he was all that I could see. I waited for someone to acknowledge him or drop him some change. Hundreds more streamed by. Nothing. Standing in the bright sun, I began to feel cold. I closed my eyes to call the energy. It didn't come.

"Open your heart to Jesus. He will save you from sin!" rang loudly in my ears. Was he crying? It sounded like he was crying. I opened my eyes to see him as I had left him; patiently listing the tenants of the Christian faith in as loud a voice as he could muster. So loud it was burdensome. Still, no one paid any attention. Then, the strangest thing happened. The old man stopped bellowing, looked at his watch, reached into his suit jacket, pulled out a cigarette and started smoking. My heart sank. I was intrigued with this character, but when he took that first tentative drag on that cigarette, I felt hatred. Maybe it was because he looked at his watch. It was definitely hatred that I felt. It was that hatred that finally motivated me to approach him.

"Are you a Christian, sir?" I was patronizing. I hated my tone, but I was driven by a deeper force than my conscious.

"Yes, I am," he was proud despite his soft tone, "and you?" He continued smoking. Somehow this calm demeanor was not what I expected. There are so many religious, fanatic, zealots that can't wait to shout the praises of their lord. I thought he would be one. He was not. I was surprised. I was so surprised I had forgotten, really, what was happening. I was focusing on him. Trying to see his eyes. They were effectively masked behind dark sunglasses.

"And you?" he repeated patiently.

"No," I finally admitted.

"You sound sad about that."

"Do I?" He nodded. "Well, I tried…Listen, do you accept donations?"

"You can't buy Christ's blessing. Open your heart to him," he took one last drag off the cigarette, put it out on the bottom of his shoe, and then put

the butt in a Band-Aid box that he had in his jacket pocket. "Jesus Christ, the son of God, died for your sins," he bellowed again. I just stood there dumfounded. I had heard all this before. Being raised an atheist in the middle of the Bible belt opens you up to "converters" all the time. This man had affected me, though. He wasn't pan handling. He wasn't distributing literature.

"What are you doing?" I finally said.

"I'm singing."

With that a total sense of contentment spread from him to me. Not so that I felt content but, so that I could feel his contentment. Then I knew it was possible and I left him with hope in my heart. And as I marched up Seventh Avenue, I felt like I was glowing. I was hoping that that glow of contentment was spreading to those around me. As I passed a particularly reflective store front, I noticed that that glow was not obvious. And when I found a mirror in that display, I knew that that glow was not apparent at all. There I was looking at myself, no different from the morning or the morning before that. Oh well, it didn't change the way I felt. Just as I was about to continue on my way, I saw those boots. They were just brown leather. They only had three pair of eyelets. They had a subtly pointed toe, and they had the most interesting pattern etched into them. The texture given off by this etching was extremely rough. As I looked closer, I found that it was just a bunch of lines maybe an eighth of an inch long. That's it. A bunch of lines, this way and that.

"Huh?" I said with delight. That's when I knew I had to have them

At first I went into my conditioned response of "wish I had the money," but then I remembered that I did have the money. So I marched into the store and asked for a pair, "Size 9". They were a little small so, I tried nine and a halves. They were a little big. Hmmm? The salesman suggested I wear thicker socks. The ones I had on were probably ten years old and extremely thin. He brought me a pair of thick black socks and they felt so good by themselves I almost forgot about the boots, but the salesman put them on me quickly and before I knew it I said, "I'll take 'em!" When the cash register stopped it said, "$258.95" and I almost reneged. That was *just my subconscious. My hands had already counted out three hundred dollars and handed it to the man.*

"Sir, your boots," he called to me as I headed out the door. He was holding up my paint covered relics. I almost yelled, "Toss 'em!" but held my tongue and retrieved them.

I stood outside that store feeling content with myself, finally. I looked down at those new boots and smiled. I wiggled my toes and felt those thick socks and laughed. I headed up Seventh Avenue again, smiling at every one I saw. The sun was just about to set and I still expected to see a glow emanating from me. All indications were against that, but I still believed it. Shortly, the stiff new leather of the boots had started to blister my feet in several spots and the discomfort was beginning to dominate my awareness. Eventually, I sat down and put my old boots back on. Part of me was defiant but my feet won out. They were in distress.

There was a tremendous feeling of relief when I stood up with my old boots on and I began to wonder what I had done. Two hundred fifty dollars to blister my feet? That wad of cash started calling again. I needed to do something with it that I felt genuinely good about. I held that cash and actually started to sweat. It began with my palm and spread quickly to my forehead. As I wiped my brow with the back of my hand, I heard Jack.

"If doing the boingo ain't fun, I don't know what is." That's when I saw the sign go on—"Tommy's Topless" illuminated brightly. I knew, then, precisely what I had to do. I wasn't that thrilled about it, but I knew that it had to be done. I wasn't thrilled at all. It was like surgery or something unpleasant that you look forward to it being over. A tension entered my system then and manifested itself as a stomach cramp. I thought about eating and that made it worse. I had to go inside.

I asked at the bar about the red head from Tuesday night. I wasn't even sure if the bartender had heard me, he just turned and slowly walked out. Red appeared, shortly, and it was obvious that she recognized me and was disgusted with what she remembered. She sat down next to me, anyways. I guess it's her job.

"You remember me, don't you?" I had to ask.

"Sure. What a ya need?" She had a cute voice. That helped me to relax.

"I was hoping to get a private show," I was sipping a beer, but I kept my eyes on her to see her reaction. There wasn't one. At least as far as I could see.

"Your not a cop, are you?" She knew I wasn't. I smiled. I'm not exactly sure why. I think it had something to do with game playing. I like playing games. Rules make for easy lanes to follow. Somehow, by her asking that question a lane had been formed. I felt even more relaxed.

"No. I 'm not a cop," I looked straight at her to make sure that she understood that I understood.

"What are you, then?" She actually lightened up a little bit.

"Does it matter?"

"Not really. How 'bout buying me a drink?" She was now coy. That made me smile—first base.

"Sure. How 'bout telling me your name?"

"I'm Mary," she held out her hand.

"Frank." I put my hand in hers. We didn't shake, we just held, hands. I smiled again—second base.

"Mary what?"

"Does it matter?"

"Not really. What'll you have Mary?" She just signaled the bartender and a glass of soda water appeared. The bartender left without asking for money.

"That was easy," I said.

"Just leave a nice tip." I threw a five on to the bar. "So, you want a private show," I nodded, "and what makes you think I do private shows?"

"Just thought I'd ask."

"Private shows cost…"

"I know. What'll two hundred get me."

"About an hour," she smiled this time—third base.

"That's a long time."

"I aim to please," I laughed, "besides we've already wasted five minutes." I stopped laughing and we just looked at each other.

"Let's get the hell out of here then."

"Let's go," she said quietly.

My heart was racing for the first time. I was at home base, but I was just starting to run. Now there were no lanes. That stomach cramp painfully made its presence. I felt a spinning sensation akin to drunkenness, but with none of the other physical manifestations like loss of muscle control. I was walking straight out the door. I followed her across the street and up two flights of stairs and down the hall into a room marked 6B. It was a dim room with a bed and a dresser and one small lamp on top of the dresser. I sat on the bed and tried to collect my thoughts. It was difficult. My palms were sweaty and my mouth was dry. Everything had a surrealistic bent to it.

"Do you have anything to drink?" Mary was looking at me as if she'd seen me for the first time. She was intrigued, though, not revolted. She went into the bathroom and brought me a glass of water. While I drank she started massaging my shoulders. Ahhhh, this was nice. Yeah, I felt pretty good.

"So, when does the show start?" Mary still didn't say anything. She just furrowed her brow. She gently pushed me back onto the bed and took her position at the foot. She started stripping very slowly. No music. No bump and grind. Just a sexy slow strip. I smiled. She smiled back. When she was naked she paraded her body in front of me while subtly caressing her breasts and bottom. She was beautiful. When she got onto the bed to remove my shoes, she gave me a close up of her red muff. I reached out and put my hands on her bottom.

"Ooh," was the first thing she said.

Once my shoes were off the rest of my clothes followed quickly. Mary looked me from head to toe. She didn't touch me, though.

"Well?" Her voice took me by surprise. I hadn't heard it for so long. I was lost in the experience. She brought me back to reality.

"Yes?" There weren't any lanes now.

"What's it gonna be?" She grew impatient.

"Whatever you want." Oh, what a stupid thing to say.

"It's your money. It's whatever you want."

I was still on my back and she was straddling me. Her nipples were erect. Her red bush had a slight sparkle.

"I want whatever you want." I was at a loss.

I felt like I had gotten my money's worth. I figured she'd take the money and run. She put her fingertip in her mouth and started biting it. Finally she said, "I want you to fuck me," in a husky voice. I reached out and touched her. She reached down and touched me. She was so hot. I was so hard. The next thing I knew, I was inside her. I watched her ride me slowly. There was a definite separation. My mind was a voyeur. Some guy was fucking Mary. She seemed to like it. She rubbed her nipples. She moaned. Her tempo increased until she was banging her hips against his. That's when my hips started reciprocating hers. Orgasm came simultaneously, I think. We looked at each other at that moment like the strangers we were, coldly. She fell on top of me and started kissing my neck. What were those sounds she was making? She was crying! That knot in my stomach returned and reached all the way up to my throat. I put my arms around her and squeezed. I squeezed so hard. I don't know why. Maybe I thought I could squeeze the tears out. It seemed to be working. She was bawling.

"God damn it," I heard her say under her breath as she jumped out of bed and started dressing. I almost laughed. She looked so cute. But she was seriously upset so I quietly started dressing. Once I got my pants on I felt that wad of cash. I pulled it out, counted out two hundred and looked to give it to Mary. She wasn't looking at me. She just went and opened the door. I put my boots on and I realized that I had left my new boots in the bar.

"Damn," I shouted. I was certain they were gone. "Mary, I left a package in the bar, can you help me?"

"Sure," she was reluctant. She still wouldn't look at me. We walked back to the bar in silence. She got me past the doorman. I rushed to the place where I had sat. No boots. I just slumped in the seat.

"Damn," I shouted again as I pounded the bar. I saw Mary talking to the bartender and gesturing towards me. Then I saw the bartender hand Mary the bag with my boots in it. I couldn't believe it. All that tension that was building transformed itself into an explosion of pure bliss. I let out a silly laugh when Mary handed me the package and it brought a smile to her face.

"Thanks so much," I was humbled. I reached into my pocket and pulled out some of that cash.

"Keep your damn money," she barked, quietly.

"What?" I thought to myself. "What?" I was confused.

"You could buy me dinner," she was coy again.

I was delighted. Absolutely delighted.

Can it be possible? A man living in Manhattan who doesn't know how to spend money? Is it believable at all? I don't believe it and I'm writing it. But, there it is, still on the page. Like so many other details that have been edited by my hand, I could've changed it. But, I didn't. And now, I'm asking myself, "Who the hell is this guy, Frank Teeman?" I'm reading his story and I'm writing his story. Sometimes these bits come down the cosmic telegraph and I stop and say, "No way."

The telegraph replies, "Yes."

So, it seems, that Frank Teeman is an unusual character. Maybe he's crazy. I mean, what's all that stuff about "soaking up the energy"? Sounds like a crazy man. But, even if he is, he's paying his bills and he's not bothering anyone. He's never been arrested. He's never even conversed with a police officer. So, maybe he's not crazy. Maybe he's just emotionally disturbed. It doesn't seem like he's dealt with the death of his parents or the fact that he's adopted. So, maybe he's hiding. It's easy to hide in Manhattan. Not physically hide, but, hide your true self behind the facade of a person. Frank doesn't seem to be hiding anything. Anyone who asks gets the real Frank. He admits to being from Kansas and talks of his adoption and mourns the loss of his parents. So, maybe there's nothing unusual about him. Still, I have a hard time with the money thing. In a day when multi-million dollar lottery winners blow everything in a year and two million people file for bankruptcy and millions of others get overdue notices from creditors, how can this man, who has relatively nothing, not be overwhelmed with desire when presented with some spending money? That's the big stumbling block. I can see wanting to hold on to your cash once you've got a little, but not to be tempted to blow it on every passing whim? That, for me, is what makes Frank unusual.

OK, granted, he did buy a couple things. That's something. But it's more like paying a bill. You get a notice, and to continue service, you send in your payment. Or you blow it off! When service is disconnected, though, you march right down to the office and pay up so that you can keep your food from spoiling. Well, Frank's music service had been interrupted and buying that tape deck was more an effort to maintain status quo than a venture into the delights of materialism. Same with the boots. Frank doesn't seem to have wondered the path of frivolous spending. "If I won the lottery, I'd buy a Ferrari…" We've all heard it. People dream about that kind of cash surplus all the time. For most it's the only motivating force in their lives. For the rest it's a major motivating factor. For Frank it's far down the list. It's not like he's anti. He admits to coveting wealth and he knows that spending is pleasurable. It's just far down the list. How unusual is that?

And what about companionship? That one seems to be pretty far down Frank's list, too. There's a lot of lonely people out there. Frank doesn't seem to be one. He does lead an isolated existence. Does that make him lonely? Most of us would assume so. Frank has his relationships. He has Mary and Brian and the McGarretys and now Jack. For him that is enough. If he were lonely he might try to buy new friends with his cash. That's what Jack said to do. Even though Frank agreed, he wasn't that thrilled with the idea. Frank's got his own methods of coping with loneliness. One of them is painting people. There's not a lot of companionship there, but it does serve to keep him in touch with humanity. His other coping mechanism is "soaking up the energy". I don't know what the hell that is all about. Frank admits to it being a cure for his loneliness.

So, the McGarretys and Brian and Ralph and Mary satisfy Frank's need for one on one interaction and "the energy" gives him that con-

nection with humanity that we all need. Painting gives him the opportunity to make new acquaintances. Actually, the people Frank meets in
day to day living, like the guy at the art store and the bartenders at the
various places he frequents and even Red, become part of the people
Frank paints. He always tries to get a feeling for the character of the
person in his paintings and through that investigation he comes to
understand individuals. All that may satisfy his cerebral needs for
human contact, but what does it do for his sexuality? No matter how
much you think about doing it, there's no substitute for sex. It doesn't
seem like Frank's getting a lot, and that in and of itself is not unusual,
as a matter of fact it's probably pretty normal, but Frank doesn't seem
obsessed with getting some. Again, he's not anti, when Jack suggests
doing the meat market thing Frank realizes it's a good idea and he
remembers sex as pleasurable, but it didn't occur to him first. It's just
far down his list of priorities. That's unusual.

There are plenty of men, mostly priests, who renounce sex. They do
it by choice. Maybe Frank is a religious man. Even the most dedicated
talk of resisting temptations of the flesh. Through a conscious effort
they sublimate their desires. They have eliminated sex from their list of
priorities. This is what makes Frank unusual. Sex is something that he's
open to, but not actively pursuing. OK, even that is not so unusual for
practicers of certain religious faiths. So, maybe Frank is a religious
man. He hasn't mentioned any particular faith, still material wealth
and sex are far down his list of priorities, I think. Maybe Frank is an
ethical man. You know, the kind who thinks about morals and moral-
ity and then shapes his life to fit his perception of what is right. Not
necessarily a religious man. Religious men often follow. Frank is not
following. He's not leading, either. He's not following so he's not a
religious man. But he could still be an ethical man. He doesn't seem to
be obsessed with doing what's right. And there's the whole drug and
alcohol thing. He talks of pot as if it were candy. And alcohol? A daily
occurrence. This hardly sounds like an ethical man. What do you call a
man who glazes over the physical pleasures of sex and the temporal

comforts of wealth, but doesn't mind getting high on drugs and alcohol or owning a stereo system? Unusual. That's what I'd call him.

Being unusual is not a bad thing, necessarily. There are probably thousands of people who fit into that category and thousands of others who are trying to fit into that category. I'm trying to say that Frank Teeman is unusual above and beyond those purveyors of angular haircuts and bright clothes. He is also unusual amongst the extremists of the right. So, Frank is unusual in a more universal way. What does that make him? Usual? Normal? Yup. I guess that's it.

Frank's just a normal guy. He's got his vices and he's got his virtues. That's normal.

PART II
▼

5/17/86

I made a deal with the devil. I hate to say it because I know it sounds absurd. I believe it's true. It happened one morning in Central Park. I was there trying to recapture some of the energy I use to feel from life. I hadn't felt it for quite a while and I was feeling desperate. Desperately depressed. It's the craziest thing. I mean, what did I have to be depressed about? I had everything; money, woman, a little bit of fame, but no energy.

From a very young age I had the ability to pull serenity from no where. I did it instinctively until I left home. Then I began to realize it was a special talent. It scared me, so I avoided it then. I did find a substitute. I became a member of the College Crusade. The CC was an organization dedicated to bringing the word of Christ to university campuses. I wasn't really that involved. I did enjoy the Sunday afternoon sessions. There, students would talk about their experiences with Christ. And more than the stories, I would get a lift from the people. Their energy was just overwhelming. Some were very mild mannered and others were all fire and brimstone. They all affected me mostly the same at first. I did develop a particular affection for the meek, though. Everyone who spoke stayed with the standard rhetoric, so, after a while, I didn't hear the words anymore. When the shy individual took the podium and everyone strained to hear their words. I would close my eyes and smile. When that room would go quiet to let them speak I would get a tingle.

When I left school, after graduating, my parents were killed and that forced me to find that serenity within myself again. From then on I was content to do just that. Until I met Irene Solomon, that is. Such a sweet woman, too. It's hard to believe that she ruined my life. Oh, it's not that she ruined my life. I don't blame her. But, after my encounter with her, I lost my ability to pull serenity from no where and that's what put me in the park that morning and that's where the deal went down. And that's where I went down.

There was something about her that didn't sit right with me from the start. I guess that's not true. When she first popped up at the grocery store, I was intrigued. She had that wealthy look about her, and I was always attracted to wealth. Not in any intense way, but it was a hobby. Then, when she bought all my work at the Purple Dragon I started to worry.

"Be careful what you wish for—You may get it"

I used to wish for wealth, but it was more of an effort at blending in than an actual wish. The only time I thought about it was when I was with other people. When I was in my loft alone, I was, for the most part, content. Then Irene came along and dropped that wad of cash on me. I spent most of my time after that trying to decide how to spend that money. It wasn't a pleasure. It was an obligation. So, when I went with Bill and Maureen to lunch with Irene I actually felt a little bit of contempt for her. Not only did she interrupt my previously peaceful, penurious life, she was talking about making it worse—giving me more money and some recognition, too.

"Mr. Teeman, I'm so glad you could make it," she squeezed my hand firmly and looked me straight in the eye. We were standing in the foyer of her grossly large estate out on Long Island. My contempt for her was as great as ever, but it was buried behind the shock I was feeling. This was the first time I had been out of New York City for years. I sat in the back seat of the McGarrety's '81 Cutlass Sierra on the way out and peered out the window constantly. As the urbanity gave way to the pastorality I drifted back to my childhood in the country. By the time we reached the Solomon's

I was a zombie. I put up a good front, but I was incapable of feeling anything. Particularly disdain.
"Thank you, Misses Solomon."
"Irene. Please call me Irene," *she was still clutching my hand.*
"Thank you, Irene. I'm very glad to be here." *I was subdued. It was actually my good upbringing speaking. I was caught up in the memories of when I was last at my folks' place. It was all the birch trees in the Solomon's front yard. My folks had a lot of birch. I discovered it was their aroma that I was attached to. When Bill stopped the car and the doors opened, I smelled that wondrously subtle odor. That's when I entered my former frame of mind. My parents had just died and I had decided to sell everything and leave.*

I was a zombie.

It all worked out well, I guess. Irene and, Bill and Maureen, had a lot of catching up to do so I sat and sipped my vodka martini and stared at the birch trees. Occasionally, the conversation would wend it's way around to me and I would smile and toast my glass and they would smile back at me and everything was wonderful. Sunny, bright, warm and cheerful.

I felt like crying.

Once lunch began, and I was halfway through my third martini, I started to focus on Irene. I needed to decide if I could trust her, so I started looking for some indication of her character. That's when I noticed that she was really very beautiful. She had an extremely dignified air about her. Her high cheekbones and well defined chin made for a nice frame of her petite nose. Her eyes were blue and pure. When there was a lull in the conversation, I piped in.
"So, tell me about your new gallery, Irene," *with enthusiasm. Irene smiled and started listing the physical details with glee. I was delighted. Her obvious joy over this project was a deciding factor. I could trust her.*

"It sounds delightful, Irene."

"We could go see it after lunch, if you'd like,"

"I'd like that very much."

We were smiling at each other and Bill and Maureen were smiling at each other, too, and there was a tremendous sense of happiness filling the room. It was intoxicating. Then, as I looked down at my plate I realized that Irene was still looking at me. And when I looked at her, our eyes locked, in what I can only describe as sexual tension. I looked down again in denial, but it was there. That threw me for a loop and I was self-conscious from then on.

The limo ride to the gallery that afternoon reminded me of the prom. I was so nervous. I was nervous because I felt that sexual expectancy. Just like the prom. Irene was smiling at me. I couldn't look at her. I was sure she was looking for an opportunity to jump my bones. The alcohol was wearing off and my mouth was dry and I started to wonder why I was so repulsed by the idea of Irene kissing me. The lip part I didn't have a problem with. It was the tongue that bothered me. I retched when I imagined it. Why?

"Would you like a drink, Frank?" Irene opened the bar.

"She's trying to get me drunk so she can take advantage of me," I thought to myself. *"Sure,"* I heard myself say. It was my dry mouth speaking.

"Vodka martini?" She had a little girl's voice! I nodded with a smile.

"Don't do this. Don't do this" was running through my head.

Irene held out the martini, *"You're very talented, Frank,"* she said with admiration.

"I'm glad you think so," I hate that word.

She laughed, *"such an artist."* I wasn't following and looked to her for elaboration. *"You don't like that word 'talent' do you?"* she said smugly.

"No. I don't," I said under my breath.

I felt angry with Irene for finding me so predictable.

"You are very talented, Mister Teeman," she said emphatically. I didn't say anything. *"To your talent,"* she held out her glass in a toast. I just

looked at her in bewilderment. "C'mon Frank. Let's drink to your talent,"
she raised her glass again.
"Please," I didn't know what to say.
"Frank, I enjoy your work. Don't deny me that," she said in a motherly
tone. "Here's to your artwork."
I was touched and flattered. I had never had so much seemingly sincere
adulation before. A wide smile forced it's way onto my face and I touched
Irene's glass with mine. We made eye contact then. She smiled, too.
"Here, here," she said quietly and we drank. Shortly we approached a
small hamlet that reminded me more of a movie set than a city. Solomon's
stood proudly on the corner of Oak and Cedar Streets. The gold letters that
spelled "Solomon's" across the awning looked newly applied.
"The exterior's finished," Irene said on her way out of the limo. A bright
ray of sunshine poked through the open door. That's when the fantasy
began. I suppose it was the alcohol, but from then on the whole trip was
like an adventure. Fiction! Here I was a "starving artist" making good.
Arriving at the gallery that was giving me my first big break with the
benevolent old woman who was making it all happen. And the air was
fresher, and the sun was brighter and the sidewalk was clean! This was a
movie set! Where were the cameras?
"The interior is shaping up nicely," Irene was unlocking the front door.
I was still looking for the cameras, sort of. A few deep breaths brought me
close enough to earth to walk inside and there, hanging in the back,
straight across from the entranceway, was "Glad". Oh, it made my knees go
weak. I missed that painting. And that sad, dispossessed face looking
straight at me seemed to be held prisoner in that posh gallery.
"It's a wonderful piece, Frank," Irene had sensed my attachment. She
had her arm around me. It felt good.
"Gladys was killed shortly after that session," the memories came flood-
ing back.
"There, there," Irene patted my back.
Time stood still for me then. I got a lump in my throat and tears
welled in my eyes. I started to think about the last time I had felt this

much loss. I was standing in the basement of the student union playing Zaxxon. At least I think I was playing Zaxxon. I had played so many times that I was on auto pilot for the first several levels and that's why I was playing. My body could burn off that nervous energy while my mind wandered through memories of Kelly. She had given me the "just friends" speech just a couple of hours earlier and I finally was accepting it and the explosions of that video game made me feel like the whole world was exploding around me. My senior year at Kansas State had started off particularly poorly.

I met Kelly at Campus Crusade. She was one of the organizers there. I used to watch her with great admiration. The abundance of her energy was obvious. She recognized me, I could tell, but we didn't actually speak until the first meeting of my junior year. For those first two years I ruled out any relationship with her based on the assumption that she was a devout Christian and I wasn't. I saw the poster announcing the meeting while registering for my junior classes and I decided not to go. That summer I had strayed far from the path and, somehow, I didn't think those meetings would hold much intrigue for me anymore. Still, I went. I did want to see Kelly again. So, I was sitting there waiting for the session to start and she plunked herself right next to me.

"Frank Teeman! Glad to see you," she said, smiling.
"Glad to be here, Kelly," I returned that friendly smile.

We sat there for that session and went out for coffee afterwards and developed a really good friendship that grew steadily through out that year. It was just a friendship, though. Kelly was very busy at school. She was no longer involved with CC as an organizer she was so busy. I kept myself pretty busy, too. Those Sundays when I saw Kelly were enough to fulfill most of my social needs. I was doing a lot of painting. That next summer I stayed on campus. She went home. We kept in touch. I wrote to her once. She wrote back—a postcard from St. Louis. I went back to Dilon for a couple weeks at the end of August. I knew that Kelly lived in Longworth, nearby, so when some friends invited me to go to the carnival there I agreed with hope. My wishes were fulfilled when I saw Kelly working the First Presbyterian hamburger stand. We went on the Ferris wheel and the "Round-up" and she won me a stuffed snake at the coin toss and it was just fabulous. Like something out of a movie. And when I kissed her good night and my head exploded in one huge burst of ecstasy, I was reeling. My friends gave me all the normal razzing about having a girlfriend. I never called her that, but part of me bought into the idea hard. When I saw her on campus we hugged and I tried to kiss her again. That's when I got the "just friends" speech.

Even though part of me knew that it was coming, the part that didn't, hurt bad.

"Did you love her?" I almost mistook Irene's hushed voice for my own.

"No," I kind of chuckled, "She was an interesting subject, though," I was answering myself. Irene didn't know that.

"Well, she should draw a good price."

"Huh?"

"I've already gotten interest in her."

"Glad?" I was confused. That wasn't such a great painting.

"Yes," Irene was proud. "We hope to open bidding at two thousand."

I just stood there bewildered. Irene was confounded by my lack of enthusiasm. She just smiled, not sure what direction to take it.

"And what if I refused?" I didn't want to be confrontational, but I was serious.

"Refused what?" Irene was angry, but didn't want to let it show. "I own that painting."

"So you do," I had forgotten about that major technicality. In an effort to keep everything cordial I let it slide by as if it were inconsequential. "Well, the place is beautiful, Irene." I looked at the door.

"I'm so glad you like it," Irene held me by the arm. I headed for the outside anyway.

"Yep, really beautiful."

Fresh air was all I could think about.

11/20/63

As a child I spent a lot of time outdoors. It was convenient for my mom; I didn't make a mess, I didn't make a lot of noise, and I was happy. Being an only child in a country house is curious. You have all this vitality while all around you is the appearance of tranquility. I say appearance because there is so much vitality in the country it's staggering. Plants are alive and they have a tremendous life energy and they're everywhere. And intermingled with them are all those animals. When you're a child you can plug into that strength easily. Some people retain that ability. Most lose it. Unfortunately, as a child, you're usually not aware of the value of life energy and if you are the subtleties of its origin and its effects do not connect.

I used to have several specific spots where I would commune with Gaya. One was in the middle of a wheat field. Because of the nature of crops that specific spot would change. Whenever those plants grew to my waste though, I could plop myself down in the middle of them and breathe. Another, more fixed, location was right behind our house, across a fallow field. There, was the forest. I had a spot there that was sufficiently deep in the woods so that I felt like my parents couldn't see me from the kitchen window. A tree had fallen and I used that to create a space to sit. The trees were tall. Infinitely tall, it seemed to me at that time. There was a canopy of leaves that would give the illusion of a roof; it would block some sunlight, but the wind would blow and there were dead leaves all over the ground so it wasn't the same as inside.

Still, it had it's own kind of coziness that made it distinctly different from the wheat field.

   I had a prolonged case of the chicken pox one fall. I remember being so ill that when I tried to get up to go to the bathroom the walls would blur and I would crumple to the ground. I was bed ridden for a long time with fever. I think that was the first time my mortality came into focus. I was seven and the exuberance of youth had placed death at a distance, but now, for the first time, I thought about it not in the abstract, but in reference to me. My flesh was losing a battle and the loss of that battle had dire consequences. So, there I was seven and scared and tripping. A tremendous sense of loneliness came over me then and I couldn't shake it. My mother was right down stairs, but I was too tired or emotionally paralyzed to cry. Instead, I made my way to the window and looked out on to the forest from my second story perch. That patch looked different than it ever had before. It was blurry, but not indistinguishable. I took a particular delight in the shades of brown and green, but couldn't make out the specific forms. Some patch of weeds at the edge of the forest had a shiny quality. I wanted to be there. The wind was blowing, but I couldn't hear the leaves rustle. Ohh, to hear those leaves rustle and maybe a bird chirp. My mom came in then and made me get back into bed. It was proba- bly a good idea. I was exhausted. When I finally laid down and closed my eyes I heard the wind blow ever so softly and there was a bird chirp- ing. It was a delightful sound and as I reveled in it I began to realize that it was chirping my name. And as I listened more closely I realized that the wind was calling me, too! When I opened my eyes to see, I saw white ceiling.

   My fever broke that night and I didn't hear those sounds any more. I was convinced that they were out there waiting for me, though. My mother insisted I stay indoors for several more days. I wanted to go outside and meet my friends. My mother won out, of course, so I was relegated to sitting at that window and wondering who had been calling me. After a couple days of that I had worked up enough energy to be restless. The pox had virtually disappeared and I was convinced that it was time for me to leave my cage. I couldn't go out downstairs; mom would surely catch me and send me back to my room. My bedroom window looked out onto a two-story drop. There was a tree pretty close to the guest room window, though. I ran there on tiptoes to find a natural ladder to freedom. I ran back to my room and dressed and when I heard the TV go on I knew mom was ironing and wouldn't be up to check on me for a while. My heart raced and I was a little light headed. I noticed sweat on my brow? Still, I went to that escape hatch, opened that window, and when that cool breeze hit me I inhaled deeply. I also shivered. Before I could even get a leg up, mom was there shrieking.

"What are you doing?"
"Mom, I wanna go out!" I whined.
"Look at you! You're sweating," she quickly closed the window and put her hand on my forehead, "well you don't seem to have a temperature, but Doc Weldon said you should stay in bed for at least another day."
"Aww mom, I wanna go out,"
"Honey, you can't," she was sympathetic, "why don't you come downstairs and watch television with me."
This was a treat. TV was rationed to me like sweets. We went downstairs and mom fixed me a spot on the couch with lots of pillows and a big quilt. Just as I was settling in it happened.

"We interrupt this broadcast for a special report. President Kennedy has been shot." Cronkite's voice was grave.

I knew what that meant, but still I looked to mom for her reaction. She was perfectly white. She had her hand over her mouth and her eyes were wide open. She kept muttering, "Oh my god." As more details came in she changed her line to "Those sons of bitches."

When they finally reported his death she let out a guttural moan and sent me to my room. I could still hear her crying.

As if the realization of my own mortality weren't enough, the death of an icon like the president had me extrapolating the eventual death of my parents. I lay in that bed stiff. Afraid to live. Afraid to die. All the while my mother's sobs echoing faintly. When the wind rattled my window I felt the outdoors beckoning once again. Now, I didn't want to go. Instead I closed my eyes and fell into a fitful sleep.

I woke up at dawn. There was still a deep gray in the air. It gave me a feeling I can only describe as hollow. Still, I had the determination that only accompanies wellness. I got dressed and went downstairs to find my folks still in bed.

"Mom," I touched her shoulder. When she opened her red, puffy eyes I was almost afraid to ask. "Can I go outside?" I said in the nicest way I could.

"Honey…" mom was reluctant.

"Let the boy go," I heard my dad grumble. After a big sigh and a kiss on the forehead, she agreed.

"But wear your winter coat and you come right back when I ring the bell for breakfast."

"I will," I said with glee.

Each step I took through that fallow field was a delight. A few birds were rising, but for the most part it was silent. The crunching of the weeds under my feet was euphonic. When I got to my spot in the woods I felt a tingle I was so happy. I sat down and looked around and reveled in every sight. The sun had just peeked over the horizon and cast an unusual light through the trees. I inhaled deeply and got a head rush. I closed my eyes and heard the wind speak my name again. A smile forced it's way until I broke out in laughter.

The trees laughed with me.

5/17/86

When I left Solomon's that day my back was against the wall. Something about this project still left me with a cold feeling, but now, I knew that I could not withdraw. Irene was going to sell those pieces she had bought. I might as well be involved. I stood on the sidewalk realizing all of this while Irene closed up the gallery. I had spooked her I could tell and I felt bad about that. I just looked at the blue, spring sky, though. And the wind blew ever so lightly and the birds were everywhere. Somehow, I was not comforted. I was coming down off that alcohol buzz. Fortunately, Irene had fed me good gin. Bad gin would have been excruciating. We mounted that limo without a word. I looked out the window and Irene left me alone. I appreciated that.

"Frank?" she tentatively piped in before we got to her house. I wanted to ignore her. The silence in that cabin was wonderful. I turned and faced her with a smile, though. To my surprise our eye contact was not painful at all. Irene smiled back. She was very sympathetic. "Frank, I've had my lawyer draw up an agreement for us. I think you'll find it very generous," she sounded like my grandma.

"Of course," I was humble.

"Then I can count on your participation?"

"Certainly," I put my hand on her knee. It was not a conscious thing and it took me by surprise. I almost yanked it away when I realized what I was doing, but Irene prevented that by putting her hand on mine.

"Oh good," she was obviously relieved, "I thought I had lost you."

"No, not at all," I smiled. I wasn't very convincing. I was focused on her hand. It was all wrinkled and the veins showing and it was touching my hand and the contrast between the two was amazing. Mine so big, hers so small. When I finally saw her fluttering her eyes bashfully, and that rosy-cheeked embarrassment, I pulled my hand back gently and looked at the floor.

I slept in the McGarrety's Cutlass all the way home only to be awakened by a police siren on my street. When I walked into my studio it revolted me. I couldn't stay there so I phoned Jack. I waited out on the sidewalk. It was a beautiful night, but there seemed to be so much noise. It was bothering me so I closed my eyes. Amongst the blackness of my eyelids an image appeared. It was Irene's face looking ever so sweet. I opened my eyes quickly. It's not that I was revolted; I just didn't want to deal with it. Jack pulled up shortly and I hopped in the back quickly.

"Hey stranger," Jack said at the rearview mirror.

"Hi, Jack," I was glum.

"Oh, Mister Enthusiasm. What happened? You win the lottery?" There was a snideness to his voice that really got under my skin.

"Just take me to Central Park," I snapped.

"Geez, sorry," he turned around and changed his demeanor, "You sure you wanna go at this hour?"

"Oh, I don't know. I just want to go somewhere," I was moaning and when I heard myself I felt like hitting myself.

"Listen, some friends of mine are having a party. Wanna go?" He had real enthusiasm.

"Sure," I absorbed that joy.

"Well, c'mon up front. I'm not gonna ride you like a chauffeur."

I felt a lift. The kind of enjoyment you get from celebrating is the best. Celebrating always involves more than one person and any get together with more than one person is a celebration.

"Hey Ernie, this is Jack," he was on the microphone when I jumped into the front seat, "ol' 47 has done it again," he winked at me.

"Jack!" the dashboard squawked back, "Don't fuck with me, Jack!"

"Ernie, the fucker's broken! Just send a truck!" Jack barked back, smiling all the while. We waited for a reply. There was none. "Ernie? Send a truck if you want your cab. Forty seventh and third."

"I thought you were on the lower east side," Ernie was clearly screaming.

"10-4. Forty seventh and third. Over." Jack switched off the radio and laughed while stomping on the gas. I guess we were going to forty-seventh and third.

"Thanks man. I was looking for an excuse to go to this party."

"You're not gonna get into trouble for this?"

"Yeah, I'll probably catch some shit. So what!" We laughed. There was a real sense of excitement for me. Every sound, every sight, was vivid. The smell of the cab even had a particular charm. I cracked the window and the auditory on rush was overwhelming. Jack laid on the horn as we bounded through an intersection that had just turned red. It gave me a tingle.

"What kind of a party is this anyway?" I giggled out.

"Just some friends. They're a wild bunch, though. It's sure to be a good time."

"Women?"

"Well my friends are these three guys. They work in the theater some where so, there's usually plenty of young actresses!" He gave me a raise of the eyebrows and an evil look.

"Actresses, huh?" I was trying to remember if I had ever met an actress.

"Finest kind!" he said savoringly.

"How so?" I was intrigued.

"You never been with an actress?" I just shook my head. "Well, first off," he affected a kind of ditzy-blonde voice, "they're really open to experiencing things, you know," we laughed, "so, you just gotta be exotic and you're in."

"I'm not exotic."

"Sure you are!"

"How?"

"Just talk humbly about your art."

"That's exotic?"

"No, but it's creative. I'll tell everyone you've been discovered."

"Please don't."

"C'mon. What's the big deal? It's not even a lie. Besides that'll turn 'em on for sure. You gotta bag one."

"Why?"

"The best thing about actresses…they do the best orgasms."

"They fake it?"

"They all fake it."

"C'mon."

"Sure! It's all a big act. And actresses put on a great show."

We parked abruptly in a bus stop. Jack jumped out, opened the hood, did, I suspect, some damage, slammed the hood, opened the passenger door, grabbed his license with the big mug shot photo and practically pulled me out of the cab. I was trying to remember all the orgasms that I had thought were moments of pure bliss for the woman I was with. They all faked it?

Jack rang apartment four's buzzer repeatedly. Eventually the latch buzzed open. Jack bounded up the stairs two at a time and I rushed to keep up. Loud music was getting louder and the rumble of a crowd conversation became more and more apparent. Jack got to the top and stopped.

"It's a party," he had a gleam in his eye that made him look like a teenager. My heart was beating forcefully, partly from the stair climb and mostly from nervous anticipation. Jack took a deep breath, fixed a smile on his face, opened the door, and entered. It was a wild event. There were people everywhere. The air above them was filled with smoke. Somebody was smoking a joint right by the front door. The music was deafening, dance music. The din of people talking was sensational. A woman screamed some where in the back. Then a bunch of people broke out in laughter. Everyone had a plastic cup in their hand. Jack started pushing his way through the crowd. I followed. The smell of body odor began to predominate as we squished into the middle of the party. A blonde girl with a bright, green, strapless dress was standing right in front of me. The crowd surged and pushed us together so that my crotch was right on her ass. I looked over her shoulder to see two large round breasts barely covered by that low cut dress. I was so close that I could smell her and she smelled like shampoo. I didn't like that. She turned and saw me out of the corner of her eye. She gave her ass a little wiggle as she giggled softly. "An actress," I thought to myself, but before I could say anything, Jack grabbed my elbow and pulled me through the crowd.

"There's plenty of time for that. Let me introduce you to my friends," and we headed out of the living room and down the hallway. This was a party! Jack headed for a door with my elbow still in his hand. When we got in it was obvious that everyone knew Jack so, the initial tension I felt waned quickly. Jack introduced me to his friends as "Frank the artist" quickly adding that I had just signed a big deal with a gallery. As soon as he had said that an exotic woman stepped into the circle. Her rich skin, thick hair, and full eyes where overshadowed by her nostrils. She had the most incredibly big nostrils. In light of her petite nose they seemed enormous.

"Frank, this is Desiree," Earl, one of the hosts, said politely, "She's an actress." She held out her hand with out saying a word. She kept her head down and looked shyly up at me. I was grinning from ear to ear. I put my hand in hers and held it. It was so fragile. I felt like I could break it with the slightest pressure.

"Nice to meet you," I hated my tone of voice. Always so God damn pleasant. Nerd.

"Did I hear that you paint?" Desiree had a sultry voice. I nodded bashfully. "I've done quite a bit of modeling."

"I'm sure you'd make an interesting subject."

Jack put his arm around me and whispered "Go". It seemed like the voice of God. I was still staring at Desiree and she was still looking at me. "Just be exotic" kept running through my mind. I couldn't open my mouth for fear of blowing it. Suddenly this awful sound broke the tension. It was Earl grolting a line. He was bent over a coffee table snorting through a short straw. He was a big guy and when he snorted anything under that straw was whisked away.

"You're next Des," Bill, another one of the hosts, held out the straw.

"Would you like to share?" She asked in a way that I could not refuse.

"Sure," I replied softly.

"Fuck that," Bill spouted, "there's plenty. Frank can have his own." He grabbed the mirror, did some quick work with a razor and lo and behold—two lines. Des did hers with the utmost grace, half in each nostril. When they flared as she snorted I was amazed to see them actually get larger. She handed me that mirror and I did likewise. Ahhhh, the serenity of numbness. My head went out instantly. I almost collapsed where I stood. Des wet her finger and rubbed the mirror clean, then stuck her finger in my mouth and rubbed my gums gently. I was still in nah-nah land and her warm finger on my lips was splendid. By the time she had removed it my head was clear enough to see her smiling face. I laughed. So did she. I was laughing, not because I was amused, but because I felt wonderful. Pure bliss.

When someone asked me about my deal with the gallery I snapped out of my haze. I wanted to under play the whole thing. To my amazement I started talking enthusiastically about Irene and the money that she intended to spend and the gallery and how nice it was and what an exciting period this was for me and everyone listened for a while interjecting "wows" at appropriate moments and Desiree was getting closer and at the same time she was getting snugglier and soon it was time for another round. The mirror was making its way. Jack passed? I noticed that my tongue was still tingling from Des's touch. I still managed to wag it extensively. After holding the mirror for Des, I snorted my line eagerly. I closed my eyes, but didn't get the same payoff. I actually felt like I had sobered.

"How 'bout a beer," Jack said to me directly. He grabbed me by the arm again, only this time I didn't want to go. When we got out into the hall we both laughed about the actress thing. Then Jack became very serious.

"Keep a grip," he was soberingly serious.

"Huh?" I felt great. I had no idea what he was talking about.

"That dummy dust will make you an idiot," he looked directly into my eyes. Suddenly, I felt my heart beating furiously and a little bead of sweat appeared. "Not to mention taken the oingo outta your boingo."

"I gotcha," I was short of breath, "let's get that beer."

We mingled our way through the crowd, found the keg in the kitchen and, thankfully, got a couple hits off that joint at the front door. I was pretty messed up by the time we got back into the room. Our timing was bad, too. Des was on the bed, mirror in hand. When she saw me she patted the bed next to her and I plunked myself down, toot suite. Another line sent me back to nah-nah land only this time in a whirlpool from those other intoxicants. I laid down on the bed. Everyone laughed and when I laughed too Des's finger began rubbing my gums again. This time that bitter taste closed my throat. I sucked on my cup, but got nothing. It was empty. When Earl filled it for me, I promptly poured it on myself. My lips were too numb to hold it in my mouth. I just wiped it on my sleeve and jumped back into conversation. I'm not sure what I was talking about, but I was talking. And I felt great. I was grinning the whole while. I really felt great.

"Tension alarm," the hippie guy who we smoked with at the front door stuck in his head. The three hosts ran out of the room. Everyone else followed shortly. There was a fight brewing and by the time I got out there the hosts had forced it outside. The living room was pleasantly empty now, and the music was still blaring. I began dancing with Des's hand in mine. The room filled again. We proceeded to dance the night away. I hadn't danced

in years. It was a ball. I felt great. Des excused herself to go to the bathroom and I plopped on the couch like a blob of gelatinous mass. Jack appeared for the first time in a while.

"Crashing?" he laughed

"Yeah, I suppose so," I was feeling tired.

"Desiree's back there crankin' it up," he was sarcastic.

"Naw, she's in the bathroom," I was feeling achy.

"Yeah, right," Jack got up and I watched him just dissolve into the party. And out of his dissolve appeared Desiree. She was bright and spunky. She held out her hand and I put mine in hers. That's when I noticed the white speck just inside her fantastic nostril. She pulled me up off the couch and put her arms around my neck. I couldn't take my eyes off that little rock of coke stuck on the edge of her nose. It was getting closer and closer until, finally, our lips met. Des's tongue injected itself into my mouth. It was so hard and strong. I was going along but my mind was on the small of my back. It was stiff. I got a chill. She broke abruptly, but didn't open her eyes. Through deep breaths she whispered, "Let's get out of here."

I was at a loss. My libido took over. We left arm in arm. I hailed a cab and we necked ferociously in the back seat from the time the door closed. She was on top of me and grinding her hips on mine and practically pulling my hair and pressing her mouth so hard our teeth were touching. I opened my eyes once to see that white speck in her nostril consumed by a big drop of mucous. She sniffed it up and that's when something deep inside of me started begging out. By the time we got to my place I was exhausted. Des was just getting started, though. She stripped on the way to the bed and started petting her pussy.

"Lick me," she said quietly. I was stunned. "Lick me," she started to moan. I dove in, fully clothed. She let out the most incredible sigh. The more I licked the more she said, "Lick me." Then, suddenly, she started in with, "Fuck me." It began quietly and by the time I had pumped a few times she was shouting. I came quickly and fell on my back exhausted. She rolled on top of me and started sucking my neck. She grabbed my limp dick and started rubbing it. I wanted to help her, but I couldn't. When that

became obvious she started rubbing me against her. That startled me so, that it actually made me less hard. I just laid there watching her use my flaccid piece to get herself off. And she did. Eventually letting out this guttural cat type growl.

Did she fake that?

11/20/73

I like people. I guess I always have. Observation is what I really like. People are really amazing things. And, some how, I always manage to be delighted by them. Interacting with people is a different story. I like it. I'm not very good at it. Well, I guess I'm good at it, but it just doesn't come naturally for me. Because I like observing people, I welcome the opportunity to interact with them. Most of the time. Some of the time I just like to watch. You know, find a perch and see what happens. Bars are particularly good for that, but actions are kind of distorted there. All that alcohol and all those over stimulated guys trying desperately to score and all those self-conscious women hoping to score enough praise points so that they can feel good about themselves. That's all interesting, but churches and supermarkets and sidewalk cafes offer an infinitely more accurate picture. It's not as dynamic, though. Nothing is more dynamic than the barroom for interpersonal interaction. Where else can you witness everything from a brawl to a zip-less fuck in the same night?

Now that I'm in New York, I have plenty of opportunity for observation. Maybe that's why I moved here. Living out in the country just did not provide that fundamental piece of entertainment for me. You'd think that TV would be an infinite source for my voyeurism. It wasn't. I rarely watched it. I don't have one now. It only serves to confuse me. On a superficial level I get that good feeling, but I never get any substantial fulfillment. It's like drinking 3.2 beer. It tastes like beer and you know there's a little alcohol in it so, you figure if you just drink

enough you might be able to get a decent buzz. By the time you're full
up to your eyelids the bloating in your stomach is more overwhelming
than anything happening in your head.

When I went to college I had my first experience with TV addiction. And barrooms, too, for that matter! My folks dropped me off at
the dormitory with a suitcase and a banana box with some stuff in it.
The dorm came furnished with an old bed and a dresser. Meals were at
the cafeteria. No cooking in the dorms, fire hazard. So, there I was in
my sterile dorm room watching my folks drive off and wondering what
the hell was going to happen. My roommate walked in. Abraham Steffens was his name. He was a tall, gangly type. He smiled when he saw
me, dropped his two suitcases and extended his hand. His folks barged
in while we were introducing ourselves. They were carrying a bunch of
stuff, too. Mr. Steffens had a portable color TV. The Steffens stayed
for a little while, abominating the conditions at the dormitory. Mr.
Steffens told us to take it easy on the girls. We laughed.

That TV got plugged in first thing. Abe was excited because we got
four stations. I had my clock radio with me. I hadn't plugged it in yet
so, I didn't know how many stations I got. The TV played a soap opera
while Abe unpacked and we chatted. I had never actually seen a soap
opera before so I was checking it out. It was boring. When I turned it
off Abe looked at me like I was crazy. I turned it back on.

Abe and I were very dissimilar. That got more apparent with each
passing day. Actually, I felt different from all twenty-nine of my hall
mates. Abe was different, though. At least I could blend. Abe didn't
care about blending. He was there to do a job and, pretty much, that's
all he did. My hall mates and I would go out in a pack scouring the
nearby village for some action. When we came back, drunk, harassing
Abe became a favorite pastime. Stuff like taking him out of bed and
carrying him through the girl's wing naked. I always felt bad about
that. What could I do? After a month of almost constant partying I

decided to apply myself a little. The first test was pending in most of my classes and I was way behind.

One night, late, there was a knock on the door. When I tried to answer it I couldn't get it open. A huge burst of laughter erupted in the hallway. We had been pennied in. Some one had taken a stack of pennies and wedged them between the door and the jam, making it virtually impossible to turn the knob. I had seen it done before and knew it was a matter of dislodging those pennies. I shook the door and heard those pennies fall. That's when everyone took off. I got out into the hallway in time to see a few doors slam shut. Abe didn't stir. A couple of those guys apologized the next day. They assured me that their prank was directed at Abe, not me. Nonetheless, about a week later I was awakened early one morning by voices outside the door. They were trying to penny us in again, I thought. I had taken some precautions, though. I had wedged myself in, so all I had to do was take that wedge out and their pennies would fall. I rolled over and tried to sleep, but then there was a big sploosh and I heard everyone outside scatter. When I jumped up to see what had happened I stepped in cold water. When I got to the door I found the mop bucket. When I turned on the light I saw the scummy old mop water all over the floor. The hallway was empty. I spent the next half-hour mopping up. Abe did not stir. Doug, the RA, stopped by to see what was going on. He asked why Abe wasn't helping. It was all I could do to control my rage. Abe mumbled something from the bed. I don't know what he said, but it made me angry just knowing that he was awake.

The next afternoon I got back to the room in a sour state. Abe was watching TV, as usual. When I walked in he didn't even move. That was pretty normal, too.

"Abe! What the hell is your problem?" I was tired and frustrated. He didn't respond. Some insipid music was blaring from the TV set. I think a game show was on. I was growing to hate that thing. "Hey man, I asked you a question." I stood between him and the TV.

"I'm not gonna lose any sleep because of those assholes." That was the first time I heard him curse.

"What?" I didn't know what he was talking about.

"I woulda cleaned it up in the morning," he mumbled, "Now get out of the way!" He tried to wave me from in front of the TV.

"Abe I'm talking about, someday, standing up for yourself so they'll stop this shit!" I was screaming.

"Fuck those guys," he wasn't very convincing.

"No, Abe. You've gotta do something. I've gotta live with this shit." I was getting angrier.

"Fuck you," he looked directly at me and then back at the TV. I was incensed. I wanted to punch him. That stupid music on the TV caught my ear and made me grit my teeth. I saw the window chock on the sill by the TV and watched myself pick it up and whack the TV. It continued spewing so, I prepared to whack it again. Abe tackled me on to the bed before I could. We started wrestling and I felt Abe's fist hit me in the ribs. I could hear the crowd gathering and the calls of "fight". Abe was getting the upper hand. He started throwing more punches. An intensity came over me then like I've never experienced. I managed to get him on to his back. I punched him in the head a few times. He was crying and had his arms over his face. Doug pulled me off. I didn't want to stop. I wanted to hurt him. I was restrained long enough to cool down. Abe just laid on the bed, sobbing. I started to feel nauseous and was allowed to leave.

I went to the cafeteria, but couldn't stomach the chicken a la king. I was upset. The last time I had punched someone was ten years previous. When I left the cafeteria I started walking towards town. I ended up at The Cask, a bar that was off limits for college kids, usually. I took a seat at the bar and they served me my JD and coke, though. I was thinking about my problems and how I was going to live with a guy who inspired the worst in me. Then I noticed two older men in an animated discussion. These guys were old, like 70 or so. They had white hair and each used a cane. Suddenly, one lunged at the other and when they locked arms they both fell to the ground. The bartender jumped over the bar and separated them easily. They were still cursing each other. Other people were laughing. The bartender made them sit in separate booths and that was the end of it. When I got back to the room it was quiet. I was liquored so, I just laid down and passed out.

My alarm woke me early. No sign of Abe. Sometimes he gets up really early. My hangover was enormous and I was convinced that it was a penance for my actions the previous day. When I returned from classes I was prepared to apologize fully. I took a deep breath before I entered, but to my surprise, Abe was not there. Neither was any of his stuff. Except the TV. It was still on the sill. The case had a huge hole in it now. Doug showed up then.

"Abe moved, huh?" I was embarrassed.

"Actually, he dropped out." I turned to see if he was pulling my leg. He wasn't. "Yup, he came and said good bye about an hour ago."

I ended up at The Cask that night, too. Those two old men where there again. This time they were laughing with each other.

5/22/86

I dreamt about nothing that night. It's not that I don't remember my dream. It was about nothing. It wasn't black. It wasn't white. It was nothing. Just this pervading sense of fear.

Des woke me up in the morning. I was so surprised to see something that it took me a while to focus. She was already dressed.

"I've got an audition to get to," she said from the foot of the bed while she pulled on her cowboy boots. I wasn't really sure who she was. I wasn't even sure who I was. "Give me a kiss," she leaned over me smiling. I recognized her then and I remembered her then and I was frightened. I kissed her, though. "I left my number by the phone. Give me a call," and she left. I never said a word. I just rolled over and fell back to sleep. The second time I woke it was with a start. The phone rang loudly and I rushed to answer it just to stop the ringing.

"Good news Frank!" Bill was on the line.

"Hi Bill," I realized I was standing in front of my open window, naked. I put my hand over my crotch and looked to see if anyone had gotten a glimpse. Nobody in sight. "What's up?"

"I took that contract to our lawyer," I had to think for a second, "he says it's great. Oh, Frank, Mo and I are so happy for you."

"The contract?" I was busy watching the rain fall past my window.

"Yeah, only one thing. It says that you need to have some more paintings that Irene approves of."

"Oh, Irene."

"Djou just get up?"

"Yeah, sorry Bill. Late night."

"Hey that's OK. You should be celebrating," Bill was so proud, "you got ten paintings, though?"

"Yeah, I got a bunch," I took a look at my storage rack. I couldn't remember if there were any.

"Well, my guy gave me the number of another guy who specializes in this kind of stuff. My guy says we should let this other guy handle things."

"Oh, yeah?" I wasn't very enthusiastic.

"So, you wanna call him, or do you want me to?"

"Would you Bill?"

"No problem."

"I'd appreciate it."

"All right. I'll let you know what he says."

"Thanks, Bill."

"Hey this is a big thrill. A big thrill," he laughed.

"OK. Thanks, bye." I was more interested in the lightning.

I puttered around the place. Did a couple bong hits. Dreaded going in for that damn C shift. Thought about the previous night's escapade. Got a chill. Then the phone rang again.

"Frank!" It was Bill again, "You got an appointment tomorrow!"

"With who?"

"That guy I was tellin' you about."

"Oh, the lawyer," I was disappointed.

"Well, actually he's an agent."

"Really?" I was intrigued. Everybody and their brother had told me that I needed an agent. I had never actually looked for one, though. Bill could sense my detachment.

"Listen, I'll tell you about it when you get to the store."

"All right. See you then,"

An agent! Just a week ago I first met Irene. That had to have been the most jam-packed week in my life. I was exhausted. I dropped Carmina Burana in the cassette deck and flopped on the futon/couch in front of that virgin canvas I had easled eons ago. Thunder boomed like the voice of God, while Orff provided the choir of angels. Pleasant images of Irene came to mind. Like the first day in the store. She has such a sweet countenance. And the birch trees at her place. I could almost smell them. And then I remembered that sexual tension I had felt at the lunch table. For the first time in almost a year, I had to paint. The elderly woman as sexual object. How interesting that I could be repulsed and attracted at the same time. I like that kind of irony.

I painted the rest of the day and into the night. Each stroke was fresh! It had been so long. When I got to work, Bill rattled on about this agent. I was distracted. It was like I could barely see something and I had to stay focused on it or else I would lose it. And that thing that I could barely see was wondrous and deserving of my full attention.

When I went to see Sal, the agent, on Tuesday I was the same way. He congratulated me on landing such a "lucrative" contract. I signed it and we made arrangements for Irene to view some more of my work. It was all busy work to me. I could see birch trees and there was Irene among them, but there was something missing or obscured. I was trying very hard to see it.

That night at work Ralph was my Remzi again. I was reminded of the tremendous amount of work he did. My heart went out to him.

"Enjoying your vacation?" I was trying to be sarcastic.

"Yeah! It's great." He was sincere. He didn't pick up on my sarcasm at all. "How 'bout you? You like the graveyard?"

"Not really," I had to be honest. He was surprised.

"Yeah, the hours are rough," he tried to relate.

"Yeah," it was the job that I hated. We shared a beer after the load and he told me about stuff he was doing. A little bit of fishing and basically lounging around. I couldn't relate.

Irene came over that Friday. I was actually looking forward to seeing her. I wanted to get another impression. I hid the piece I was working on and spread all the other ones around the studio. To my surprise there were twenty. I had never done that before—spread all my pieces out so that I could see them at once. It was great. It gave me just the boost I needed to get over the anxiousness. I had never showed all my work to some one, either. That was frightening. As I sat there soaking up all those images and as the memories behind each piece filled my head, I got this paranoid sinking feeling. Someone was watching me in disapproval. I told myself that was ridiculous. Still I couldn't shake it. When I made eye contact with myself in that damn self-portrait I realized that it was me that was watching me. I took that painting and put it back on the rack. I placed myself back in front of the other nineteen. And I felt good once again about what I had done. After a short while, though, my eye drifted to that lone painting on the rack. Even though its back was to me I could feel those eyes piercing me. Besides it looked so conspicuous on that rack by itself. I decided to stash it. That made me feel better, much better.

And just in time. Sal showed up first. He was very business like. He just wanted to make sure everything was ready. He said something about artists being flaky. Irene was right behind him and for some reason I hugged her when she walked in. I don't know where it came from. It wasn't a big bear hug or anything, very polite, but, that brief moment when our chests and cheeks pressed together was exhilarating. Now that Irene had become the subject, she took on a different character for me. The touch of her skin. The frailty of her bones. These elements were at the forefront of my thoughts. I was making progress on that painting already. I almost wanted to dismiss them so I could get back to work. I contained myself.

"Frank, these are wonderful," she had an awe-struck tone. I just smiled. I was thinking about that painting. And her delight provided me with one of the essential elements that had been missing—joy. Joy is utterly attractive. At least it is for me. At the same time melancholy turns me on, too. I guess it's just emotion that revs my engine. Even more than that it's the capacity for emotion. Irene definitely had that. Still, she was an elderly woman. Even if I could work up a temporal attraction for her, my body

was having nothing to do with it. This provided the major element of irony.

I watched Sal and Irene conduct business. I was silent. Irene picked ten pieces. Sal moved them all over to the same side of the room. One of them was that leg thing. The last session with Gladys. I was reminded of her and her death and her visage staring blankly from the walls of Solomon's gallery. It made me sad.

"Frank, will you come visit me some time again soon?" Irene interrupted my memories of Gladys.

"Well," I wasn't sure what to say. I wasn't sure if I wanted to or not, "I'm pretty busy."

"Of course. I want to have a dinner party the night of the opening," there was a pause, "Can you make it?"

"Oh, sure. Sure," I was surprised.

"Good. I want all my friends to meet you."

"I'd be delighted to meet them."

"Do you have a tux?" she tried to whisper so Sal couldn't hear.

"No," I couldn't help but laugh.

"I'll get you one. You're going to be needing it," she beamed proudly, "Ta-ta for now," she kissed me on the cheek and left, waving.

"Where did you find her?" Sal was delighted. I was embarrassed. "Never mind. Good get, though," he patted me on the back.

He spewed something about getting the paintings framed and shipped.

I don't know. I just was not that interested.

I was ready to get back to work.

Time flies. If you let it. I let go of everything for a while. Well, not everything. I still showed up for work and of course there was that painting. This one turned out to be particularly difficult. I would stare at the sketches and the little bit I had done for days. Sometimes it seemed like a half an hour would pass between every glance at that canvas. I couldn't escape thinking about it, but I relished the chance to get out of its sight. Work provided a welcome respite. It was raining a lot then. That, combined with my self-induced isolation gave me a feeling of encapsulation. Sometimes that's comforting. Sometimes that's stifling.

The business of my debut went on without me. Sal and Irene were happy to take care of it all. The pieces for the gallery were picked up. All I had to do was answer the door. A tailor came and measured me for a tux. It was delivered promptly. One day Bill and Maureen practically jumped on me at work. Solomon's Gallery had run it's first ad in the Times. They were so excited. I looked at that quarter page ad and particularly the line "Introducing Frank Teeman" and felt a detachment. It really didn't make any sense to me.

"Isn't that great?" They were both a glow. I just stared at it trying to make some sense. That was my name all right and it was all a part of this little fantasy that I was living through for the past month. It was the first thing that made me wonder if I was ever going to wake from this bizarre dream. I actually felt a little nauseous. I was glad when work ended that day. Every time I saw Bill or Maureen I was reminded of the reality of the situation by their brightly smiling faces. I hurried home only to find Desiree at my door. She is a beautiful girl and when she smiled she was even more beautiful. She smiled brightly when I walked up, but I wanted to paint. When she put her arms around me I could smell her cigarette breath. I kissed her on the cheek.

"Well, aren't you going to invite me in?" She was sweet.

"No," I wasn't. I didn't say anything else. I didn't know what to say. All I knew was that I wanted to be alone. I guess I made that painfully obvious. Desiree looked hurt as she slid away. I felt relief. When I got inside and saw that painting I felt like hugging it and kissing it on the cheek. I was glad that we were alone together. The phone rang. I let it ring. It kept ringing. I tried to ignore it. I couldn't. It was Sal. He had lined up an interview for me.

"An interview?" I couldn't imagine why any one would want to talk with me.

"Yeah, you know, the guy asks you questions and you answer them. Can you handle that?" He was pedantic.

"I don't know," I was reluctant.

"Listen, Frank. This is a business. I am your advisor. If you're not going to listen to me you might as well get some one else," he was gruff.

"OK, OK," I didn't want to deal with the tension.

"All right. This is my advice. You listening?"

"Yes," I wasn't happy, but I was listening.

"You have a tremendous opportunity here, but it won't mean shit unless you're willing to work. It'll all fall apart as quickly as it came together if you don't do the right things," he was serious.

"Interviews," I understood.

"Yes, among other things. Are you with me on this?"

"Yeah, yeah. What do I have to do?"

"This guy's name is Al Rosenstein. He's gonna call you tonight to set up a time."

"OK, I'll be here."

"Frank, this guy is important. If he likes you he can be a tremendous asset."

"OK, OK, I understand." I did understand all too well.

"Hey, great ad in the Times today, huh?"

"Yeah, not bad," I moaned.

"Listen Frank," he sighed, "This is a great thing. Try to be happy about this," I didn't know what to say, "I know what you're thinking 'Sellout' am I right?

"Not really," I was reluctant to admit it.

"Artistic integrity is vital to being a success. I'm not going to do anything to compromise that. All right?"

"All right…"

"Trust me on this Frank."

"All right."

"And try to be happy"

"I was happy until you called," I didn't mean that the way it sounded.

"OK, I'll let you go then," he was insulted.

"Sal, thanks a lot," it wasn't until I said that that I realized how much I meant it. There was a pause.

"You're welcome," he was obviously touched.

"Talk to you soon," I was actually smiling.

"Take care."

I was still smiling after I laid the phone down. This was a great thing. I was lucky to have met Irene and Sal and even if nothing did come of this it was an opportunity of a lifetime. I had myself convinced of that, now. I was delighted. I called Mary Everett. She wasn't in, but I left a message inviting her to the opening. Then I started to think about some other people that I wanted to invite. Brian Mosten! Where was Brian? This would thrill him. I never did know how to track him down. Go to McSorley's and wait? And what about Red? I didn't know what to think about her. Why didn't she charge me that night? Why was she so distant during dinner? I thought of her often, but felt like I shouldn't. I guess another trip to Tommy's was in order. John Rogers. If he could see me now.

If only my parents were alive to see this.

That damn phone always rings at the wrong time.

"Hello," I was not particularly bright.

"Frank Teeman?" a dark raspy voice.

"Yes,"

"This is Al Rosenstein." That was the name Sal had given me.

"Hello Mr. Rosenstein. I was expecting your call," I changed my tone.

"Good. Please call me Al," he changed his.

"All right," thunder rattled the window.

"Can I ask you a few questions right now?"

"Sure," I was looking to see if the rain had started.

"Good. Do you have a portfolio and a resume that I could see?" he was quick.

"No, I don't." I was embarrassed.

"Have you ever showed your work before?" He became slightly patronizing.

"Yes, at the Purple Dragon," I was proud.

"Where?"

"The Purple Dragon," there was a pause, "it's a cafe here on the lower east side." I was hurt.

"Oh. What about school?" He had obviously lost interest.

"What about it?" I was defensive.

"Did you show your work at school?" Now he was pedantic.

"No, I was a communications major." I stood my ground.

"I see. What school was that?"

"Kansas State." I hated to admit it.

"Are you from Kansas?" He didn't sound xenophobic.

"Yes." I resigned.

"I see. And how long have you been in New York?"

"Eight years now." Why did he continue?

"I see. And did you take art at Kansas State?"

I heard the rain on the window.

"Yes. It was my minor." I didn't know what to think

"I see. Do you have a job in communications?"

"No, I work at a grocery store." I hated to admit that, too.

"So you came to New York to be an artist?" he sounded genuinely interested.

"Not really," I didn't know what to say.

"Why did you come to New York?" He was getting frustrated.

"Well, I'm not really sure." I was defensive.

"Mr. Teeman can I be frank?"

"Certainly. And please call me Frank." I almost laughed.

"Well, Frank, I don't normally do previews of unknowns," a nice let down.

"I see," I was relieved.

"And that's what Mr. Montrallo contacted me about." He sounded genuinely sorry.

"Sal?" I was embarrassed.

"Yes. He assures me that you are very talented and it's obvious that Mrs. Solomon is doing a wonderful job. How did you land this show anyways?"

"Well, Irene was in the grocery store I work at and saw one of my paintings behind the counter and that's how it started." I was proud.

"One of your paintings hangs in a grocery store?" he laughed.

"Yes, it was a gift to the owners." I was confused.

"Frank, I'll be at the opening, but I'm not going to do a preview," he changed his tone.

"OK. See you then." I changed mine.

"Listen, Frank, I know this is exciting for you. I'm sorry I can't help you out."

"I know." I was smiling.

"You know?"

"Yeah," I wasn't particularly bright.

"Well, I'll be looking forward to seeing your work."

"Thanks for calling."

I felt cold when I hung up. I felt like curling up.

Still, I was determined to get the most out of this opportunity.

11/20/83

It rained practically everyday of November 1983. I still remember that month. The rain had a sinister timing. At first it was refreshing. You know that wonderful, clean smell that rain provides. That was great for a day or two. At least it was something different. God, I was in such a rut. The third day the wind picked up and thrashed my umbrella. I got soaked. Suddenly, I was not enjoying the rain so much. It was cold in my studio when I got back from work. I didn't turn on the heat. I didn't have the budget for it. I fixed myself a bowl of Ramen Pride, wrapped myself in a blanket, and sat in my dark apartment. I figured it was going to save money...the lightning provided spectacular glimpses of my studio for me. And the rain! And the cars in the rain! What a sound. Once the soup was gone and I was warm inside, I felt conspicuously cold outside. I wrapped my arms around my knees and buried my face in my legs and pulled the blanket over top of me. It wasn't coldness that I was feeling, but loneliness.

The lightning, the sound of liquid everywhere, the encapsulation, the warmth in my belly—womb simulation.

For a second I relaxed. It was just a brief moment, but I *was* there for a second. Then I began to realize that my shoes weren't dry and my jacket was wet and I had to be to work early in the morning. I took a second shift. I had bills to pay. And that's when I started thinking about being stoned, but I knew I didn't have any weed. Something inside me said "Get up. Go check." So, I found myself scrutinizing the bong for any pieces that might have gotten caught in the crotch of the stem. There weren't any. But what about that film canister I used to take to the park? Nothing there either. Well, there is always pipe mung. God, what a disgusting thing, though. Scraping all that goopy black shit out of the bowels of every piece of paraphernalia you own? I did it. I only had the bong and the pipe. There wasn't much in either, but there was enough to smoke. This was disgusting but it would be over with quickly. If only I could find some fire. I could've sworn I had some matches in that box. Ah, I left them in my coat pocket when I went to the park. Yes! Here they are, but they're soaked. That damn rain! It was still coming down in sheets. By the time I lit the newspaper on the electric stove and got the fire to the bowl, it was out of control. I sucked on the bong trying to encourage the flame to light that mung. As the newspaper disintegrated, fire went everywhere but in the bowl. I stomped it all out cursing the black spot on the floor.

Now, I really needed a bong hit.

I crafted a little wand out of newspaper and got that mung lit. I could taste the nastiness and it burned my throat. I made sure to hold it in, but it wasn't expanding. I exhaled barely anything. I got a little head rush from the oxygen depravation and the THC in my body kicked in.

I was glad I had smoked that shit.

That mung hit worked for me that day. The rain continued. It was a miserable time for me. It was cold and wet and I was poor and bored. I had been working at the store for a couple of years and it had worked for me nicely. Not only did it give me a budget, but it gave me something to do. By this time, though, I had over extended my budget and I was tired of stacking canned goods. I hadn't sold a painting in over a year, not that I focused on that; it's just that it gave me confidence or at least a sense of purpose. No, more like a sense of belonging. I was participating in the system. That kind of thing, anyways. Not to mention the cash it provided.

It's amazing to me how my frame of mind is directly related to the amount of cushion, cash that is, that I have. Take November '83 for example. I had nothing. Well, I had bills; so, my income was all used up. One of those deals where you get your check and within an hour it's completely spent. At least I didn't have to worry about being evicted. So, there I was in my paid for studio sitting on the ever so hard wood floor trying to feel good about my life, eating a nineteen cent package of Ramen Pride wishing I had a burger. Just a burger! That's all I wanted. I fingered through my little box full of change and figured out I had enough to go down to White Castle and have six and a shake (my minimum order) but, that god damn rain! It wasn't worth it. Besides that change was my laundry money so, I was stuck. I had finished up the pipe mung a couple days earlier so that artificial sense of well-being wasn't even an option.

After I cleaned the kitchen sink and swept the floor and scrubbed the tub, I flopped on the couch. Nervous energy was still building, though. It was time for a change. That was all I could think. I couldn't take this shit anymore. What to do? What to do? Well, I did have my degree in communications. It was time to put it to use. How to do that? I guess a TV or radio station or maybe a newspaper? What could I do there? Nothing. I guess it was time to get my painting career moving. I could advertise for portrait commissions or maybe do some store front window painting. God, all those fluorescent colors and block letters, though. That would drive me crazy. There was still the portraiture idea. Who would hire me though? And where would I advertise? And how would I afford it? I guess that's a dumb idea. I might as well get used to this. It's my niche. At least I've got a place and I'm not out on the street pan handling. That's one thing.

But what about that persistent cavity? Maureen did mention something about a group dental program for the store. Ah, well, things aren't that bad. I got up and saw that clean kitchen and smelled that Pine-Sol residue in the bathroom. It made me feel light. Not light-headed, but light in general. That's when Ellen Tamoritz came to mind. I started to think about what my life would have been like had I taken Ellen up on her offer.

I imagined us living together in the house that I grew up in. Her son playing in the yard while I sat on the porch drinking a beer. Ellen in the kitchen preparing our Sunday meal. A certain amount of contentment in the air. Ellen calls out that dinner is ready. I grab the boy and we laugh as we race to the house. It's quiet. I imagined that it was quiet. It always was at our farmhouse, but I never had an appreciation for it. Now it struck me as blissful.

I imagined Ellen sitting at the dinner table with her brown her hanging about her shoulders and she smiles when her boy and I enter from the bathroom where we have just washed our hands. And I realize that I love her. Simply by making that request five years ago she had instilled in me the self-worth that is so vital to survival. And if I had taken her up on her offer I would be standing at the head of my dining room table looking at her and loving her. Still, there is a certain amount of tension between us. Perhaps it's because of the subservient role that she has taken. That lack of equality makes it difficult for me to respect her entirely. We have a good life, though. Nothing is ever perfect. Or maybe that tension comes from me. I never felt like I belonged in Dilon and I had stayed for some wrong reasons and now, maybe, I felt trapped. But, because I had made a commitment, and because our life is pretty good, I don't feel enough stress to rock the boat.

We eat quietly. Her son does all the talking. I imagine the food to be really good. Nothing like Ramen Pride. Nothing like anything I eat in New York. A real Kansas style home cooked meal. But, I imagine that I'm thinking about Chinese food. Ellen turns to me and asks about the store. It's doing all right. We're not getting rich off of it, but it's all right. She then tells me how Jeff, her son, is performing in kindergarten. He's a bright boy. I know that. We have him count to twenty for us. He needs a little prompting on thirteen, but he keeps going past twenty. Jeff asks to be excused and Ellen tells him to go outside and play. That's unusual. We usually make him finish his dinner. That's when I realize that she has something to tell me.

"Frank?" her voice is soft.

"Yes?" I'm curious.

She lifts her head and looks at me for a while trying to draw strength to say, "I'm pregnant."

A loud thunderclap provides enough of a distraction so that I don't have to deal with that idea. My own child! It just seems such a distant possibility. I can't stop thinking about it, though. A sheet of rain furiously pelts the window. It gives me a chill. The force of nature reducing my already miniscule self-image to nothing. I've never been able to wallow in self-pity so when I hit that bottom point I jumped up. I started flipping through my cassettes. It was time to paint. All those cassettes seemed boring to me. I had heard them a million times. Paint with out music?

Why not.

I picked up my sketch pad. That was always the first step. Once the pencil was in hand it started moving magically. It's so easy if you let it. What was this? A sun? Yes, the sun. I could almost feel it's warmth. I closed my eyes and I could see it. My back yard in Dilon. The sun shining brightly. The wind rippling the weeds in the field. I could feel the warmth. And there I was loping through that field, laughing. And some one was chasing me. Ellen! I opened my eyes. Why was Ellen dominating my thoughts? Maybe she was trying to get in touch with me. I went to the phone, dialed information for Dilon, Kansas, and asked for a listing for Tamoritz. Nothing. Nothing? Not even her parents? Nothing.

Hmmm.

I continued sketching. Now, I wasn't so delighted, though. My sunny day had transformed itself into a dark day. Still, there was the sun. How could it be dark and sunny at the same time? I was possessed with an image of a dark sunny day. Yes, black sky with a yellow sun. Hmmm? Something like that. Maybe it was more like dusk that I was thinking of. Kind of this glow on the horizon, but with ominous black clouds flowing in from the east. No that wasn't it. It was definitely an abstract thing. A sunny, dark day. By this time it was 2 AM. I decided to go to bed not because I was tired, but, because it was time. I laid in my dark studio, listening to the rain hammer the building. When I closed my eyes I saw light. When I opened them—dark. When I fluttered them I got this curious combination. That's when it struck me. I needed to contrast lightness and darkness on a miniscule scale. That's when I fell asleep.

6/12/86

It was here. It happened so quickly. June 12, 1986. The debut of Frank Teeman "The Artist". I felt a growing sense of helplessness as the day approached. Now that it was here I was feeble. This was an event that would transform my life in one way or another, but I had no control over the outcome. I pretended to myself that it really didn't matter. That I could go back to my normal life if it all fell through. That I could handle whatever came with success. But when it came to actually thinking about that time after, my mind was blank. It was like the negative version of amnesia. I realized the vitality of this event even if I couldn't admit it to myself. I kept on painting and going to work as if nothing extraordinary was on the calendar. I did invite Mary Everett and Jack. And I tracked down Brian Mosten. He flipped.

"Frank," he sat with his mouth open staring blankly, "Frank! God! This is great!" I had showed him the ad as proof. We got really drunk that night. He kept talking about not forgetting him when I was famous. And the more we drank the less resistance I put up. At first I wouldn't buy into his assessment of the largeness of this thing. That would mean I would have to admit it to myself. But when I was sufficiently blotto and "myself" was almost completely unaware, I played along. I told Brian about Irene's mansion and all the rich folk that wanted to meet me.

"God damn it you bastard," he slurred, "how the hell did you get this gig anyways?"

"She saw one of my pieces in the grocery store."

"One of your paintings hangs in a grocery store?" He burst out laughing. Why did everyone find that so amusing?

"Yeah," I was defensive, "And she loved it."

"And you don't have to service the old prune?"

"She's really quite pretty."

"So you do have to service her," he punched me in the arm, still laughing.

"No!" I was revolted

I went and saw Red again, too. She was dancing on that same platform when I showed up at Tommy's. I smiled at her, but she wasn't happy to see me. She left abruptly. I was extremely disappointed. Another girl took her spot shortly and I started to finish my second beer so that I could split. Mary appeared, in street clothes, her hair up, smoking a cigarette.

"Let's go," she said dejectedly.

"Well, hello to you too," I was flip.

"You don't have to do that," she was bitter.

"What?" There was tension.

"The niceness thing. You wanna go or what?"

"Yeah, let's go."

Not exactly what I had in mind. We marched, silently, back up to 6B.

She wouldn't even look at me.

"Listen," she said to the wall when the door was shut, "full price this time." She turned and looked straight at me.

"Mary," uttering that name made me shiver, "I didn't come here for that."

"Oh God," she headed for the door.

"Wait! I wanted to make a reservation." I don't know where that came from, but it stopped her. "I need an escort." She turned and looked straight at me. "It's a formal dinner party and art opening," I showed her the ad.

"This is you!?"

"Yeah. Can you make it? Next Friday?"

"I don't know," she didn't trust me.

"I'll buy you a dress…"

"I got a damn dress."

"I'll send a cab,"

"I can take my own cab,"

"Good. Then you'll be there?"

"Yeah, I suppose. Three hundred, though."

"Fine, you got paper and a pencil?" She fished one out of the dresser. I wrote my address and phone number, "We need to leave at three," she snatched the paper, "see you then." I was happy.

"God damn you," I heard her mutter. Not at all what I expected.

So, now it was here. I was wearing my tux waiting for Red's arrival. I was starting to doubt whether she would actually show. I was staring out my window at the rental car Bill and Mo had gotten for me wondering how I was going to get it, and me, out there if she didn't show. The cab pulled up, though, and when she got out in that sexy black dress I felt the first exhilaration of the day. She turned around and looked at the building. Her hair was all done up on the top of her head and she was adorned tastefully with diamond jewelry. For the first time in a week I was glad that I had invited, hired, her. I ran out the door, keys in my hand, and met her at the front door with a kiss on the cheek and a hug. She was very business like. I was very happy. I handed her the keys and pointed at the car.

"I'm driving?" she was insulted.

"I'm too nervous," I was still beaming at her.

"Whatever," she resigned with the slightest hint of a giggle. The ride out was quiet. I was too nervous to speak. As we approached Irene's house I started to freak out.

"What's our story?" I insisted. She wasn't following. "What are we gonna tell people about you and me?"

"You mean what are we gonna tell people about me?"

I was embarrassed. "Well, yeah. What do you want to say?"

"How 'bout the truth?"

That idea made me really uncomfortable, but I was always an advocate for truth.

"Please be diplomatic."

"Don't worry about me," What was she insinuating? We had arrived, no time to deal with that.

Smiling bright faces greeted us. The valet was smiling. Irene was smiling. All her friends were smiling. As I shook the hands of those rich men and nodded my head ever so slightly at their wives, I was smiling. Red was not smiling. It was obvious that Irene and her friends were looking down their noses at her. She was tactful. I loved that. Everyone kept smiling.

By the time we sat down at the dinner table, I had collected myself enough to get a bit of perspective. Like looking off a cliff. My heart started racing. I took a big pull off of my third martini. Everyone laughed. I had missed the joke. I was distracted. More like oblivious. I wasn't really thinking about something else, I just wasn't computing. I saw the faces of all those overly dressed guests. They were looking at me. I guess they were waiting for one of those obtuse artistic quirks that signify greatness. I wondered if I were doing one unwittingly. Whatever, I couldn't understand what they were talking about. I smiled.

Red was on my right. She looked down at her plate constantly. She really was beautiful that night. The more I looked at her, the more I realized that. She caught me admiring her and she smiled. That made me happy. I took another haul off that martini. That's when I felt Red's naked toe touching my leg. I looked at her and she tried not to laugh. She ran her foot up the inside of my pant leg and I let out a giggle. It tickled! The room went silent and all eyes were on me!

"Good joke," I slapped the table and kept on eating. The group started buzzing, I'm sure about stereotypic artist eccentricity stories. I was laughing aloud at myself. I couldn't believe I had just done that. Red's toe found it's way back to my leg. It didn't tickle anymore.

Maybe because numbness was setting in. It did give my balls a tingle, though.

I started to think about that session we had in 6B. It made me hot and I looked at Red's naked shoulder longingly. She knew she had me. I didn't mind. I put my hand on hers. She looked at me in utter disbelief.

"Mr. Teeman," a nasally man's voice beckoned. I turned to see the entire table looking with eager anticipation. They were all older than me, and cleaner, too. Amazingly clean. "May I call you Frank?" a man who was introduced to me as "Phil Jankow, the banker" asked.

"Sure, Phil," I was flip even though I felt like I was on trial.

"Irene tells me you're from Kansas," patronizing.

"That's right," smiling right back.

"How do your folks feel about this?"

"Well, Phil" I didn't know what to say. All of those smiling clean faces. "They're dead," I said it. I don't know how.

"Oh, I'm terribly sorry," he turned red.

"Don't be, Phil, don't be," I actually chuckled, "It was their death that prompted me to come to New York. Mom and Dad," I lifted my glass towards the sky and downed it. The room was eerily silent. My eyes kind of rolled in my head so I couldn't see how people were reacting. "I was adopted anyways," I continued eating. The clinking of everyone else's silverware resumed gradually. I realized I had put a damper on the party and in a desperate attempt to make amends, I stood. "I'd like to make a toast," I noticed my glass was empty so I grabbed Mary's, "To Irene Solomon, the best mom any adopted kid could want." The response was less than enthusiastic. I didn't know that Irene had never had kids and that that was a great source of sorrow for her. When I looked at her I could see the melancholy plainly. That made me sad. I motioned the waiter to fill my glass.

Irene had me limo-ed to the gallery. It was nice to get away. I slumped in the back trying to muster the strength to continue. Red just rambled on about how amazing this all was. She fixed us both a drink, but we had arrived. There was a bit of a crowd on the sidewalk and my first thought was that something was wrong. I got out before the chauffeur could let me out and the crowd erupted into applause. I was stunned. Literally stunned. I stood on that walk, agape until a large shiver went up my back. It was so immense it forced me to drop my drink. I laughed. Irene escorted me into the gallery like a Thorazine patient. Finally, there were some familiar faces. Bill and Mo, and Brian, and Mary Everett and some one who I recognized, but couldn't place. And Sal came up and introduced me to Al Rosenstein. People were patting me on the back. The place was just a din of voices. I was so drunk I was on the brink of losing it.

"Congratulations, Frank," it was Jack.

"Thank heaven you're here," I looked at him in distress.

"Oh, don't tell me you're not loving the hell out of this."

"No, I'm not," I kept trying to smile.

"What the devil's wrong, now? Too much attention?" there was his sarcasm.

"Yes, as a matter of fact, I need…"

"Ladies and gentlemen," Irene spoke from a podium with a microphone, "I'd like to welcome you to the first featured artist auction at Solomon's Gallery. Before the bidding starts I'd like you to meet this very special talent."

"Oh no, Oh no," I dreaded this.

"Ladies and gentlemen, Mister Frank Teeman," she pointed me out. As every one started applauding she waved for me to come up to the podium. It was then that I realized that all my paintings were hanging on the walls. And all the memories came rushing back. I was filled with a tremendous desire to cry. I hung my head. And as the applause quickly waned the crowd was abuzz.

"Frank's very humble," Irene spoke with a slight jag, "So let's start the bidding!" It sounded like the beginning of a race. I raced to leave.

I got myself outside amazingly, and blissfully, alone. I sat down on the sidewalk and tried to ignore the whole thing. It was impossible. My memories and feelings were being auctioned off in there and even though my eyes were closed my ears were open. I heard a man's voice. "We'll start the sale with this wonderful study—Untitled number one."

What the hell was this? I didn't have anything untitled. I had to look. I peeked in the window and saw that leg thing. I never did like that. It's amazing how much a nice frame adds, but nobody would buy that. Would they? It was a diddle. A jot. Look! Gladys' gnarled toenail.

"We'll start the bidding at five hundred dollars," and the auctioneer went into his spiel. To my amazement a thousand had been reached in a matter of seconds. I sat back down on the curb and prepared to puke.

"Frank Teeman, you little pigfuck," someone was out on the sidewalk with me. I turned to see the silhouette of a man that I knew. Who was this guy? Tall, gaunt, curly hair. Pigfuck? I hadn't heard that since...

"John?"

"It's a long way from Dilon squirt," he laughed.

"John Rogers?" I still couldn't believe it. I got up and approached him. When I finally got a look at his face I was shocked. He looked so old.

"Yeah, it's me. Eighteen years later." He held out his hand.

"John Rogers..." the surreality of this whole day had just kicked into high gear. I shook his hand. He was real.

"So, you're doin' pretty damn well for yourself,"

"Yeah, I guess,"

"Whatta you mean 'I guess.' This is phenomenal."

"Listen, I know this must seem great to you, but I'm still trying to believe it myself. What are you doing here?"

"I saw the ad in The Times."

"You've been in New York all this time?

"Yup."

"I knew it. I told my folks..."

"How long you been here?"

"Eight years," that was a harsh realization.

"You live out here?"

"No," I laughed, "What the hell have you been doing all this time?"
"Ah, never mind about me," he looked down, "tell me how this hap-
pened for you."
We sat down on the curb and I tried to relate the story to him. I started
with his "disappearance". We laughed about that. We almost cried,
though, when I told him about my folks. We laughed about Ellen Tamor-
itz proposing to me. And then I started telling him about New York like he
had never been there. He listened quite patiently. That was so therapeutic.
It made me feel so good. Maybe I was sobering up a little bit, too. When I
finished I noticed for the first time how sad John was. He sat there on the
curb hanging his head barely moving or saying anything. I felt so great. It
was like he had taken my sadness from me and bore it himself.

"Frank," a voice from the gallery door pulled me from this dream, "You're missing it." It was Red. She was drunk. John and I looked at each other and I felt twelve again. My mother used to interrupt our little adventures in the same way.

"You better go, squirt," he used to say that then, too.

"Yeah, I'd better," just like 1965. I got up and shuffled in without looking back.

Glad was on the block and bidding was furious. Red held my arm and stuck her tongue in my ear. She was drunk and laughing. I was sober and straight faced. That's how we appeared when Al Rosenstein's photographer snapped us at close of bidding on Glad.

"Hot new artist, Frank Teeman and unidentified companion show surprise and glee at the sale of his painting "Glad" (in the background) for the remarkable sum of $155,000," read the caption on that photo which ran in next Monday morning's Times.

When I heard that figure out of the auctioneer's mouth I was confused.

"One hundred fifty five thousand going once,"
Did he say fifty five thousand?
"One hundred fifty five thousand going twice,"
One hundred fifty what?

"Is everyone satisfied? One hundred fifty five thousand?"

Glad I'll miss you.

"One hundred fifty five thousand three times," he had reached a fever pitch, "SOOOLLD, for one hundred fifty five thousand dollars to the gentleman number fifty seven."

The crowd erupted. People were congratulating me and people were congratulating Phil Jankow. He was number fifty seven. I saw him hug Irene and I could swear a tear came to his eye. Irene made her way through the crowd.

"Frank, I never dreamed this would work so well," she was on the brink of tears.

"It's all because of you, Irene" I had to shout to be heard. We hugged. I felt her tremendous warmth. I thought of the piece I was in the middle of. I felt her glow.

11/20/68

I heard the knock on my window and I awoke from a dream that had me climbing through a rocky terrain looking for my pet cigarette butt. There it was again. It was definitely a rock against my window. Unless that blustery wind was knocking somehow. I went to my bedroom window and looked down on our backyard to see him there looking back up. I pointed to my left and he nodded and ran. I went to the guest room and opened the window in time to let John Rogers fall in. I was so afraid that he had awakened my parents I just stood there, with my eyes closed, waiting for the hammer to fall. He stumbled out of the room and flopped on to my bed. After a sufficiently quiet period, I followed him.

He was in a peculiar state. It scared me. He was laying on the bed, feet still on the ground. His eyes were huge and wide. He was smiling. I remember that the most. John never smiled. But now he was smiling. And it was a warm smile despite the stubble.

"Thanks little man," he said in a husky whisper, still focused on the ceiling or the wall or some place else.

"You're drunk!" I'd seen him drunk before and knew this was different, but wanted to show my savvy.

"Yeah…" he giggled, "I'm drunk," he sat up quickly, "But I haven't had any booze." He tousled my hair. I hated when people did that.

"Don't," I whined.

"I'm sorry squirt," he was holding back laughter.

"Your folks kick you out again?"

"Na. I didn't even bother going home."

"You're drunk," I laughed, but I couldn't get over how different he seemed.

"Being drunk like this ain't so bad," he laughed and fell back onto the bed.

"You drinking moonshine?" I didn't know what that was, but I remembered hearing my dad talk about how crazy people got on it. John definitely looked crazed. But in a benevolent way.

"Man, there is one, big, whacky world out there. And I can see it all on your ceiling."

"Where?" I looked. "I don't see nothin."

"Look hard," he had such a soothing tone. I strained to see.

"I still don't see nothin."

"It's a funny thing about looking. To look harder you've got to try less."

"What?"

"Just leave your eyes open, but don't look at anything."

I tried, but couldn't.

"How do you look at nothin with your eyes open."

He laughed. "It takes practice, it takes practice. One of the most important things is not to think about it. Don't think about anything."

"How do you not…"

"Shush, shush…just try it." We laid there side by side staring at the ceiling. He would let out a "wow" or a giggle occasionally so I was convinced he was doing it. Just like climbing the silo, I was determined to follow.

I never did see anything on that ceiling, but I was still trying when he said, "God damn it, this is a boring town," he took out his Lucky Strikes and lit one.

"John," I whined, my heart racing.

"What?" he mimicked me.

"I'm gonna get in trouble,"

"Why?" he was still mimicking me.

"My room's gonna smell like smoke."

"OK, how 'bout we open the window," he walked to the window and cracked it and stayed there looking out on to our backyard. "Damn, it's windy out," he blew his smoke out the crack, "You member the kite we flew?"

"The Purple Dragon?"

"Yeah, the purple dragon."

"What about it?"

"That was just beautiful, soaring up towards the sun."

"I thought it was going to burn."

"I remember. Do you know how far away the sun is?"

"Ninety three million miles," I was proud. I had just learned that in science class.

"Ninety three million god damn miles away," he took a drag on his cigarette.

"You think we'll ever send rockets to the sun?"

"Nah. Too far."

"People said the same thing about the moon."

"Fuck outer space," he said venomously. I pulled my covers up. I still wasn't sure what he was going to do. He spit on his cigarette, tossed it out the window, and came back over to the bed. That benevolent crazed look he had had changed.

I was scared.

"Blinded, narrow-minded..." I think that was what he said.

"You're drunk," I peeped out.

"No, I'm high," his melancholy scared me even more.

"You're smoking grass?"

"Yeah, but I'm high on life." I wasn't sure what he meant by that. I was too afraid of the revelation.

"Are you an addict?"

"Listen squirt," he was serious, "don't buy any of that shit about grass. It's no worse than alcohol."

"Really?"

"Yeah, really. It's peaceful."

"Why do they say it's so bad?"

"It's the establishment. They don't want us to have any fun."

"Why not?"

"They need slaves for their factories."

"Slaves?"

"Listen, you wouldn't know by hanging around this hick town, but there is a big, beautiful, wild world out there. And there's more than one way to live your life. And there's more than one god to believe in. And some people never get married or work a normal job." I was just gawking at him. "Frank, promise me that you'll check it out. You might end up here in Dilon. You might decide you like it and you might take over your father's store and get married and have a little pigfuck all your own, but promise me that you'll check it out.

"I promise," I wasn't sure what I was promising I just wanted to placate him.

"What do you promise?"

"I promise to check it out."

"Check what out?"

I had to think then. I was afraid to say the wrong thing so, I just shrugged.

"I'm talking about the world, Frank. Other people. Other cultures."

"Cultures?"

"Art…and…music"

Art? I liked painting at one time. "I promise I'll check out art," I said proudly.

"Thanks Frank," he threw open his arms and smiled brightly, "C'mon give me a hug."

I hugged him, but I felt funny about it. He squeezed me so hard and so long.

I didn't know what to make of it. I pushed him away.

"You're drunk!"

"Yeah, yeah. It's terrible, I know, but you love me anyways. Don't ya?"
He almost seemed like a different person. He had never talked like that
to me before.
I didn't know what to say.
He tousled my hair.
"Jo-o-ohn," how I hated that. He just laughed.
"OK, gotta go," he popped up and headed out.
I followed him instantly. I didn't want him to go. When I realized that,
I realized that I did love him. He popped open the window and hopped out
on to the tree. I watched him dissolve into darkness and waved. He never
looked back.

I started to think about what he had said. The wonder of the world
and all that stuff about culture and people. For the first time in my
young life I started to get a sense for the proportion of my life. I started
thinking about all the places in the world and all the people in all those
places and I started to wonder how many of them were wondering
about Dilon, Kansas. And it occurred to me that most of them didn't
even know about Dilon, Kansas. I started to think about all those little
towns that I didn't know about and I was overwhelmed by the thought
that maybe there was a twelve year old boy in China looking out his
window at that precise moment wondering precisely what I was wondering. I closed my eyes and I could see him. It sent a shiver up my
back.

"Franklin Teeman! What on earth are you doing?" Mom had
caught me standing in front of that open window.

"I'm checkin' out the world, Mom!" I had never been so proud.

6/16/86

That straight-faced photo of me in The Times was appropriate enough. I was in shock from that point on. Al Rosenstein did an impromptu interview with me that night. The whole time I was remembering that John Rogers had showed up. I kept an eye out for him, but never saw him. Consequently, Al was convinced that I didn't care much about the interview. I didn't.

He wrote—"Normally, I would chalk up the sale of studies on the elderly to a group of wealthy elderlies as the perfect incestuous relationship. Normally, I would label the artist an opportunist who paints the elderly when he knows he'll be selling to them. After talking with this particular artist, I have to conclude that the art world is blessed with a rising young star…"

Blah, blah, blah. I guess Al's word is valued. I never heard of him before. Suddenly, I was the painter of the aged. Sal was able to "score [me] any interview [I] wanted!" Well I didn't want any interviews. That frustrated Sal. He would call me periodically with a list of rags that were willing to do a story on me. I declined them all. I was enthralled with the painting of Irene that I was working on. I guess I was hiding. It worked for me. Sal opened up a bank account for me. I never asked about it. He kept asking if I needed anything. When I told him that I was painting he would almost lose it. "That's great! You keep on doing your thing. Don't stop now. Keep up the good work." I thought about having my phone disconnected. I kept hoping that John

Rogers would call. I showed up for my next scheduled day of work right on time. Bill and Mo were there all smiling and proud.

"Frank? What are you doing here?" They were almost afraid of me.

"I'm on the schedule," I felt like I was talking to strangers.

"Frank? What do you mean? Your career has started. You don't need to work. Mo and I'll cover it."

I didn't know what to say. I had never thought about that before. I was actually looking forward to working. "No. That's OK. I don't mind."

"Aw, Frank you're a good boy. Don't forget us now," Mo was on the verge of tears.

"Listen, I don't plan on quitting this job. I'll give you two weeks notice when I do!" and I went to work. I felt bad about snapping at them, but never had a chance to apologize. When I clocked out we said "tomorrow" to each other. That was it. Bill and Mo just watched me like I was going to school for the first time. Arm in arm and all aglow. Huh? There was that glow again. How could I capture that? I was staring at them and they were staring at me.

I waved. They waved back. Wild.

I was feeling particularly alone not being able to communicate with Bill and Mo, so I found myself on the stroll. I had taken so many different paths home I was surprised to find a street that was unfamiliar. In the middle of that block was a beautifully ornate, old gothic church. The organ was filling the streets with a wonderfully sonorous current. I stopped long enough to realize that the organist was practicing the same four bar pattern over and over.

"Are you Christian, sir?" a strong deep voice broke through the organ. I turned to see a priest. A young priest. So young I looked hard. Maybe harder than I should have. "Father Frank," he extended his hand. I shook his hand, but couldn't look him in the eye. "You seem troubled," he waited for a response. I didn't give one. "Have you asked for Christ's blessing?"

"Oh, yeah. That was a long time ago," I was still reveling in that rich, reedy, repetitious sonority.

"Maybe it's time you renewed your faith," he smiled. Priests' humility always touched me.

"I think it's too late for that," I chuckled and started to walk away.

"It's never too late," his voice was filled with as much richness as that organ.

"If money is the root of evil, like they say, I just fell into a pile of trouble," I said over my shoulder.

"Resist temptation brother. You are loved," he raised his voice to be heard. I smiled and waved. He smiled and waved back. Wild.

It was time to hide again. I wasn't so lucky. Jack was waiting for me on my stoop and not only Jack, but Des, too. I got a big hug and a kiss from Des and Jack was laughing and cheering. I was less than enthusiastic.

"What's up?" Jack was incredulous.

"Aw, I just got off of work," I was tired.

"You need to relax," Des was sympathetic. I thought she had gotten the hint. I was wrong. "Let us help you relax," she was suggestive. Those fabulous nostrils flared and my mouth said, "C'mon in," before I knew what was happening. I was planning on painting, but what the hell!

I saw that Sapphire in Jack's hand. "Pour me tall and dry," Jack took the hint and headed for the kitchen with glee.

"That was a great write up about you in The Times," Des had already started massaging my shoulders and I was just beginning to realize how tense I was.

"Yeah," was all I could muster. It was a great write-up. Was it about me?

Her kisses fell lightly on my nape. I hadn't gotten a tingle like that since my first line of coke. She giggled.

"Here you go, Maestro," Jack handed me a tall martini. It was quenchingly dry. "Life's rich pageant," he toasted. We all drank. "So," he was hesitant, "You made out like a son-of-a-bitch Friday, huh?" that hyena laugh.

"I suppose I did."

"Well either you did or you didn't, and you did!"

"Did I?" I wasn't convinced.

"Even if you didn't make any cash on this one, the junk lyin' around here just quadrupled in value."

"Who would wanna buy this shit?"

"Good question." Martinis are wonderful at these moments. I indulged. And as I was reveling in the onslaught of alcohol intoxication, Desiree unbuckled my pants and began massaging the small of my back.

"Mmmm," I took another haul off that martini.

"So what are you gonna do with that loot?" Jack was just making small talk, but it aggravated me. I just looked at him wide-eyed. "Oh, I forgot, the man who couldn't spend money," Des's kisses had me enthralled, "Real estate's always solid."

"Jack! We're trying to relax," Des spoke my thoughts.

"OK. No more business…..Who was that redhead?"

"Mary," I remembered how great she was that night, "She's that stripper from Tommy's I told you about."

"You took a stripper to that bourgeois bash," that hyena laugh, "Frank you crack me up!" he clinked his glass on mine and we drank.

"Did she fuck you good," Des whispered in my ear. It tickled so I giggled. She started nibbling my ear, "Let me do you right," that husky whisper. I just looked at her. "Let me do you like you deserve," she said more loudly. Her eyes were closed and her nostrils…

Damn those fabulous nostrils.

"Oh, you've done it now Frank. Desiree is on," he took my empty glass and left the room. Desiree's sexual energy exploded on me. She pinned me down. Her tongue was almost machine like. By the time I was inside her mouth I had figured out what was going on and began to reciprocate. Sex with Des is intense. I have never been with someone who had so much enthusiasm. When I would get tired she would take up the slack while I just laid there reveling.

"Fuck me," started quietly from her mouth and had reached shrill levels by the time I finally entered her from behind. I looked up to see Jack standing over me handing me a new martini. I took it and quaffed without missing a beat. Jack winked and gave me the thumbs up. I proceeded to pump harder and harder. I winked at Jack and gave him the thumbs up. All the while I was more confused.

"Yes!" Des screamed.

"You like that?" Jack was standing in front of her smiling.

"Yes!" Des reached for her clit.

"Do it Frank! Do it!" that hyena laugh. I just came and collapsed. I opened my eyes to see a naked Desiree and a fully clothed Jack standing side by side, smiling down on me.

I smiled and waved at them. They waved back. Wild.

RRRinggg. I had fallen asleep where I had collapsed. RRRinggg. The phone beckoned and I stumbled to answer it. Jack had beat me to it. He handed me the phone with a smile and a limp wrist. I had forgotten that I was in the middle of a gin buzz so it took me a while to figure out why everything was so fuzzy.

"Frank?" It was Sal, "this is your man Sal. How the hell are you!?!" I had just spoken with him that morning.

"What's up Sal?"

"I'm workin' for ya…"

"No interviews," my head throbbed.

"Listen, Frank, you gotta work with me…"

"Sal…"

"Just hear me out, hear me out."

"OK, OK," there was a pause.

He was subdued, "Time magazine."

"Time magazine?" Jack and Des popped up.

"Time fuckin' magazine," Sal was so happy.

"What do they want?"

"They want to talk to you. It's part of a thing on the elderly."

"I'm not old!"

"This issue is about how the elderly are growing and invading society and culture…"

"Culture?"

"Yeah. Like that Cocoon movie."

"What?"

"It's a movie with a bunch of old folks," I didn't know what to say, "at least say you'll think about this. Work with me Frank," he sounded pathetic.

"OK," I resigned.

"OK you'll think about it or OK you'll do it?"

"I'll do it." I felt like I had just volunteered latrine duty.

"You'll do it!?!"

"Yeah, I'll do it!"

"Good decision Frank. I'll give them your number. Good decision. Will you be home tonight?"

I looked at Jack and Des who were anxiously trying to figure out what was happening from my side of the conversation. "No. Tomorrow morning."

"Eleven?"

"Eleven."

"You won't regret…" I just hung up.

I have to admit I was jumping and laughing along with Jack and Des after that one. We went out to celebrate, but I was called home by that painting. We'd only had a couple drinks and then, suddenly, that image of Bill and Mo standing arm in arm, waving…that glow. I didn't even try to make excuses.

"You two have a good time, I've got to go home," they had seen the image forming in my mind.

"We'll come with you," Des begged.

I just shook my head and waved. They waved back, perplexed. Wild.

RRRinggg. That damn phone woke me up again. And I stumbled over it in an alcoholic daze, just like before.

"Hello," I croaked out.

"Mr. Teeman?" a chipper young woman's voice put a little spark in my brain. "This is Sally Weitz, Time magazine."

"Oh. Hello. I thought you weren't calling until eleven?"

"I know I'm late. Please forgive me…"

"Late? What time is it?"

"It's 12:05 by my watch," I had thrown her off.

"Damn! I have to get to work!"

"Mr. Teeman what about our interview?"

"Some other time."

"I just called to make an appointment," she was indignant yet polite.

"How 'bout never?" I hung up. Before I could get three steps…RRRinggg.

God that was annoying.

"Mr. Teeman please don't hang up," it was Sally and she sounded desperate, "Mr. Teeman this is my first day on the job, actually this is my first job, I'm sorry if I upset you, but I just need to make an appointment for my boss."

"Who's your boss?" What was this about?

"Roger Mondrake," she had such a sweet voice.

"Is he a good boss?" I was melting.

"He's very nice," she giggled.

"I'd be glad to meet with him then," I smiled.

"Oh, thank you so much!"

"You're welcome," and we set a date.

I had a tremendous feeling of dread then. But I was doing Sally (and Sal) a favor. So, I convinced myself it was the right thing to do.

I met with Roger Mondrake two days later. He came to my loft and I was busy working on that painting of Irene. I had decided to use the same technique I had used in "Shine On" to get that subtle illumination. It surprised me how that technique worked equally well on animate objects as inanimate.

"I can see how you got your moniker. That is superb." Ralph was agape. I was determined and therefore distracted. "Sally call Jim," he barked, "We can photograph. Can't we?" his tone changed noticeably.

"Sure," I figured it would be easier than arguing. Sally dialed diligently as I finished up that one segment which seemed most difficult.

"Thanks for seeing me on such short notice," Ralph was plaintiff.

"Thank Sally. I'm doing it for her." I flopped on the futon, exhausted.

"Most artists would consider this a major opportunity," he was smug.

"I suppose," I was smug.

"Do you mind if I ask a few questions?"

"Not at all," I smiled at him. He proceeded to ask, what seemed to be routine questions. I gave him what I thought were routine answers. His photographer showed up and took what seemed to be routine photos. Then they left.

Thank God that was over.

Being ethical in today's society is forbidding. Most people don't even take up the challenge. They just subscribe to some religious faith and hope they'll be forgiven in case of errata. Being raised an atheist I found myself floating, ethically, as a young adult. When I learned of Kant's categorical imperative—to treat others not as means to an end, but as ends in themselves—it sounded like a good idea. It reminded me of what I had learned as "The Golden Rule"—Do unto others as you would have them do unto you. Kant seemed to take the Golden Rule a step further. Further towards the metaphysical, that is. The Golden Rule assumes that every one wants to be treated ethically. What about those people who seem to enjoy abuse? Under the Golden Rule they would be justified in abusing others. At least in their own minds. When I talk of abuse I do not speak of it in the physical sense, although physical abuse is also contained in the type of abuse to which I refer. When I talk of abuse, I'm talking about the abuse of power. Each of us is imbued with power. Power that can be used against each other. Again not physical power, per se, but the power of understanding. Understanding that each of us is vulnerable. Abuse of that power comes from utilizing that vulnerability for individual gain. Using people as means to an end. Being ethical, for me, is treating people as ends in and of themselves. And, as Kant said, this is categorically imperative whether you enjoy abuse or not. Nobody puts much stock in Kant anymore.

So, is that what this is all about? Is Frank Teeman's voice—that voice that I hear telling me this story—is Frank Teeman's voice my voice? Am I just grappling with ethics? Am I trying to work out Kant's Categorical Imperative in the context of post-industrial society? The answer would appear to be "Yes". I mean, look at Frank. Gladys was vulnerable. Mary Everett was vulnerable. I don't know, those aren't great examples, but Frank hasn't showed a propensity for putting his needs first. Actually, he seems to have tailored his life so that his needs don't force him to forgo other people's needs. I still have a real problem with the idea that this is some kind of "autopsychography". Maybe it's because I'm afraid of exposing myself to unknown readers. But the parallels are there. I can't deny them. I, like Frank, am involved in the art world. I am consciously struggling with the idea of making money. Most importantly I have chosen a life and lifestyle that allows me to focus on my art. That gets back to what I was talking about at the end of the first part—priorities. Everybody has to deal with very similar impulses in the context of very similar situations. Nobody can have everything. So, one must prioritize. And when I say Frank is normal, that is what I mean. He prioritizes.

Are there commonly accepted priorities? I mean, if everyone must prioritize, are there commonly accepted things, goals, ideals that are commonly held so as to define normalness. This is what I'm getting at—I have this image of Frank Teeman as a normal guy, but as I hear his story, I'm not convinced.

First there's the money thing. Money has to be the most wildly addictive substance known to man. So many people are addicted to the stuff that a whole country was formed that would tolerate its abuses. People are still standing in line for that kind of toleration. Here is a guy, though, who grew up in the midst of that, he even had a little surplus, budgeted himself, and when he ran out? No big deal. That kind of lack of income is the most perilous feeling most of us get. It's the same kind of loneliness that is described in opium withdrawal!?! Frank is undaunted.

Then there's the sex thing. The second most addictive. People will go to just as many extremes for some regular action as they will for a regular income. Some even further! But not Frank. We know he has a libido or maybe he's just got a prosthetic. Whatever, he's managed to satisfy a couple of partners. At the same time he's not obsessed. At least that's the way it seems, doesn't it?

And what about all those substances that everyone admits are addictive? Alcohol? Frank seems to have a dependency or at least an intimate relationship. Cocaine? I've personally seen people go off the deep end on that. Frank? He seems to be able to take it or leave it. Tobacco?? Not even a consideration.

So what's the point? The point is that being addicted in and of itself is not a bad thing. Let's face it there are millions of addicts alive and well (at least functioning) today. The problem is that addictions have a way of screwing up your priorities. Once your priorities are screwed up it is only a matter of time before you wander off the path of well being and straight into the hands of misery.

Maybe Frank is addicted to art. His priorities have been shaped by his passion for art. Most people become addicted to something that makes them feel good and, more over, something that they can manipulate to make them feel good at their whim. Should Frank wean himself of art then, simply because he may be addicted to it? I guess it's kind of like being a workaholic. There are treatment programs for that, too! But if that's the case are any of us free from addiction?

I dated a woman once who said she had not found her passion. She had tried several occupations and dispensed with them all. Thirty years old and still searching!?! And when I asked her, "Isn't there anything that you feel genuinely motivated to do?" she said, "No. I haven't found my passion." She was then a secretary for an accounting firm and she disliked it. She didn't even hate it. I suppose that would have been a passion. I don't spend much time with "9to5'ers", but I got a feeling that her lack of passion is common for that set. Maybe that's what being normal is. I call it addiction she called it passion.

If being passionless is normal, being normal in today's society is incredibly difficult. Isn't it? There are so many things that are open for abuse—money, power, drugs, alcohol, food, sleep, even work. So many people consider "normalness" to be that straight clean ideal. Doesn't being normal mean succumbing to those temptations of abuse sometime?

We all have our vices.

PART III

7/11/86

I made a deal with the devil. I didn't think so at first. But now I'm convinced. It seemed like such a good deal, at the time. When you're jonesing for energy you'll do anything for a fix. And anything that'll give you that fix is your friend. So, there I was walking through Central Park, desperate for energy. All the elements were there—the sun just barely peeking from between the buildings, the birds chirping, even a little breeze. So I closed my eyes and waited for it just like I had done so many times before.

Nothing.

"I don't know what you're doin'" he said, "but it sure looks funny," he laughed.

I couldn't reply. I didn't know what I was doing, either. That made me sad. But I tried again. And as I sat there with my eyes closed an image came to me. It was Irene Solomon. No. It was my painting of Irene standing in the birch trees, all-aglow. I saw it then. Clear as day. God, I loved that painting.

I know I said that Irene ruined my life or was, somehow, involved in my decline. Well only in the fact that she was there to witness it is that true. I often say to myself, "What if I had never met Irene?" Somehow there's comfort in that thought. I doubt it would have changed my life much. I just have a tremendous attachment to the past. Or at least to the way things were. That time when I thought I was happy. It is much easier going around pretending to be happy. And in the end you may actually convince yourself if you do a good job of it. Too bad I didn't know that then.

The one who was most responsible for my decline was Roger Mondrake. Yes, Roger. He came over to interview me for a piece he was doing for Time magazine. It was on the culture of aging America and I was supposed to be a little side bar piece because I had just been labeled the painter of the aged or some other thing. Well, Roger decided to expand my piece and it became a full-fledged article. When the release papers were sent over I just signed them without reading. Maybe that would have given me a hint.

Maybe I could have prepared myself.

Maybe.

Once that magazine hit the stands my life was never the same. Sal was the first to call me and he was simply ecstatic. "You gotta see it Frank. It's beautiful!"

"I thought it was supposed to be a sidebar," I was sure he was stretching.

"Well it's not. I'm looking at a full page picture of you."

"Full page?"

"Full page!"

"How do I look?"

"Great! You gotta see it Frank. Go find one."

"All right, all right."

Before I made it half a block I ran into Maureen. She had a copy in her hand. We hugged. She was jubilant as I ruffled through the magazine. Then I found it. Me. Full page and in color. And there was Irene behind me all aglow. I was so proud of that painting, even if it wasn't finished. My eyes flowed directly from the picture to the text. Roger made the connection between me and the elderly. He talked about "Glad" (I wonder when he saw that) and a bunch of stuff about respect. Supposed respect that I had for these older people. I guess I did, but I never really thought about it. Then the article went on to describe me as an unusual character, intensely dedicated to my work blah, blah, blah. That's when I stopped reading.

"Isn't it wonderful," Maureen *was ecstatic.*

I wasn't that thrilled. "Yeah," *I had to play along.*

"We have more copies at the store, would you like 'em?"

"Sure. I'll pick 'em up tomorrow. Save me a couple."

"OK Frank. You know, you don't really need to be comin' into work."

"Mo, I don't mind. I like it."

"Well, Bill doesn't want me to tell you, but we're having some problems," I was confused, *"Financial problems."*

"Mo! How long has this been goin' on?"

"Well, you know the grocery business."

"A long time."

"So, we're lookin' for ways to cut some corners."

"And if I left you wouldn't replace me?" I was getting the picture.

"Well, we may get someone, part-time."

"I understand."

"Don't tell Bill I told you."

"I'll give my two weeks tomorrow. He won't suspect."

We hugged and parted and I felt more sad then than I had in a long time.

I think it was that look in Mo's eyes. They were in big trouble, I could tell.

By the time I got back to my place I had realized what had just happened. I told Mo that I'd quit. This was the end of an era. This was the beginning of…

All very frightening. So much uncertainty. And Des is waiting at my door.

"Hi Desiree," I smiled and waved. I didn't want her to know that I was sad. She gave me a big hug. And we kissed.

"Have you seen the article?" she asked.

"Yeah," I thought I smiled.

"You don't seem very happy about it." I was trying my hardest.

"Well, I just got some bad news."

"Awww. That's rough." Those nostrils! "You need to take your mind off that." She put her hand on my…Oh I so wanted to feel good. And the way she touches me. And the feel of her hair. I kissed her hair.

She giggled. I smiled.

That afternoon we reran the first night we had spent together. She had her clothes off before I knew it. And I couldn't do my part. I didn't even try. It didn't seem to matter. She went on without me. Well, I was there, sort of. Boy I was glad when she was done. I waited what I thought was an appropriately polite amount of time and then went and got myself a bong hit. Maybe that'd make me feel good. Des heard the gurgling.

"I don't know why you smoke that shit," she raised her voice.

"You'd rather I snort it?"

"I have some tooters if you want."

"Tooters?" I laughed. She came out of the bedroom completely incredulous and totally naked.

"Yeah, tooters!" She looked so cute with her hands on her hips.

"Yeah, whip it out. Why not." I laughed. Maybe that'd make me feel good.

RRRinggg! That damn phone. "Hello,"

"Hey Frank," it was Mary Everett.

"Mary?"

"How are you?" she sounded uncertain.

"I'm all right. How 'bout you?"

"Yeah I bet you're all right. I'm looking at your article right now."

"Is that something?" I chuckled.

"It's great Frank! You should be happy."

"No big deal."

"Well, I'm happy for you."

"Thanks. I appreciate that. How are you?"

"Let's not talk about me."

"OK."
"   "
"   "

"Thanks for inviting me to the opening."
"Listen, I apologize for not talking to you."
Des held out the bullet. I waved her away.
"You were drunk."
"I was," I was ashamed.
"You played the part perfectly, though."
"What part?"
"The part of the artist. All mysterious and decadent."
"I'll have to make a note to stay sober at openings."
"Do you have another show?"
"Not yet."
"Let me know when you do."
"I will."
"All right then. Bye."
"Bye."
Des started massaging my shoulders. "Who was that?" I couldn't get over how sad Mary had sounded. Des handed me the bullet. I took it and tooted both sides. That felt good. For a second.

RRRinnggg.
I woke up the next morning with a start.
RRRinggg.
That damn phone.
It hurt to talk so I just grunted.
"Frank!" it was Sal, "Great news!"
"Not so loud, Sal" it hurt to listen, too.
"We got a commission"
"We?"
"Well, I got one for you. Maybe."
"A commission?"

"A big one."

"Who?"

"Some army big wig."

"What's he want?"

"A portrait."

"Me?"

"Yeah. He wants to meet with you."

"OK, tomorrow," I was so hurt.

"Don't you want to know how much?" he was so happy.

"No." I hung up.

There's nothing like trying to piece together a drunken night's events. I sat there reveling in the emptiness of my memory. I remembered going to the Blarney Stone with Des. We got hammered there. And that little bullet just kept popping. After that was blank. And you wonder if you really are alive or if you're just part of someone else's dream and when they wake up you disappear. The headache I had seemed real enough. Back to bed. When I got to my room I saw her in my bed. I stopped.

"Are you coming back to bed," she said with her face still in the pillow. Thoughts of Des revolted me. When I didn't answer she sat up. It was Red! She saw the look of shock on my face. "You don't remember, do you?" I just shook my head. "You were drunk," she was emphatic, "When you jumped up on the platform and started dancing with me I decided to bring you home."

"I'm sorry."

"Don't be. It was a scream."

"I made a real fool out of myself, didn't I?"

"Don't worry. You're friends made a bigger fool out of you."

"My friends?"

"You don't remember at all?" I just flopped face first on the bed. "That Mediterranean bitch and that creepy cabby kept yelling 'It's OK. He's a famous artist.'" I looked up in horror. She just nodded.

"Thanks for getting me out of there."

"You're welcome," she kissed my neck. And she kissed my shoulder. Oh, that felt good.

And I so wanted to feel good.

And I felt so bad.

RRRinggg. Aaggh.

"Don't answer it," she put her hand on my…

RRRingg. I had to stop the ringing.

"Hello," I was short.

"Hi Frank. It's Irene." Such a sweet voice.

"Hi Irene. How are you?"

"I'm just fine. I saw your article."

"Isn't that something."

"It sure is. Congratulations!"

"Well, I have you to thank, Irene."

"You're very talented Frank."

"   "

"What was that painting in the photo with you?"

"That's my current project."

"It looked wonderful. Is it for sale?"

"Oh, I don't know…"

"I understand. Frank, we must do another show soon."

"OK, I'd like that."

"Great! And you know, Phil Jankow wants to commission you."

"Have him call Sal. Have you got his number?"

"Yes, yes, I do. Oh Frank, I'm so happy for you."

"Thanks Irene."

"Will you come visit me sometime?"

"Sure."

"You know that you're welcome to stay as long as you like if you need to get away."

"Thanks, Irene. I'll keep that in mind."

"All right. I'll let you go then."

"Bye."

"Bye, bye."

Mary started massaging my shoulders. "Who was that?"

"Irene. You remember her?"

"She want to do another show?"

"Yeah."

"Frank, that's great!" She hugged me from behind.

"Yeah," I just wanted to go to sleep.

Maybe that'd make me feel good.

7/7/83

"Today is the first day of the rest of my life!"
It's amazing how despair more than anything will drive you to absurdities.
"I will not drink to excess ever again!"

It's amazing how despair more than anything will send you reeling between extremes. July 7, 1983 (the first day of the rest of my life) was very much the same as the days that preceded it. I sat in my studio, sweltering. It was a particularly hot day. So, I sat there, naked, on the floor. I felt like I could feel more comfortable only if I entered some kind of meditative state. I just wanted out. You know, "Stop the world! I want to get off!" type of thing. And after I had spent all that time getting into the middle of things.

This is what I mean…

I found myself sitting on the sidewalk early one morning. I had awakened at six, which is normally an ungodly hour, but this day I was awake. I didn't look at my clock, I just went to the bathroom for my morning drainage. And as I made my way to the kitchen I was captivated by that orange glow. What the hell was that? It was the sun coming up like a big, bald head. Wow! That was cool. I went out onto the street, not to get a better view, but, to get a better feel. Feel for the energy. I sat on the sidewalk in those navy blue gym shorts. Those same shorts I had worn at Roosevelt High oh so many years before. I sat there and closed my eyes and waited. Eventually, the energy came.

It seemed like a mild dose, though. That was unusual. I went inside and had some corn flakes. I stared out the window and wondered if there was, somehow, less energy in the morning.

I couldn't ever recall waiting for it in the morning, before…?

The next morning I woke at 6 again and did my normal urination. Half way through I realized that it was that time again. I found myself out on the sidewalk waiting again. It came again. This time in an even lesser dose. How frustrating. I concluded that energy must be at a low in the morning. I worked at the store that day and was constantly distracted. What was going on? I used to get such a buzz off that stuff. Now it was there and that was nice, but nice is not a buzz. I almost felt like I was impotent. I didn't say anything to anybody all day. I waved a couple times. I tried to smile at a few customers. I punched out. Jim Jacobs, one of the tellers, invited me to a party. I smiled and waved. On the way home I started to think about that party. When was the last time I had gone out? I honestly couldn't remember. Oh, sure there had been a couple of obligatory holiday things. But when was the last time I had gone out? Amazingly I had led a clean and isolated existence for over a year.

Time really flies.

If you let it.

I showed up at Jim's almost unwittingly. I looked up and saw the number plate on his apartment door. What was I doing here? Better go back home. Sounds like a party inside.

A party?

Knock, knock, knock.

"Hi, Frank!" Jim was surprised.

"Hello," so was I.

"C'mon in. Let me introduce you," Jim's friends were all pretty young. Not that I was old, but Jim's friends seemed particularly young. They looked at me like they had never seen anything quite like me. Particularly the girls. I touched my nose, convinced I would find a stray buggar. It wasn't there. After I had met everyone, Jim got me a beer and sat me next to a particularly wholesome looking young blond girl. Her name was Kathleen.

"Where are you from, Frank?" She was chipper.

"What makes you think I'm from somewhere?"

"I know that accent. Huntington, right?"

"No, Dilon." She searched her memory and came up blank. "It's in Kansas."

"Kansas! Hey Marjorie. Frank's from Kansas!" You would have thought I had said the French Riviera.

Marjorie came over quickly. "What's Kansas like?"

"Have you ever been out of New York?"

"New Jersey," Kathleen resigned. "Upstate!" Marjorie was proud.

"It's flat. Kansas is god damn flat. Kansas is…" I looked up to see them aghast. Politely so, but still aghast.

"How do you know Jim?"

"From church," they answered in tandem. A-ha. A slight switch of social gears was in order. I know this crowd, though. No problem. I sat there entertaining them for the rest of the evening. Jim kept feeding me beers and I kept making them laugh.

Once I remembered what a delight the female laugh can be, I was hooked. I started visiting all my old haunts. There, I could be raunchier than in front of Jim's friends. I was so hooked on that laughter I had turned into a clown. I couldn't believe it myself. It's amazing how many free drinks you can get by being funny. The staff likes you so they float you. Patrons like you, after all they're there to have a good time. I never drank so much or so many different kinds of alcohol as that month. I was "Mr. Popularity".

But then one day, I started to think about who I had become. And I looked in the mirror and saw what I recognized as me, but I didn't feel like me. So, I went outside and I closed my eyes and I waited. That energy came and it came strong and by the time I got back inside I was back. Back to the way I had been. The way I thought I should have been. I still went to those bars. Why couldn't the real me be just as popular? People still bought me drinks, for a while. It's not that I was depressed or introverted, I just wasn't "on" all the time.

"Where's that Frank we all know and love?" people at those bars would say. I would just look at them like I didn't know what they were talking about. When the Fourth of July weekend hit, parties abounded. I was invited to them all. And everybody was having such a great time and they were all looking at me. For what? I don't know.

"C'mon Frank," I must have heard it a million times. I just drank more and more. I thought I was having a good time. I was laughing and dancing and falling down. That's fun, right?

Then I woke up with a pile of puke for a partner. I had no idea where I was and certainly didn't want to be conscious to endure the agony.

"Today is the first day of the rest of my life," I thought.
"I will not drink to excess ever again," I proclaimed.

I heard someone laugh. "Frank the comedian," he said.

7/11/87

Head down. Keep those legs pumping. I learned that when I tried out for the football team. Keep those legs pumping! That little piece of advice came in handy several times throughout my life. But when you start extrapolating the concept to different areas of your body, like your brain, you may be in trouble and I started applying that idea to other parts of my body, like my brain, and it got me into trouble. For one thing if you break through the line you only have to pump your legs in quick bursts. Shortly, you will stop. Either someone will tackle you or you'll be in the end zone. And even if you don't have that kind of finality, legs have a way of just giving out. When they get tired, they stop. The brain has a funny way of keeping going long after it has the where-with-all to do its job adequately.

OK, let's say life is one big football game. Those little bursts of "Leg" pumping would be months, maybe years long. The metaphor breaks down somewhere, though. There's no tackling or end zone in life. Well, actually there is, but they're so much harder to recognize. In football, when you're down, you've been hit, and there's some one on top of you and the referee blows his whistle and you know you're down. In life, you often get a feeling like the entire opposing team is on top of you. There's no referee blowing the whistle, though. If you're a well-trained footballer you know that you don't stop until the whistle has blown. And if the whistle doesn't blow you keep those legs pumping until you get to the end zone, a clearly marked area, and then the referee blows his whistle and you can stop pumping those legs. Making it to the end zone is such a wonderful experience. Even when the end zone is marked by the two elm trees in your backyard you can get the thrill. I did it once at a freshman scrimmage! While people were watching! And they cheered and my teammates were ecstatic. It was the first time we had scored against an opponent as a team. I later got cut.

Well, I felt like I had broken through the line after that Time article ran. I finished up at McGarrety's soon enough and I became a full time artist. Suddenly, things seemed easy. Sal was filling my calendar. I did that commission for General Jenkins, that army guy, and I did Phil Jankow and his wife, and I painted and I partied and I painted. It was a lot easier than I expected, actually. When I was doing those commissions I felt like I was at the store. Stacking those cans in neat little rows. The General was a wild man. We drank Jack Daniels at most of his sessions. The Jankows were very serious. Almost nervous. I drank gin at most of their sessions. Still, it was interesting for me and I was proud of the work and they both loved their portraits. They gave me bonuses!?!

I was cruising down the sideline and I was keeping those "legs" pumping. In between my commission sessions I was working on a piece that had me really perplexed. It was the first time I didn't have any idea about what it was about. Des used to sit around naked trying to get me to paint her. I didn't feel it. Sometimes I would get really frustrated because I didn't know what it was about. Des always broke out the cocaine. Or the tequila. When I was done with the Jankows I became obsessed with completing it. Where was the end zone? I thought I was there once or twice, but then I would hear the roar.

"Keep going. Go! Go! Go!"

And off I went.

The year after that article ran was the fastest in my life and my "legs" were getting tired.

"I'm gonna spend some time out at Irene's," I said matter-of-factly to Des, one day. She had been hanging around this whole time. I didn't feel like we had anything going. I guess she did, though.

"You need a weekend away," she tried to be supportive while pouting.

"Nah, I need a month away," I wasn't trying to be hurtful. I just didn't realize. I was stupid. I mean, the woman was there for a year. And the whole time I took her for granted. We were good friends. I knew that. That's why I was telling her about my plans.

"What about us?" That's when I first started to realize and before I could say anything, before I could even think of anything to say, "I have to stay here," the whine, "I have to work still," the sniffle, "Not that you ever gave a damn about what I needed!" Then the realization of what was happening weighed heavily. I hung my head. "I waited around here for fucking ever," she was crying, "and I never complained once," oh, this hurt, "and when you were puking that tequila and I had my arm around you," I started to remember. I still couldn't say anything, though. "Go ahead and leave," she was bawling, "Fuck you!" She got out the bullet and snorted both sides and I just stood there like the vegetable that I was.

"Well?" She looked at me with fire. "Say something you fucking idiot!" She screamed. I opened my mouth to say, "you could visit", but realized that wasn't right. I just looked at her. I don't know what kind of expression I had. I felt pain. A genuine pain. What ever my expression was it added fuel to her fire. She ran at me with both fists clenched and started flailing. I took my blows. I didn't blame her. She landed one square on my nose and it knocked me down. Blood splattered far and we both laid on the floor. She was bawling. I was reeling. Blood was flowing. Her ring had cut the bridge of my nose and the blow had broken some vessels. There was some pain, but in comparison to the angst, it was barely noticeable.

All I could think was "I WANT OUT!"

"I WANT OUT!"

"I WANT OUT!"

"I WANT OUT!"

I made it to Irene's all right. And I was glad to be there. I wasn't particularly happy, but I had this overriding sense that it was a good thing. Irene could sense my woe. And she would look at me with the most compassionate eyes. I tried to smile. I sipped my gin and stared out on to the huge yard. Those wonderful birch trees rustled. And the odor. I gulped my gin.

After about a week, "It's time for us to do another show, don't you think?"

Irene is so sweet.

"Yeah, I suppose it is," I was still glum.

"We could make it an annual event!"

"If you wanted. It is your gallery."

"What do you think of the idea?"

"Annual?"

"It bothers you."

"It does."

"Well, let's do this one and see how it goes."

"OK"

I got up and headed for the woods before she could try to cheer me again. Once outside I started to think about the last show. John Rogers. I sure would like to see him again. I started to feel good about the show. And Red. I should invite her, too. Such a sweet heart. I set my martini glass on an angled piece of rock. Gray rock. And sunlight shown through it and cast this really unusual shadow on the leaves below. Brown leaves. Every which way. And that shadow had that prism effect, sort of. I went back to the house and got my easel and set up all my stuff there in the woods. There was a creek near by and when I finally got set up and had the brush in hand, I paused for a moment. I heard that gurgling of the brook. What a wonderful sound. And as I stopped to listen, my nose was filled with the most wonderful scent. And that glass on that rock. I smiled and I painted. The more I painted the more I smiled. But soon, it was dark and then I was sad.

I spent every day from then on at that spot. Irene would bring me food and watch for a while and then slip away quietly. The closer I got to completing it, the more difficult it became to be happy about it. "What is this?" It was a glass on a rock. How boring. But I continued, confident that something would appear and make this image fresh again. It did, too. Late one day. I don't even know what day. I saw him there in the middle of the glass. Floating in the gin. Not casting a shadow. Not even really there. But a human form in the gin. Was it me?

That night, as I sat in the study staring out the window, listening to Debussy, Irene approached tentatively. She smiled when I looked at her. I smiled back. What a sweet face.

"I've set up a date at Solomon's for you."

"Sal's cleared it?"

"Yes. September sixteenth."

"How far away is that?"

"A month." She was puzzled.

"Good." I tried to smile.

"Will you be done?" She gestured towards the woods.

"I'll be done tomorrow," that made me sad. It made her happy.

"Can we use it in the show?"

"Certainly."

"Oh, that is wonderful!"

Solomon's the second time was not exactly like the first. I was almost bored with the whole thing by the time it actually happened. I was still staying at Irene's so I heard about all the details. I didn't really care, but felt obligated to listen. After I finished "Sapphire Dream" I took a train ride back into the city. I found my flat exactly as I had left it. My blood had stained the floor in the shape of a daisy. A black daisy! That damn abstract thing still on the wall. It was huge. Too big to put on the easel. What was that thing? I saw Des, naked on that canvas. I had to get out. I called Jack and he was there quickly to escort me around town. I was passing out invitations to the show. It was Irene's idea. Mary Everett's was the first stop. The last time I spoke with her she seemed so distant, but I remember her asking to be invited.

When she answered the door, she was surprised. So was I. She looked so different. When she stood in the doorway and didn't invite me in, I suspected that her boyfriend was there. When the child started crying her artificial smile disappeared. I started to realize. She invited me in and marched to the kitchen. There was Terra her six-month-old daughter. Infants are the most amazing things. Terra was happy to see me. So delighted. Her father, that PD Mary had been seeing, was now married. He paid child support. Mary looked worn, but she had a great attitude. Her love for Terra was obvious. I stayed there for hours. When Terra fell asleep Mary was ready to also. I called Jack. I did have plans to see some other people. When Mary's door closed behind me, I hopped into Jack's cab and had him take me to Penn Station. I caught the first train to the Hamptons.

So, there I was sitting on the curb outside Solomon's wearing a tux for the second time, thinking about little fingernails. Amazingly tiny fingernails. Attached to tiny fingers. Attached to tiny hands. I was thinking how those tiny appendages would steadily grow and how Mary would be there watching that process. I imagined Mary crying while telling her fourteen-year-old daughter how fast fourteen years can fly by. Then I started to think about the last fourteen years of my life and what an eternity that seemed to be. Still, I had imagined Mary telling her daughter how quickly fourteen years can go by. I wondered if the next fourteen years of my life would be as agonizingly long as the previous fourteen. That was a dreadful thought. I decided to go back into the gallery not because I thought I would enjoy it, but because I hoped it would help me to stop thinking these horrible thoughts. Why did I stay sober for this thing?

"YO! Beave," came a voice down the street.

"John?" De ja vu. His silhouette came sauntering into the street light. "John! You made it!" I felt like I was ten again. I gave him a hug. I was so happy to see him.

"Good to see ya, squirt."

"God it's good to see you, too."

"Still pumping right along I see," he looked into the gallery.

"Yeah," I wasn't proud.

"Who would've ever thought? Little Frankie Teeman—a famous artist."

"Famous?"

"Time magazine."

"Oh, you saw that."

"Pretty impressive."

I wasn't impressed with myself. "Do you ever hear from anyone back in Dilon?"

"No. Do you?" he asked matter-of-factly.

"No," I was sad.

"Are you missing it?"

"What?"

"Dilon"

"Yeah, I guess so," I never thought I'd say that.

"Don't. It's not like you remember it."

"Have you been back?"

"Yeah, for my father's funeral."

"Oh."

"It wasn't like I remembered it."

"How was it?"

"Dismal."

"Dismal?"

"Dingy and dismal."

"Well I certainly don't remember it that way."

"How do you remember it?"

"Quiet. And the smell of birch. And the leaves in the fall. All those colors. Rich, full colors. Certainly not dismal."

"Well I was there for my dad's funeral…"

"That probably had something to do with it," I was trying to be optimistic.

"No," he got those far away eyes, "You can never be young again, squirt." I just looked at him "That's what you remember, youth."

"Do I?" I wasn't buying it.

"That richness. Those ephemeral 'smell', 'quiet' things…that's youth. Fascination with life and nature."

"You sound a little jaded…"

"And you're not?" I shut my mouth. "Aww Frank, here I am still being your big brother after all these years."

"I don't mind." We paused. It was strange how quickly we could fall into those roles after a twenty-year hiatus. "You got any kids?" I asked after thinking how little I knew of him.

"No. Not really," he seemed sad.

"Well, either you do or you don't," I tried to laugh away the tension.

He remained distant, "No I don't," but came back quickly, "How 'bout you?"

"Nah. Are you kidding? A bohemian like me?"

"What? Are you celibate?"

"Nooo. I just could never…I don't know…it just seems so remote."

"You sound sad."

"I don't know. My career is really…" I always hated that word, "career", and there I had just spoke it. I stopped short.

"Caught in the middle?"

"Huh?" I wasn't following.

"You have an opportunity to do something really special, Frank."

I still wasn't following. "Art?"

He smiled that facetious smile, "Or?" He was teasing me just like when I was ten.

"Or what?" I was starting to get pissed, just like when I was ten.

"There you go!" he concluded.

"What are you talking about?"

"Be the artist, Frank," still smiling that grin.

"I am an artist, John!" he was really pissing me off.

"If you don't live it, it won't come out your horn."

"What?"

"Charlie Parker…"

"I live it John," I was insulted.

"Resist temptation, Frank. You are loved." He hugged me.

I just tingled all over. What was that supposed to mean? Then I remembered Father Frank! Whoa…

7/7/84

She dropped on me so unexpectedly. She just showed up one day with Brian. And I looked at her and those crystalline eyes. And she presented her hand. And I placed mine in hers. It was warm. I smiled.

"I'm Ellen," with a wide smile.

"Hi Ellen. Frank," I smiled even wider.

"Nice to meet you."

"Likewise," and I thought to myself "what an interesting girl this was". She had energy. A different kind of energy than I had ever felt before. And then the voice, "Don't get sucked in again." I had to listen. I was just getting used to being alone. I couldn't afford to be trampled.

And then she showed up the next day. And she was by herself. That felt good.

"Just thought I'd drop by."

"I'm glad," I was painting.

"Don't let me disturb you."

"Not at all," I stood there with brush in hand as we talked. I didn't paint anything. A couple of times I tried, but I was too busy listening to her Coney Island story. We laughed a lot that day. I remember that. And the more she talked the more I listened. And the more I looked the more I liked. She wasn't my type, though. The black hair? Something. It was all very surprising—my attraction to her. And then she stood up and announced her departure and I felt that panic feeling like I might never see her again.

"Thanks for stopping by!"

"My pleasure," and she kissed me. She kissed me.

And then the voice, "Don't get sucked in." I couldn't bear to get trampled. I broke.

"Stop by again."

"I will." That moment. Part of me tried to ignore it, but another part knew that that moment had happened. That moment between two people where that visceral communication happens. It happened. It was undeniable.

And then she came back a third time, two days later. "Third strike and you're out" that little voice had changed its stripes over the last forty hours. And by the time we had gotten back from dinner it was simply saying, "Yes." And when I woke up that morning and saw her sleeping and that voice still said "Yes!" I had to stop and think. The sunlight was peeking through the living room window and it seemed so peacefully quiet. I smiled. I was looking at this same hole that had revolted me for so long and now, after five years, it struck me as pleasant. I should have been scared.

I was delighted.

And then the next day at work I was thinking about her and how I wanted to be with her and how I had planned on doing some work that night, but I could do that later. I needed to be with her! I got a chill. And I wasn't even working in the frozen foods. And I started to think about how she would be waiting for me at my home. I so like flopping after work. Doing a bong hit and flopping. Was I going to be able to do that tonight? Doubtful. I had been sucked in. The panic.

So, I went to McSorley's after work and I was trying to calm down. I had set myself up for a heartache. Brian sauntered in right then. I wasn't sure what to say.

"You look glum," he was matter-of-fact.

"Yeah," I sighed.

"Are you in love?" he teased.

"God! Did you have to say that," I was bitter.

"Who is she," he was still teasing. I just stopped. I figured Ellen had told him that we were together. After all she had just come to town and she hardly knew any one else. I looked him square and said with a certain reluctance, "Ellen Turner."

He was surprised, but not bitter, "Good luck."

"What?"

He paused. "Ellen is a free…Just don't get too attached."

"What's that supposed to mean?"

"I did my Ellen thing back in Seattle. She's a great girl. She just scares me a little."

"Yeah. I know."

So, I went home with dread. And she was in the shower when I walked in so I flopped on the couch and scraped up a bong hit and closed my eyes. "You've got to tell her," the voice said. And I felt her sit down beside me and I exhaled and I was glad to be stoned. She touched my head ever so lightly. She kind of cupped the back of my head and patted ever so gently. God that felt good! And I opened my eyes and I saw her. She looked so innocent. She couldn't possibly hurt me.

"Long day?" and her voice was so sweet.

"Yeah. And it's your fault." What was I saying??

"My fault?" she was playing.

"Yeah," I wanted to tell her. She made me smile, "I was thinking about you all day." I teased.

"Good thoughts, I hope."

"Sometimes."

"What were the bad," she looked down.

"Ellen, I don't even know you. I feel like I know you. But I don't."

"I don't know you either."

"I know. That's not a good thing."

"I know you're special. That's good."

"Ellen, I know that you're special, too. And that is a good thing. I didn't say it was all bad."

I tried to be bright.

"You want me to leave?"

"Oh come on," I actually giggled she was being so cute. And then she snuggled up beside me and I could feel her warm breath on my neck. I stroked her hair. Black hair. I never liked black hair, before.

Hers was beautiful.

So, periodically I would voice my reservations, but she remained. And I just kept telling myself that I was safe. That I had expressed my doubts and she understood and wouldn't stay unless she was really enamored. After all, we were so happy. Only something real could spawn this kind of joy.

And with each passing day I grew more attached and when I saw Brian he would say "Good for you," but the enthusiasm was a put on. I didn't care. I was in love and she loved me and this time it would be different. I didn't care if she had dumped a million guys before me. I was different. And we had something special and the world was right.

So, for months I would wake up early just to watch her sleep and she would wake up and catch me watching her and she would put her head on my chest and I hoped it would never end. And that canvas I had started right before she had showed up? It stayed in its infancy. I would think about doing some work on it but we would go out, some-where, and I would have a great time and in the morning her face would eliminate all outside input. It was just her and me alone in the world. And I found myself telling people about it. And I would think, "Is this me talking?" and it was me talking and everybody was so happy for me and I was so happy for myself. Life took on a different dimen-sion for me, then. It seemed like those moments when I got home from work were not part of that new dimension, though. That was when the voice would say, "Don't get sucked in," and I would answer, almost aloud, "It's a little late for that." But, if she wasn't home already, she always made it a point to show up right around that time. And she always seemed so happy to see me. And that felt good. I quickly blocked out the voice.

Then one day she got a job.
It was a happy day.
We partied hard that night.

But then, I would come home from work and she wouldn't be there. And I would start painting. I had forgotten how much I had loved that. And eventually she would come home from work and I would be painting and I would be distracted and she was sour and needed some attention but I wouldn't notice and she would get angry and leave. And the voice would start to talk and I would shut it down.

Soon, she got a place of her own. That was a happy day, too. I helped her decorate it. But, that gave me even more time to work. And I got involved with the painting on an emotional level and she couldn't relate to that and we argued. It wasn't the first time. But, shortly after that I showed up at her place and she wasn't as happy to see me. I could tell something was up, but couldn't get her to explain it. I showed up with flowers the next day. I feared the ennui. It was too late. She had met some one else. She had gotten involved emotionally with some one else! She didn't feel the same about me.
"[She] still loved me, but…"
But what!?! That's when the voice took over.
"I didn't get sucked in," it kept saying.

It wasn't until that Christmas that I admitted that I had been sucked in. The Christmas of '84 at the McGarrety's house. I will never forget that feeling of loneliness. Surrounded by friends and still that intense feeling of loneliness.

7/11/88

Sal Montrallo did his work. Or maybe it was luck that all those art beat reporters were at that show. Maybe it was just coincidence that there was no other event to speak of that night. September 16? I wondered why Irene had scheduled a Tuesday. She said it was Sal's idea. So, Sal had done his work and it had paid off. At first I was upset that some of the articles were negative. "As long as they're not all negative!" Sal had a fierce determination. That was exciting. And I needed a boost. I mean he was more excited about my "career" than I was. So when AM New York showed up at my place at five AM I told myself "Sal knows what he's doing." Besides, I was engrossed in completing that abstraction that I had left. I still saw Des naked when I looked at that thing. I heard John Rogers spouting Charlie Parker, too. When I woke up that morning I thought I could see Des naked amongst all that vagueness. I couldn't get over it. At that hour it looked like I had actually painted her in there!?! I was almost completely oblivious to the cameras and the crew from the start. Still, I turned to that guy in the tie and said, "Do you see that girl," pointing at the painting. He just laughed a little chuckle, looked around for some assistance, got none, and said, "Not really."

"She's naked. She's haunting me," I didn't realize that we were live. I stepped closer to the canvas.

"Is this your current project?" the guy in the tie said to his microphone.

"Well, I've been trying to avoid it for a long time," still looking closely at those lines.

"You don't enjoy your work?"

I stopped. I hadn't thought of enjoying the painting.

"Sometimes it really sucks," that caused a stir amongst the crew.

I woke up after that, to the roar of the masses. Sal gave me some figures on the number of calls my comments had elicited. It fell on deaf ears. I was still looking for Des in that painting. I couldn't see her anymore.

"That many?" some abstract figure.

"That many!" Sal was ecstatic.

"They're upset?" I know she's in there.

"They loved you!"

"For saying 'it sucks'?" Was that curved line her breast?

"Well, there were some people who complained about that. But most of them loved you!"

"Why?" That doesn't look like her at all.

"Who knows? Who cares? Carson's people called."

"The Tonight Show?" I faced him for the first time.

"Every affiliate picked up that AM segment!" I wasn't sure what that meant. Sal sure seemed happy about it. "Listen kid you've got something that really comes across." Was he speaking Russian? "Frank," he was suddenly serious, "as your manager I've got to know if you're up for this."

"I'm up for this," I guess I wasn't convincing.

"Are you really in for this?"

"I'm really in for this."

"You're fastened in? You're ready to do some work?"

"Painting?"

"Painting and other things,"

"Interviews?"

"Precisely."

"I'm ready," apparently I still hadn't convinced him.

"OK," he finally resigned, "but I'm gonna remind you of this conversation and I'm gonna hold you to it."

I just smiled and nodded.

Sal had me on the plane within a month. That abstract was in cargo. I kept thinking that Des was in that bay. I didn't tell anyone, but that was my first flight. Not that anyone needed to know. But I made it a point not to tell anyone, still. Pride. Once we got up to cruising height, the magnificence of this experience began to impress me. The clouds are so dynamic. And the speed barely noticeable. And the perspective. What a perfect opportunity! So much perspective.

I got bumped from my first scheduled appearance on The Tonight Show. I was relieved. They put me up so, I was on vacation. Me!? I had never been on vacation. I was at a loss for a while there. I tried TV in the hotel, but I could hear something else calling. I just walked out on to the street and I could feel it. The energy lives in LA, too! And as I strolled down that street, where ever it was, the fact that I was three thousand miles away from NY served as constant amazement. I felt like I had just turned one of those obscure corners in Manhattan. Like the one where I found Father Frank. Eventually I saw several things that reminded me of the truth. Palm trees are pretty rare in NY. And then I saw the most incredibly black man that I've ever seen. Black men are not rare in NY, but this man was blacker than any I had ever seen. He was sitting on the sidewalk leaning against a store door, reading. I stopped and looked. He stopped and looked at me, too. I smiled. And when he smiled at me he turned his cheek and I saw the abrasion. Such rich colors. The contrast of his white eyes to his dark skin. And the red blood…glistening.

"God bless you," he was earnest.

I just nodded and kept walking.

"Christ loves you," he called after me.

I am loved.

I don't remember The Tonight Show. I was on. It went by so fast, though. I vaguely remember the unveiling of Des. A painting on TV? I was just as confused by that abstract as everyone else. And when I got up to take a closer look at it? That caused quite a stir. And then when I said, "I like it," everyone laughed. The next thing I really remember was sitting on that plane again. They flew me out right after the show. By the time we had reached cruising height and that stillness comes over the plane and everybody started to settle in, I started to think about what had just happened. It seemed so surreal. All that adulation?! It must have been a dream. I ordered another scotch.

"Frank!" Sal met me at the airport. "You're beautiful!"

"I love you, too." I was sauced. And when he wrapped his arm around me it knocked me slightly off balance, just slightly, and I fell down and banged my head on the window. And it bled. And there was such a commotion. The guards pulled Sal away thinking he had attacked me and before I knew it some medical type person was there all dressed in white and she took my head in her hands and cleaned the cut and it stopped bleeding quickly and I finally looked up. When our eyes met she smiled. I smiled back, I think. At least I tried.

"I know you," she said with awe.

"Frank Teeman," I extended my hand.

"You were just on The Tonight Show not an hour ago."

"That's me,"

"I thought you were great."

"Was I?"

"Are you all right?"

"I'm fine," I got up to see a ring of thirty or so people.

And that blood still on the window.

"Famous artist's blood," I pointed and laughed.

"You are beautiful," Sal put his arm around me and we left.

While I was away having such a wonderful time, my friends were not faring so well. McGarrety's went into hopeless Chapter 11. A couple weeks later I got a call from Mo. She told me about the bankruptcy and the imminent foreclosure. She wasn't tearful, but she was sad.

"You know Bill, always trying to keep prices down."

"Yeah, you don't deserve this. How can I help?"

"Oh, I don't know. It all seems hopeless now. I just thought you'd want to know."

"Well, something can be done. Can't it?" I had no idea what, exactly, was happening.

"We're looking for a buyer now."

"Aw, Mo."

"Our lawyer says it's all we can do."

"Any prospects?"

"Well, we've had an offer for your painting," she laughed a forced, sad laugh.

I got a chill.

"Ahhh?" I was confused.

"Yeah. A generous one, too." That forced laugh again. I didn't know what to say. I could tell that part of her wanted to sell it. That thought hurt me. Genuine pain.

"Enough to make a difference?" I couldn't believe it.

"Oh, don't worry. Bill won't let us sell it. It's a gift!"

"Don't be silly, Mo. If it'll save the store,"

"We'll work it out some how." She wasn't very convincing.

"All right. Keep in touch, huh?"

"We will. We will."

"Bye."

The higher you ride, the harder you fall. The longer you ride, the faster you fall.

I decided that night that I was going to buy that store. I didn't really know if it was possible, but I decided I was going to do it. How could I not? I just kept thinking about that day in Dilon when I was sitting in Sam Selman's office that contract from Kroger awaiting my signature Sam staring out the second story window.

"It's a good offer, that's for sure," he was melancholy, "Of course they won't be retaining me," he laughed his coughy laugh. I was just staring at that line with the ex by it. I wanted to sign it, but couldn't.

"Mr. Selman?" I felt awkward calling him that, but it's what I had always called him, "Don't hate me for this."

"Oh, don't be silly, Frank. It's the right thing to do. I'm advising you to do it. I just…" he turned and looked out the window again, "Everett was more than a client to me. You know that."

"I know," I sighed and signed. I slapped the pen down on his desk. He didn't move. "It's done," I felt like I had finally laid my father to rest. Sam still didn't move. I headed for the door.

"Frank," he called just as I got to the door, "What are you going to do?" he tried to smile.

"I don't know, Sam. I don't know."

So, here I was staring out my second story window, fighting the notion that this was some kind of opportunity for divine retribution. Whether it was or not became less and less important as I became more and more convinced that I would do it. And that tremendous sadness that I was feeling slowly gave way to joy when I came up with the idea of buying it anonymously through Father Frank. It just seemed right.

Terra squeezed my finger and smiled at me. Those huge blue eyes. And I melted and Mary laughed. I felt cold. I had thought about getting in touch with Mary several times over those intervening months. This was why. To hear that gurgly laugh and see that tremendous openness to the newness of everything.

"You must be very happy," Mary was talking to me.

I wasn't really following. "She is adorable." Mary was confused. And when she looked at me, that way, I finally heard her words, "Oh, yeah. Things are going well."

"What's next?" She had an eager anticipation that was invigorating.

"A grocery store," I hadn't told anyone else yet.

"What?"

"I'm buying a grocery store," I was proud.

"What about painting?" She was shocked.

"Huh?"

"What are you going to do with a grocery store?"

Somehow I had expected her to be excited about this. She wasn't. That threw me. Once I was distracted, Terra wanted mom back. "Oh, I don't know. Just a crazy idea. Haven't really given it much thought." Trying to cover up like that was the surest sign. Suddenly, I wasn't convinced that I should do it. And when I saw child nestled comfortably in mama's cradle, suckling ever so sweetly. And mom looking down at baby, smiling ever so radiantly—the bottom fell out. Maybe because "Mom" happened to be the woman I had proposed to, however offhandedly, but mostly because this was a snapshot of emotion at it's finest. And once the snapshot is taken it never leaves the screen. Not until it's on canvas.

So, the canvas went up. And that image was locked firmly in my gaze. And now the interpolation of emotion. I got those images all the time and most of them ended up on canvas. Except not precisely. Something happened in the process. My hand didn't do exactly what my eyes saw. Some details came out remarkably similar. Gladys' nose. Irene's ear. Trees, sometimes. It's not that I couldn't do exactly what I saw. Somewhere between the eye and the hand something was added. Emotion.

The process of that interpolation had begun. So, I sat there, in that apartment and my mind would wander wildly. And other times it would focus intensely. But only on that image. And Jack would stop by. With gin. Sometimes I would be glad to see him, other times I would barely recognize him. And I'd get cravings for strange food. And I'd have a real craving for alcohol. And I would puke in the morning. And I would hate myself. But then I would see the sketch from the night before and I would feel light. When the painting actually began all those things doubled in intensity. I didn't have to work. I could devote my whole to that project. That only meant that each turn around the roller coaster, I would go farther in an ever-widening gyre. I would look at that painting in it's half completed state and agonize on my knees. "How does this end?"

Sometimes there would be no answer and I would hate myself for thinking that I could even attempt such a thing. But when the paint flowed again—euphoria. The pot and the alcohol only kept me going, like a fly wheel, while I didn't have the emotional energy to continue. Unfortunately, the dosage had to increase to maintain the speed. The last two weeks of that painting were one long spiritual hallucination.

When I broke the brushes on that one I had the most tremendous sense of relief ever. But that only lasted for a short time.

Soon, that painting beckoned me. "What?" I would scream at it. And that child's face would just look at me, unwaveringly. I had to get it out of my place. It intimidated me. I thought about giving it to Mary, but she was the subject and that was pretty obvious even though I had tried, desperately, to conceal that. So, her having it didn't work for me. I thought about Irene. I couldn't bring myself to call her, though. I thought about Jack. I thought about throwing it out. There was no way I could do that. Then I thought about Sal. I could have him dump it in some exceedingly businesslike way. That would be all right.

Sal came over right after I called him. He was absolutely energized. "Frank, this is…" he stood there staring at it, arms outstretched. "You like it?" I was in the kitchen frying some bologna. "Like it? It's…It's unbelievable." The toast popped up. "Huh?"

"It's unbelievable!" He shouted still standing in front of that thing.
"You think you can do something with it?" I mayonnaised the toast.
"Definitely," he came into the kitchen. "Definitely!"

"OK. But nothing under a million." I stuffed my mouth and laughed through my nose.

I was wasted.

The movers came and got it the next morning. Sal didn't understand why I was so anxious to part with it, but he made the arrangements. Sal Montrallo does his job.

I was sad. Very sad. The kind of sadness that presents itself in visceral form. A pervasive sadness. Kind of a dull aching. Mostly in the abdomen. I was aware of it for two days straight. I called Jack and he ferried me to Tommy's at my request. And there was Red jiggling her breasts and smiling so radiantly and men were whooping and laughter everywhere. I smiled. I actually smiled when she recognized me. She didn't wave or wink or anything. She just looked in my direction and our eyes met and she was happy to see me. I just know that she was happy to see me. I smiled. She disappeared backstage and I dreaded not seeing her but she appeared in a red robe and brought me to a table in the back. We drank and laughed. Mostly she talked about all the crazy things that had happened to her since last we spoke. She was so alive then. When we hugged to say good bye a tear drop came to my eye. And that dull pain in my gut waned. Suddenly I was whole again.

Jack took me to Central Park that night. He followed me around convinced that some harm would come to me. I had this tremendous desire to touch trees. So, I went strolling, fondling trunks of long lost friends. Trees are so majestic and nothing makes me reflect like bark. And in the middle of that park that night I paused briefly at a peculiar sight. A black man sat in an open field, reading a book by moonlight. When he looked at me I saw that abrasion. The red glistened like a jewel. And the contrast to his dark skin!?! Oh, I had that feeling again. I gripped the tree harder and I closed my eyes and I let it begin.

The black man spoke.
I strained to hear him.
What was he saying?
It sounded like truth.
"Hey, you all right?" Jack called.
I savored a moment.
"Yeah, I'm all right," I shouted.
"I am loved," I whispered.

7/7/85

Roosevelt Park is littered with them. I spent quite a bit of time there so, I know. I usually went there out of a desire to commune. Sometimes I would feel like the only person in the world, cooped up in that studio. So, I would go to the park and sit on the bench and all those other solitary folks would come out, too. I liked it for a while. For a long while, actually. Until the street crazies invaded. I suppose they were there all along, but I didn't notice them, really. They didn't bother me. I wasn't bothered by them.

I was sitting on that bench one hot day, July of '85. One excruciatingly hot, bright, day. My studio was an oven so I had come to the park to escape. Not to commune. Mistake. I noticed him after a short scan of the inhabitants. He was old. He had that decrepit look; all hunched over and wrinkled. His white hair went every which way. But what I really noticed were his clothes. The sweater with the zigzag stripe and the wool pants and the gloves with the fingers cut off. His hands were so filthy it took me a while to see that the fingers of his gloves were cut off. It must have been ninety degrees and I was sweltering, but there he was—long sleeve sweater, sitting there quietly. He almost looked content if it weren't for that vacant stare. I wondered how he could stand the heat. He didn't even seem to be sweating. And then it occurred to me that he might not have any other clothes. Those clothes were probably stuck to his body. Years of sweat and unwashed skin had probably fused those clothes to his body, I thought. His decrepit nerve endings couldn't even feel the heat through that thick hide. And for a second I envied him. I needed relief from that infernal heat! And he had it. He was just sitting there staring blankly, occasionally forming a new and more interesting hair design by scratching his head. "What I wouldn't give for that kind of bliss," I thought. When he got up I couldn't resist following him. He didn't go far so I didn't even have to get up. He slowly hobbled over to a bush, unzipped his pants and brought out his brown stump of a penis. It shocked me. He didn't even seem to care. He was by a bush, but in plain sight. Standing there with his one-eye staring right at me. And then the piss started to flow and I became suddenly uncomfortable. But I couldn't stop watching. First there was a little spurt of urine, but it quickly dropped to a slow dribble. That guy stood there, hands at his side, pissing on himself! All the while staring blankly, straight ahead. At me? But I couldn't stop watching. And then I realized that I was no longer overwhelmingly hot. I swear there was a chill in the air. I almost shivered. He finished up and tucked himself in and returned to his position. Only now he was smiling. I finally looked away, but everywhere I looked…street crazies. There was an old oriental woman who had that exact same skin dirt tone. She had her arms crossed over her and her fists pounded her shoulders while she rocked back and forth, spouting nonsense. Periodically her fists would stop. Her voice would rise and she would bend way down so that her head went between her legs. Then the pounding and rocking would resume. I watched a young black man dressed only in gym shorts and torn sneakers with no laces chase a one-inch piece of hot dog across the sidewalk. He would get it in his grip and then it would squirt out or he would kick it just before he grabbed it, like a comic. I almost laughed. He finally caught it when he kicked it into the dirt. He plopped himself down in that dirt and made three deliberate bites out of that small piece, savoring each for quite a while. I thought I was hungry, but to see his satisfaction with a dirt covered piece of nothing? I wasn't hungry. I wasn't thirsty. I wasn't hot. I wasn't cold. I had disappeared. None of those things that seemed so vital just fifteen minutes ago mattered at all. Least of all my desire to paint. Why was I so obsessed with such a trivial occupation? Why had I put myself on the verge of homelessness? Just to arrange some colors into an abstract pattern? To, somehow, communicate with the masses? What would that old piss stained man think of "Glad"?

I got up to leave. A force, deep inside me, yanked my body up off that bench. It wasn't a conscious thing. My consciousness was drowning in the futility of my life. My consciousness wanted to stay there, in the park. My consciousness wanted me to piss on myself. Instead I got up and walked away. And as I made it to the edge of the park, my consciousness beckoned me to look back. It was sure that those people were laughing at me. They had won. It was their sole pleasure in life to remind people like me of their reality. I didn't look back. I just kept walking. I stared at the ground. I couldn't look up. I was afraid that if I did no one would make eye contact with me. I had disappeared. I was nothing. I didn't want any confirmation of that. That force that yanked me up? It was something. It propelled my invisible non-body forward desperately looking for a place to hide. For a place to rejuvenate.

I found that place in a coffee shop. As I walked by I heard that shrieking atonal violin music and smelled that dark, burnt smell of espresso beans. Here I could find respite. It was so hot I couldn't fathom the idea of hot coffee so I ordered an iced cappuccino. And as I sat sipping that cold coffee, I felt that something inside me rising to the surface and inhabiting the shell that had ambled into the shop. Even iced coffee has a kick.

And as I lifted my head to reaffirm my humanity by looking at other people, and smiling and exchanging that recognition that we were both alive, I finally noticed all the wonderful images adorning the walls. There was a familiarity about those images. They reminded me of my own work! I got up to look closer. The first piece I looked at was a dramatic abstract. Lots of obtuse angles and sharp contrasts. And what was that? It looked like something human. Yes, it was definitely some androgynous human figure squirreled away behind all those flagrant designs. Boy, I loved that! And as I looked closer I saw yet another form that struck me as human. Yes, there were definitely two figures, hardly noticeable at first glance. And they were touching. They were almost touching. Like God and Adam on the ceiling of the Sistine. I smiled. This was the work of a true artist, I thought. I would buy this. I moved on to the painting to it's immediate right with eager anticipation. It was an equally gratifying experience. Again those androgynous abstract forms. This one had some texture. Some fabulous texture. There appeared to be some material in that paint. Some fine material that provided not only texture, but also very subtle contour. Those human forms seemed corporeal. There was a flesh-like turgor. How did he do that? I wanted to touch it. I thought maybe he had used flesh. It looked like flesh, but he couldn't have. Who was this guy? I couldn't look any further until I found out who this artist was. I scanned the walls for the obligatory bio sheet. It was not there. There was definitely an insignia on those paintings. They hadn't been created in a vacuum. Some one had done them. I searched the counters for some literature. Then I saw that woman smiling at me from behind the counter.

"They're not for sale," she said proudly.

"Are you the artist?" I said with desperation.

"Noooo…" she chuckled.

"They're wonderful," I took another look around.

"Thanks." She was shy.

"You are the artist! Aren't you?" I tried to catch her eye.

"No," she looked down, "They're my sister's."

"Your sister?" I was surprised. "Where does she show?"

"Oh, she doesn't show."

"Huh?"

"She doesn't consider herself an artist."

"How do you explain these?"

"I got her to do these for the shop."

"Hmmmm," I didn't know if I understood.

"She's good. Isn't she?"

"I think so," I was flabbergasted. I couldn't take my eyes off of them. "Well, if she's not an artist what is she?"

"A wife. And a mother," she smiled.

"Oh," my heart swelled, "And she paints on commission?"

"Well, I suppose."

"Then I'd like to commission her!"

"Really?!"

"Really."

"Why don't you give me your number."

"Gladly." I scrawled down my name and number and left that shop with a sense of hope. I couldn't wait to hear from this woman. That gave me strength.

I waited for her call from the start. And as I waited I looked at my current work in progress. I couldn't continue. I just looked. And with each passing day, I hated it more and more. It was terrible. I was convinced. And then I started to wonder if I had done anything worthwhile. I went to my rack and started pulling pieces out. They were all terrible. And then I pulled out "Glad". Well, I lucked out on one. I got drunk that night. And when I got home that awful, half-finished monstrosity slapped me in the face. I went to pull it down and it ripped ever so slightly. I got a tingle from that tear. So, I tore it again. This time on purpose. What a rush! I tore that thing into pieces. Each tear, though, had an accompanying guilt pang so that by the time it was done and I was lying on the floor, canvas as my blanket, I was crying. Tears flowed and my throat was in a knot. I didn't make a sound.

The next morning I went back to that coffee shop. I had to. I didn't know what I was going to say or do, but I went. Fortunately, the girl behind the counter recognized me.

"Hello," she beamed.

"Hello," I tried to be happy.

"Did Claire call?"

Claire? That was the first I had heard the name. What a beautiful name, too.

"No," I looked away.

"Oh," she could tell I was hurt. "I didn't think that she would," I looked puzzled, "she just isn't interested," I still didn't understand, "She just doesn't think it's possible to be an artist and have a family."

"She's right." I turned to leave. "Is she right?" I thought aloud.

7/11/89

I woke up in a museum some where in St. Louis. A little boy was tugging on my pant leg while I snoozed in an incredibly uncomfortable chair in the lobby. Sal had me zagging all over the country doing "appearances" of one sort or another, and it was wiping me out.

"Are you an artist?" the little boy asked so innocently.

"Yes, I am," I smiled. I was in St. Louis doing a "Meet the Artist" thing. It was an opportunity for kids to meet people behind the work. Some hair brain idea to get kids to come to museums or something.

"I thought so," so much venom in his voice. He turned abruptly and left before I even collected myself. Ouch! That hurt. I cursed Sal. These appearances always turned out to be a drag in some way, whether it was the interviewer who asked stupid questions or just unbearable amounts of waiting around. I was dreading this particular date. My tour (that is the tour of my work) had just been installed in St. Louis and I was making an appearance in conjunction with that. It was always hard for me to be surrounded by "Glad" and "Shine On" and "Sapphire Dream" and "Irene" and have people ask me questions about "my motivation" or some other absurdity. I just didn't ever know what to say. I couldn't tell them about the energy or the agony. I couldn't tell them about inspiration. I didn't have any artists who "inspired" me. Except maybe Claire. Claire. It always left me feeling incomplete somehow. And now to have this little boy, maybe seven years old, snub me!?! That's what he did he snubbed me. And now I was supposed to stand in front of a group of those irreverent little snots, for what? Am I supposed to tell them that being an artist is great and that they should all grow up to expose their emotions to a largely uncaring populous. OK, so maybe traveling was getting to me. All I can remember is wishing this little session were over so I could get back to the hotel and have a couple of drinks before the night's fiasco.

"Frank?" Haddie Nelson called across the room. She was the matron who was assigned to me.

"Yes, Haddie. I'm ready." I stood and turned to find her with a pretty companion. I smiled. The young woman smiled.

"You have an admirer," Haddie was delighted. That young woman extended her hand. Our hands clenched and our eyes met. There was that moment. "Ellen this is Frank Teeman," that name always made me stop, but she was just beaming, "Frank this is Ellen…"

"Hi, Frank. How are you?" That voice?

"Ellen?" I looked harder. "Tamoritz?"

"Frank Teeman!!" She was ecstatic.

"Ellen Tamoritz," I felt cold.

We hugged.

I was particularly distant during that "Meet the Artist" session. The kids seemed enthusiastic, but Ellen was sitting in the back beaming so. Like the Cheshire cat. This big, white smile. I didn't get to talk much with her before Haddie dragged me into the museum's auditorium. I did know that Ellen's daughter was in that group, somewhere. That girl who was still in the womb last I saw her, stood up in that auditorium. I knew it was her, too. The resemblance was blatant.

"Do you remember my mom?" she asked.

I looked and saw Ellen's hands go up over her face. I laughed. "Yeah, I do. What's your name?"

"Terra," she was proud. I thought of Mary's Terra.

A melancholy filled me then. "Terra, your mom is a wonderful woman."

The girl who was sitting next to Terra stood up abruptly, "Did you love Mrs. Winger?" So, innocent.

"Kathy," a voice of authority scolded, "That's personal."

"No. That's all right," everyone looked with eager anticipation, "I didn't love Mrs. Winger then," sadness weighed heavy for an interminable second. I saw that Cheshire smile disappear. "I do now," I practically whispered. But that room was silent enough to let it be heard. I looked down. I was blushing.

Dinner that night at the Winger household was like a trip back through time. That colonial ranch style house in that clean suburban tract. Was this where they filmed Ozzy and Harriet? Nonetheless there was a tremendous amount of warmth and happiness in that dining room.

Chuck Winger was a painter, too. He sat at the head of the table paint speckles covered his hands. I had the feeling they were permanent. He was telling me about spraying the exterior of buildings. I couldn't really listen. I was engrossed in watching the girls. Across the table from me they sat side-by-side Terra helping her younger sister to eat. Annie could obviously handle the task herself, but she endured Terra's play at motherhood. Fucia, the Irish setter, sat patiently at my side while Ellen kept everything in order. All the clanking of dishes and flatware. And Chuck going on about paint (I guess he thought I'd be interested). It all made the happiest din.

I reveled in it.

And after the Chicken Picatta. And after a few good laughs provided by the children being silly. And right about the time the coffee came with the mint chocolate chip ice cream. There was the lull. Chuck was still laughing and playing with Terra so, it wasn't an auditory lull, per se. It was more of a personal lull. Maybe it was the beer and the travel. But I didn't feel tired. Just…settled. You know, content to be sitting in that spot. And the gravity feels good because if you never left this place that wouldn't be such a bad thing.

And you smile.

And you pet the dog.

And you have another bit of ice cream.

"More coffee?" Ellen beams.

"No. This is great," I beam.

"When was the last time you saw Dilon?"

"That day. You?"

"Oh, I get back every now and again."

"Has it changed much?"

"No."

"You have!"

"So have you."

"Have I?"

"I suppose not. Have I, really?"

"Yes," I remembered that pony-tailed five year old, "You're such the woman."

"Well, thanks, I think," she blushed.

"You're welcome," I smiled.

"Frank!" Chuck had stood from his throne, "Let's go out back."

"Chuck!" Ellen had that reprobative tone.

"Frank'll be interested in this," he admonished.

"Well don't be forever." They kind of bumped hips and kissed. Not just a peck, but a nice kiss. When they parted they exchanged words, but nothing I could understand.

Chuck led me out to the back patio; a small slab of concrete that over looked their fenced in yard. It was a beautiful night. The temperature was just right and the stars were the only light. The moon wasn't out that night. And I breathed deep the fresh, countryside air that was wafting ever so lightly over that fence. To my delight the scent of birch filled my nose and I opened my eyes to see that wonderful birch tree there in front of me.

"You are so lucky," I envied Chuck tremendously at that moment.

"Me?" He was rooting around in the bar-b-cue, "I was about to say the same thing to you."

"That's funny," I laughed.

"Here check this out," he handed me a coffee can, "Grade A sativa."

I didn't know what that meant. But when that skunk hit my nose shortly after lifting the lid and Chuck lit that corncob pipe I knew I was in for a ride. We smoked and we chatted. And the buzz came on, and I started to laugh. I couldn't stop thinking that if I had married Ellen Tamoritz back then, this would probably be my life. It's not often you get a glimpse of a branch of your life that you passed on.

"You are the lucky one," Chuck finally submitted after we cut through the small talk. He sounded so defeated.

"That's nice of you to say, but sometimes I don't know," I felt so defeated.

"Well I'd give anything to be in your shoes. Wanna swap lives," he chuckled.

"Yeah, that would be great," I was dreamy.

"You sound half serious," he was incredulous.

"I'm fully serious," we both looked at each other as if the other were crazy.

"Listen to us," he laughed, "never satisfied." He lit the pipe and passed it. I took a long draw and held it in. I was trying to work up some enthusiasm for my life so that I could respond with some positive affirmation.

"Yeah, never satisfied," was all I could come up with.

"I know why I'm not satisfied. What the hell is your problem?"

"When I was sitting there, in your dining room, I had this feeling. It was almost like gravity had increased or, I was, somehow, more in touch with it, but there was this weight. I haven't felt that kind of groundedness since...since I left Dilon."

"And that's a good feeling?"

"That's a great feeling!"

"I hate that feeling."

"Are we talking about the same thing?"

"Every morning when I get up, I know what my day's gonna be. I could probably do it in my sleep."

"I'm not talking about being in a rut. I've got plenty of that. I'm talking about a rootedness that comes from family, home. You know, that kind of thing that answers that early morning question 'why am I gonna do this again?' Ya know?"

"I don't ask that question anymore."

"You used to?"

"Yeah, I did. I stopped about five years ago. Maybe longer."

"What happened?"

"I don't know. I guess it happened when I set up my studio again."

"Painting?"

"Yeah. After Annie was on her feet and out of diapers I decided to start painting again. So, I set up a little space in the basement, bought myself all the stuff and threw up that first canvas and went to work. But then the job just went nuts, lost a couple of people, had contractors breathing down my neck. I was working ten or twelve hour days. Terra got the mumps. I didn't get to the painting for a while and then a while had become a couple of weeks and then a month and finally one Sunday night I was determined to do some work on it so, I locked myself down there and proceeded to fall asleep in front of that thing. I started telling myself that once the kids were grown, then I would have the time. That's when I started counting the days. Twenty-five years left on the mortgage, four years left on the car loan, fifteen years 'til the kids were grown. It was like a prison sentence," he hit the pipe, *"Still wanna swap?"* I didn't know what to say. *"Oh, I exaggerate. I love Ellen and the kids. And you're right the family thing is wonderful. I just never thought I'd end up just turning a buck."*

"Well, you know, that's what I'm doing." He just looked confused. *"Yup, I'm on a promotional tour. My agent booked it. It's all an effort to increase my marketability."*

"But you still get to do your art."

"Yeah. But now I'm always thinking about what other people are gonna think about it."

"You didn't think about that before?"

"No. Actually not. Not until I was discovered."

"C'mon you guys," Ellen stuck her head out the door, "The kids are asleep. It's safe to come in."

"Sorry honey," Chuck kissed her on the cheek.

I was a zombie for the rest of the night. I'm sure the weed had something to do with it, but more than anything, it was the fact that I had vocalized the discomfort that I was feeling ever since that event. So, we sat in the living room and talked about everything from New York to Dilon. I was sitting in the Lay-z-boy and Chuck and Ellen were on the couch arm in arm. I felt like an alien then. The plush carpet and the new, cushy furniture and the beautiful TV and all the gold-framed photos of the kids. I was an alien zombie.

I had the cab driver wait for me when I returned to the hotel. I ran upstairs, grabbed my bag and jumped back into the car. We got to the train station at the stroke of midnight. One of the last things I had seen at the Winger's was a TV ad for Amtrak's "45 days anywhere in the U.S." deal. I thought once about my next scheduled appearance—a gallery in El Paso—"Oh well!"

The next train out of St. Louis was heading east. Not exactly the direction I was headed, but it was the movement that really mattered, not the direction, so, I plunked down that American Express card. And within a matter of minutes the ticket was in my hand. I wasn't accustomed to making spontaneous purchases. That was so fun I knew I had done the right thing.

I watched the countryside roll by. The excitement wore off quickly. When I woke up we had just arrived in Memphis. "Should I get off here? Home of Elvis!" We rolled on. The daylight countryside was only slightly more interesting than the night. Sure there were those rich colors, but no people. I quickly realized that nobody got close to those tracks. The thing was just too damn loud. And, unlike the airplane, you could only see things close to your path. "Maybe this wasn't such a good idea."

I had left Jack to sit my loft. When I walked in there three weeks early, I took him totally by surprise. There he was all naked, his mouth wide open. I quieted him with the finger to the lips and went straight for that box in my closet. That girl screamed. I was oblivious. I got that bankbook and left Jack standing right where I had found him. The bank wasn't exactly prepared for a twenty five thousand dollar cash withdrawal. They asked me to come back. Once I hit the street, that sinking paranoid feeling hit. Some one would surely recognize me and tell Sal where I was. I went to hide at Our Lady of Sorrows. Father Frank took me into his office and started to tell me how wonderfully the community development project I had sponsored was working.

"Bill and Maureen have you to thank!"

I was oblivious. All I could think about was how I was going to effectuate my disappearance.

7/7/70

There are times when it all comes together. And when you're young, and when that happens, life seems the richest pageant imaginable.

I'm walking down the concourse. The huge motor revving the Ferris wheel deafens me in the left ear while the screams from the Round-up pierce my right. There is a general euphoria that is palpable. My cohorts and I frolic with teenage abandon. In the midst of a hormone induced growth spurt you feel capable of anything—Godlike.

I used to tag along with John Rogers at the fair. As long as I could anyway. He would lose me and find me at his whim. Now that he had been gone for a couple of years I was hanging with kids my own age. The little experience I had gotten from John made me the chief innovator amongst my peers. I knew about the change that fell out of people's pockets as they rode the Round-up. Or better still the fan in the spook house that exposed the panties of unsuspecting girls with dresses.

The 1970 fair had a bonus—a beer tent. Not only did they drink in there, they gambled, too! The energy coming from that place drew me and my cadre magnetically. It was an open tent with a fence around it so you could see the excitement. We tried to watch but invariably the men would throw beer at us and laugh hysterically. We finally found a dark spot where we could watch with out being doused. The cheers we were hearing centered on a white rat. They had a table-like, hollow wheel that spun. It had several pie shaped wedges painted on top in varying colors. Near the edge of the wheel was a hole for every color. The rat was put inside through a door in the center of the wheel and it would be given a spin. After a while the rat would appear through one of the holes on the edge. If he had come out on the color you had bet on—you won. We watched with fascination. Everyone was drunk and the thing with the rat made it excitingly bizarre. After a few spins my friends started betting amongst themselves. One time the rat came out of a green hole almost instantly. Bob Benjamin let out a huge "Yeah!" He had bet on green. We saw several heads turn our direction. It was obvious they couldn't see us. The rat handler put the rat on his shoulder, like usual, and called for bets. Then he left the table and headed our way. He had his eyes peeled for us so I scooted. Everyone followed shortly. As I looked over my shoulder, I ran square into a stack of beer cases. They were on a hand truck as some one was wheeling them into the tent. Beer bottles went everywhere. I managed to roll and keep running. My friends, who were trailing, just dispersed the bottles wider. The guy with the dolly cursed us loudly.

We all gathered by the stream, laughing and out of breath. Jim Evans was the last to show and he had a beer with him. When he wouldn't share we all made our way back to look for other strays. Just as we got there I saw the guy with the hand truck heading away from the tent. He parked those tousled beers outside of the trailer, unlocked the padlock and went inside. Soon, he appeared with a new case plunked it down on the dolly and returned to the trailer. This was our chance. He came out with a second case and put it on top of the first and turned to go back. I headed for the trailer on tiptoe, my friends followed. As soon as he was inside I grabbed two of those tousled beers in each hand and took off.

How we laughed and cheered with the crack of each new bottle. And even though those beers were warm and foamy, they were the veritable nectar of the gods. I was relatively new to drinking so I downed my first one and was halfway through the second before the buzz started to hit. And when it did come I was so intoxicated with the moment, I barely recognized it. So when Fred Paschel was passing out the Pall Malls that he had taken from his dad's carton, I took one too.

And the fire lit. And the burning leaves transfer that fire to your mouth. And you blow it out at your whim. YES! Then, to take that fire into your lungs and feel your body consume it. What a feeling! I had to sit down. But I heard some of the guys jeering at my wasted state. I stood right back up. That's when I knew I was drunk.

With each passing sip our energy level rose. First it was the harmless sparring and then the breaking of the branches for mock duels. When the cigarettes ran out we headed for the parking lot like a pack of dogs. It was my idea to go to the parking lot. John used to get cigarettes out of unlocked cars there. Once we got to the cars all that energy was channeled into the exercise. We fanned out and combed the lot all the while making believe it was the jungle of Vietnam. As I crouched behind a big Buick my heart raced with excitement. There in front of me, on the dash of a new Plymouth Valiant, were two packs of Lucky Strikes. Those red circles were beacons. I moved in for the kill. I crawled up beside my prey while Bob watched my back. What luck! The door was unlocked. I tried to stay as low as possible so that just my hand was up on the dash groping for those smokes. I couldn't reach them at first so I lay down on the seat. I saw the keys and stopped. My head was still cloudy from the beers. I blinked my eyes a few times and refocused. The keys were in the ignition! The opportunity presented itself. I paused. Then I passed. I just grabbed those smokes and got out. I couldn't keep the secret, though.

I knew it was a mistake.

"Let's take it for a spin!" Jim went for it as soon as I let it out. Everyone followed. I had that slight, sinking, paranoid feeling that grabbed my stomach and wouldn't let go. We snuck in, Jim fired it up, everyone was quiet. We took it out the back entrance. Next thing I knew we were doing sixty on route seventeen, whooping it up. My nausea had waned. Jim was driving all right. His older brother had taught him. Still, I couldn't stop thinking about the stupidity. But every one was cheering and singing. I got caught up in the good time.

Fred found the bottle of whiskey in the glove box just as we were passing the Tamoritz' place. I remember I was glad to see their barn. It gave me my bearings. And then Fred held up that bottle. Seeing that amber liquid sent me back into my nausea. That bottle started making it around. I pulled off it, too. How could I not? The ensuing tingle made me laugh. After a couple times around it was dust and so were we. Seven piles of dust doing seventy down route seventeen.

I stared out the window. The countryside flashing by. The alcohol buzz. I felt like I was in a big, hollow, spinning table and I couldn't find my way out. Finally the spinning slowed. Jim had pulled the car over. I just fell out the door on all fours, reveling in relief. But, before I knew it, I was back in that thing. And the spinning began. At first I just tried to deal with it. When the idiocy began—Bill Bellamy putting his hands over Jim's eyes, Jim swerving intentionally, yelling "I can't see! I can't see!" everyone laughing—I started looking for a way out. We pulled over again this time to piss. I couldn't get over the firmness of the earth. The weight of gravity. Ahhhhh. I didn't want to get back in the car. I guess I was scared. I know I was drunk. I was going to walk back to the fair, but Jim promised he'd drive straight back. So, there I was again inside that spinning wheel, desperately searching for a way out. My heart was racing, my nose was twitching. That sense of impending doom occupying every thought. And every time I looked at the clock on the dash, only ten seconds had passed.

We made it back to the fair all right. For a while I thought we'd get busted in the parking lot, still we pulled that Valiant right back into the spot we had found it and left as if nothing had happened. After a brief respite I was strolling the concourse again reveling in the sounds and the sights and the smell of those Belgian waffles. All that terror seemed like a dream.

Had I ever left the fair?

"Frank!" my mom called my name. "Oh no," I thought. I was still drunk. By the time she grabbed my hand I realized she was happy about something. She pulled me away. I just waved to my friends and rolled my eyes.

"Look," she pointed when we got to the judges tent. What she was pointing at was my watercolor "Sunset". It had a huge blue ribbon affixed to the upper left corner. When she kissed my cheek a huge chill went up my spine, and an even bigger smile appeared on my face. I had submitted the painting on Mom's insistence. I thought it was terrible. So much so, that I had forgotten that I had even entered it.

"Is that your work son?" An elderly man piped in. I just nodded. "Very nice. Really nice." He handed me an envelope that said "First Prize". I opened it to find fifty dollars. My head swam as it had never swum before. Not even close to the whiskey swim.

Just pure delight.

7/11/90

Father Frank smiled down at me. I looked past him. I didn't want him to see my fear. And over his shoulder—Christ on the cross, all bloody and anguished. That image grabbed me and increased my terror. So, I looked at Father Frank. But his smiling face was unbearable. I looked away.

"Frank you seem troubled."

I was never very good at hiding the truth. "Oh, just tired," I tried anyways.

"Frank...?" he wasn't buying it.

"Something's not right."

"How so?"

"I don't know," I couldn't escape that image of Christ, "just not right." I definitely couldn't look at Frank. I just put my head down.

"Before I entered the seminary, I had a pervading sense of unrest. Something wasn't right for me then. You know, I had a good job. I was working for Eastman Kodak. Kodak's a decent place to work. No union, but still they take care of their people. I made a good wage, had a nice apartment, drove a sixty eight mustang," he tapped me on the arm and gave me a little raise of the eyebrows like that would intrigue me. I wasn't sure what a Mustang was. "Well, anyhow, most people would have been happy in my place. I thought I was happy there for a while, at least I thought I should've been, so, I convinced myself that I was." I didn't really want to hear this. I couldn't stop thinking about that cash and how it would get me away from everything. "Then my cousin Dave died, rest his soul. I realized then how afraid of dying I was," I looked up to see Father Frank suddenly serious, "Fear can be a tremendously stifling force," that crucifix behind him captured my view, "What are you afraid of Frank?" The clock struck three.

"Gotta go," I stood, still looking at that symbol of anguish. "Thanks for stopping by. You are loved," he was smiling again. "Got an appointment," was all I could say.

I sat on that bundle of cash. Literally sat on it. Head in my hands. I was almost out. When the bank handed me that case and asked me to count all that money, I felt light again. But I had to come home. Why? I don't know. I was planning on grabbing some clothes. I don't know. I could've bought new clothes, but I stopped home. When Jack handed me that note I couldn't help myself. Some "mysterious" stranger had dropped it off while I was away.

I had to read it.

> Frank,
> Urgently need to see you!
> I'll stop by again after you return.
>
> John
> Rogers

Well, I knew I couldn't hang around New York for three weeks. And I couldn't leave without seeing John, so I went back to work. Sal was a little pissed. He got me out to Phoenix toot suite, though.

When I got back from the West coast I was hoping to see John waiting for me at my door. No such luck. That suitcase full of cash was still at the end of the couch. I sat on it and waited. Still, no John. The whole time I was sitting there I was thinking about Christ on the cross. That image from Our Lady of Sorrows hadn't left me. Only now, Christ had lost that anguished look. He seemed bored. In my mind's eye, Christ was an old man for whom crucifixion was just his last tedious task. The image was set. The canvas went up.

John stopped by a couple days later. I was in the throws of interpolation so I couldn't really feel the joy I knew was present. John looked positively awful, so that didn't help. We sat in my kitchen sipping tea. My image of Christ staring down on me. It was only a sketch, but I couldn't help looking past John with curiosity.

"I'm dying," were the first words of his that I really heard. I looked at him and saw the illness for the first time. I still didn't know what to say. Neither did he, evidently.

"How can I help?" was the only thing I could break the silence with.

"You can't," he was grim, "I just wanted to see you."

"Will this be the last time?"

"Probably so."

What could I say? I thought about asking how or why. I thought about telling him about Ellen Tamoritz. I couldn't say anything, though. The knot in my throat made that impossible.

"Christ?" he nodded toward the sketch.

"Yeah," I had almost forgotten about it. I thought about telling him more. What else could I say? He put out his cigarette and stood up. I had that panic feeling.

"Resist temptation, Frank," he held out his arms. When we embraced I just sank. The unbearable weight of sadness was pulling me down from the inside out. I wanted to say how much he had meant to me, but I couldn't. I just held on. Don't go. If I just held on he wouldn't go.

Then Jack popped in all glib, that hyena laugh seemed particularly irritating. When Jack popped in I let go. That was it. John just turned and left. I watched him for as long as I could.

He never looked back.

"Friend of yours?" Jack had sensed the gravity.

"I grew up with him," I was surprised that I could croak out anything.

"In Kansas?" I just nodded, "Wiild." Jack sounded just like John. Somehow that made me feel better. I smiled. He caught me. "Yeah, no reason to fear death," a stilted hyena laugh. That gave me a chill and when I shivered I spent all my energy. I just flopped on the futon; gravity's massage soothing my angst. I cried.

Irene Solomon died when John and I were embracing. Stroke. I was surprised how deeply that affected me. Jack was also there when Mo called me about that.

"Some consider death a beginning, not an ending," he almost seemed disgusted with my sorrow.

"Yeah, yeah," I didn't want to hear it.

"As a matter of fact, most artists aren't recognized until after they're dead."

"I thought you were talking about the great beyond!"

"I am. The future's the most concrete form of eternity known to man."

I looked down at my sketch of Christ and thought about how the eternity of future had immortalized him. How ironic if there was no form of eternity other than the future. All those Christians talking about heaven and hell all the while Christ being the supreme example of the eternity of future.

"Maybe I should knock myself off, then," I tried to laugh.

"No need, no need. Simulated death works just as well. That way you can have the best of both worlds."

"Heaven and hell?"

"If you want to call it that."

"Who would want hell when they could have heaven?"

"Some people want it all."

"I just want a little," I said under my breath and began painting.

Even though I couldn't stop thinking about making that break, my determination to finish this painting kept those thoughts on the back burner.

I got quite a bit done on the day of Irene's funeral.

Bill and Mo begged me to go. I couldn't.

The notice of John's death arrived the very next day.

"Donations can be sent to The Haemmeker Home for Retarded Children in lieu of flowers."

I got a lot of painting done that day, too. At the end of that day there was Christ, old, and black. I don't know how it happened. He wasn't Negro. He just had dark skin and the blood on his hands glistened so. And there on the hill behind him a young man on the cross. Christ was bored; the young man was anguished. Who was that man?

I was stalled.

I sat there for a week.

Rrringgg.

I was still trying to figure it out.

Rrringgg.

"Hello," I had answered unconsciously. I usually let the machine get it.

"Frank Teeman?" a woman's voice.

"Uh-huh"

"This is Claire Hodges."

Claire? Where do I know that name? "Claire!?" I finally focused.

"You gave my sister your number."

"Yes, yes. Claire!" The excitement! My heart raced.

"Are you…Frank Teeman…the painter?" she said tentatively.

"Yes," I had to think about that one.

"You wanted to commission me?" in disbelief.

"Certainly," I was smiling. I almost laughed.

"I could never," she was flustered.

"I think you could."

"No."

"Let's get together and talk about it."

"I don't think so. I just called to see if it was really you. I love your work."

Now I was flustered. "Are you doing any painting?"

"Oh, not really."

"Either you are or you aren't."

"Well, I am…"

"I'd love to see it."

"It's packed. I'm moving to New Mexico."

"I see," my heart sank, "with your family?"

"Uh-huh. I've held on to your number all this time."

"Thanks for calling," I didn't hear anything after that except "Merry Christmas."

Such a sweet voice. I thought about tracking her down. Those thoughts only lasted a couple days. I just returned to my depression. Only in addition to the pervasive, dull, aching there was now that heart ache. A tightness in my chest that accompanies longing. I painted while I thought about Claire and her home life. I painted horns on that other crucified man, and a tail. Yes! Now it was clear—Beelzebub was on that cross next to Christ. But, why?

I was stalled again.

When Mary called two months later with the invitation to Terra's third birthday party, I was still trying to figure out that damn painting. "Why would the devil be crucified?" I kept asking myself. It must be a mistake I kept telling myself. But there it is. It's plain.

Still, I was stalled.

I kept the flywheel running, though.

It took me a while to adjust to the frivolity of Terra's party. All the balloons and bright colors and unabashed happiness were a distinct change from the frame of mind I had brought. Not to mention that there were a bunch of kids there and most had parents in tow. And there I was all unshaven and sullen. There must have been a dark cloud following me. Mary took me aside the first chance she had.

"I saw your portrait of me and Terra."

"Where did you see that?"

"You don't know?" I shrugged my shoulders; "They've got it in the big window at Bloomingdale's!"

"Bloomingdale's?"

"It's the center piece of their maternity display."

"Display?"

"It's in all the ads, too."

"Ads?"

"You didn't know about any of this?"

"I've been busy."

"It's a beautiful piece, Frank. I'm so touched." She kissed me on the cheek. I was so emotionally exhausted I barely mustered a smile. A wail went up from the kitchen table and she left. The mother in my painting was plain to me then. I almost cried. Ad copy!?! But the joy of youth is so infectious I was smiling again within minutes. And then we sang Happy Birthday and the cheer went up afterward. All that joy. I closed my eyes just for a second. The energy came and it was a blast. A huge dose. I could barely stand. And my spine tingled so, I must have been wriggling like an epileptic. And then that painting appeared. I saw clearly what needed to be done.

"Mother and Child" went big. The T-shirts, the calendar, the whole deal. Sal had done his work, though. My bank account was huge. I was still finishing up "Two of a kind" when word of Irene's inheritance came down. She had left me her house in the Hamptons. "Sell it," I told the lawyer. I was in the throws of interpolation. I couldn't be bothered. The media went nuts. They portrayed me as some kind of saint, spurning the comforts of life for art. Pictures of me in my flat were in every tabloid, Roger Mondrake leading the charge. Pictures of me opening the Roger's library at the Haemekker House followed.

That sealed the deal.

That made the unveiling of "Two of a kind" all the more sensational. I had kept that painting hidden. Only Jack had seen it. He had no comment. I had agreed to unveil it at the new community center Father Frank's parish had built with my donations. Every one I knew was at that unveiling. Except for Red. I searched past Ralph and his wife, Jim Jacobs was there with Kathleen, Phil Jankow the banker…No Red. Mary and Terra, Jack and Des. No Red. The happiness began to slip. Roger Mondrake and his photographer, Al Rosenstein…I could see them all with their eager anticipation. I felt sick. All that drinking and hardly any eating. I hadn't had a good night's sleep in months. Bags under my eyes. The beard. I was a wreck. But, still, there they all were looking at me to pull that sheet and give them something. So, I did. And there was a murmur. And a few people clapped. But still, there was a lot of chatter. People started to file by to get a better look. I looked close, too. It was like I was seeing it for the first time. Lucifer was a woman! And at her feet a throng of mourners. Christ had one vigilant person watching him. The rest were on their way to mourn the crucifixion of the devil-woman. Some looked at Christ but showed no emotion. And then I realized all those people were filing by me, but they weren't looking at me. They were looking at her—"The Queen of the Jews" (that was the inscription on her cross). And as I looked back and forth between the still image and the moving one, I could see that the faces were the same. Where was my one mourner? I should've guessed. Father Frank was standing next to me on the dais, that's why I didn't see him at first. While everyone was fixed on that painting, his eyes were on me. Once I realized that, the end was near. A nervous energy grew in me until I couldn't control it. I grabbed that painting off the easel and fled out the back. The crowd erupted in astonishment. Camera flashes exploded. "It's blasphemy," several people called out.

Yeah, I sold that painting. I didn't want it. Didn't need it! That image was fixed firmly. Sal had so many buyers after all the hype I could name my price. So, I did. I wanted out. Jack found the guy for me who could get me out. Sure, I could've bought myself a fortress and shunned society. How would I get the energy? I wanted in, yet I wanted out. And, fortunately for me, that painting was just the ticket. Johnny Angellini took it in exchange for one genuine disappearance.

Jack and I drove down to Central Park after a couple of days of bingeing. When you're about to die, gin and cocaine have a wonderful way of making you feel alive. When we got to that part of Central Park where I told Johnny to meet me, I closed my eyes and waited. Nothing. I tried to summon the energy. Still, nothing.

"I don't know what you're doing, but it sure looks funny," Jack laughed.

Suddenly, gunfire. I hit the dirt. Jack kept laughing. His cab got rifled and exploded. I almost screamed. Still, that hyena laugh. "Be careful of what you wish for, you may get it."

"Jack?" I did scream.

"Hey! Can I have your flat?" he yelled. The roar of flames was deafening.

"Sure," I was out of breath with excitement. I looked around. The light was blinding.

"This is it?" Suddenly, I was scared.

"This is it." He was suddenly solemn. "Pleasure to have met you."

A blow to my head.

Nothing.

A little knowledge is a dangerous thing. Fear is based in knowledge. You can't be afraid of that which you are ignorant. Fear can be one of the most stifling forces, too. Interestingly enough, the antidote to that fear based paralysis seems to be more knowledge. Some think that returning to ignorance is the way out. After all, ignorance is such bliss. And then the awareness creeps in and ruins it. So, why not just eliminate the awareness and return to that wonderful state? How to do that?

For some, the awareness is so deep that trying to eliminate it becomes a full time job. We know these people as problem addicts. I say "problem" addicts as opposed to adjusted addicts. The people who let their addiction subsume their life. They have a problem. Most of those have a large element of denial in their mix. The adjusted addict admits that their behavior is in response to fear, not just verbally, but on an inner, subconscious level. Through that admission comes the perspective.

For others, the awareness is so pervasive that more drastic measures are needed. These people need to sufficiently alter their reality so as to controvert the awareness. For them denial is their addiction. Anything that doesn't sit gets explained away. There are so many acute awarenesses, explaining them all away is a tremendous task. This has been so for thousands of years and in response to that difficulty, systems for explaining away life's harshnesses have been developed. We know these systems as religion.

In the same way that addicts can be functional or problematic, religious people can be functional or problematic, too. The basis for the distinction in either case is the same. If you can admit on a fundamental level that your beliefs are a coping mechanism, the perspective gained from that is a tremendous asset in keeping it in check. All too often people need to distort their reality in such an extreme fashion that such an admission would be shattering. It would no longer serve as relief if it weren't all encompassing.

The need for both these coping mechanisms comes from the same place. It's about the anguish over the loss of a perceived ideal. That ideal is not just some material thing that is never attainable; it is a frame of mind that comes from being in an environment conducive to happiness. How cruel to be able to see that which is most desired and not feel it? And how to ameliorate that pain? Religions seem more suitably adapted to that purpose.

Distorting reality to suit your perceptions is not, in and of itself, harmful. Sharing your perceptions with other people? There's the rub. That's where religions come in. Rather than forming your own perceptions, here are ready-made ones. Those of your ilk require no explanation, just faith. If you are surrounded by people who share a common delusion there is no immediate problem. With the advent of religious tolerance, explaining your perceptions has suddenly become requisite. The dialogue between groups does present a problem. Allowing other groups their opinion would be a shattering admission for some.

Addicts don't really have that problem. They're trying to escape reality rather than redefine it. This implies that they are operating in reality and attempting to get out. It could be that they have distorted reality in such a way that there is a perceived need to escape a nonexistent harm. There must be a few of these, but for the most part, I think not. If you are prone to distorting reality, eventually you will distort it into a source of comfort. If not, suicide quickly intervenes.

For all those non-denial addictions, the flight from reality is only temporary. Even for the most hardened alcohol or drug abuser that effect wears off. Not only does it pass through your system, its efficacy is minimized with each usage. Larger doses are required. Abuse of substances does have a deleterious effect. Increased dosages will eventually be destructive enough to warrant a change. In that way the substance abuser is less of a burden on society than the religion abuser.

Whether you're trying to escape from it or redefine it, reality has a nasty way of sneaking up and biting you on the ass. Particularly if you don't stay on top of it. So, ultimately both coping mechanisms have a fundamentally problematic nature. That's why I say that increased awareness is the cure. On the surface there are a lot of frightening things. Most, if not all, shrink under the microscope. If only it were as simple as looking through a tool. It's not. It's a long process that frequently dissolves into hopelessness.

Where does one get the strength needed to endure the torture of ignorance? From family. I don't mean family in the limited, nuclear sense. I'm talking about anything that gives you that feeling of togetherness. Anything that works to reduce the aloneness. Fear of loneliness has to be one of the most deeply rooted and pervasive of all fears. If that one can be stemmed, the foothold for all other fears is dramatically curtailed.

A spouse offers the most direct form of support, affirming your existence by buying into it in a wholesale fashion. A child offers a genuine kind of perspective not only about your own origins, but also about life in general. That combination of support and perspective provides the necessary atmosphere to proliferate a knowledge capable of overcoming fear. While the emoluments from the nuclear family are particularly potent (especially when kids are introduced) the strength can be derived from other forms of kinship.

Art offers the same kind of benefits. Just like watching a child grow, the transformation of an artistic endeavor from inception to completion, frequently leaves the artist astounded. Having an idea, exploring your feelings on that topic, comparing those feeling to others', seeing how people respond to your evaluation...The interpolation process is all about perspective. Having others buying into your life in a wholesale fashion is the ultimate goal of all artists. Some denounce cash purchases, but all long for the affirmation associated with admiration.

BOOK 2

FACING FATE

Security is mostly superstition.
It does not exist in nature,
nor do the children of men as a whole experience it.
Avoiding danger is no safer in the long run than outright exposure.
Life is either a daring adventure, or nothing.
To keep our faces toward change and behave
like free spirits in the presence of fate is strength undefeatable.

Helen Keller—Let Us Have Faith

PART I

▼

I made a deal with the devil.

For the longest time I honestly thought he was an angel.

Now I know the truth.

That fiery scene with Jack's hyena laugh seemed like a dream when I finally woke from that blow. The room was so dim and quiet I wasn't sure if I had died or what. The door cracked and the light peeked through. I knew I was alive with the squinting of my eyes. She didn't notice that I was conscious at first, but I was still too weak to speak. I recognized her, but couldn't put my finger on it. When she came over to the bed and saw the glint of my eyes a huge smile appeared and that's when I recognized Red.

"Frank!" she came to the bed and caressed my forehead. I tried to ask why. The tube down my throat made it impossible. I flopped my arm out next to her. She took my hand. Her smile was infectious. There was a tremendous amount of happiness amidst all the confusion.

So, I had gotten what I wanted. Shortly, I was up and out of the hospital and living in my two bedroom, 1 1/2 bath, raised ranch in Levittown, Pennsylvania. My new name was Frank Kunstler. Mary, my wife of twelve years, and I were in an automobile wreck. A fiery crash. I suffered several injuries to my face. All had been repaired very nicely. The grocery store I had just purchased was almost out of escrow. I would be strong enough to run it when the time came. Yes,

Johnny had come through. Birth certificate, credit history, new face—
the whole deal. One thing I had a hard time getting used to was the
grey. My hair had turned a whitish grey. I thought it was dyed. It
wasn't. After a while I came to embrace that, too. I had embraced every
other aspect of this transformation so, it wasn't that much of a leap.

Mary and I didn't talk of our past for the longest time. There was
one episode early on where she told me about how she had come to my
place all battered and teary eyed. I was away so Jack took her in. She
told him, then, how much she wanted out. When he eventually asked
her to go with me she jumped at the chance. Once I knew that she was
there by choice all apprehension was eliminated and I dove into my
new life headfirst. The whole domestic thing was so new to both of us
we were like two kids playing house. And the freshness of everything? I
could just sit on the back porch in my folding, webbed lawn chair and
watch the grass grow. The quiet, the clean air, breathing the clean air!!!!
I felt like a kid again. There were still some tremendous adjustments to
be made. At night Mary and I would sit together and talk. A lot of our
conversation centered on the town and it's surroundings. She was more
adventurous than I so, she would tell me all about it. Through that we
had occasion to share childhood memories. Mary's Upton, Minnesota
sounded just like Dilon. The acquaintance process had begun.

Eventually we worked out our fictional past. During those times I
always felt apprehensive. It was more like a chore. We made up some
funny stories, though. Stuff like Mary locking herself out of the house
while she was in her bathrobe, and courting stories like me serenading
her outside the wrong apartment. We rehearsed until we thought we
had it down. The conjugal side of our relationship took longer to grow.
One day we went to the mall to buy a TV. We both had an aversion to
TV, but we felt like we should have one for appearances sake. The
salesman at Sears kept referring to us as "Mister and Missus Kunstler"
and every time he would say that I would look at her and she at me and
we would hold hands and smile.

"How long have you two been married?" he asked once.

"Twelve years," she had that line down.

"Twelve years and the honeymoon isn't over yet. That's so nice."

"What do you mean?" I was confused.

"Look at you two. You're like newlyweds."

We ate dinner in front of the TV that night. When you don't watch a lot of TV it seems wondrous. Particularly a new color TV. The image!?! So vivid. We were transfixed. Even the commercials were fascinating. Casablanca was on that night. Mary fell asleep on my shoulder about half way through. I had never seen it so I was riveted. Once it ended, I was ready for bed.

"Missus Kunstler," I whispered to Mary. I felt nervous. Her eyes fluttered open.

"Yes Mister Kunstler," a sultry whisper.

"Are you ready for bed," I kissed her forehead.

"MmHm," she was still drowsy.

I picked her up and carried her upstairs.

We were husband and wife from then on.

We met the neighbors soon enough. Shortly after our arrival Edith Johnson had dropped off some cookies. She left an open invitation for dinner, too. The morning after our "honeymoon" we were sitting on the couch.

"Think we're ready for dinner at the Johnson's?" Mary asked during a commercial break.

"Look at that!" I was transfixed by a razor commercial that had several men's faces blending from one to the other. So quickly and so smoothly.

"That is wild," she thought I was ignoring her.

"The Johnson's?" I was teasing, "What's he do?"

"Fred's a postal worker."

"Fred Johnson the mailman," I drew it out, "I think I can relate."

She gave me an excited squeeze and a kiss.

I smiled.

I was fascinated with the Johnsons from the start. When we arrived at their door that Tuesday night an air of festivity captured us. Maybe it was the kids and their youthful exuberance. I think it was my youthful exuberance, though. Life is thrilling when you're stocking your memory banks. With my slate cleaned I was eager and happy to do something that was a genuine Kunstler memory. The kids, Jeff and Julie, made the experience festive, though. Fred was a barrel of laughs, too. When you're throwing the ball with the dog, sipping a beer, marveling over an eleven-year-old's ability to run and run and run, you laugh. I laughed. Fred laughed. When Ralph, the black lab, crashed into Jeff we all laughed, hysterically. And with each deep breath of fresh cut grass scented air, a certain element of joy crept in. I remember watching Fred Johnson play with his son in that back yard and thinking that I had done the right thing. Not only had I done the right thing, but Jack and Johnny had done a supremely righteous thing.

I remember thinking that.

Bright Star Burns Out

by Al Rosenstein

Special to The Post

Frank Teaman, one of the fastest rising stars in the art world, died this morning in a bizarre shoot out at Central Park. At an early hour, Mr. Teeman had taken a cab to Central Park for an as of yet unknown reason. The driver, Mr. Jacsun Pranesh, said that Mr. Teeman had requested they simply park when, suddenly, the cab was riddled with bullets and exploded into flames. Mr. Pranesh was able to escape, but Mr. Teeman was not so fortunate. Thus ends the life of a promising young talent. Mr. Teeman was "discovered" by Irene Solomon, a wealthy art enthusiast who opened a gallery in the Hamptons, in June of 1986. The Teeman show was her first and his brand of unabashed portraiture

captured not only the buying public, but the critical art world as well. His "Glad", a simple yet haunting portrait of an elderly woman, sold for an unheard of price for an unknown artist. That particular sale began speculation by this critic that good art had value beyond the hype of the art market.

Mr. Teeman went on to be canonized by the press for maintaining his spartan lifestyle while amassing considerable wealth and fame. Several television appearances, most notably The Tonight Show, established him as a personality as well as an artist. Through it all he seemed largely unaffected, keeping his residence in a shabby flat on the lower east side and donating large sums to

(continued on pg.9)

TEEMAN

(cont. from pg.1)

local redevelopment efforts. In 1990 his "Mother and Child" was bought by Bloomingdales and became the centerpiece of their maternity ad campaign. There was a lot of grumbling in the art world about his selling out, but the shear artistry of that painting hushed most would be detractors. Mr. Teeman was characteristically silent on the topic. Some wondered if he even knew what was happening.

Most recently Mr. Teeman unveiled his "Two of a Kind". The scandal surrounding this painting was on an epoch level. His portrayal of Christ on the cross with a devil-woman labeled as his wife crucified next to him brought scorn from the religious community and feminist

groups. For some he had gone from saint to demon, from gentleman to misogynist with literally the stroke of a brush. At the same time some religious groups found inspiration in the work and others found it intriguing outside of any religious or socio-sexual connotations. A politically incorrect scandal that would have ruined most careers, launched Frank Teeman to the fore front by making him the topic of all the hot discussions.

Frank Teeman was an artist in the truest sense. He had a rare commitment and vision that hasn't been seen in the modern world since Picasso. His contribution was great, but only beginning to develop. The loss of his potential is the saddest part of his passing.

Grab can, lift arm, stack can, turn around. It was actually fun to be doing this again. Maybe it was because it was my own store. More probably it was the filling-the-slate thing. Or maybe I had done the right thing. I had never felt that pervasive happiness before. It led me to believe that I had found my calling.

"Hey Bob, where are those green beans?" I shouted to get over the radio.

"Look behind the back door. Or maybe under the paper towels." Bob Brelen shouted back. He was my night manager. Hell of a guy.

Normally I didn't see much of Bob. I did days. But one of our stockers called in sick so, I stuck around to help out. When you see all those empty spaces on the shelf you start to get an idea how much stuff goes out these doors. That made me feel good. Not that I was selling a lot. I had seen the balance sheet, we were doing all right, more that I had helped to provide food for so many. The store was located just on the south edge of town. The poor part of town. That meant I saw a lot of elderly and a lot of black. That was fine with me. I was already on a first name basis with a couple of customers. Such nice people, too. Ah, there's those beans. Under the paper towels just like Bob said. Hustle 'em out onto the floor.

"Hey boss! You don't have to do that. Aren't you coming in at six?" Bob stopped me on aisle six. I hadn't thought about that. I looked at my watch; ten 'til twelve. "Get home and get some sleep." He flashed me that huge smile. In contrast to his dark black skin his teeth seemed illuminated.

"OK, after these beans."

"Isn't your woman waitin' for ya?"

"Yeah, I suppose."

"Mine would be waitin' with a rollin' pin."

"She's jealous?"

"Nah, she just crazy," I was confused, "she afraid a losin' me," he laughed.

"What's her name?"

"Rosalie," he could see her then, "Sweet Rosalie."

"You love her don't you?"

"I sure do," that lighted smile.

And more green beans. And more coffee. And more WIC. UGH, that damn paper work. But you get up in the morning and you've got some place to be. And that is enough. For a while. And then your payroll deposit doesn't clear because too many customers have written you bad checks and your employees are complaining because their checks haven't cleared. So, you spend all morning hustling up a deal with the bank so your people can pay their rent. But through it all you had forgotten to call Eastern Supply to cancel the order of paper towels. So, they showed up. Those things take up so much room. Special on paper towels! And Elijah catches a shoplifter. A young girl. Already got a kid. Zero tolerance, though. Elijah had called the cops. That policy was a left over from the previous owners. Sometimes it was nice to have a smooth running machine. Sometimes not. I wanted to go soft on the girl, Zita. The cops didn't think so. They knew Zita. She needed to be taught a lesson, they said. So, a lesson I gave. Credit. Yes, I extended Zita a credit account for the stuff she had taken. We were clear. She had thirty days to pay it. If she did, her credit would go up. If she didn't, well, my loss. I didn't want her responding out of some threat. I wanted her to learn. To learn a lesson about credit. The flexible dollar. The most useful tool known to mankind.

"That was cool, what you did for Zita," Elijah caught me on his way out.

"Thanks," I smiled.

"You don't think she's gonna pay, though?" he was so bitter. I didn't know what to say. "Well, she won't. I'm tellin' you right now."

"My loss then," I was smiling again.

"Mister Kunstler a word of advice?" I waited eagerly, "Don't do this."

"Do what?"

"You know, the whole good Samaritan routine."

"What's wrong with that?"

"I'll tell you. Zita is, right now, telling everyone what a chump you are."

"A chump?"

"A pushover. Pretty soon, all those crackheads'll be here looking for some credit. And they'll be laughin' just like Zita if they get it cause none of them is gonna pay it."

"Maybe they just need a chance."

"Man, these people are gone. Forget about 'em. You do more good by keepin' your store open for the good folk here," I hadn't thought about that, "When Mister Sanders announced he was retiring we figured nobody'd buy in this neighborhood. The nearest grocery is over in Watkins Heights. That's a forty-minute bus ride, one way. You're doin' a lot of good just keepin' this store open. Don't start losin' money on lost causes. It almost wiped Mister Sanders out."

"So, I should've let the cops take her away."

"Yeah. You should have."

"There's got to be a better way."

"That's what I'm talkin' about."

Sure enough Elijah caught two shoplifters the next day. He looked at me sternly when the first one was in his grasp. I just stared at my shoes. The cops came and, I'll be damned if he wasn't hollering about credit when they took him away. The second one came late in the day.

When Elijah brought her in, I marched right over. Elijah just kept his head down.

"Elijah, you know the man," she was saying when I got there, "Get me that credit deal." I went cold.

"I'm the man," I took her wrist, "let's talk about credit." Elijah gave me that stern look. She was happy. I just took her away.

"That was cool," Elijah caught me on the way out.

"Yeah, I feel real good about that."

"I'm tellin' you, it was cool."

I knew that he was right. Somehow, throwing his cousin in jail didn't make me really happy. Not that he was happy about it. I just couldn't work up the same enthusiasm. Elijah had been fighting the war all his life. To him every battle was important. I was still attached to winning the war without any battles.

Grab can, lift arm, stack can, turn around. Robert, the stocker, had called in sick again. Time to start doing some interviews. Lots of corn sold today. I wonder why that is? People are eating. That's a good thing.

"Hey boss," Bob Brelen had snuck up behind me. No sign of those electric teeth.

"Bob," when you're tired very little comes to mind.

"Rough day, huh?"

"You said it," I kept stacking cream corn.

"Well, you did the right thing."

"How's Rosalie?" He couldn't help let a little smile out.

"She's pregnant," that huge grin.

"Hey! That's great!" Both knees cracked when I stood.

"Yeah. Not exactly planned, but we'll deal with it."

"God, that's great!" I thought about Fred and Jeff Johnson.

That tremendous abandon.

What a lucky man.

FRANK TEEMAN MEMORIALIZED

Al Rosenstein

Several hundred people showed up at the Bowery Street Community Center on the lower east side last night to mourn the death of Frank Teeman. The art world's fastest rising star died last week in a fiery shooting in Central Park. His untimely death brought out friends and admirers to pay tribute to a man they considered a saint. Unfortunately not everyone agrees with those people.

In June of 1986 Frank Teeman first caught this writer's eye with an exhibit at a new gallery in the Hampton's. Irene Solomon, long time benefactor of the arts, had opened her own art gallery and she chose Frank Teeman, an unheard of painter, to head her opening. Mr. Teeman's work, while unknown, held enough charm to dispel the "Tax write-off" nay-sayers critiquing the show. Even if that was Mrs. Solomon's original intent, which is still open to speculation, her taste in art effectively ruined any chance of that. Frank Teeman's paintings don't grab you and shake you like some contemporary artists, but they are possessed with a certain amount of humanity that gives them an enduring quality. There are those who doubt the public's ability to recognize "good" art. Mr. Teeman's story should put an end to those pessimistic rantings.

After Mr. Teeman's "Glad", a touchingly sorrowful portrait of an old woman, sold at Solomon's opening for a robust fifty thousand dollars, several of his other works slowly captured the American masses. That combined with a few public appearances, most memorably "The Tonight Show", transformed this Kansas farm boy into a media icon. His unassuming, distracted nature lent a real honesty to his paintings and his persona. For the first time since Warhol, the art community had a media all-star.

Three months ago, Teeman unveiled his "Two of a kind" at the same community center that housed his wake. The painting was a graphic depiction of Christ's crucifixion only this scene had a demonic woman on the cross next to Christ and an inscription that implied that she was Christ's wife. Various elements in the Christian community took exception to the painting. The implication that Christ and the devil were, some how, consorting or equals qualified as heresy of the worst kind for them. Several women's groups disparaged Teeman for simply depicting the devil as female. Frank Teeman had suddenly become the villain. His supporters tried to emphasize the passion and the religious nature of the painting. They tried to point out his good works and his simple lifestyle, but to no avail. Frank Teeman had become the latest victim of political incorrectness.

Father Frank Berger delivered the most moving eulogy at Mr. Teeman's memorial last night. A room full of supporters sat silently while this Catholic priest trumpeted the goodness of this, so called, demon. "Frank Teeman was a Christian," the father opened up his sermon. "He gave of himself, unquestioningly." Father Berger went on to announce that the community center, which was on church property and financed by Mr. Teeman's donations, would be renamed The Frank Teeman Community Center. Father Berger did address Teeman's detractors. "Certainly Frank struggled with the devil. All mortal men do. He accepted the challenge, though, and asked some hard questions," referring to "Two of a Kind", "perhaps if he had lived he could have given some answers, too."

The father seemed oblivious to the reports that Frank Teeman is, indeed, still alive. His body was cremated when the cab he was in exploded in Central Park after being riddled with gunfire. What was left of his body was identified by a sole coroner and then disposed of. The city does dispose of some "John Does" quickly, but only when they are suspected of being contaminated with a communicable disease. The official explanation for Mr. Teeman's hasty disposal has yet to surface. With no surviving relatives to push the case, it is unlikely that any explanation will. Whether he is alive or dead, Frank Teeman is gone. There are some of us who are saddened. His work touched a spot that few can touch

Her essence enveloped me. Standing in the kitchen, fixing a cup of tea, she was all around me. Not surprising since our intimacy had become so intense. What was surprising was how it had changed me. It really hadn't changed my behavior, but it had certainly influenced my thoughts. Standing in the kitchen I was thinking about that particular shade of red in her hair. And how that hair was attached to her head and how that head had produced such wonderful thoughts, like, "Honey, let's get some fish." That one popped out at midnight one night. I thought she wanted some trout for dinner. "Sounds good," I was on the brink of sleep. I came home that next day to a glorious fish tank filled with assorted plants and animals. I'm not sure why that fish tank brought me so much delight, but it did. And whenever I thought about that tank I thought about her bringing it to me and that made me feel so good in a way I had never felt before.

Mary stayed home while I went to work. Yes, the whole housewife trip. Cooking, cleaning, sewing. I used to say to her, "You don't have to do that." She would just smile and say, "Thanks." I had a wonderful home. Smartly decorated. Her urban sophistication showed through in her decorating. Our guests were usually astounded. That house was an enormous source of comfort.

There were days when I was literally numb from work. So much thinking. So much labor. I would arrive at the house and drop into my chair like the gelatinous mass that I was. And she would take my feet in her delicate hands and rub them ever so gently and I would be inside myself. Totally encapsulated. Returned to the womb. I would hear her voice, though. She would be telling me about the plants on the side of the house or the new curtains in the bathroom. That house kept her busy, for a while. When it was all pretty much together she dove into cooking. Again, her worldliness showed through. She was pulling off Thai dishes and the like. Invariably our guests were overwhelmed. Entertaining was our passion. I guess it was more her passion, but it brought me a great deal of satisfaction to see her happy.

Once the domestic thing had played itself out Mary was depressed. Not in a big way. But I could tell. Through the candle light at the dinner table, I looked into her eyes, I didn't see her happiness. That had me worried. She enrolled herself at the community college, though. Shortly, she was back to her happy self. Interpersonal Communications became her major. She had quite a bit of field experience. Her experience earned her praise form her teachers. Her grammar was not so stellar. At night I would review her papers. Some things she was adamant about keeping. They would come back marked incorrect and slowly she began to take my word. She always wanted to know why, though, and that was a challenge for me. I managed to explain things pretty well.

When we retired to the bedroom our teacher/student roles were reversed. I was so enthralled with her that I would follow her hushed directions reverently. I seemed to be making her happy although I often wondered how, considering how often I was gone and how often I was exhausted and how many partners she had had. Thrust into married life. Admittedly by choice, but suddenly to be in your twelfth year of marriage!?!

On a particularly quiet night somewhere between Thanksgiving and Christmas, Mary turned to me with a distant terror.

"Think we'll ever wake up?"

"Huh?" I knew what she was talking about.

"I'm just tripping out," she said through a sigh.

"November 20, 1983," I don't know why I thought of the rain.

"Huh?" She didn't know what I was talking about.

"Where were you on November 20, 1983?" I had to know. She thought. She looked at me and thought again.

"I was in Kansas," she thought I was testing her.

"No, no, really. Where were you? Where was the real Mary?"

"Frank! The real Mary was in Kansas. That other Mary, that other Frank, those are someone else's memories. Mary was in Kansas in 1983." She was intense. Not angry.

"You really hated it didn't you?"

"Yes I did. That's why I left."

"I loved it."

"What?"

"I loved it in New York."

"Why'd you leave?"

"I loved what I had. I hated what I was becoming."

"What you were becoming?"

"Alone."

"I was alone from the start. That's why I hated it."

We looked at each other. It was Frank Teeman looking at Red. We hadn't had a moment like that yet. What to do?

"What happened on November twentieth?" She fell back on to her pillow.

"It rained. It was a glorious rain. Sheets and sheets and bright lightning and loud thunder claps…" I remembered.

"I was in 6B," it was another voice talking. I didn't know what to say. That was something I didn't really want to hear about. "Some fat fuck from Indiana. Drunk. He could barely talk. Most of the time we considered his kind easy work. If you worked it right they'd be passed out before you tricked. Not this one, though. He had his pecker working just fine. Could barley talk, but hard as a rock. And he got on top real quick and started banging away. Fat. God damn smelly fat all over me. I thought he was a passer or a squirt so I wasn't ready yet. At first I felt like I was drowning in blubber…I finally let go. I remember the rain. I could see it pounding against the window and I could hear it whipping the street. I watched the lightning bolt. And the thunder?…It enveloped me. The whole time he was going and going. A giggle would come out like a little boy. He drooled on me. I felt rain. That three hundred pound fat ass wasn't even there."

I watched her through it all. She had really suppressed those memories. They came from deep. I searched for something to say. I couldn't find anything. She sat there for a while, stone faced. I expected a tear. There was none.

"Whew, I hope we never wake up," she broke the tension, "What'd you do on that day?" She even smiled.

"I opened my heart," after a long pause.

"I thought I had a bad day."

"Now, Missus Kunstler, no need to be jaded."

"And why not Mister Kunstler," we giggled.

"Because we'll never wake up," I tried to be serious.

"Never?"

I just shook my head. I knew I couldn't promise that one.

"I love you, Frank."

"I love you, too, Mary."

Oh, to be loved. There is nothing sweeter. I went to the store that next day with a spring in my step, a smile on my face and a good thought for everyone. I counted the last few minutes. Of course Mary wasn't home when I got there. I had forgotten about her Thursday night class. And as I sat in the living room, the bubbling fish tank filling my ear and the TV filling my eye, my mind wandered.

I wandered to that day when Mary and I separated. It was hard to see. Death? Divorce? All I knew was it scared me. It grabbed me by the bones and shook me. So much so, that I held extra tight that night. And I breathed her scent and I felt her skin and her being. I stroked her hair and I kissed her nose. I was filling my slate and remembering. In the morning I watched her eat and when she smiled—it was like a snapshot. The sun behind her. The steam from the coffee, the image was locked. No easel this time. It didn't matter.

As I was scurrying to fill the deposit bag, that night, I caught Bob Brelen smiling at me.

"Got a date," he chided.

"With a peach," I played along.

"You sure do love her, don't you?"

I could see her then. "Yeah. I sure do," I smiled, too.

"You give that peach a kiss for me."

"I certainly will. And you give that peach and peachette a kiss for me."

"Sure will, Boss."

We laughed as I ran past him out the door. Running, like a kid, through the parking lot. Running! So that I could be with her.

Mourn the Passing of a True Artist

Today we mourn the passing of Frank Teeman. When I say we I mean me. I realize that there are those who do not join me. I know there are some who do. Perhaps, this diametric is the most significant aspect of our loss. Mr. Teeman challenged us. He challenged us in an inviting, comforting fashion. Not in a confrontational way. All too often those confrontational challenges are simply too easy to dismiss. Or rather neglect. Consequently the artist never reaches any one new. They are preaching to the choir. When an artist can present challenges in a way that is accessible to those not accustomed to grappling with aesthetics, the full potential of art is realized. Frank Teeman was such an artist.

Frank Teeman's origins are as mysterious as his death. He was adopted by Eleanor and Everett Teeman as an infant, but any traces of his biological parents are nonexistent. Apparently he was abandoned. It is not clear whether he was left with the Teemans or whether they adopted him through an agency. None the less he ended up in the small town of Dilon, in eastern Kansas. His father owned and operated the only grocery store in town and young Franklin led a normal middle America life. He showed promise as an artist early on, winning a prize at the Howard county fair for a painting he did at the age of fourteen. There is mention of a piece being displayed while he was an undergraduate at Kansas State, but until his "discovery" by Irene Solomon in the summer of '86, Mr. Teeman's work was unknown. Following his introduction to the art world by Mrs. Solomon, I wrote a piece about Frank. I was doing an article on the culturalization of the elderly and the subject of his paintings, at that time, were mostly older people. From our first meeting, I can still remember the humility of the man and his surroundings. He was totally involved in his current piece and totally uninvolved with me. At first I took it personally, but I began to realize that it was his nature. He was telling me that he was only doing the interview as a favor to my assistant. Her first assignment with me was to make an appointment with Mr. Teeman. Evidently he was very abrupt with her on the phone when she first called. She came to find that relatively commonplace. Frank was reticent, though, and finally agreed to meet with me. Our interview proceeded in a rather perfunctory manner, all the while he was scrutinizing his painting. Soon enough I found myself fascinated with that painting, too. That abstract turned out to be "Gravity". When he unveiled it on The Tonight Show the whole nation became enthralled with his vision. He had done the same thing to them as he had done to me. By getting out of that chair next to Johnny and walking over to that canvas he not only forced the camera on that image, but he forced the eye on the image, too. He didn't merely stand in front of it. He stood with his back to the camera, looking at his own work as if he had never seen it before. There was an awkward moment there when it was obvious Frank wasn't following the plan, everything is always so staged on TV, and then there was this purely honest moment. It allowed the viewer to open up, to relax, I think, and to look at that image without prejudice. In that mode the viewer is never disappointed with Frank Teeman's work.

It's hard to understand how anyone could disparage Frank Teeman. His detractors are numerous, though. At first they seemed mostly jealous of his mercurial rise. With the commercialization of his art, the purists joined the ranks of the jealous. Then, Mr. Teeman posed some particularly hard questions with his "Two of a Kind", an unflattering view of Christ's crucifixion. He won back many of the purists with that step, but lost more of his loyalists at the same time. Any accusations of pandering had to be put to rest at that point. Why would a panderer take the risk of alienating so many? Still, there were those who thought it a clever media stunt. Those people are now saying that his death is another one of his clever stagings designed to make "an untalented artist famous". With the mysterious disappearance of his remains, perhaps there is some room for speculation as to the where-a-bouts of Frank Teeman. Some of his loyalists have joined the calls of "He's still alive," perhaps they are still in the denial stage of grief. I, for one, can not subscribe to such a theory of duplicitous behavior. Mr. Teeman's pure honesty and simplicity were evident to me. Those traits were what allowed his public persona to be spun in so many different directions. It is true that I contributed to this. I realized I was doing it at the time. It is my job. It is sad that he did not live long enough to weather the storm. Time would have bourn his consistency out. ∎

Zita Anderson didn't pay her bill. Thirty days, forty days…sixty days! I could have written it off. After all thirty-five dollars was hardly worth losing sleep over. It was the chump thing that I couldn't get past. So, I decided to go see her. The address she had given me was in an industrial part of town, but sure enough, there was a house at 411 Lambert. A small, weather beaten cottage standing amongst the concrete behemoths. It looked pretty in comparison. Even though it probably hadn't been painted for ten years. When I knocked I heard the child cry. Zita answered the door reluctantly.

"I know why you're here," she started right in, all the while looking down. "I'll have the money soon." She was a mess—hair all frazzled, clothes old and wrinkled. The kid wailed on.

"May I come in?"

"Watcha wanna come in for?"

"I want to talk about a payment plan."

"Well, start talkin'."

"Don't you want to see to your child?"

"Sandra!" she called over her shoulder, "Shut that kid up," she turned back to me, "That ain't my kid." She was proud. I saw someone go into the kitchen.

"Do you get a welfare check every month?"

"Yeah,"

"How much do you have left over?"

"Left over?"

"After your bills. How much does it leave you to spend?"

"It don't leave me nothin'."

"How do you make ends meet?"

"Mr. Grocery man why you doin this to me?"

"I want to help."

"Well, you could leave me alone. That would help."

"Zitaaa?"

"What!?"

"I'm trying to help."

"By makin' me pay?"

"If you pay you'll have credit at the store," she just looked at me like I was crazy, "and you'll be able to get some food and not pay 'til later."

"Really?" she screamed, but the child's wail had suddenly stopped. I heard her excitement. I saw her thinking about it. "How would that work?"

"Just come in and ask for me or the night manager."

"And you would let me have some food without paying?"

"As soon as you pay this bill."

"Hang on," she went inside and shortly returned with cash. "Thirty five dollars." She held it out. I put my hand on it. "You got a receipt?" I chuckled.

"No. I don't," she pulled it back, "You're right, you're right. I'll write you one. Got a pen and some paper?" She looked at me hard and waived me in with her head. "Thank you."

I was thanking her?

Zita's house was immaculately clean. Not only was it free from dust, it was empty. An old, green, crushed velvet love seat and a black and white TV on a stand were the only encumbrances to a large living room. I followed her into the kitchen, which was also spotless except for an orange that seemed freshly squeezed. Sandra and the wailing kid were strangely absent. Zita laid a piece of paper on the kitchen table and I wrote her a receipt. I handed it to her with a smile and an open hand. She snapped it back and read it thoroughly.

"All right," she admitted finally. I tried to get her to smile. No such luck.

The Johnson's were over for dinner that night. Edith and Mary took up their position in the kitchen. Jeff and Julie were frolicking and Fred and I sat in the living room sipping our beer watching the tube. The wonderful aroma of chicken something-or-other coated my nostrils. I was still thinking about Zita.

"How 'bout those Steelers," Fred pointed at the TV.

"Huh?"

"They just traded Bubby," I was confused, "Football!!" Fred searched for some sign of recognition. There was none. "Not a fan, huh."

"Nope,"

"What do you do, Frank?"

"The grocery store. You know that."

"No. For fun. Got any hobbies."

I had to think. "I like to help people."

"Salvation Army or something?"

"No, just independent," he was confused, "Today I went to see a girl who had been shoplifting in my store."

"Jail?"

"No, I let her go."

"Really?"

"Yeah. Gave her credit for the stuff she took, too."

"What's the logic there?"

"I just figured she was desperate and needed a chance. She didn't pay for the longest time, so I went to see her today and she gave me the money."

"Really? That's great."

"Yeah, it worked out well."

"You don't seem that thrilled."

"I was just thinking about her. She had nothing. Except a child, I guess. Didn't see the kid. The place was so empty."

"You know, our church sponsors needy people."

"Really?"

"Yeah. It's a new thing. It's not charity. You know, we don't give them money. They have to apply and we help them with a project."

"Sounds great."

"It's working out well. We've got this young black girl who's got a kid. Fresh off that crack stuff, anyhow, she's got a job and needs a car, so, we lend her the money. She doesn't have to pay it back, but the car's in the church's name till she does."

"What church is that?"

"First Baptist over there on Elm. You should come to services this Sunday."

"I should." It did sound interesting.

"Great bunch of people. You'd like 'em."

"Dinner, guys," Mary called from the dining room. Jeff said grace and I said, "Amen," at the end. I hadn't done that in a long while. Mary heard me. She was surprised.

We went to services that Sunday. Pretty boring. But the Johnson's introduced us around. There was a definite warmth in that apse. I basked in it. At times I was so busy looking at all the folk that I lost track of the sermon. Afterwards when Joel Tierney called me by name, I smiled. Joel wanted to know if we had any need for carpet cleaning at the grocery store. Of course we didn't. Not a stitch of it anywhere. Still, we talked and exchanged "nice to meet yous". Mary met a woman who ran a beauty salon. On the way home she talked and talked about Evelyn and how cool she was. She was excited and that made me excited.

"Can you believe it? Us! Church goin folks?" Mary giggled as we pulled into the driveway.

"You wanna go next week?"

"Definitely. Did you hear what the pastor said about persevering through the hard times and eventually finding your true self under the lord?"

"No. I missed that."

"It was like he was talking to us," what I had said had finally registered, "Did you fall asleep?" she teased.

"No, my mind just wandered."

"Where do you go when you wander like that?"

"Huh?"

Transcript from Hard Copy
March 11, 1991

Voice Over: Today on Hard Copy -- The mysterious death of Frank Teeman, innocent victim or wily con artist.

Jim Lang : [seated at desk] Frank Teeman made an explosive burst onto the art scene in the spring of 1986 when Irene Solomon, a rich widow, featured his work at the opening of her art gallery in East Hampton, New York. Frank Teeman was an unknown artist at the time and there were plenty who questioned his relationship with this innocent heiress to millions. Now, after a bizarre shooting that supposedly claimed Teeman's life, the doubters have surfaced again. Is this just another scheme in this wily con artist's incredible rise to fame and fortune? We'll have more when we return.

****

JL: You probably know him as the mild mannered artist behind "Mother and Child" the serene portrait that washed over the world in front of Bloomingdale's. Or, perhaps, the shy, introvert, who graced the Tonight Show and touched millions. But from the beginning of his renown, vicious rumors have surrounded this mysterious recluse. Now, with a special report, our Audra Barkley.

Audra Barkley: Thanks Jim. I'm standing on Devonshire Drive on the lower east side of Manhattan in front of number 342, the now famous home of Frank Teeman, the art world's latest rage. You can see the evidence of his fans who have come from all over the world to pay homage to this anti-hero. [pan of graffiti] You can also see signs of those who call Frank Teeman the world's biggest con artist. Back in 1986 when Frank Teeman met Irene Solomon, he was a poor stock boy working at a small grocery store near his dilapidated studio in Manhattan. She was a rich heiress who had come to visit her humble beginnings and find a tax break. Together they turned the art world upside down. After she sold his painting "Glad" for an incredible one hundred fifty thousand dollars the artist and the heiress took center stage.

(cut to montage of background clips)

AB (voice over): On the surface they maintained a professional relationship, but when photos of the two of them, drunk in a limousine, ran in the tabloids, people began to scream. While he managed to keep scoring points with the public, stories of drinking and drugs and wild times began to be heard.

(cut to MCU)

[title: Bill "The Brute" Rogers – Doorman at Tommy's Topless]

"Frank used to come here a lot. He liked the girls all right, but I think he liked the booze better."

(cut to ext.)

AB: Here's Tommy's today, closed down by the hunko squad for running a prostitution ring. One of the dancers here, simply known as Mary, was Frank Teeman's favorite. Her where-a-bouts are unknown. She coincidentally disappeared shortly after Frank.

AB (cont.): Frank Teeman's body was badly burned in the fire that supposedly took his life. The remains were disposed of by the city of New York under a Doe alias because no dental records were available for comparison. Fans say he opted for a simpler life. Others warn against a megalomaniac who would do anything to increase his fame and fortune.

(cut to montage)

AB (voice over): Did Frank Teeman stage his death and run away with his girl? There may be a least one man who knows for sure. Jacsun Pranesh, was the last man to see Frank Teeman. He refused to speak with us. He was a friend and the cab driver who took Frank to the park where he supposedly died. The police have exonerated him from any wrong doing. He has refused communication with the press since his first statement after being released by the police.

(cut to ext.)

AH: Mr. Pranesh now runs tours here at 342 Devonshire. He has made a decent profit off of Mr. Teeman's legacy prompting accusations of his complicity. Teeman's work continues to sell at high prices and his memorabilia at high volume despite the chorus of boos. Definitive proof of his existence has an equally high price tag. None has surfaced as yet. Is this mysterious character alive and well or is he simply another myth of mass media?

(cut to int. studio)

JL: Thank you, Audra. I'm sure we'll be hearing more about this bizarre tale in the future.

Johnny and Jack set us up pretty well. The house, the car, the basic furnishings, the bank account, the credit…Yup, we were all set for our new life as consumers. The only problem was that we didn't know how to do it. Granted it's an easy thing to do—you see something that you like and you plunk down the money and you walk out with it. That's what I thought, anyways. I didn't realize it would be so difficult to find something that I liked and of course many of those things had to be something we liked.

Well, we knew that we didn't like the couch that had been provided. So, that was our first shopping experience. We went to an all sofa store and to a discount furniture warehouse and, of course, Sears. Nothing. I mean, they all had couches, but nothing that really grabbed me—us. We looked through catalogs and Mary got some magazines and we tried to figure out what we wanted. When we finally had that figured out, we went back out on the hunt; Fromme's Home Furnishings downtown, Ethan Allen, back to the Sofa Factory. I was starting to like the one we had more and more. It was an awful orange tapestry type thing, but it was comfortable, I mean, I had fallen asleep on it. "So, let's get the thing covered," that's what I said one day. Then we started looking through books of material. There it was. Some kind of bluish, purplish, crushed velvet. Yes, we agreed, that was it. Call the upholsterer! "Sure [he] could get it. [He'd] have to order it, though." Damn that shit is expensive. That's about the price we were going to pay for a new one. And the upholsterer's not sure this material will work so well on that frame. And besides that frame is hardly worth covering with anything, let alone something so nice.

"Let's get a new couch." Mary had said one day.

"OK." I figured we'd come home with it that day.

Here it is three weeks later and nothing.

The couch was a tough one. There were plenty of things that spending came easy for. You know, all the bills and the property tax and the food. When you first get a house there are plenty of expenses. Shower curtain, lawn mower—a myriad of "essentials". I never put much effort into shopping for those items. I wasn't good at it. I bought the first lawn mower I saw. It worked, great. I did feel a little pang when I saw a comparable mower for considerably less. I had paid for quality. I kept telling myself that.

Once I took over the store there wasn't much time for shopping. Or much desire. Unfortunately my lack of shopping knowledge was a detriment to my selling abilities, too. Fortunately, for me, groceries are not as much a subject to the whims of consumers. Still, the balance sheet was not looking fabulous and our initial nest egg was dwindling. When we decided to get another car I needed to get a good deal.

I went to the lots to find a used car. Probably a mistake. I figured I could handle it, though. All it takes is intelligence, right? I had $4,000. That's it. No more. How could I go wrong? I had underestimated the power of the automobile. I had never had one before and even though Johnny had set us up with a nice Pontiac it never really did much for me. Mary drove it most of the time. After all, I had to learn. By the time I was comfortable enough behind the wheel it had become Mary's car. Consequently, I never felt that attachment between a car and it's owner. Mary was getting tired of taking me to work every time she needed the car so, she sent me out to get my own. I was reticent. She couldn't understand. She loved her car.

"Get your own car! It'll be good for you," she counseled.

Good for me? I didn't understand.

Thompson's Toyota was a large lot on Grand Avenue. I passed it every day on the way to work. They had used cars, I saw the sign, so I stopped there first. They had a bunch of used cars. I was standing in the lot looking up the row of assorted colors, that's all they were to me at that time, just a bunch of colors.

"Good afternoon," a bright voice came from behind me. I turned to find a man in a polyester suit. "Bob Bradley," he smiled and extended his hand, "Looking for a used car?"

"Yeah, Bob, that's why I'm here," we laughed. My heart raced. I was swimming with sharks. Fred had warned me and sure enough here I was. Don't let him know how scared I was.

"Well, let me know if you see anything that you like," he was still smiling.

"Will do," I smiled back and turned to continue looking. I couldn't focus on the cars, though. What was Bob doing? I looked over my shoulder to find him gone. Well, this wasn't so bad. Let's see what they have here.

A blue Toyota two door? Too small. A green Ford LTD? Too big. Too ugly. Another small one. HELLO! What is this? A red Camaro. This, I like. Sporty, but still not too small. That shade of red is fabulous. Body's in good shape. Interior looks all right. What's the price? $5,795.00! Ouch.

"It's a beauty isn't it?" Bob popped up.

"Yeah," I was hesitant. I didn't have the money.

"Want to take it for a spin?"

"Sure," Bob opened the door for me. I plopped into the leather bucket seat. Wow. The engine roared when I started it and we took off with just a touch of the pedal.

"Take it easy! This 386 puts out a hundred eighty horse!"
I smiled. The speedometer flowed up to fifty. We were on a cloud. I took my first corner. What a dream. So effortless. The tires spun a little on the way out. What power. Bob was listing all the specs. I didn't really know what any of it meant. It sounded great. "Anti-sway bars." I liked that one best.

Once we got back to the lot I just sat there. It was so comfortable and the angle of the windshield and the layout of the dash, the feel of the big knob of the shifter. Yes, this was a car.

"Well, I can tell you like it," Bob was smiling, too, "Can we do business?"

"I do like it, Bob, but I've only got four thousand."

"C'mon into my office. I'll talk to my manager. I'm sure we can work something out."

I sat in that office forever while Bob checked with his manager. 4,000. That's it. I kept telling myself that. He came back with a smile and a little slip of paper.

"This is as low as we can go," he handed me the slip. $4, 700 it said.

"I told you I've only got four thousand," I was proud of myself.

"We can finance the balance," he handed me a credit application, "Go ahead and fill this out and I'll put some figures together for you."

"What's another seven hundred dollars," I thought. I wanted that car. I scrawled the application. I tried to bargain. Tax? Licenses? Warranty?

As I lay in bed that night, the red Camaro in the drive, I couldn't sleep. I was too upset. How did I agree to $5,700?

The green grass of the other side is filling Frank's nostrils with the scent of joy. But, as is so often the case, new life is sprouting on the side he's standing on. What is that strange mechanism in man that fills him with unrepentant desire? A force so strong it can make life changes that seem impossible to the conscious mind? A longing that occupies your thoughts and derails your train in an instant. It is the curse of imagination.

Dan was a musician. A talented musician. When his band rehearsed he always started the songwriting. He could whip off interesting bass lines in a second. His band, The Ravens, couldn't get a gig in Modesto. They didn't play cover tunes. Their parties soon became the rage, though. So much so, that the clubs opened their doors to them. Still, it was those private parties that packed 'em in. Five years of that had made The Ravens stars. They kept crankin' out the Rock 'n Roll. Dan had discovered other types of music—funk, R&B, baroque. The Ravens didn't play that stuff. They did Rock 'n Roll and it was fun. Lots of fun.

I met Dan in Santa Barbara. He wasn't playing music anymore. He worked as a Telemarketer. In Modesto he had gotten involved with his roommate/meth dealer's ex-girlfriend. Dan did a lot of crystal meth, then. A lot of cocaine, heroin, too. It was fun. Lots of fun. Anyhow, his meth dealer didn't take kindly to Dan's attachment to his ex so he had someone beat on Dan's head with a lead pipe. Took all his stuff, too. Dan came to Santa Barbara as a fugitive. He stayed off that stuff for quite a while, too.

One day I ran into Dan on the street.

"I am never going back to Modesto," he said with as much conviction as I've ever heard. I was confused. "I just got back from there and it is the worst."

"Why'd you go back?" I was still confused.

"I had an idea for a new tune and..."

"Yeah, right," I wasn't buying.

"Well, that was the initial reason. But as soon as I got back I started in on that junk. I swore that I wouldn't. But, I did. Next thing I know I was broke and homeless. I got in a fight with that dealer. I was miserable. But high. So, it was all right. Until Joe Baker rigged up. Joe never used. The small town finally caught up with him. That's when I knew I had to leave."

"How'd you escape?"

"This guy gave me forty bucks to go to the grocery store. I went to the bus station."

"Good thinking," I said trying to chuckle.

"Not a lot of thought involved." He looked down.

"Animal instinct?" I felt cold.

"Survival instinct."

I know it's been said before, but I'm going to say it again—The creative tool that rescued our kind from that primitive state is probably our single biggest curse as well. That's why life is so tough. You have to fight fire with fire. And every time there is the attendant risk of the opposing fires joining forces and obliterating their masters.

With risk comes uncertainty.

With uncertainty—fear.

Uh-oh.

PART II

▼

I started off '92 with the flu. I guess I should have taken it as a sign of things to come. It didn't cross my mind then. I just laid in bed wondering if I would ever get well.

"This is it," I muttered to Mary, delirious with fever.

"Huh?"

"This is the big one." I was sure I was dying. Maybe I hoped that I would die. I was so uncomfortable.

"Don't be silly," Mary patronized. Maybe she was scared. It just pissed me off.

"You'd like to see me go," I was half serious.

"Get some sleep, Frank," she patted my brow with a damp cloth. Oh, so soothing.

"Jack put you up to this didn't he?" I teased.

"He certainly did," with that patronizing tone.

"Lucifer!" I shouted, "and you're his agent," I mellowed, "Oh, so pretty." I focused on her. It was an effort. "You are so very pretty," I touched her hair. A tingle went up my spine. A smile came to my face.

My fever broke shortly after that. I fell asleep and when I woke I could feel the difference. Still, I was exhausted. I lay in that bed and watched the clock. I wasn't sure if I had died, or what, so I watched that digital clock.—9:16—I figured if I were dead it wouldn't change. And it still didn't change. Certainly a minute had gone by! Why wouldn't that damn thing change?—9:17—I was alive and I was glad to be alive. I closed my eyes and listened to my heartbeat. A wondrous sound. And then the wind pressed against the window and the rustling of the trees. Yes, I was alive and it was a good thing.

I sat in my Lay-z-boy watching the neon tetras. They were my favorite fish. Maybe it was the wide eye. Maybe that fantastic streak of colors. Mary liked the angelfish. The tetras seemed less afraid to me. And when those flakes hit the water, they'd come right up to the surface and get some food! So, I'm sitting there watching them, waiting for Mary to return, and for a moment there, I actually felt bored. The store could run itself. My sick leave proved that. The house was assembled. We hadn't made an improvement in months. "Maybe it was time for me to take up a hobby." That's what I thought to myself sitting there zoning on the tetras. "What would I like to do?" I asked myself between sips of beer. When I answered "paint" it took me by surprise. Mary walked in just then and I jumped up to greet her. When I closed my eyes during our embrace, that image of her sitting at the table, smiling, steam rising from her coffee, sunlight behind her head, appeared. It left me cold.

"Mister grocery man," Zita called up to me from the floor. I could tell she was wasted from the sound. The sight made it apparent.
"Hello Zita," I dreaded this.
"I need some food for my baby."
"Got any money?"
"No. I ain't got no damn money."
"No money, no food."
"Why you doin' this to me?"
"What am I doin' to you?"
"You teasin' me."
"Zitaaa…"
"You said I could get food with out payin'!"
"Not until you make a payment."
"I need some food for my baby. He sick."

"Go by the Baptist church on Elm. They'll help."

"Fuck you. I ain't goin' to no Jesus asylum." She stormed out. I just kept counting the money. Head down. Cold.

"Hang in there, boss," Elijah gave me the thumbs up. I smiled back at him. I was still sad.

"Eternity for the damned..." Reverend Jones was prattling on. I sat there in that pew waiting for something to come to me. Mary sat next to me riveted. I just couldn't care. I had lost that feeling of community I had once felt in that church and now was attending just out of obligation to her. I looked around and saw those images of Christ. I was bored. Same old thing—poorly rendered, too. When I closed my eyes the energy came. Oh, it had been so long. The newness was beautiful. After I got past the newness I realized that the energy itself was cold. These people are afraid.

I opened my eyes. What did I see? I didn't see fear. I saw stoic, complacency. Joel Tierney was facing the pulpit. His eyes were open. He wasn't looking at anything. Edith Johnson? She was right down the aisle. She seemed to be paying attention. Still, she was afraid.

"Those who accept Jesus into their heart..." more prattle. I couldn't accept Jesus into my heart. I had tried. I thought I had tried. I wanted to accept Jesus into my heart. He wouldn't come! Fred Johnson was facing the pulpit. He was hanging on every word. When Reverend Jones' voice would rise, Fred's eyes would open wider. When the reverend was hushed, Fred looked asleep.

"That was a fantastic sermon," Mary broke the silence on the ride home.

"Huh?" I was watching a snowball fight.

"I really liked the sermon," she was earnest.

"I didn't follow it."

"Why do you come anyway," she was angry.

"I like..." I was fishing.

"Aren't you afraid?"

"Huh?"

"Don't you feel fear?"

"Well…"

"I'm afraid. I'm afraid that I will be damned to eternal anguish."

"Where does that come from?"

"I have been eternally anguished and I'm afraid it will never stop. Not even in death. I probably would've killed myself if I didn't think I would be eternally damned."

"The church makes you feel better?"

"Yeah, it sure does," she almost sounded surprised.

We traveled the rest of the way home in silence. I kept thinking that she was trying to tell me something. I was afraid of what it was, though. I mean, I guess I didn't make her happy. At least I didn't take away that anguish she spoke of. I thought I had done that for her. I hadn't tried that hard, though. I wanted to do that for her. She turned off the car in the driveway. I could see the fear in her eyes. I reached out to touch her. She didn't respond. I stroked her hair. She turned sadder. I put both arms around her and squeezed.

"Thank you, Frank," she whispered.

Excerpted from --
Running With the Devil
by Desiree Montano

Frank Teeman is capable of anything. He didn't seem so dastardly at first. It was precisely that unassuming, little boy, look that gave him that ability. He led you in. You began to trust him. That's when he had you. He did that to me. He did that to the whole world!

We were at a party together. That happened every weekend. It was a typical New York style party. Lots of dancers, lots of freaks, and cocaine in large amounts. Frank always kept up the pretense of not liking cocaine, but he always seemed to find it at those parties. We were always locked away in those back rooms, ignoring others and indulging ourselves. This night's party was at Jungle Jim's. His exploits at The Bend were legendary. His warehouse flat was enormous. We were in a bedroom, as usual. The volume was still pervasive. He had all the lights and a particularly powerful sound system. The thump of the bass rattled that bedroom loudly. It made the floor seem liquid. My already drunken knees had a hard time maintaining balance on that sea of low end vibrations.

As was also usual, people in that room recognized Frank. It always took a while, but one art enthusiast would recognize him and I could see the word pass around the room. And like that party game, the people at the end of the line would turn and look at Frank as if some one had just whispered "That's God over there." So, the eyes were on us, all waiting for something spectacular. Frank never did say or do anything spectacular. It was part of his act. This particular night, as was usual, one brave (or stupid) individual finally piped up with, "Aren't you Frank Teeman?" Frank always smiled at these times. Smiled and looked down and nodded ever so slightly. Then the questions would begin.

"Tell us what you're working on."

I snorted a big line then and a huge surge of bass guitar from the stereo swept me off my feet. I went crashing against a dresser and ended up on the floor, pinched between the furniture, my skirt up around my shoulders, my naked legs jutting out into the room. Everyone went silent then. Frank started laughing. He started roaring with laughter and every one joined in. He grabbed my ankle and dragged me out from between the furniture, my head bumping the whole way. A couple of his admirers helped me to my feet while he tried to collect himself.

"That will be my next work," he proclaimed through giggles, "Look out! Gravity in effect!" The whole room burst out.

I was hurt that night. Still, I got over it. It probably was pretty funny. What wasn't funny was that he went through with it! "Gravity" he called it. It was an abstract thing. Every time I looked at it I knew that he had immortalized my gaff. Frank did have a cruel side.

I took a deep breath. I had to summon the strength. Sitting in that little booth, overlooking that little store, doing the same little tasks, one more time! I took a deep breath. One, two, three, four, five,…One hundred thirty eight in ones! One, two, three, four, five, six,…Three hundred ninety five in fives. One, two, three, four, five, six, seven,…Five hundred ten in tens. Who cares!?! I'll only deposit it so that my creditors can have it. Damn that Eastern Supply. Always changing their prices. I can never keep 'em straight. How am I supposed to make a profit if I don't know my overhead? How am I supposed to make a profit indeed?

"I got a thirty seven on four," the PA rang out.

Damn that register four. It's on it's last legs. Why do we keep using it? Hustle down there. Oops, forgot the key ring. Bob keeps telling me to get a caddy. Gotta keep the customer happy. Yup, that same old jam in the paper feed. "There you go Joy."

"Mr. Kunstler," Frieda the bag girl called, "Broken pickles!"

Damn those pickles! I gotta find a better place for those things. Mop that stuff up. "Thanks Elijah," always so helpful. There's that white spot from the vinegar. Huh? De ja vu.

Ok, back to the paperwork. Count the money? Fill out the form? I took a deep breath.

Why did I want to do this? I mean, I didn't just choose this. I wanted to do this. Desperately! What was I thinking?

"Hi, honey," Mary called from the floor.

What was she doing here? She never stopped by. Not in a long time, anyway.

"Hey," I rushed down to meet her, "What's up?"

"I was just in the neighborhood," we kissed.

"It's great to see you," I was surprised to find my heart racing ever so slightly.

"Business seems good," she looked around.

"Yeah, not bad." No eye contact? She sighed. "What's up?"

She took a deep breath. "I crashed the car."

"What?"

"Totaled," she choked out, a tear running down.

"Are you all right?" I hugged her. Stroked her hair.

"Mmhm." She was crying.

"Anyone hurt?" I could feel her lungs grabbing air, desperately.

"A little boy. He's in the hospital," her face pressed against my chest.

"Oh, Mary," I hated the pity in my voice, "C'mon up to the office and tell me about it," my heart was in my throat.

It turned out that Mary had hit some ice, spun around banging both front and rear ends, and ended up rear-ending a car waiting at an intersection. The boy was in the front seat with no seat belt. He had banged his head and was in for observation. Our Pontiac was totaled.

She sat there in that office, pouting and waiting for me to finish up so that I could take her to the hospital to see that boy. She was in no condition to drive. Unfortunately, I had a lot of things to do so; she was there for a while. Every time I stopped by to check on her my heart sank. The shipment of baked goods arrived and I had a talk with the driver about all those squished hot dog rolls that managed to make it on the shelf. Then there was the issue of the invoice from three weeks ago.

"I'm just doin' my job," he said defiantly, "If you gotta problem with the paper work you gotta call the office."

"I did call the office and they said talk with you."

"What do you want me to do?"

"Just make the correction."

"I can't do that."

"Why not?"

"It'll come out of my pocket."

"Your office said that if it was an error it could be worked out."

"Really?"

"Really. Now, you and I know that you didn't deliver 222 sour dough flutes to this store," I pointed to the invoice.

He looked at it long and hard. "That ain't right," he conceded.

Now that I had that worked out maybe I could get away.

"I got a thirty seven on four," the PA rang out. Damn that number four.

"Joy, we're going to have to move you over to number six."

"I hate number six," she whined.

"Well, that's tough," I snapped. She looked at me like I had actually hit her. "What is so bad about number six?" I tried to be sympathetic.

"It's too close to the door. My hands get cold."

"Do you have a pair of gloves?"

"Sure."

"Why don't you wear them?"

"Really?"

"Really."

"All right."

Mary was hunched over in her chair. Sadness was everywhere. It brought me down. I took a deep breath. There was a tightness in my chest that bordered on pain. Mary was so sad it affected me? I just wanted to grab her and hug her and make every thing all right.

"Let's go," I interrupted her daydream. When she looked up I could see the dread. She didn't really want to go. Time ground to an excruciating halt, then. I held out my hand and she put hers in mine. I could feel her skin. Every little ridge. The scar on her forefinger. The slight callous on her palm. The moisture of her sweat. The heat of her tension. The softness, the frailty. She gripped my hand and I inhaled and I saw her begin to rise. Th, thump. Th, thump. My heart was knocking. I was in love.

"Hey boss." Bob Brelan popped up. "Mary!" His electric smile. And on his arm sat his little Petunia.

"Bob," I smiled. I didn't want him to sense the sadness.

"Hi, Bob," even Mary smiled. It didn't matter. He could tell that he had interrupted. He looked down. "Petunia-a-a," Mary dropped into her little girl's voice. She held out her finger and Petunia grabbed it. She smiled and the smile of that infant lifted the weight of the moment out of the place. Soon we were all laughing and playing. Bob handed his little girl over to my big girl and they both forgot about us.

"I hope I'm not interrupting anything," Bob whispered to me.

"Nooo," I scrunched up my face and waved my hand, "Mary was just in a crash and she's pretty blue."

"Damn, that's too bad."

"What are you doin' here?"

"Just thought I'd stop by and show off my precious."

"She is a darling," I looked at her and saw life.

"Light of my life."

"You are a lucky man," I was jealous.

"God blesses me," he was reverent, "God could bless you, too."

"Please."

"What? You never gonna have kids?"

"It's just so much."

"Well, when you're in the middle of it, you deal. You can't hardly ever see the big picture, you can't even see the medium picture. You just wake up cause she's crying and you just follow her around 'til she falls asleep. I ain't saying it's easy. It has a strange way of workin' itself out."

Mary looked up at me then.

She knew what I was thinking.

I tried to hide it.

I couldn't.

She looked away.

St. Louis American
4242 Lindell Bl.
St. Louis, MO 63108

To the editor:
Your recent articles about Frank Teeman have prompted me to
respond. The departure of Frank Teeman has really made me
wonder. I can't help but think that this man's life stands
as a great metaphor. I say "stands" and "departure"
intentionally. You see, I met Frank Teeman. My wife and
he grew up together so, when he was in St. Louis in the
fall of '89 we had him over for dinner. As most would
guess, he was a very likable, very quiet guy. As we ate
dinner he seemed like a tourist. He just seemed unused to
the whole experience. His eyes were wide and every now and
then a huge smile would burst onto his face, delighted with
the gravy boat, or my two young girls playing. After
dinner I got a chance to talk with him privately. I have
to admit I was in awe. His reputation had preceded him. I
was a fan. At one time I had aspirations of being an
artist, but I had settled into middle America before any of
that could happen. I was telling him that when he
earnestly asked, "Wanna swap lives?"
Frank was not happy when I met him. He envied me my wife
and kids and my mortgage and my job. We stood out on my
back porch comparing our wish lists and they were
completely opposite. I envied him his fame and his fortune
and his freedom. I was not happy when Frank met me. It
was when we both realized this that the silence fell, there
that night. We were smoking a little pot, the universal
salve for disenchantment sores. He exhaled a big cloud of
smoke and let out, almost as effortlessly, "Never
satisfied."
"What's that?" I wasn't paying attention.
"Listen to us! Leading charmed lives and not satisfied."

"Yeah," I chuckled.
I went back into the house that night and put my arm around
my wife and felt our love anew. And the next morning when
our kids woke us with their youthful clatter, I liked it.
I loved it! After Frank's visit, every time I would feel
the rut or look longingly over the fence, I would hear him
and I would be reminded to appreciate what I did have.
I had hoped that Frank had found solace in his life, like I
had in mine. When, I first heard about the fiery explosion
in Central Park that took Frank's life, I was tremendously
saddened. I know that he had a lot to offer and hadn't

given much of it. The waste of potential was sad to me.
When I heard of his last tormented months I was depressed.
Why couldn't his wisdom have lightened his load like it had
mine? Reports of his existence soon crept in and I began
to wonder. Had he found a way to "swap lives"?
Frank pursued his dream and it had worked out nicely for
him yet he was not happy. What would you do if your dream
came true and it turned out to be a nightmare? Some might
be tempted to escape through suicide or drug induced
obliviousness. Unfortunately, we hear those stories all
the time. Although it's not glamorous and it's not
lucrative, there is a tremendous amount of happiness that
can only be gotten through family. You hear the voices
calling for "traditional family values," where are the
role models? Cosby or any of those other TV families?
Hardly. Unfortunately, those who call for "traditional
family values" are also the ones who seem to think that TV
and other forms of fiction have some kind of impact on
people's way of thinking. That's bunk. All those forms of
mass media are too removed from the reality that those of
us in day to day America experience. To have an impact on
us, there needs to be real role models and real stories
about real people. Frank Teeman's story is just one of
those stories. I'm certain that he has transformed his
"ideal" existence into one of true happiness.
Frank, if you are out there, and I believe that you are,
you should find a way to share your experience. You had
achieved the American dream. The supposed bliss associated
with fame and fortune, such as yours, is often touted as
the brass ring of this country's carousel. You know that
it's not. You pulled that ring and found it was made of
tin, didn't you?

Chuck Winger
St. Louis, MO

She slept next to me so silently. I tried to cuddle but she denied. I guess it was inevitable, those nights when she wasn't in the mood. This was the first, though. That made it hard.

Breathe in. Breathe out. I could see her chest expand with air. I wanted to touch her. I wanted her to touch me. I didn't care if our genitals touched. It wasn't a sex thing. Somehow, through touching, the pain was ameliorated. Mary had described it as fear. I felt it as pain. Not pain in the literal sense of that feeling, that hurting feeling that comes from your cells. More of the thought of pain like when you think about that hurting feeling. When I try to imagine what it feels like to get your finger cut off, I don't feel pain in my hand, but there is a murkiness that overcomes my mind and I wince and my stomach curls. That's the pain I was feeling that night. That's the pain I felt every night. Every night? Every night. But when she touches me, I'm soothed. When her hand touches my shoulder and caresses my back my eyes relax my stomach unfolds. I can see clearly!

Mary couldn't do that for me that night. She was exhausted. Life had worked her. That little boy being injured was more than she could bear. He was fine. We went to the hospital and they said he was fine. Mary had brought him a stuffed bear and he laughed. That saved her. If he had been seriously injured she might have died. Not physically, but emotionally. Now, she was just exhausted. So, I sat awake, jonesing for a fix. A fix of love. The stars outside my bedroom window beckoned me, that night. I stood from my bed with fright and approached the window slowly. I could see the trees rustle ever so slightly with the passing wind. A crescent moon lit a small cloud. I watched it etch its way across the night sky first obscuring a particularly bright star, then revealing its beautiful white light. A gust of wind pressed against the glass. I felt it caress my thigh through my flannel pajamas.

She tossed and mumbled. I turned to see her naked breast peeking out through her gown. That dark circle perfectly topping her soft suppleness, that crescent moon casting its spotlight. I smiled. It seemed that she did, too. But when she rolled over and dropped into darkness, I was alone again.

I strolled through the house, the silence overwhelming me. In the living room the gurgling of the fish tank was deafening. I switched on its light. The neons darting everywhere. The angelfish drifting effortlessly by. The guppy giving birth!?! Yes, those were tiny little guppies appearing from the womb. Thrashing their little tails. Getting no where. Mom turns and gulps. Suddenly they are eaten! I switched off the light.

There, in that dark, I remembered. I remembered the freedom I had felt during those days in New York. Even through the worst of the puking after the drinking binges, and the umpteenth ramen dinner in a row, there was a certain lightness. Life was a river that I was riding. Sure it dunked me occasionally, but that was refreshing in a way. I stood there in my living room, that night, and I felt dry, and heavy. I wasn't in the river any more. The dryness was palpable. The weight unbearable. I rubbed my fingers together and licked my lips and I yearned to be drenched and floated again. It's not surprising, then, that that paper and pencil seized me. There it was on the dining room table; a piece of notebook paper and a number two pencil - - - - ->

Mary always signed her notes with that smiley face.

That crescent moon was projecting its spotlight on that piece of paper. I grabbed the pencil and started to draw. I drew late into the night. Mary woke me at the usual time. I peeled my eyes open and moaned.

Honey,
I'll be late tonight.
Got a test

¨‿

"What's wrong?" She was scared. She remembered my illness, still.

"I couldn't sleep last night," my phlegm covered voice eked out.

"I slept fine," she sounded surprised.

"I know," I smiled.

"Sorry," she smiled at me and that was enough energy. I jumped out of bed and felt remarkably well, considering.

"How ya doin'" I tried to cuddle. She denied.

"I'm all right," not very convincing.

"Pretty scary, huh?"

"I'll say," through a big sigh.

"Mary," I caught her eye, "let's have a child." I surprised myself with that. It wasn't premeditated. It just jumped out.

"What?" the terror was obvious. I just smiled. "You're serious." I nodded. "God, I can't tell you how that just made me feel."

"You looked scared."

"Well, sure, but, at the same time it just threw me into a…a warmth. That's got to be the nicest thing that's ever happened to me," it almost seemed like she was going to cry.

"So, is that a yes?" I was feeling that warmth myself. I thought my face would burst from the grin.

"It's not that easy, Frank."

"I know."

"No, you don't." She looked down. The heaviness fell. "I don't think I can."

"I know it seems like a lot," she shook her head, "but we can do it." She looked up at me with those sad eyes. The same ones I had seen the day before at the store.

"I don't think I can," that scratchy voice that precedes tears.

"?"

"Frank, I had several abortions when I was…"

Her voice had changed for me. I had forgotten about that Mary. Suddenly, I saw the wrinkles in her face. I didn't quite grasp what she was getting at.

"My plumbing's all fucked up," she ran away. I sat down on the bed. The heaviness pulled me down on to the bed. My lack of sleep went straight to my head. But when I heard her sob, I ran to her side.

"Mary, I'm so sorry. I didn't know." I had said the words, though, and now the idea was intractable. "How bad is it? Let's have it checked out."

"You don't understand," she laid face first on the couch and cried. I stroked her hair and stared blankly. I was beginning to understand.

Passing your seed is the most basal instinct. I never really thought about it outside of the context of why men are so horny. Now, confronted with the real idea of not being able to do it, I was devastated. For the longest time the thought of having a child was the most terrifying one in the book. The responsibility…the cost…all those years…all that work. Then to suddenly find the inspiration to dive into that morass, it's like…it's not like anything I felt before. I felt whole for the first time in my life when I uttered those words. And now emptiness has taken on a new dimension. Missing part of an incomplete is nothing compared to a hole in the whole.

An empty shell of a man walks out to his Camaro. Sitting behind that incredible engine, encapsulated in all that glass and steel, there is nothing. A bag full of salt water. Squish, squish, the bag makes it's way, amoeba like, to it's job. Plop in the chair.

"Why can't I be a normal man?"

I closed my eyes. I saw Mary's naked breast under the crescent moon. What a pleasant image. The stars in the sky and me standing at the foot of that enormous tit praying. Kneeling and praying. The image was set. Where was my easel? I tried to forget. Just count the money. Get those drawers full. One, two, three, four,…twenty ones. One, two, three, four, five,…ten fives. One, two, three, four, five, six…ten tens. Boy was I tense. Two rolls of quarters, a roll of dimes, one of nickels, two rolls of pennies. There! Whew! One drawer done. Wait a minute I forgot the twenties.

"Elijah!" I called out over the PA. He popped up shortly. "Can you count the drawers?"

"Sure. I was pricing peas."

"OK, well, do this first. I've got to take care of something."

I made my way back to the stock room in a panic. I could barely breathe. Yes! There it was. The butcher paper, the brush, the red paint. I set out a sheet on the floor in front of me, opened the can…the glistening of the red. Mmmm…the pure liquidity dripping from the brush. I sat amazed as those red streaks transformed that stark whiteness. What was it, though? I thought the image had been set. This wasn't what I had seen. Was that my hand pushing the brush? It was. Ah yes; now I could see. The wavy streaks, that square chin, the button nose. It was Mary! I do love her so. I had almost forgotten.

JJ: Now Joining us is **Mary Everett.** Mary was a friend of Frank Teeman's and some of you might recognize her as the subject of his tremendously popular painting "Mother and Child." Thank you for joining us Mary.

ME: Thank you.

JJ: How did you come to know Frank?

ME: I'm a social worker and one of my clients had been murdered. She was an elderly lady, . . . anyhow, Frank's name and address were among her affects so, I paid him a visit to see if he could tell me anything.

JJ: What were your first impressions?

ME: He struck me as a very nice guy. He was obviously moved when I told him about Gladys' death.

JJ: Gladys was the elderly woman?

ME: Yes. He pulled out a painting of her. He paid her to sit for him. He called that painting Glad. It made me cry. I remember he hugged me and it was so refreshing.

JJ: Was that the same "Glad" that he sold for one hundred fifty thousand dollars?

ME: Yes, only he sold it for seven hundred. Irene Solomon sold it for a hundred and fifty thousand.

JJ: Did you see him after that first time?

ME: Oh yes. We dated off and on for quite a while.

JJ: What was a typical date like with Frank?

ME: He was always a perfect gentleman; opening doors and holding chairs. I always felt very relaxed with him. There was never any pressure.

JJ: What happened?

ME: Excuse me?

JJ: He sounds like a nice guy; tender, artistic, gentlemanly . . . Why didn't things work out?

ME: I asked myself that when he asked me to marry him.

JJ: When was that ?

ME: It was a beautiful, warm spring day and he asked me to meet him at a deli nearby work. We had met there quite a few times. He was so excited. Irene had just bought her first painting. I don't think he even believed it himself, when he said it.

JJ: What did he say?

ME: Will you marry me? (Laughter)

JJ: What did you say?

ME: I had to say no.

JJ: Why?

ME: It just wasn't there for me.

JJ: No romance?

ME: Nope. No romance.

JJ: Did you see him after that?

ME: Oh sure. He invited me to his first opening, he visited several times, he was at my daughter's third birthday party . . .

JJ: When was the last time you saw him?

ME: He came to visit me about a week before his death.

JJ: What happened then?

ME: Oh, not much really. We spent a lot of time playing with Terra, my daughter. He seemed very happy. Really very happy. I asked him about the unveiling . . .

JJ: Two of a kind?

ME: Yes

JJ: You were at the community center that day?

ME: Yes

JJ: Could you describe what happened that day for our viewers who might not know.

ME: A large crowd had showed up at the lower east side community center to see the unveiling of Frank's new painting. It was really quite strange. I mean, all those people to see one painting. Frank was on a stage with a couple of other people and he pulled the drape to reveal his "Two of a Kind".

JJ: How would you describe that painting?

ME: Intense. Particularly compared to his other work.

JJ: So what happened at the unveiling.

ME: People started pushing forward to get a better look and the whole place was abuzz with chatter. I was looking at the painting and Frank just snatched it off the easel and ran out the back door.

JJ: What did Frank say when you asked him about that night?

ME: At first he just thought. And then he became serious and he looked at me with these eyes. Eyes like I had never seen on Frank. And then he said, "Mary, I just couldn't stand to see it scorned." And then he smiled and we started playing with Terra again.

JJ: Do you miss him?

ME: I certainly do. He brought something to my life that will be hard to replace.

JJ: When we return, we'll talk to Mary about all the rumors surrounding Frank's death and we'll open up for your questions. Please stay tuned.

Life is hard. Here I thought I was solving all the difficulties. Maybe I was sticking my head in the sand. I thought it would be easier that way. I guess what it really comes down to is that once the Kunstler slate was filled the extrapolation process began. Once that started the images appeared. The offspring one was the hardest. It wouldn't leave me. I tried to forget about it, but there it was, everywhere. At the gas station a young blonde girl gazing dreamily into a baby's eyes. And the look on her face. At the K-Mart a middle age man holding the hand of his twelve year old daughter.

"Honey, we'll be done soon." The girl fidgeting impatiently.

On the street where I live. Every other home dotted with squealing voices of delight with life. The grocery store—a din of youth interacting vivaciously with their parents. And then there's me.

"What about adoption?" I tossed out to Mary one day. She could sense my lack of enthusiasm.

"Frank, please don't do this."

"Do what?"

"Put us through this."

I stopped. We stopped.

After a long pause Father Jones intones solemnly, "Friends, I don't need to tell you of the crisis facing the religious community today. We need to talk about it, though. I'm referring to the proliferation of abortion clinics through out this country and particularly here, in our home town." I felt the collar on my neck then, the tie cinching it tight. Why did I put myself through this every Sunday? Where else could I see and feel the real action? When Father Jones mentioned abortion every one sat up and listened. This was something that they knew about. The details of gestation had been scrawled over every rag in sight. Yes, it is against the lord's plans; the taking of a gift from above. Did we really have to do something about it?

"It is up to us to protect those children of the lord who can not protect themselves," Father Jones demanded. Oh great, another group to sign up for. Or rather, not to sign up for.

I headed for the door at the conclusion of the service just like always. Waving. Smiling. Mary headed for the sign-up sheet this time. I waited for her outside. What was she thinking? If abortion was a sin then she was damned to hell.

Ah yes, Eternal damnation.

She appeared, shortly, with a group of women all obviously very excited about something. As they approached I could hear. They were excited about saving the lives of God's defenseless children.

"You think I'm a fool, don't you?" She didn't even look at me on the way to the car.

"What?"

"I can see you looking down your nose."

"Is it that obvious?"

"It's that obvious."

"I'm just concerned."

"You think I'm a fool."

"Why are you doing this?"

"It's something I feel strongly about."

"Mary, you can't bring those babies back."

"Fuck you!" she yelled, "I know that. You think I don't know that. I know that. That's why I have to do this. Some of those girls might not know how terrible that is."

"I'm sorry, I understand now."

"You don't understand. I don't understand."

I slept on the couch that night. Mary didn't ask me to or anything. She went up early and I sat there watching the tube. I thought about going to bed. I just couldn't do it. A silence had befallen our house that night. The distance between us seemed enormous. It scared me. The strange thing was that the closer that we physically got, the more uncomfortable I felt. So, that's why I couldn't bear to go to bed that night. To be next to her and feel that distance? I could stand being downstairs. There, I could think about her so she was with me in a way. To be next to her and feel that distance, though, that's the worst kind of loneliness. She woke me with a kiss. I was still in my clothes. I still felt cold. Her lips on my forehead. I felt warm.

"Frank," I heard her voice and peeled open my eyes, "time to get up," so soft and gentle. My first hazy sight in that dim light was her smiling. It was that crude painting I had made in the store that day. I stared hard trying to make reality come into focus. "You don't have to be so surprised," she caressed my head, "Thank you, Frank."

"For what?"

"For putting up with me," she laid down on top of me. We hugged. She moaned a guttural moan. I saw that painting, still.

Zita showed up, child on her arm, belly protruding. She wasn't her normal vociferous self. She just stood down there until I noticed her. I saw her son first. Wide eyes, fresh skin, soft hair. I melted. I gave Zita some food that day. She was so sad. I asked her about the father. I asked her about the crack. She just shook her head to both.

"Zita, did you ever consider abortion?" Her eyes got wide. I thought she might scream.

"That's wrong," she whispered, her head shaking. "That's wrong," she looked down.

Bob showed up shortly after that.

"Did you and Rosalie ever think about abortion?" popped out first thing. Bob was a little surprised, but not too.

"Yeah, we sure did," he was solemn, "just couldn't do it."

"There's a lot of 'em being done, I hear."

"Oh yeah, people fucking like it's the end of the world."

"You know anyone who's done it?"

"Abortion?" I nodded. He thought. "Don't know. It's not the kind of thing people talk about."

"Suppose you're right."

I sequestered myself in the store that night. I laid out the paper and opened the paint. My heart raced. I felt like a junkie rigging up. I was looking over my shoulder the whole time, afraid to be caught. I painted a few lines and caught a buzz. After that I just sat for the longest time staring at that sheet. Nothing came. When I got up to take a piss I saw the roach. Not a cockroach. That, unfortunately, wouldn't have been surprising. There was half a joint sitting on the back shelf, right under a ventilation duct. Somebody was smoking pot on the job! I don't know why I was surprised, but that surprise manifested itself in anger. I felt the blood rush to my face. Maybe I was embarrassed. Whatever, I stood there holding that roach and it dawned on me that I used to like smoking pot. I used to like being high. Frank Teeman that is. Maybe Frank Kunstler would like it too. I scratched that match and the flame ignited. "What a wondrous thing fire is," I always thought. I dipped that stub and it started to glow. That pungent odor filled my nose and I rushed it to my lips and soon it was in my lungs. What a strange flavor. I took another, looking over my shoulder afraid to be caught. By the third its effects crept in. My eyes open. My stomach unwinds. A wonderful cloud envelops my mind. I smile. I'll leave this roach for who ever left it. Back to the painting. Still nothing comes. That's all right this time.

"Why'd you ask me about abortion?" Bob caught me on the way out.

"Abortion?" I thought to myself.

"You're not thinking about doing it, are you?"

"Nooo. Mary's just joined Right to Life," I tried to say with a smile. Somehow, it made me really sad.

Excerpt from *Death Becomes Him* by Brian Mosten

The thing that I remember about Frank Teeman is his singularity. I still remember that day when he ambled into McSorley's. I said to Frank, the bartender, "Look at this one. A real prince." Frank just nodded. We used to call all those rich-boy Columbia undergrads "princes". They would eventually stroll into one of those downtown gin joints in a terrible effort towards communing with the down trodden masses. Frank looked like a prince all right, but I should've realized he wasn't. He came in alone. Princes always traveled in packs. It was something they had been taught from early on – the buddy system. When they were at those bars they were in dangerous territory. A Prince would have never come in alone. Frank Teeman sat down at the bar next to me, that night. Jim McGilley came over. He sensed a touch. Those princes were always good for a free drink or two, if you knew how to work 'em right.

"Hey stranger! New around here?" Jim must have been broke, he started to work right away.

"Yeah, as a matter of fact," Frank responded wryly. That wasn't the normal prince response. They used to always try to make it seem like they were born and raised.

"Want to make some quick friends," Jim was undaunted.

"No thanks."

"Don't mind him," I tried to rescue Jim, "Jim's just looking for a free drink," we laughed.

"A free drink! Is that what you want?" Frank called Jim's bluff.

"If your feeling so inclined." Jim was an old poker player.

"I'll buy you a drink, Jim." That always drew a crowd.

"Well, thank you stranger."

"But first you've got to do something for me," the crowd hushed while Frank smiled, "Tell me about Christ," the groans went up. He's not a prince he's a pusher! That's what we all thought. Jim scratched his head unsure of whether it was worth playing this guys game just for a drink.

"*Jesus* Christ?"

"I believe that's the fellow."

"He's the son of God. Uh, two thousand years ago he was crucified for our sins, he died for our sins!" Jim was sure he had hit the jackpot with that one.

"Have you ever met him?"

"No."

"How do you know all this?"

"Church! Now where's my drink?!" Jim was exasperated.

Frank paused, "Whiskey or beer?" He chuckled.

"Whiskey," and the bartender poured while Frank laid down cash.

"I can tell you about Christ," Louie the Lush snuggled up for a touch.

"Can you?"

"Yeah. And I can pay for my own drinks!" Louie was far more pragmatic than Jim. His plan was to get on a roll. Instant friends we used to call that one.

"Is this guy for real?" Frank turned to me.

"Quite," I laughed. Louie was a master of the taboos; politics and religion. If he wanted to put you off he could say just the wrong thing. If he wanted to snuggle up he would say just the right. Louie had figured Frank for a pusher so he started in hard with the rhetoric.

"I don't buy that bullshit," Frank exasperated after Louie went off a bit. I looked at Louie, Jim looked at Louie, Jim looked at me. Frank was ordering a drink. I just laughed and with that, laughter erupted. Louie paid for Frank's drink, that time.

From that day on I would look forward to running into Frank. He always was out when he wanted to be. As soon as he felt like leaving he did. If he didn't feel like coming out at all he didn't. That was rare amongst us barflies. The last time I ran into him, the day he died, he was in rare form. We talked and talked over the din of the bachelor party at Lilly's. We even talked about how dying was the only way to make a buck in our business. We had laughed about that so many times before. He seemed even more tickled by that irony that night.

"Brian, don't ever die." Those were his last words to me. I was telling him my new address. I had just moved in with a woman friend. She had a kid. I knew how much he loved kids so I had invited him over. We were sauced. I just laughed when he hugged me. Now I think about him every day wondering if, indeed, I have died.

The TV blared and the blender roared and Jeff Johnson's toy something-or-other clanged. Yes, this was the proverbial bar-b-cue with all the technological accouterments to make all our guests happy. There was a moment there, when I looked around and I couldn't believe all the stuff we had accumulated. Still, despite my disgust with the things, I was having a good time. It was the people. The kids. Kids are great. We pigged out on all kinds of stuff and the gluttony continued. And as we sat around the tube waiting for dessert, it happened. The news was running, nobody was paying much attention; I was half in, half out. Most of my energy was down in the stomach. It's nice to be full.

"Today the art world's latest scandal reached a new high," the TV blared, "A hero for some, demon to others, Frank Teeman's self-portrait sold for six million dollars."

My eyes bugged. They flashed it on the screen. My self-portrait!!!

"Look at that," Fred Johnson exclaimed, "that looks just like you, Frank," he laughed. That picture just lingered. And lingered.

"That does look like you," Joel Tierney exclaimed.

"Kunstler means Artist in German," Josh Tierney was taking German in High School. And that painting just lingered. I could barely breathe. I flashed back to that day when I had stashed my image and with that single act of self-denial I had forgotten. Suddenly, my stomach felt empty.

"Son of a bitch!" I practically yelled. "Six million dollars!?!" Mary had come into the living room agape. Every one else was laughing.

"Who would pay that much?" "I heard he was a Satan worshipper." "What about the Mother & Child?" "That was so beautiful." "I've got the coffee mug."

It was a din of Teeman gossip. I sat transfixed. The clashing of my two different identities had stunned me. Why did I feel such animosity towards that image on the screen? It is a fine line between love and hate.

Somehow I managed to respond to some question or statement from the Kunstler reality and that's when I began to feel the Frank Teeman inside of me looking out. And now, for the first time, I had been shoved into the Teeman mind. There was Jack on the tube glibly describing how he had discovered the painting. I hated Jack then, too. It sure was nice to see him, though. Mary touched me on the shoulder. I looked up. I saw Red smiling. I smiled, too. She gave me one of those circular rubbing massage-of-the-shoulder things. I could tell. I could see her arm moving. I couldn't feel it, though. I wanted to feel it. I wanted out of Teeman mind. I wanted to feel full of food and beer, and laugh with kids! And love Mary. Teeman couldn't do that. Could he? Why could Kunstler do that and not Teeman?

"Not only is the man an artistic genius," I heard Phil Jankow spew from the TV, "I believe he's a saint."

"Do you believe he's still alive?" The woman with the microphone asked.

"Certainly! His spirit lives on through his work," Phil was beaming like a proud father. Good old Phil.

"What about the story that Mister Teeman staged his death to escalate the price of his work and he is profiting from your purchase," that perky reporter asks unabashedly.

"That's just absurd and so what if he is," Phil turned sour. So did I. And then that damn self portrait comes on the screen.

"And the saga of Frank Teeman continues," that sweet voice over, "as the art world holds its breath until another Teeman piece surfaces. And the question remains—Is this elusive artist still alive and painting?"

Click.

"Dessert!" Mary called out after turning the TV off. Everyone rushed to the dining room table.

"Spooky seeing yourself on TV, huh?" Bob Brelan looked down on me. I panicked. I thought he was calling my bluff. I didn't know what to say. I just looked at him, begging for mercy. "That painting did look an awful lot like you, don't you think?"

"Yeah, I guess so."

"Spooky," he shook his head.

"Weird," we headed for dessert.

The house emptied after a spirited game of Michigan Rummy. I collapsed.

"Pretty wild," Mary was massaging my shoulders.

"Yeah, it was a fun game."

"I'm talking about your painting!" She hit me on the head.

"What was all that stuff about me still being alive?"

"You don't know?"

"Know what?"

"They've been talking about you ever since you died."

"Who has?"

"The press."

"Shit," I resigned, "Why didn't you tell me?"

"I thought you knew."

"Shit," I was pissed, "You think anyone suspects?"

"Nah. Don't be silly," she put her arms around me. The warmth of her cheek on mine. I could close my eyes.

"Mary?"

"Umhm."

"Let's adopt," I tried to be sincere.

"Oh, Frank," she moaned, "It's not that easy."

"Why is everything so damn hard," I was too exhausted to be pissed anymore.

"They do exhaustive background checks at agencies!"

"You don't think we're covered?"

"I don't know. We'd have to hire a lawyer."

"Let's hire a lawyer."

"Frank, we can't afford that."

"What?"

"We're broke."

"How'd that happen?"

"You spend more money than you make."

"Shit."

"The store's not doin' that well."

"I know."

"And Jack just made six million off of you."

"That, fuck."

A tenuous feeling came over me then. A perilous feeling. Almost like falling. Falling in ultra slow motion. More like, the ground had taken on a liquid quality. And I could feel each breath. And I could feel her breath. And the gurgling of the fish tank was enormous. And the smell of the coffee was pervasive. Life was huge for me then. And when I closed my eyes...the child. Some infant smiling at me and I look at him and feel the weight of the world is on me.

If only to have some one to pass it on to.

I was open once. Life had beaten me down so, I was open. I was open to anything that built me up. Drugs and alcohol had beaten me down. I knew that. What could build me up?

I left town with one of my oldest friends. He dropped me at my new school on his way to divinity school. I was running from the grasp of the devil. He was running straight into the arms of the lord. For five hundred miles we were going in the same direction. This old friend of mine and I, after spending our childhood together, we had separated there for a while just to come together for an instant. Right when I was open. Hmmm.

We had all the furniture in the U-Haul and my cat in tow, too. As we headed out I began to realize how long those four years had been. Not far down the road we got to the big issue. I was still looking for some tangible proof. Yea, I was young then.

He started telling me about a book. This guy, Alfred something, could prove it through "Bible Numerics". One of the theories went something like this—

If you assign a number to every letter in the alphabet and you total the value of each letter of a word and you took that sum and totaled the digits of that amount and kept totaling the digits until you reached a single digit you had reached some essential element. Each single digit having a particular significance; one representing God, the one and

only; two being his son—"#2"; three being the holy trinity; four representing nature (or reality)—"Four sides to a house" he gave as an example (I didn't point out that there was really six); Five representing
man—five fingers, five holes in the head etc.); six being the number of
the beast "Look how easy it is to transform a six into a serpent";
seven—a combination of the holy trinity and natural man. This was
the significant number. Alfred Something had gone through the original Hebrew bible and done his calculation for every sentence and they
all totaled seven. This was the objective evidence of God's hand at
work. God authenticating his work. A plan so complicated only God
himself could have wrought it. And the fact that it was the number
seven indicated that the bible was the instrument to connect the holy
trinity with nature. This certainly transcended coincidence.

What can you say to that? My friend dropped me in Ohio with a
copy of Alfred's book. I read it. It was short. He went on to describe
several other phenomenal calculations, like the fact that Moses is mentioned a function of seven times and the solitary mention was in the
book of John, written hundreds of years after the original sites. God
had worked his magic again. There it was—emphatic proof. I had a
couple of days to think about it and every day I would try to work up
some enthusiasm for the idea. After all, I was new in town. I could be
anybody I wanted to be.

My friend called me a couple weeks later. We talked about moving
and what a chore that was.

"Have you found a church?" he asked after a break.

"No," I knew what he was asking. I had to think. How could one
argue against such hard proof? "I have had a revelation, though."

"Really? Want to tell me about it?"

"I used to think that my atheism was based in an intellectual rejec-
tion of the concept of God."

"It's not."

"I know. It comes from the heart…"

"Amen!"
"And I just don't have it in my heart."
"Have you asked for Christ's blessing?"
"I have. Nothing."
"I'll pray for your soul."
"?"

PART III

I made a deal with the devil. I didn't want to admit it at first, but now I can't deny the truth. Once I had seen that image on the TV screen, the harsh reality of my situation was all too apparent. The rug had been pulled out from underneath me and I scrambled to get my footing. When there's no solid ground there's no solid footing. You scramble for as long as you can, but eventually, you fall down.

I carried that tenuous, perilous feeling with me from that moment on. I don't think it showed. Not at first anyway. Not except for the lack of my smile. When Time magazine came out with my self-portrait on the cover, I couldn't hide my tension. Everywhere I looked there I was. In living color. And the inevitable connections were made. My employees, my customers, the guy at the 7-11. I tried to smile about it, but every time one of them said, "Teeman" I cringed. I took comfort in the thought that it would pass. While it was on, though, I was a wreck. Those two or three weeks were the longest of my entire life. I woke up every ten minutes expecting hours to have passed. I would catch myself staring at the slightest reflection like a long lost brother. One I hadn't seen since childhood. I would try to relax. I would focus on my breathing. Each breath an eternity. Mary would try to get me to relax. She would fix these beautiful dinners and she would be so pleasant. I couldn't converse. I was too distracted. She didn't let it bother her, though. She would tell me all about what she was doing. It was great to see her so excited about her life. The church group was going full steam. They were running counseling sessions and trying to get clinics shut down and, most importantly to Mary, they were facilitating adoptions. I was restless. Invariably, I would get up in the middle of one of her monologues and stare longingly out the back door.

"I should go to New York," I piped in one night.

"Frank, I don't think that's a good idea," she was justifiably scared.

"No. I could talk to Jack…"

"What?" she shrieked.

"Listen," I rushed back to the table, "he could help us to adopt."

"Frank?" she was incredulous, "What if you're found out?" She threw out her hands.

"   " I threw out my hands.

"There might be charges."

I just furrowed my brow.

"Even if there aren't, you'll never live in peace again."

She had a good point there.

I did the right thing. I rode it out. I ran the store. I tried to make a profit. I just stayed out of sight. That meant I could do a little painting. I had a neat little corner where I wouldn't betray my secret. I found some watercolors and brought some markers and I worked on Mary. She was a tremendous source of inspiration for me. I felt free at those times. One night I brought some house paint in. A light blue. It was the final touch. I broke the brush after that one and sat there smiling. Reveling and smiling. I didn't hear Elijah approaching. He's the only one who would come back that far. I would have pulled the cover over the thing if I had heard him coming. He never did come but that one time.

"Wow," was the first thing he said. He was reveling and smiling, too. I realized it was him and realized what he was seeing. I couldn't do anything. "Mr. K," he turned and looked at me, "you did this?" He saw the broken brush. I saw that he saw. I still couldn't do anything. "You are that dude!!"

"Elijah," I tried to demure.

"You tellin' me you're not?"

"Elijah?" I was still paralyzed. I went to put the cover over Mary.

"Holy shit! It is you."

"Elijah, I'm not saying it's me, I'm saying you have to stop this silliness. Please, for me?"

"That's cool. You know, everybody's sayin' what a crook you are," he caught himself, "he is, fakin' his death." I tried not to react. He saw my reaction clearly. "I always said, though, I didn't think you were in on it. And I was right! Runnin' a grocery store! You bailed out!" He was delighted.

"Elijah." Why couldn't I think of anything else to say?

"It's cool. It's cool." He calmed himself down. "I knew you were cool when you showed up. I really admire you for what you did." He hugged me.

He hugged me! I stood there in his grasp, warm. The weight of gravity firmly pulling. Pulling me down to solid ground.

"What are you gonna do with that?"

"It'll be our little secret, huh?"

"Right on."

When I got home Mary was sitting in the dark. She was slumped in a chair, sadness everywhere.

"Hey," I turned on the lamp. Her swollen, red eyes revealed the level of hurt. "Honey what's up?" I knelt in front of her. She grabbed me and held me as if she would be swept away.

"It's so hard."

"What is?"

"We were intervening at the clinic today, and to see all those sad girls, mostly girls, that's bad enough, but then Marianna pulls up," that name broke the gates. I just held on as tight as I could. I felt the current pulling her. I didn't want to lose her. "Marianna came in for counseling," she pulled herself together, "I spoke with her. We talked about adoption. I thought I had her convinced. She just looked so sad." It was good for her to get it off her chest. She calmed quickly. "How was your day?"

"Not so good."

"It's still hard, huh?"

"I got busted," I finally revealed. I couldn't keep it from her.

"What?"

"I've been painting in the store room."

"Painting?"

"A picture of you," she wasn't soothed, "Elijah found me and now he's convinced that I'm Frank Teeman." I tried to laugh.

"Oh great," Mary separated herself from me, "I hope you told him he was wrong."

"I tried."

"You tried?"

"He caught me with a broken brush. It's a habit. He promised not to say anything. He hugged me!"

"I can't take this anymore," she stormed into the kitchen and started slamming pots around, cooking something.

I just stood where I was, thinking, "Neither can I."

Remembering the Man
by Jim Evans

Frank Teeman was always in a different class. When I knew him at Roosevelt High he blended in nicely, but we knew that he was different. In our adolescent clique Frank was always the visionary. He wasn't necessarily the leader, he was the idea man. He seemed to be able to see the big picture with out straining. Sometimes, it seemed, the big picture was all that he could see. He planned an extravagant camping trip, but didn't include toilet paper. He helped me build a huge rabbit hutch in my garage. We had to disassemble it to get it outside. We drove to Philo for soft shell crab without enough gas money to return. There was never any idea for Frank that wasn't worth considering. Somebody would make a silly suggestion and we'd all laugh. Five minutes later Frank would pop out of his trance, "It could be done." We constructed an enormous jock strap and hung it on the high school to protest football hysteria. We sneaked rum and coke into the prom by puncturing coke cans and refilling them. We actually managed to find a Willie Mays baseball card to make a friend's birthday complete. All these were one of those silly suggestions laughed about by our gang as absurd and realized through Frank's vision.

I saw Frank the day he left Dilon. He was standing at the bus station watching the sky. I almost stopped to say good bye. I knew that Frank had already left. I felt sad that day. I knew then that Dilon had lost a wonderful citizen. Now, I know that the world gained one.

TEEMAN continued on pg. 12

TEEMAN continued from pg. 12
Whether Frank liked it or not, he had become a symbol. For many he represented the success of innocence. The nice guy finishing first. That was such a joyous happening for those of us who had witnessed the advance of vanity, greed, and sloth. Others, who had given up hope, accused Frank of exploiting our fears. After all, anything that ended up with a profit must be a form of exploitation, right?

Whatever the truth about Frank's rise to fame and the subsequent turn of events surrounding his death, Frank opened a dialogue. At first it was about the beauty of age, then the topic moved on to the success of innocence. After his unveiling of "Two of a Kind" he had the whole world talking about faith and now we are contemplating the price of fame. Regardless of how these things were done or whether he intended them or not, I believe these are great contributions. The ability to stir debate on grand topics should be one of the ultimate goals of art. Only art is able to simultaneously touch the abstract and the concrete with one fell swoop. These topics, and all subjects of a grand nature, necessarily combine elements of extreme abstraction with fundamental real life. Now that I realize that, I realize that Frank Teeman was destined to do that job. Unfortunately, there is still more work to do. Every day I pray that Frank is out there, still, waiting to spring on us a huge jock strap or better yet a giant 1966 Willie Mays.

Dilon Post, 7/7/91

Manhattan is alive. My heart races from the moment I see the skyline. I sit behind the wheel of my Camaro, passing through the Holland Tunnel, shaking. My back aches I'm so nervous, but once the light of day hits, I feel the energy. I roll down the window. I breathe deep again.

Maneuvering the streets of New York is decidedly different than Levittown. Cars pass me left and right, honking and cursing. I laugh, "Yeah, Fuck you, too!" and rev the engine. A bicycle courier whizzes past maybe a couple of inches from me. My back is tense again. I pull that behemoth into a lot. It'll cost a fortune. Oh, to be on foot again.

There's a spring in my step as I gobble up sidewalk. A smile on my face. I'm overwhelmed with stimulus. The proverbial kid in a candy store. Yes, this was the right thing to do. I knew it would be. I've got my big hat and dark glasses. No one recognizes me! Even if they did, this is New York, they couldn't be bothered by some tabloid character.

"Open your heart to Jesus. He will save you from sin!" The singer! That invisible old man.

"Hello my friend," I was glib.

"Mister Teeman!" he was delighted. I lost my energy. He recognized me?

"How did you know my name?"

"You are very well known. Have you found Christ?"

"No!" I was angry that he knew me, "No!" Why did he have to ask that?

"You sound sad about that."

"You're not surprised to see me?"

"Why should I be surprised?"

"Reports of my death have been widely circulated."

"Not in my circle."

I ran. I mean, I didn't run, I fled. I had to escape. The old man just smiled. I looked over my shoulder. He wasn't looking at me. He was staring straight ahead, smoking a cigarette and smiling.

When I rounded the corner of my old neighborhood I was surprised to see graffiti. Shocked! Not that graffiti was unusual there. It had never been on my building before. Now, it was all over and it was mostly about me.

"Home of Satan" "We love you Frank, Beth and Moira"

There was even a crude rendition of my self-portrait. Both a halo and horns had been added. I wondered if one artist had done it that way. I hoped that one artist had done it that way. I approached my front door. I was just going to pass by. The sign on the door stopped me in my tracks.

OPEN FOR TOURS 3-5 P.M. DAILY

Tours? Ho-ly shit. I tried to look in the window to see if anyone was in. Who would be giving tours? Who would go on tours?

"Here it is." A young voice was relieved. I heard those kids coming towards me. I wanted to bolt, but found myself frozen. They had come to see me. I had to know. I turned just in time to pass them as they were gawking at the facade. Wide, bright, eyes. One with a shaved head, the other with green hair. Both had pierced eyebrows and paint covered clothes.

"Not like I imagined it to be," the skinhead said.

"Nothing ever is," replied the other.

Somehow, the fear was gone.

"You kids paint?" I had turned back around. The green hair turned and smiled, "I try." I realized for the first time that she was a girl. That short, butch haircut and those loose clothes…"Good, good," I nodded, "you live around here?"

"No. We're from Toronto," the skinhead joined in. That's when I realized she was a girl, too. I was surprised. Pleasantly surprised.

"We came to see Frank's house," the green hair said in a decidedly gruff tone.

"What on earth for?"

"We were stalled."

"Frank used that word to describe the block."

"I saw you checkin' out Frank's house. You a Teemanite?"

"I don't know. Kind of an enigma, huh?"

"Nah," the skinhead took a cigarette from her flannel shirt pocket and lit it. "Look at the eyes." I just tilted my head.

"Teeman's eyes are heaven sent," the green hair answered.

"His eyes?" I was being facetious.

"The eyes he paints," in unison.

"Uh-huh," I nodded. "You think he's dead?"

"Yeah, he's dead," the skinhead.

"No way," her friend.

"He's fucking dead!"

"I don't think so."

"Whether he is or not he's heaven sent," the skinhead looked skyward.

"You sound like Christians."

"We are."

"We have our own relationship with Christ."

"You've accepted him into your hearts?"

"That's right,"

"Blessed are those…"

"Do you ask Christ to help you paint?"

"Oh yeah,"

"That's why we're here."

"Christ told you to come here?"

"Christ loves Frank."

"Frank loved Christ."

The thought of those girls brought me equal amounts of joy and ter-ror as I strolled aimlessly through those city streets. I left those kids with a friendly "Nice to meet you." They were just going to wait there for the tour to start. I had to keep moving. I called Checker and asked for Jack. "He's not driving anymore," I recognized Ernie's growl. So, I just started walking. Those girls wouldn't leave me. They seemed so happy. Content. They didn't seem sad. They made me sad.

I had to sit down.

"May I ask your name," the receptionist at the Social Services office asked.

"I'm the brother of Gladys Rowe," I told her. I hoped Mary would get the hint. She came out into the lobby. I saw the eager anticipation on her face. She stopped to look at me. I took off my sunglasses. She smiled. Such a wonderful smile.

"C'mon back to my office Mr. Rowe," Mary watched the reception-ist to see if she suspected anything. She didn't. "Frank," she hugged me hard as soon as her office door closed.

"Mary," I hugged her hard back. When I said her name visions of Red appeared. I had to let go.

"It's so good to see you," she seemed genuinely happy. That warmed my heart like nothing could.

"You don't seem surprised."

"I always knew you were still alive."

"How'd you know that?"

"At first it was just a feeling," she made her way to her desk. I just watched her and felt joy. Pure, unequivocal joy. The kind that fills your head with clarity and your heart with warmth. Th-thump, Th-thump. I was in love. "But when I found out the truth..." her words echoed in my ears and when I finally interpreted them they brought me down.

"What?" I was getting cold.

"Frank," she had that hushed tone that precedes bad news, "I'm living with Jack." She looked away. My heart collapsed and left a cold hole in my chest.

"Jack!?!" I eked out. I didn't want to believe it.

"I went over to your place for a tour…we just started talking…you were what we had in common!" She tried to laugh.

"Jacsun Pranesh?" We couldn't be talking about the same Jack. She just nodded. My mind went cloudy. I was swimming in confusion. My heart beat frantically, but to no consequence. I was short of breath. My legs took my befuddled mind away. I had to get out. I needed to breathe.

ASKING TOUGH QUESTIONS

When I first met Frank Teeman he struck me as a very ordinary guy. That particular day he was struggling. I could see it in his face as he passed my church. Life's burdens were written plainly on his face. I see those signs all the time. Frank's burden marks were the same as everyone else's I see. That's why I thought he was just an average New Yorker. I reached out to him that day, "You are loved," I proclaimed. He turned with a slightly sardonic smile that seemed to say "I know" and "I don't care" all at once. I was intrigued. Christ's love usually goes a long way. Particularly for those who are just discovering it. Frank's smile convinced me that he knew Christ's blessing. I sensed that was part of the problem. I watched him walk off into the distance (after he sheepishly waved at me) anxiously hoping that he would turn and engage me. Being a priest, my job is to help people lose those burden marks. Frank faded into traffic, not once looking back.

Frank did return soon enough , though. My prayers had been answered, I thought when I saw him that day. I would have that same thought about Frank many times. When he first donated a thousand dollars to rescue our day care, and then again when he set up the trust that would become the Lower East Side Redevelopment Fund, I thanked the Lord for answering my prayers. One day Frank had stopped by the church for one of his social visits. We were chatting very politely, since we were just getting to know one another, and Frank just let loose with, "Can you believe that bullshit with Koch?" At first I was a little surprised at the expletive, but then it dawned on me that it was the first time I had been talked to like a real person in a long time. Frank prattled on about Mayor Koch and had fallen into such a comfortable tone, I just sat back and listened. When he broke into his imitation I burst out laughing. We sat there and yucked it up for the longest time. Even though we're encouraged to balance our lives as priests, it's difficult. It's very difficult in a city parish. I had lost sight of that and Frank brought it back to me. I thanked God for Frank that day, too.

In a way my prayers were answered the day Frank unveiled his "Two of a Kind". Two days previously I had been talking with another priest about how people did not talk about what it means to be good or the difference between good and evil. "We need to prompt the imaginations of our people to see the enormity of the ethical dilemma," I said to my fellow preacher.

"I try to do that every day," he was almost insulted.

"I do to." I reassured him. "I just think that people look to us for answers, not questions." I looked for some understanding.

"What's wrong with that?" He was perplexed.

"To learn, you've got to ask questions. You can't just be given the answers all the time. In life, every situation requires a slightly different response. Rote answers only fit rote situations."

"So we need to start asking questions?"

"No. They need to start asking questions."

We both sighed.

Frank Teeman's "Two of a Kind" got people asking questions. When Frank unveiled it I started asking questions. I stood there next to him on that platform asking myself, "What is this man thinking?" I knew Frank as a noble man so, I wasn't so quick to condemn him as many in the audience that night were. Still, I didn't understand. Now I do. His departure is a mystery to most. If Frank were still a stock boy at McGarrety's Market his death would have died with his obituary. Only because of his singular character is there any doubt. ∎

When you hurt you cry. When you know you shouldn't hurt you suppress tears. But still you cry. Pain is undeniable. You can't wish it away. You can't hope it away. You can't pray it away. You just have to wash it away. Of course you can try to ignore it, but that means dulling your senses enough to not feel it. That means eliminating your humanity. There are an awful lot of walking dead out there, aren't there?

When I left Mary's office the pain was huge. My whole upper body was consumed by it. My legs were noodles. I walked briskly, though. It was the only way I could keep from screaming. The devil had gotten my angel! First he got my life and then he got my paintings and then he got my angel. And she looked so happy too. That hurt worst. Aaaagh. I just wanted to yell. Guttural, primal sounds. Aarrgh. I just kept walking. Huge strides, pounding my feet down. After a while it stopped helping. Fortunately, by that time, I was at Central Park.

The smell of the trees. The brilliant green. The rumble of a passing truck. The energy. I breathed deep to feed my decrepit body. I felt like I was aging rapidly. Cells breaking down. Tired. Oh, so tired. I laid on the ground and relished the gravity. The weight was the only thing that let me know I was whole.

It felt so good.

I laid on my back in that park watching the sky for a sign. Birds would fly by. Planes would appear. I wanted to see God. I wanted something, someone, to tell me what to do. How to find Jack. How not to kill him when I did!

"Frank Teeman!" a robust voice came from that black man's face that appeared above me, "How the hell are you?" I got up. He was smiling. I just turned and started walking. "You are loved," he called after me. Spooky. Did everyone recognize me? I was so paranoid. New York's not a good place to be when you're paranoid. It was time to get this trip over with and get out before something bad happened.

I camped out near my loft. Maybe Jack was still conducting tours. I was in luck. Somewhere around three he arrived. Those two punk girls were still there and Jack wouldn't let them in. I didn't want them to see this, but I had to do it. I went up to my door and pounded.

"No tours 'til three," the skinhead girl said, a lit cigarette dangling from her lip. I kept pounding. Finally the door opened and there he was in front of me. He smiled. I went to push my way in. He stepped aside.

"Frank," he was beaming, "What the hell are you doing here?"

"I came to talk to you," I tried to control my anger.

"My lucky day. The dead walk."

"Listen you…" I almost cursed, "Listen Jack, I need some help."

"Frank you shouldn't have come here."

"I had to come here!"

"You could really screw things up."

"Fuck you," I finally yelled.

"Settle down," he lit a cigarette. I looked around for the first time. My place had not changed. The blood stain on the floor from Des, that folding futon with the black cushion, the hole in the wall where I had fallen. It was exactly the same. Except it had a museum like quality to it. Too clean or something. No life.

"Mary told me you were here." I cringed. I literally felt my whole body tense up instantly. "Sorry about that Frank. It wasn't planned."

"Jack," my back still to him, "I want to have a kid."

"So have a kid! Whatta ya need me for?"

"We need to adopt. We don't have money for a lawyer. Mary's afraid we'll be found out." I stated the facts through gritted teeth.

"Shootin' blanks, huh?" That hyena laugh.

"No," I growled.

"OK, OK. That's not a bad one. We should be able to do that for you."

"You've got to do that for me."

"Or what?"

"Or I'll come back."

"Frank," patronizingly, "You wouldn't want to do that."

"I'll do it."

"Frank you made a deal. Besides, you're far more valuable to us dead…than alive."

"Can you arrange it?"

"I think I can. Let's go talk to some people." He put his arm around me and escorted me out.

"Hey, what about the tour?" those girls called out to us as we walked past.

"No tours today," Jack snapped back.

"Go home," I yelled over my shoulder. I saw those girls looking at me. The disappointment written all over them. They kept watching me and slowly, the recognition crept in. I turned hoping they would forget.

I was in a cloud.

My head was swimming.

I just kept walking.

Focusing on getting this done.

I needed to get this done.

"You seem angry Frank." Jack piped in after we were silent for a while. I couldn't say anything. "I've never known you to be angry Frank." He smiled at me. That understanding, comforting smile I first saw in his cab. I didn't know what to say. "Didn't get what you wanted?"

"No I didn't."

"Domestic life not all it's cracked up to be?"

"It's fine."

"Fine? That's what you say to the waiter when he asks how your food is and you want to be polite."

"It was really cool there for a while. The security is great. It's still got some great moments."

"Women are nutty, aren't they?"

"We're all nutty. I'm surprised there are any marriages."

"You two not getting along?"

"We're getting along."

"What's the problem then?"

"You're fuckin' me up, Jack."

"How's that?"

"My self-portrait's all over. People recognize me."

"That is a problem."

"Yeah. The kid thing really sucks, too."

"What's up with that?"

"Mary's not able."

"We screwed up on that. We'll take care of it for you, though."

We ducked into a bar. A dark, quiet, clean bar. Jack sat me down at a booth and told me to hang on a second. A scotch rocks was delivered in his absence. I started sipping that whiskey, my mind drifting back to Kansas. I thought about my folks for the first time in a long time and it occurred to me that they must have been in a similar situation as I was. The adoption. My adoption! How did they come across me? Where did I come from? Why weren't my parents listed on my birth certificate? Did I just pop up out of no where? Or was I simply abandoned? The whole "leave the kid in a basket on the doorstep" thing? I took a big gulp. It didn't fill the gap. There was a hole deep inside.

"No prob," Jack plopped himself down in the booth, "I knew that would be an easy one." He handed me a business card. I couldn't read it. I couldn't focus. "There's your lawyer. It's all taken care of. No charge."

"Thanks Jack. Now what about people recognizing me?"

"You want more surgery?"

"I want you to stop."

"No can do."

"What am I supposed to do?"

"Once this kid comes you'll be layin' low."

I took a look at the business card. "This guy can do it?"

"It's in the bag."

"How long?"

"Give him a call."

I smiled. I smiled! Yes, this was the right thing to do!

"There's the old Frank," that hyena laugh.

I put that business card in my shirt pocket and pressed it close to my heart. Mary would forgive me once she saw this. I closed my eyes and polished that scotch. Visions of Red appeared. I heard the laughter of children, Jeff Johnson running through the back yard. Terra's birthday party...? I opened my eyes with panic. Jack was gone. I hated him then. Not only did he have my angel, he had the life I had sold my soul for.

And I still didn't have it.

"Why can't I be like normal men?" I heard myself say. I was tired of feeling that way. Now, I had the power to do something about it. I had all the right parts and this lawyer was going to add the missing element and I would be normal. A happy normal man. I gritted my teeth. Nothing would stop me.

Nothing!

Excerpted from *Teeman Travelogue* by Beth Monnay

We're standing in McGarrety's market. This is where it all happened. Irene Solomon came here to see her old friends and that's when she met Frank Teeman. Maureen and Bill McGarrety are still running the store when we dropped in. "Ahhh . . ." is still behind the register, our eyes glued to it.

"You recognize Frank's work?" Maureen McGarrety beams from behind the counter.

"Uh-huh," we both nod.

"Well get a good look. It won't be there much longer."

"Did you sell it?" I was shocked.

"Heavens no. Not that we haven't had offers. We're closing up," she said matter-of-factly.

"How much have you been offered?" I couldn't contain myself.

"Oh, you wouldn't believe the offers we've had." Bill McGarrety, a big teddy bear of a man steps from behind the counter wiping his brow. "We thought about selling it plenty of times." Bill and Maureen smile at each other

"Remember the day when Frank first walked in?" Bill looked at Maureen. He didn't remember. We were lucky enough to witness their reminiscing. "It was a cold day. A bitter, cold day," she prompted him.

"And I was trying to fix the heater," he remembered.

"Frank walked in smelling of liquor," she turned to us demurring.

"But he fixed that damn heater, didn't he?" Bill was defiant, "And when I offered to pay, all he wanted was some heat."

"Yes, Frank never did know how to take care of business."

"No, I suppose he didn't."

"He did all right for himself, though," Moira piped in.

"Well he didn't spend himself to death, that's for sure," Bill.

"He had as hard a time spending money as he did making it." Maureen laughed. "Can you imagine that?" she asked us.

We all paused for a moment trying to reconcile that piece of irony.

"Frank was a lot like Irene that way," Bill seemed to realize for the first time.

"Maybe that's why she left him that house," Maureen was realizing, too.

"Were they lovers?" I had to ask.

"Heavens no!" Maureen.

"Don't be ridiculous!" Bill. "I don't think he even liked her."

"What?"

"Their relationship was strictly business."

"You don't think he slept with her just to get her money?"

"You kids have been watching too much TV." Maureen was disappointed.

"I remember once asking Frank, 'You're a nice young man. How come you haven't settled down yet?' and he looked at me like I had just spoken Russian. 'I am settled, aren't I?' he says. He was really sincere. 'Most people settle with a member of the opposite sex.' I informed him. 'Oh that,' he says. He says, 'I don't have anything to offer women.' I had to think about that one. 'You mean you're gay?' I asked him straight out. I didn't have a problem with that. Frank insisted he wasn't. 'So whatta ya mean you got nothing to offer women. If your impotent they can cure that.' I was jokin with him. 'Is that what women want?' he asks me real serious. 'Well sure!' I tell him. 'Isn't that what it's all about?'" Maureen gives him an elbow to the ribs. "I'm tellin the story just like it happened!" Bill bellows.

"Was he . . . you know, . . . incompetent," Moira blushed.

"Well I asked him that and he assured me that wasn't the problem."

"If that Desiree woman is tellin the truth it wasn't a problem at all." I had read her book.

"There you go. Frank turns to me, that day, and says, 'I guess I'm just emotionally impotent,' and I'm not following. He says, 'Love and love making just seem so absurd to me.' I think he was whatta you call, asexual."

"Whatever he was," Maureen broke in, "he was a good man. Don't you believe any of that crap they're saying about him. He was as good as they come." She went back to work. Bill nodded while he packed a box. "Ahhh . . . " hung effortlessly above them, almost glowing. We drank it in.

As I marched through New York towards my car I had a growing feeling of determination. It was a strange feeling, for me. I guess what was strange was all the doubt around it. I usually only attempted what was probable. My move to New York; my subsequent departure—both financed, both a must situation. The fear of remaining outweighed the fear of changing. All that time in New York—que sera, sera. Sometimes I would long for a change but the urgency wasn't there. I had rationalized that letting things happen was somehow healthier than trying to control those massive forces. It's certainly easier. But there I was, grabbing the proverbial bull by the horns trying to make change in my life with out changing my life. And I was gonna do it! But I had to have Mary's help. Relying on another person? That certainly throws an element of uncertainty into the mix. That's where all the doubt came from. I didn't care, though. I was tired of everything. I just wanted to be fulfilled. Full—filled. Saturated. I wanted it all and I wanted it now!

I fired up that engine. I could feel the explosions. They were at my fingertips. I touched the accelerator with my toe. ROARRR. I had control. I shifted into gear. I turned the wheel. I made that two-ton crate move forward, with the slightest flex of my leg. Now was the time. I cranked up the radio. Rock 'n Roll!! Yes! This determination thing was definitely strange. Wonderful, but strange. And the feeling of cruising at 65 with the thump, thump, thump of the drums and the powerful wail of the electric guitar? I could feel my muscles. It wasn't a tension, per se, I could feel them and I knew that they were at my beckoning and I knew that they could do incredible things. If I willed it.

After you get accelerized and the Rock 'n Roll has hammered your ears into submission, there is a calm unlike any other than in a fast moving car. Maybe the drone of the engine has some kind of hypnotic effect. Maybe it's the scenery whipping by. Maybe it is the endorphin power buzz. Maybe it's the solitude. Whatever it is, I felt that serenity then. Sitting there watching the world go by, hurtling towards my destination, moving undeniably toward my destiny? Content in the knowledge that I was going to rescue my existence from its present miserable state. I started to think about being happy.

When happiness pops up it transforms those moments into a certain iconographic unreality. A larger than life memory. "Is that true?" I thought to myself. And the reel began. My life started passing before me. I remembered a general kind of happiness that transcended moments as a kid. One particular image did jut out, though. It was winter and it was cold. That night we had a fire going in the fireplace. I remember Dad telling me to crawl up into his lap, and me sitting there reveling in him. His big arms, his five o'clock shadow, his body odor. All exhilarating. And then Mom walks in and Dad tells her to sit down, too. She plunks herself on top of us and we groan while she laughs. Mom's laugh. I can here it there in the car over top of the Led Zeppelin.

And then, somewhere around puberty, happiness becomes not a higher spot, but a completely isolated moment. Happiness outside the context of that general euphoria associated with youth, is intoxicating. I'm hanging out in the bleachers all dressed in my football gear, covered with dirt and sweat. We had just scrimmaged and we kicked butt! The coldness of the Coke was so nice and the laughter amongst my friends, infectious. I remember the setting sun and the smell of cut grass. And then Farrell O'Connor walks up in her glow of blonde hair.

She congratulated me on my touchdown with a smile. That feeling of being appreciated combined with that hormonal urgency thing, that was nice, but when I saw that locket my head blew off. I had developed a crush on Farrell and gave her a heart shaped gold locket for Valentine's Day. She didn't want to take it. After all, we weren't dating or anything. In such a small town you can't help but know each other. But it was a total surprise—my Valentine's gift. I insisted she keep it. And that summer day near the end of August she was wearing it.

"I really like it," she said when I asked her about it. That's when my head blew off.

I sat there in my Camaro some twenty five years later still smiling and feeling good about it. But then I started to wonder if it were possible to feel happiness in an isolated way. I searched for that feeling in my memory—sex with Ellen Turner, Coney Island with Mary, that time when Ellen Tamoritz was giving me support, that family outing we took on my sixteenth birthday—these were the things that came to mind. Does happiness lie solely in the realm of interaction? I was pretty happy when I first started painting Mary in the storeroom. I was all by myself back there. Still, Mary was there. My thoughts were about her. And what about that incredible moment at the Rolling Stones concert? Standing in the middle of Arrowhead stadium looking at all those people. Amazed at how brown the sea of heads was. Sure I was buzzed, but something unique happened there. I wish I could say it was the music. It wasn't. It was during a break and some crazy fucker had climbed up one of the light poles and was parading around on top pumping his fists in the air. Slowly, the whole crowd began to notice him and there was a tremendous buzz. Some people were concerned, some applauded, some people thought he was an asshole. Everybody was watching him, though. 50,000 folks concentrating on that one thing. And the cops gathered around the base and eventually he started to descend and there was a hush. He was just hanging on to the rungs, unprotected, unsecured, hundreds of feet above the parking lot below and we all watched. That's when it happened. A tremendous surge of happiness came over me then. A smile erupted on to my face and the top of my head tingled and there was this feeling of rightness. He got down and the cops took him away and people alternately booed and cheered. I just made my way through the crowd, beaming. There, amongst all those people, I was alone and I was happy.

What was that? Flashing lights in the rear view mirror, the chirp of the siren. I guess I should've pulled over. I didn't want to pull over, though. I was on a mission. Eventually reason prevailed, and I had come to a stop on the side of the highway. I guess I was speeding. "So right the ticket!" Why was he just sitting in the car?

"Step out of the car," his car belched. What was going on? I got out. I thought he was supposed to saunter up to the window and ask me for my license. "Put your hands on the roof of the vehicle and spread your legs," it was like the voice of God. Or the devil. Who ever it was, his minion got out of the cruiser, gun drawn, and approached me slowly. When I saw that barrel pointed at me, my life really started to pass in front of me. "Keep your hands on the car, your head down." I pressed my hands hard against the car. I kept my head as low as possible. He patted me down. I was shaking. I tried to think of something to say to make it all right. "I'm on a mission," was all I could think of.

"Why didn't you stop?" he asked while he cuffed my hands behind my back those metal bracelets cutting my wrists and my will.

He wrote me a ticket for speeding after checking my sobriety, and giving me a stern warning. I sat in my car trying to breathe. I felt weak. I was back on the road soon enough. My determination was buried under a mass of fear. It was still there. Now, somehow, I was even more convinced I was going to make it. With each passing mile that determination worked it's way out from under. By the time I hit Levittown it had consumed me.

If I asked you to come, would you not run? I am he who allays your grief. I'm the one who'll soothe you eternally. Frank Teeman sought eternal relief. He was constantly fixated on eternity. That's why he was drawn to painting. That's why he dropped out. His time frame had been distorted in order to bring eternity into focus. And once the future part of eternity became slightly clearer, the past part came into view. That's when he opened his heart to me. Yes, I've known Frank Teeman a long time. Eternally, you might say. He knew me, too, although he had trouble admitting it. One day I appeared to him, in Central Park, a large Negro man.

"You are loved," I assured him, blood glistening from my chin. He smiled at me a sardonic smile that seemed to say, "I know" and "It does me no good".

"Love does you no good?" I read that smile. He stopped.

"I don't understand it. Can you explain it?"

"No I can't." Who can explain love?

"Are you OK?" He approached me.

"There you go!" I smiled.

He saw me again on the streets of L.A. He was wandering, feeling alone.

"You are loved," I assured him once more. He smiled that smile again and walked away.

"Love is everywhere," I heard him say.

I saw him again in Central Park early one morning.

"I don't know what you're doing, but it sure looks strange," I chortled. His eyes popped.

"Do I know you?"

"We are acquainted."

"Don't tell me..." he had trouble admitting. I nodded. "Well maybe you can help me then."

"I'll try."

"I would give anything to be normal."

"Yes?"

"Can you tell me what normal is?"

"You would give anything to become something that you don't know?"

"Yes."

"That sounds pretty desperate."

"It is."

"Well, I can't tell you what normal is."

"What good are you then," he lashed. "I'm sorry, I'm just a little crazy, now." He quickly withdrew.

"What makes you think you're not normal?"

"People look at me like..." he demonstrated with furrowed brow and tilted head, "and I look at them, you know, the same way, and I see them all worked up over nothing. I mean killing themselves over...nothing. Or what seems like nothing and when they look at me they're amazed and they all talk like I'm setting some kind of unattainable goal and they ask me 'How do you do it?' I feel like asking them the same."

"Well then, maybe I can help you."

"Please do."

"Look," I pointed to a couple of Latino children running around the base of a tree, "do you remember?" He looked at me with that furrowed brow and tilted head. "Look there," an elderly black couple strolled arm in arm ever so slowly. "Now look at yourself. Are you them?" I pointed back at the kids. "Are you them?" Back to the old folks. He looked at his hands.

"I am neither."

"You are both."

I left Frank then, never to return. He watched me walk away. He was neither happy nor sad. Angry nor pleased. He watched the elderly couple as they rounded the bend and then saw those children disappear in a sprint. He looked at all the people in the park and saw himself there, too.

"You are loved," I called to him.

By the time my foot hit my driveway I was high. I was so high I was inside myself. Every breath deafening. My heart pumping forcefully. Tunnel vision!?! I was so high. I checked my pocket for that lawyer's business card. It was still there. I had checked every ten minutes or so, but I was still relieved every time I felt it. As the front door approached me, I rehearsed my spiel. Should I be happy and spring it on her? Should I feel it out and slip it in? I hadn't decided by the time I turned the knob. The house was dark. "Mary honey?" I called up the stairs. No reply. I hadn't planned on this. I plunked myself in my Lay-Z-Boy. "Where could she be?" The fish tank bubbled away. I pulled out that card.

Robert Halstrom, Esq.
Family Law

Maybe I should call first. No, Mary needed to be in on this. Where the hell was she? How could I forget? Operation Rescue was in town. They were down at the clinic "intervening". I couldn't wait for her to return. It might have been hours. That determination grabbed me again and whisked me out the door and back behind the wheel. Once again that tremendous inertia hurtling me towards my destiny. I almost felt like I could have let the car go and it would've ended up at the clinic anyways. I ran a stoplight I was so oblivious. All I could think about was Mary and what I was going to say to her.

What was I going to say to her?

There was a circus atmosphere at the clinic that night. The sun was hanging low over the horizon. The television lights like the stars. Huge stars. The roar of the crowd, the tension in the air. They all contributed to the surreality of the event. Operation Rescue people were trying to block the entrance by laying down in front of it. The police, dressed in their riot gear, carted them off like fallen soldiers. Pro-Choice people shouted chants in angry voices. Some even confronted their opponents face to face with harsh tones and nasty words. No one noticed me when I pulled up. I just got out and watched for a while trying to take it all in. I felt like I was watching a show. There did seem to be some patients trying to get in. They had escorts, but that didn't matter. The police couldn't clear a path fast enough. I started walking towards the action. I had forgotten why I had come. I was simply drawn to the drama.

The din…
    The passion…
        The energy.

Once I got closer it became more real. A child cried at his mother's hand. She was on the Pro-Life side of the field wearing an Abortion is Murder T-shirt, yelling "Murderer, Murderer" at the escort in front of her. Her boy just wailed. She didn't seem to care. She held his hand though.

"Maybe she did care." I thought, noticing the tightness of her grasp. Hey! That was Sue! I knew Sue from church. That's when I remembered Mary. Once again my right hand checked my breast pocket for that card. That wonderful ticket to heaven nestled securely in there. The crowd began to shrink for me. Or I began to grow. I felt my determination again. I sifted through the masses looking for my betrothed to tell her…? Yes, I was going to tell her, right there that I had the key, that I was in control, that I was going to wrest our existence from despair and place it squarely in the center of bliss. If only I could find her. Joel Tierney!

"Have you seen Mary?"

"She's here some where," he shouted above the din.

I was right on track. I made my way through the whole crowd. I figured her red head would stand out. No where. I got back to my car and took a breather. "Why isn't anything easy?" I closed my eyes. The energy came strong. Oh, sweet bliss.

"This is absurd!"

I heard her voice poke through the din. I opened my eyes. I saw a red head across the parking lot near the back of the building. "Was it her?" My heart raced. I made my way across the parking lot. I checked my pocket once again. I still had the ticket. Her back was to me and she stood in a crowd so I wasn't quite sure if it was her. Just as I was certain, a large dark car pulled up and parked between us. I ran around. A tall grey haired man got out of that car and came between us, again. We bumped into each other I was so oblivious.

"Excuse me," he said and he let me pass.

The shot rang out.

Or maybe I saw him before. It was Bob Bradley, the car salesman, pointing a gun at me.

Then the slug hit.

"Bob?" I remember thinking.

Then that tremendous blow to the chest.

I fell back on to that grey haired man.

The screams erupted.

"Frank!" I heard Mary.

It was all very distant compared to my breathing.

I saw Bob fall down on his knees, still pointing the gun, shaking madly.

I woke up laying on the ground, enveloped in a warmth and a haze, gravity pulling hard. Mary knelt over me, tears flowing from her eyes.

"I was looking for you," I smiled.

"Don't talk," she groaned.

"I couldn't find you." She looked so beautiful, then.

"I'm here Frank," she was growing desperate.

"Look Mary!" I reached for that business card. I found blood.

"I know. I know," she wailed.

I saw past her to the throng of horrified faces.

"I had the ticket to heaven." I felt around my chest until I found it. I pulled out the remains of that card. Bob Bradley's 9mm slug had shredded it. It was soaked with blood.

"You're not going anywhere Frank." Mary squeezed my hand.

That tall, grey haired man pushed through the crowd. His black bag clanged when it hit the ground.

"You're not going anywhere," he repeated, "You saved my life. You're not going anywhere."

"Mary look! I got a lawyer." I held out that bloody shard. "Everything's going to be all right."

"Yes it is. Yes it is."

I felt a pain then like none I've ever felt. It was everywhere. A full body pain. My mind began to swim.

I couldn't see.

"He was trying to shoot the doctor!"

"He saved a murderer!"

"Frank stepped in the way!"

"That looks like Frank Teeman!"

"He's a hero!"

"He's the devil!"

"Everybody clear the area!"
"That murderer deserved to die!"

The din of the crowd ebbed. My mouth became totally dry. I tried to lick my lips.

Nothing.

"We could name him John or Roger…or if it's a girl, Kelly. I always liked that name. Kelly."

The ambulance came I remember that.

I heard the scream of the siren.

I heard the tires on the pavement.

"In the morning when I rise, I can feel the energy. In the morning!" I tried to laugh. I only coughed. "And in the afternoon…we're so tired. But we still smile. And in the evening all is quiet, even inside. Than at night that's when I get high. When I see you smiling in your sleep. That's when I know I've done right. Look Mary! I've got a lawyer. We'll have our child." I tried to see if she could see the ticket.

All I saw was that beautiful shock of red hair.

"I made it. I made it home."

Everything went black
        and my muscles relaxed
                and my arms flopped out to the side
                        and the cameras clicked like mad.

Even in death I was immortalized.

Well, Frank's done it again. He befuddled those intent on establishing absolutes. It's easy to do when you don't try. The photo of Frank, laying in that parking lot—arms spread, feet together—ran on every news wire. A few papers ran his name as Kunstler. Most recognized him as the elusive artist Teeman. And as the news media tried to work out this convoluted story, cries of "Hero" rose up from those convinced he had stepped in front of that bullet.

"There were witnesses who said that he cried out the name of his assassin before the shot was fired!" His advocates claimed that this proved his heroism. His detractors weren't so willing to make a martyr out of a villain. While they didn't support Bob Bradley's action they were convinced that Frank was sent by the devil to keep that "baby butcher" in business. Then, of course, the whole mystery around his corpse. Cremated.

"He's not really dead." A green haired, teenage girl painted on a billboard in Toronto.

The whole cycle began again.

Frank Teeman died in that spot, sprawled out, his arms spread, his feet together. He still lives on, though, in a tiny voice that tells me this story. It is the story of a man trying so desperately hard to do what's right. And when he speaks I cannot help but listen. I'm hoping that in his tale I'll find the strength to continue. To type this thing up and pass it on to other people. Sometimes I hate him for speaking to me. Sometimes I love him. All the time I wish for him to get what he wants. To escape the madness. To live in the bliss of anonymity. I know that he won't.

That's sad.

Frank Teeman is alive. Bloomingdale's reissued "Mother and Child". "Shine On" works for a battery company. T-shirts, calendars, mugs, watches—everyone wants a piece of Frank. Even those convinced that he was the Antichrist keep him alive by referencing "Two of a Kind" ad nauseam. In some ways he's more alive today than he ever was.

You can see Frank today. His "Self-Portrait" hangs in a brightly lit room. People come from all around to see this hero. This devil. He can be seen on a postage stamp, too. Transforming the most banal correspondence into a work of art. Or at least one little corner of it. Some people look at his image and cringe; the fear of loneliness runs deep in their veins. That is what he is. He is not an artist. He is an icon of loneliness.

Some one who is "blessed" with a talent separates themselves from the masses. It's not a matter of choice. It's an inevitability. Talent is not so much an extraordinary ability rather, it is an extraordinary inability to ignore certain elements of life. All forms of creativity are attempts at explaining those perceptions. "I see this. Do you see this?" People see it. That's why art perseveres. Most can simply dispense with it. That solution proves too harsh for artists. They seek cover, literally and figuratively.

When talent is recognized the separation becomes all the greater. Suddenly, it is obvious because society's attention is on them and they can't deflect it. Try as they might they just can't understand that voyeuristic need and consequently it penetrates them. This is not a bad thing. It's not even necessarily a sad thing. It just is. And it always will be.

People need each other.

0-595-26522-7